D1241845

Scarlet Scars Book One

J.M. DARHOWER

ISBN-13: 978-1-942206-21-7

To Princess Leia, the most badass woman in all of the galaxy… you'll always be royalty to us.

Menace

men·ace

/ˈmenəs/

noun

noun: **menace**; plural noun: **menaces**

1. a person or thing that is likely to cause harm; a threat or danger.

synonyms: danger, risk, threat; jeopardy

"a menace to society"

1

"Wake up, sunshine," a voice called out in a frantic whisper as the little girl was shaken, roused from a deep, dreamless sleep. *"Please, wake up for me."*

The little girl peeked her bleary eyes open, blinking a few times as she gazed up at the face hovering above her. "Mommy?"

Her mother smiled—a big, wide kind of smile—but it wasn't the kind of smile that meant happiness. Rain fell outside, a steady, heavy downpour, battering the windows as the trees blew all around. Their shadows danced along the wooden floor, visible thanks to the glow of the soft nightlight in the room. Banging echoed through the house, so loud it reached the second-story back bedroom, coming from somewhere downstairs. It sounded like something ramming the front door, merging with the sound of thunder rumbling in the distance.

The wind screeched. No, wait... that wasn't the wind. The little girl's heart pounded hard. Someone was *screaming*. Her mother's smile was frozen in place as she gently, pushed the hair back from her face, caressing the little girl's warm cheek.

"It's time to play a game," her mother said, voice shaky as tears fell from her deep brown eyes. "We talked about this. Remember? *Hide & Seek*. You and me."

The little girl sat straight up in her bed. She didn't like this. She didn't want to play. She shook her head, her small hands grabbing her mother's face, squishing her cheeks as silent tears coated them. "No, Mommy. No! I don't wanna!"

"We talked about this," she said again, her voice firmer as the banging downstairs seemed harder. "Trust me, okay? You trust me, don't you, sunshine?"

The little girl nodded.

"Then hide," her mother said. "Just like we talked about. Hide *really* good, and do just like Woody and Buzz do, remember? Don't make a sound, don't move at all, no matter what, if someone comes near you, okay?"

The little girl knew '*okay*' was what her mother wanted to hear, but she couldn't get that word to come out. Her voice didn't like it. Her mouth wouldn't say it. "Mommy, I'm scared."

"I know, baby," she said, "and it's okay to be scared, but remember what we talked about? Remember what Mommy said about what to do when something scares you?"

"Name it," she whispered.

"Exactly." Her mother's smile softened. "If you give the monster a name, it takes away its power, because we're really just afraid of what we don't know. If you name it, if you know what it is, you can be stronger than it. So face your fears and wipe your tears, remember? *Face your fears and wipe your tears.*"

The commotion downstairs grew louder, a bang rocking through the house, this one different. Her mother's smile fell as her gaze darted to the doorway of the bedroom, the screaming closer.

Her mother turned back around, unable to hide the fear in her eyes. "Hide. I'll find you. I *promise.*"

Soft lips pressed against the little girl's forehead, lingering there for just a moment, not nearly long enough, before her mother pulled away. In a blink, she was gone, running from the bedroom, leaving the little girl alone.

Hide, she thought, *so only Mommy can find you.*

Snatching up her teddy bear, the little girl jumped out of the bed, her bare feet quiet against the wooden floor as she hurried out of the bedroom in her favorite pink nightgown. They'd played this game so many times, but never in the middle of the night, never when it was storming, and never when someone was downstairs screaming. It had just been practice then, like the fire drill they did in preschool, but this was for real.

She ran from room to room, the noise downstairs making it

hard for her to think. Things were breaking. Her mother was begging. "Please don't do this... *please!*"

Think, think, think.

The little girl came to a stop in front of the linen closet, making the split second decision to hide in it. She climbed the shelves, not for the first time, going way up to the top and shoving things aside to crawl onto it. She pressed way against the back, wedging behind a stack of towels, too big to completely disappear. But it had taken her mother almost an hour to find her in that spot one time when they'd practiced, and it had been daytime then, so maybe the darkness would hide her.

No sooner she settled into her hiding place, a crack of thunder rocked the neighborhood, light blasting through the windows. The rumble shook the whole house as her mother let out a piercing shriek, the noise silenced in a blink.

It grew quiet.

So quiet.

The electricity even went out, all of the light disappearing.

All the little girl could hear was her own panicked breathing.

"Face your fears and wipe your tears," she whispered to herself, repeating those words again and again and again, as she clung to her stuffed bear. *Face your fears and wipe your tears. Face your fears and wipe your tears.*

Footsteps started through the house, but they didn't belong to her mother—too heavy, too measured. It sounded kind of like a robot.

Made sense, since she called him the Tin Man.

The little girl didn't know if he was missing his heart, too, like the real Tin Man from the story, but her mother called him heartless once, so she thought it might be possible. She wondered if he rusted in the rain, since it was storming. *Maybe that'll keep him from finding me.*

"Come out, come out, wherever you are," he called out, searching the house. "I know you are up here, kitten. You cannot hide forever."

That's what you think, Tin Man.

She was good at this.

Her mother had made sure of it.

He walked down the hallway, right past the closet, dripping water onto the floor. He was soaked from the storm, his dark hair lying flat, and his white button down clinging to his chest, only halfway tucked and mostly ripped open.

An hour passed as he searched the house. It felt like forever to the little girl. How much longer would he look for her? When would he go away? *Ever?*

"Fine, I give up," he said eventually. "You win, kitten. Game over."

His steady footsteps went back downstairs. Everything remained silent until the electricity flashed on, the house coming back to life as the storm outside faded. *Game over.*

The little girl waited another few minutes, cramped in the closet, before her muscles ached and she grew even more tired. Quietly, she climbed out and crept downstairs, wondering why her mother hadn't tried to find her.

Still carrying her bear, she held onto the creaky wooden banister, finding the front door wide open. The locks were torn apart, the red-painted wood splintered, the hinges broken. She wandered past it, her stomach all queasy, and stalled in the doorway of the kitchen. "Mommy?"

Her mother lay on the floor, eyes closed, not moving. The little girl sat down beside her, pushing the hair from her mother's tear-streaked face. Her cheeks were all puffy and her head was bleeding, a mark on her neck, like someone had finger-painted on her pale skin.

"Mommy," she whispered, shaking her. "You can wake up now. We don't have to play no more."

"Let her sleep, kitten."

The little girl tensed, her heart racing as she looked to the doorway, seeing the Tin Man lurking there. She froze and held her breath.

Be like in Toy Story.

She didn't move, not at all, but it wasn't working.

The Tin Man strolled closer and knelt down, caressing her mother's swollen face before pressing his fingertips to a spot on her discolored neck. Sighing, he pulled his hand away and leaned over her, pressing the softest of kisses to her silent, parted lips. It looked sweet, like *love*, the little girl thought as she watched, not at all like the anger that had broken down the door.

Maybe he *did* have a heart.

She couldn't tell.

"Come on," he said, standing up, not giving the little girl a chance to argue as he yanked her up in his arms and hauled her over his shoulder. "We have to go."

Sirens wailed in the distance.

Scared, the little girl struggled, trying to get away from him, losing her grip on her teddy bear. It clattered to the floor, right there in the kitchen where her mother slept. The little girl shrieked, panicking, as he carried her through the broken front door without it.

Stepping outside, into the light drizzle, the Tin Man said, "It is time to go home, kitten."

2

Lorenzo

Manhattan. Dead of winter.

It's so cold I think my balls have closed up shop and gone home. Home, back in Florida, where it's a beautiful seventy degrees this time of year. They're basking in the glow of the warm southern sunshine, while I'm stuck here, freezing my cock off out by the East River.

Two o'clock in the morning. Twenty-one degrees. It feels closer to zero with the way the frigid air seeps through my thick black coat, the fake-ass fur-lined hood not enough to keep me warm. My ears are frozen. My nose is running, it's so goddamn cold. It's like tiny needles jabbing my skin, over and over, obnoxious little pinpricks, stinging and numbing me.

I'd rather be stabbed with a knife than deal with frostbite.

Snow from a recent storm is still spread out along the worn, wooden dock, layered over patches of slick ice... ice I almost busted my ass on not once, not twice, but *three* times as I walked along it. I wasn't made for trekking through slush, that's for damn sure. My boots are wet, my toes about to join my nutsack far away.

You've gotta be a fucking fool to be out here at this time of day.

Fucking fool.

That's what I am.

That's me.

Lorenzo 'Fucking Fool' Gambini.

Say it with me.

Because here I stand on the dock, hands shoved in my

pockets, fingertips tingling, struggling to pay attention to the schmuck five feet in front of me as he yammers away about a card game that was robbed last night, like I give a shit about some small-time gamblers in a city rich with, well, *riches*.

"So, like I said, my boss says the deal is—"

He's still talking. My teeth are chattering.

How has my life come to this?

"Are you homeless?"

My question comes out in a cloud of breath that lingers between us, like the words are caught mid-air, frozen in the cold night. It cuts off his tireless rambling as he looks at me for the first time since arriving, his eyes widening with surprise... or *horror*, maybe.

Given it's me he's here with, I'd say the latter is likely.

He stares at my face for a second too long and he knows it, because before I have a chance to say anything about it, he averts his gaze, his eyes going straight to a pile of snow by his feet that he nervously kicks at, like a bad little boy that knows he's about to get a whipping.

"Uh, no, I mean... why would you think...?"

"Because you asked me to meet you *here*." Pulling my hand from my pocket, I wave around us, at the graffiti-riddled, bum-infested area. "We could've met anywhere... a bar, a restaurant, a fucking all-night Laundromat... but no. You ask me here. Nobody comes here unless they've got nowhere else they can go. So tell me, are you homeless?"

"No," he says. "It's just, you know... safer here."

"Safer." *Seriously?* "You think it's safer to meet me right by the river, when it's so dark that I could just toss your body in and nobody would give a shit?"

"But my boss—"

"Is a fucking fool," I say, cutting him off again. "More of a fool than I was for agreeing to come to this bullshit charade of a meeting with some underling when I could be at home... in bed... with the gorgeous little blonde still riding me that I had to kick out an hour ago in order to make it here on time, which is saying something, you know, because that's starting to rank as the second biggest mistake of my life, and I don't even *like* that woman. She talks too damn much."

The guy looks at me again. It's just a flickering glance, but it tells me that somewhere deep inside of him, he's got guts. He's got balls that haven't yet tucked tail and run. The kind of balls that can withstand all of this goddamn cold. Balls of steel.

He came alone on the instructions of his boss, a man by the name of George Amello. Ol' *Mello Yello* was one of many so-called 'bosses' to spring up after the great 'Mafia Massacre', as the media oh-so-poetically dubbed it, when the heads of the notorious New York crime families were executed in a room over in Long Island, paving the way for me to take over the city.

The competition nowadays? *Pretty goddamn dismal.*

They're so inexperienced, so melodramatic, that it's boring. They think they're playing a game of *The Godfather,* pretending to be Michael Corleone when they'll never be more than a weak ass Fredo. They're pussies, and quite frankly, I'm growing tired of dealing with any kind of pussy that doesn't come attached to a shapely female form. *That* pussy, I'll spend my life worshiping, but these guys? These buffoons?

They're not worth losing my balls over.

I happen to like my balls. They accentuate my cock quite nicely, you know. I'd show you, but well... you've got to earn that first. So pay attention, okay? There's work to do here.

"Look," I say, having had my fill of this winter bullshit. A few flakes trickle from the cloud-coated sky, which is my cue to take my ass inside somewhere. "There's a bar right down the street, called Whistle something or whatever."

A throat clears behind me. "Whistle Binkie."

I almost forgot I brought Seven along tonight. He's always there to flank me when I need cover but never one to get in the way. I appreciate that. People in my way tend to get run over, and I'd hate to have to run over one of my best men. He's a bit older than me, mid-forties, and has been calling these streets home since he was just a kid. Dressed in all black from head to toe, he blends into the darkness just like he intends to do.

The man is my shadow.

"That's the one," I say. "I'm going to go get a drink at Whistle Binkie before they close. You want to finish this conversation? That's where I'll be. But this?" I motion around us again. "This ain't happening, man."

The guy just stands there, saying nothing, as I walk away, heading back to my car parked near the dock. Seven keeps up with my stride, not even wavering as I slide on the ice, damn near falling yet again. *I hate winter.*

Annoyed, I climb in the passenger seat of my black BMW, not bothering with the seatbelt. It's only a block away. I could walk, sure, but I have a feeling it would be more like ice-skating, and I don't ice skate.

Not willingly, anyway.

Seven drives. He was smart enough to wear gloves tonight, black leather clinging to his long fingers as he clutches the steering wheel. A ski mask is shoved up, perched on top of his head, mostly concealed by his hoodie, the oversized hood of it up, dropping down over his forehead. Seven's an average-sized guy, about my height and kind of lanky, his skin a deep olive tone that looks like leather.

He stops the car in front of Whistle Binkie, double-parking and turning the hazards on. "You need me to come in with you, boss?"

"Nah, it's fine," I say. "Find a spot, I'll call when I'm ready. Don't go too far."

"Yes, boss."

Getting out, I step around the parked cars, up onto the sidewalk, and pause there as Seven drives away. He doesn't drink. It's against his religion, he says. Raised Mormon, he still adheres to some of the principles, like not drinking alcohol or screwing around, although it seems the 'no killing folks' aspect is more negotiable with the guy. After he rounds the corner down the block, I push the door open and step inside the bar.

It's somewhat busy, but that's not really a surprise, is it? It's

Saturday night in the city that never sleeps and the beer at this place is dirt cheap. I find a stool along the side of the bar and sit down, motioning to the bartender, a young guy, barely old enough to drink.

He wanders over, eyeing me like I'm a rabid animal that might maul him if he comes near.

I'm used to the look. I've been getting it for years, ever since I was sixteen and my stepfather beat me half to death with a shovel. Part of my face never recovered, a scar covering the right half, slicing through my eye and running down my cheek. I'm blind on that side, the eye cloudy, a lighter shade of blue than I'd been born with.

So I'm used to it, you know. I've had twenty years to get used to it. To get used to the judgment, the harsh glances, the repulsion. Strangers gawk. Kids cower. Most are afraid to look me in the face, like I'm something out of their nightmares.

But while I might be used to it, that doesn't mean I *like* it. Doesn't mean I'm not tempted to gouge their fucking eyes out and ask them how it feels.

"What can I get for you?" the bartender asks.

"Rum," I tell him.

"A shot?"

"A bottle."

He hesitates, like maybe he's thinking about not getting it for me, which would be a mistake. With the mood I'm in tonight, I'm liable to hop behind the bar and personally *take* it. He obliges, though, unknowingly saving his own ass some trouble, considering I'd be inclined to knock a few teeth out of his mouth if he made me serve myself.

Grabbing a half-empty bottle of rum from below the bar, he slides it in front of me before handing over a shot glass.

He walks away to tend to someone else.

I carefully pour myself a shot and toss it back.

I shudder. It burns. My insides are coated in flames as I swallow the liquor down. I can feel it thawing me out, smothering the coldness. It's the cheap shit, so bottom shelf that it doesn't even deserve a spot on the display along the mirrored wall behind the bar. It's so vile, in fact, that it's probably eating away at my insides as we speak.

"You'd be better off just drinking paint thinner," a voice says. It's playful and feminine with a tone that makes me think of home. Not that we talked like her in Florida, no, but her voice reminds me of warmth. It reminds me of sunshine. It reminds me of starry nights and cloudless days.

That's *way* too sappy, I know.

Don't tell anyone I said that shit.

My attention drifts to the source of it, diagonally across the corner of the bar, just a couple seats away, meeting a woman's gaze.

She's young—early twenties, I'd say—with wild brunette hair, the kind that looks like hands have been running through it, like someone wrapped it around their fist and held on for dear life as they fucked her senseless. Her face betrays that, though, with a set of wide brown eyes, *innocent* eyes, and a quirky smile, almost sheepish with the way only one side seems to curve. Blood red color shines from her lips, matching the skin-tight, long-sleeved red dress she wears. Either the girl is classy, like a modern day Marilyn Monroe, or she's the type that'll suck my cock in the alley if I buy her some liquor.

I've found there's really no middle ground for a woman who wears that much red out on the town.

"You know what they say," I tell her. "That which doesn't kill me—"

"Only makes me stronger," she says, finishing the sentence.

"I was going to say *isn't trying hard enough*, but that works."

Her smile grows, genuine amusement crossing her face as she looks at me... *really* looks at me.

She isn't turning away. *Huh.*

Maybe this night isn't completely fucked.

I eye her and the dingy pint glass she holds onto, half-filled with what I assume to be whatever's on tap. She doesn't look like a beer drinker. I would've taken her for a tequila girl, if anything. Margaritas. Body shots. Salt. The whole fucking pizzazz.

"So, what's a woman like you doing drinking cheap beer at a dive bar all alone at this hour?"

She regards me for a moment before saying, "What makes you think I'm alone?"

I look to either side of her. The guy on her left, wedged between us, is so drunk he's passed out in his seat. An empty stool sits to her right. It's been empty since I walked in. If she isn't alone, whoever she came with sure as hell isn't concerned about her well-being. "Because a guy would have to be a fool to leave you sitting here by yourself, looking how you do, considering he's liable to lose you."

"You think so?"

"Oh, without a doubt. I'd steal you in a heartbeat."

Color rises into her cheeks. She blushes, soft pink accentuated by the crimson on her lips as she tries to fight back a smile but loses... miserably. "*Smooth.* That line usually work for you?"

"Every single time," I say, "but I wouldn't call it a line. It's true. If you don't take good care of what you've got, someone will be *more* than happy to take it away."

She lets out a light laugh, shaking her head as her gaze goes to her beer. "Tell me about it."

Before I can take the conversation any further, the door to the bar opens and the guy from the dock steps in. Took him long enough. I was beginning to think he wasn't going to come, that I'd been wrong about his balls, that his boss had already confiscated them.

As much fun as playing with the pretty brunette would be tonight, there's still business to attend to. I know, I know... my cock is mourning, too.

Sliding off the stool, I snatch up the bottle of rum and the empty shot glass, nodding to the brunette before strolling the guy's way. I grab a small two-seater table by the door, sitting down in a flimsy chair as I motion to the one across from me. "Sit."

He listens. He's obedient. He'd probably roll over and beg if I barked those commands, all in his quest to please his master.

Who's a good boy?

"So, uh, like I was saying," he mumbles, picking back up right where we left off. "These card games are important to my boss. The people who play in them... they're important, too. All this trouble that's been happening is scaring the guys away, so my boss wants to make a deal with you."

"He wants to make a deal with me," I say, pouring myself another shot, splashing liquor out onto the table. "What kind of deal are we talking?"

"He's willing to cut you a share of the profits."

"How much?"

"Ten percent."

I nearly choke on the rum as I swallow it down, coughing, the burn taking my breath away. Ten percent. The fucknut is offering me ten percent of practically nothing. *Pennies.* "Let me get this straight. Your boss got a little problem with thieves busting up his card games. So in exchange for ten percent of what he makes off of it, he wants me to, what? Provide protection? Security? This ain't a fucking rent-a-cop service I'm running. What does he want from me?"

He pauses. "He wants you to stop robbing him."

I stare at the guy. *Hard.* I stare at him until he starts fidgeting, and I wait for him to retract that statement, but he says nothing.

He's not taking it back.

"You calling me a thief?"

"*I'm* not calling you anything. My boss is."

"Like I said... your boss is a fucking fool." I rip the plastic pouring spout out of the bottle of rum and toss it onto the table, giving up all sense of propriety. Not like people expect it, anyway. Who needs manners when you've got a face like mine? They expect the worst, and what can I say? I don't like to disappoint. "I have no interest in his petty little games of *Go Fish* with the brats he does business with."

"Yeah, I told him as much," he says. "Told him it wasn't your M.O."

I take a swig straight from the bottle before pointing it at him. "What do *you* know about my M.O.?"

"I know it's not about the money to you," he says. "The money's a plus, of course, but that's not why you do it. For you, it's about the power. It's about the respect. You're not going to waste the energy on something that isn't worth attaching your name to."

Huh. He's got me there. I do happen to be a fan of grand gestures. Go big or go home. He might have more balls than I gave him credit for out on the dock, but it's obvious, looking at him, listening to him, that his boss takes that for granted. Georgie sent him out here tonight knowing there was a good chance he wouldn't survive to see sunrise. He's expendable, a simple go-between, and despite the cliché, everyone knows I'm the type to shoot the messenger.

"Tell me something." I take another swig of rum. "What did your boss give you for coming here? How's he compensating you?"

He hesitates. "He's not."

"No?"

"It's my job. I'm here because that's what I do."

"You deliver messages?"

"Among other things."

I can hear the hidden meaning in those words. The messages he's used to delivering aren't verbal. They aren't warnings. They aren't stupid little deals. He delivers messages in the form of a bullet to the eye, telling the world, *'I see you, motherfuckers. I see you.'*

He's intuitive. He's got to be, if he was able to read me. That's a rare quality these days. Nobody trusts their gut anymore, but they ought to. Sometimes wires get crossed in the brain, things get all jumbled, everything gets confused, and your heart... you can't trust that son of a bitch. It'll be the first to betray you. It'll make you feel like the world is a beautiful place. It'll make you forget all the darkness. It'll make you hope, and believe, and then it'll destroy you, just when you start to think maybe it's okay to not be so goddamn frigid.

But the gut? The gut knows. The gut remembers. You should always listen to it.

After taking one more swig of rum, I shove the bottle aside and lean across the table, closing some of the distance between us. He blanches as I do. Ballsy and perceptive, yes, but the guy is uneasy, nervous about how this is going to end, worried that I might kill him for the things he said.

I can't say the thought hasn't cross my mind.

But I'm going to give him a chance, maybe because I'm feeling generous, or more likely because I'm a conniving son of a bitch. Besides, I'm bored. Might be fun to poke the bear a bit.

"Here's what's going to happen," I say. "You're going to go back to your boss and deliver my counter offer, because this deal he's offering just isn't going to work for me."

He stares down at where his hands rest on the table, clasped together like in prayer, and is quiet for a moment before he asks, "What's your counter offer?"

Reaching into my coat pocket, I pull out my worn, leather wallet. I shift through the wad of cash, finding only hundreds, and toss one on the table to cover the cost of the rum before sliding my wallet back away.

"Tell your boss he can suck my cock," I say, shoving my chair back to stand up. "If he does a good enough job, maybe I won't blow his fucking brains out for calling me a thief."

Tingles creep along my skin, the hair on my arms prickling from a rush of adrenaline. I should've never left my house, should've never bothered with this meeting, should've never given those schmucks the time of day.

It's pushing three o'clock in the morning now, the sky pitch black when I make my way outside, the snow coming down harder. I just want to get home and forget I was ever stupid enough to go along with this shit. I curse under my breath when I step out into the air. The cold slaps me in the face, nearly taking my breath away, as I yank the hood of my coat back up over my head to try to block some of the assault.

Grabbing my cell phone, I dial Seven's number as I pace a section of sidewalk in front of the bar, my gaze out along the quiet street.

It rings once. Twice. Three times.

The door to the bar swings open just as Seven picks up. He greets me, but before I have a chance to say anything in response, something rams into me from behind. I stumble, nearly losing my footing, skidding on ice as the phone drops from my hand.

Shit.

It hits the sidewalk with a thud, landing in a patch of snow. I snatch it back up, cursing as I wipe it off on my pant leg. Anger rushes through me as I turn around, about to make some unfortunate asshole's night something to remember, when a flash of red greets me.

The doe-eyed woman from inside.

The moment I lay eyes on her, she starts stammering. "I, uh, I'm so sorry, I wasn't looking when I walked out, I didn't see you..."

Flustered, she wraps her black coat around her tighter. It's thin, not nearly warm enough to fend off cold of this caliber. Her red dress falls well above the knee, the only thing covering her legs a pair of black pantyhose. She's petite, shorter than I imagined, barely eye-level wearing heels.

Shivering, she takes an immediate step back, putting a bit more distance between us as she clutches her coat closed defensively, like it's her armor.

"It's fine," I say. "No harm done."

She pauses for just a beat after I say that before turning to head down the street, scurrying away, like I scared the daylights out of her just by existing. *Figures.* She had more guts inside the bar. Guess she might be a Marilyn, after all, instead of an alleyway cocksucker.

Pity.

Sighing, I bring my phone back to my ear. "You still there, Seven?"

"Yeah, boss."

"I'm ready to leave now."

I end the call and slip my phone back away, grateful the thing still works. My hand lingers in my coat pocket, something off.

25

It takes a second for it to strike me: the pocket's empty. *No wallet.*

My gaze darts to the sidewalk, and I search all around my feet, figuring I dropped it, too, like the phone, but there's nothing.

Nothing but snow, and ice, and battered concrete.

You've gotta be kidding me.

I pat myself down, looking like even more of an idiot, but I know better. I'm not going to find it. It's not here. My gaze shifts down the street at where the woman hurries away from me. She turns her head, as if she can sense my attention, looking back at where I'm standing.

And just like that, it clicks.

She knocked into me, catching me off guard, distracting me for the moment...

She fucking pick-pocketed me.

Me.

I'm so damn stunned I almost don't react. My brain, it just can't seem to make sense of it. It's doesn't compute. How the hell did she pickpocket me? *Me.* It's impossible. Unbelievable.

Nobody's balls are that big.

But yet, there she goes, looking back again, hurrying her steps even more the moment I start to move. My brain is still far from catching up, but gut instinct kicks in, forcing my muscles to work. I head for her, breaking into a sprint, slipping and sliding all over the goddamn place but managing to stay on my feet. She keeps glancing back as she starts to run, nearing the end of the block, that wild hair all over the place, whipping into her face.

She's fast; I'll give her that. Even in heels, she manages to navigate the ice with ease. That might impress me if I weren't so goddamn angry.

Pins and needles jab my face, the coldness stinging. I run as fast as my legs can carry me, closing the distance, each stride sending her more into a panic. As soon as she hits the corner, she kicks off her heels, sending them flying, and runs through the slush out in the street in her bare feet.

Jesus Christ, the woman is crazy.

She's fucking insane.

She has to be.

I dodge across the street, following, and catch up to her just as she rounds another corner. I'm close enough to snatch a hold of the back of her coat, fisting the material and yanking her to a stop so hard that she barely manages to stay upright. Before she can think to struggle, I swing her around and shove her back against a crumbling brick building, pinning her there, standing right up against her, so close her body heat surrounds me.

She gasps, eyes wide as she stares me dead in the face, like she just can't believe this is happening.

Me, too, woman. I can't believe this shit, either.

"I'll scream," she says, her voice a breathless cloud between us. "I swear I will."

"No, you won't."

"What makes you so sure?"

"Because if you wanted to scream, you would've just done it," I say, patting down her flimsy coat, feeling for some pockets. "Now give it to me."

She tries to block my hands. "Give you *what?*"

"You know what."

"No, I don't... I don't know... ugh, what are you...? Get your hands off of me!" she growls, pushing me. "What do you *want?*"

"My wallet," I say, grabbing her hands when she tries to push me again. I press her hard against the brick, brushing the tip of my nose to hers as I lean down, smelling a hint of beer on her breath, but it's not as strong as the scent that clings to her skin. *Vanilla.* "I know you swiped it."

"I didn't—"

"Don't play dumb with me," I say, an edge of anger to my voice as it drops low. "It's cold as fuck and I'm fresh out of patience, so this isn't the time to play games. It's in your best interest to just hand over the wallet before I drag you into an alley and strip-search you for it."

Her eyes narrow. "You wouldn't."

"Just try me. I *dare* you."

A second passes. Then another. And another. Her

27

expression shifts, the shock melting away as those bright red lips let out an exasperated sigh. She yanks from my grasp and pushes away from the wall, her chest bumping against me so hard that it forces me to take a step back, giving her room to move. She reaches into her coat, into her dress, and whips my wallet out from somewhere along her bra, holding it up between us. "Fine, you caught me. Happy?"

"Fucking ecstatic." I snatch it, also grabbing her hand, pulling her toward me. Her sleeve moves up her forearm, exposing a tattoo on her wrist. It's simple, nothing more than a cursive red 'S'. "What's this, huh? Your own little *Scarlet Letter?* What's it stand for? Sneaky thieving bitch?"

She rolls her eyes. *"Funny.* If you're done manhandling me, asshole, I've got somewhere to be, so I'd appreciate it if you'd, you know..." She motions with her head toward my hand. *"...let go."*

I hesitate before loosening my hold, letting her slip from my grasp. I start to say something about how she's getting off lucky tonight when a car whips around the nearby corner, coming to a stop.

I turn, spotting my BMW, before my attention goes back to the woman. I barely catch a glimpse of her face, a flicker of a smile on her lips, before she's gone again, *running.* She turns the corner of an alley, disappearing.

That was easy. *Too easy.*

She seemed almost amused by it.

My gaze turns to the wallet in my hand. I flip it open, finding the billfold empty. No money.

Son of a bitch.

After all that, she *still* robbed me.

Nobody does that.

Nobody.

I walk over to the alley and glance down it, but it's empty. I'm not surprised. She's long gone, having slipped into a building or climbed a fire escape or ran out the other side.

Shaking my head, I shove the wallet in my pocket, where it belongs, and make the trek to my car. I pause when I cross the street, collecting the pair of red high heels discarded in the slush, left behind in her haste to get away with my money.

"Boss?" Seven hollers, stepping out of the car. "Everything okay?"

Is everything okay? *Hell no.*

I turn to him as I approach. "Got a job for you, Seven."

"Yeah?"

"I need you to find someone."

"Who?"

"A woman," I say. "About five and a half feet tall. Brown hair. Brown eyes."

"That describes half the women in New York."

"Yeah, well, the one I'm looking for is twenty-one or so," I say. "She's good-looking, kind of curvy for being so petite... got a red 'S' tattooed on her wrist..."

He stares at me, like he expects more. "What else?"

I shrug, glancing at the high heels, flipping them over to look at the red soles. "She wears a size thirty-nine shoe."

"That's it?"

"That's it."

"Shouldn't be too hard," he says, blinking a few times as he looks at the ground. "Only a couple million people in the city."

"That's the spirit," I say, slapping him on the back. "Now let's get the hell out of here so my nutsack can start thawing."

I climb in the passenger seat of the car, the heat blasting me, bringing feeling back into my fingertips. It takes Seven a moment to join me. He climbs in quietly, putting on his seatbelt.

He starts to drive. I can tell something's on his mind. He fidgets, drumming his fingers against the steering wheel, as his eyes flicker all around. I try to ignore it. I try. I do. But I wasn't kidding when I said I was out of patience, and I don't like my shadow being distracted.

"Say what you're thinking," I tell him, "before I take the wheel and shove you out of my car."

He instantly stills. "I'm just curious, you know, why you're looking for this broad."

"She robbed me."

His head turns my way so fast that he accidentally swerves into another lane. "She robbed you? How?"

"It doesn't matter *how* she did it. All that matters is that she pulled it off. So I need you to find her, so I can do something about it. You got me?"

"Absolutely," he says. "Just one more question."

"What?"

"Are you going to kill her for that?"

I shrug. "Guess we'll find out."

3

Morgan

A thousand dollars.

I count it out—ten crisp, new one-hundred dollar bills—as I slip in the back entrance of Mystic, passing through the metal door someone propped open with a broken cinderblock (yeah, because *that's* safe...). Thumping bass rattles the dark, winding hallway, music coming at me from every direction as I pass by a dozen rooms, a few with the doors closed. Every room has a different vibe, a different song playing, and it all kind of converges out here in the middle. Lights flash, a multitude of colors, so intense as they meld with the music that it's almost like you can *feel* them running through your system.

From the corner of my eye, I can see shadows moving, but I don't purposely look in any of the rooms, giving them privacy. It's a matter of respect. Nobody really *likes* being back here, so the least I can do is let them keep whatever shred of dignity they manage to dig up.

I make my way to the front, to the wide-open club space, the music from the hallway drowned out by whatever vulgar rap song is playing.

Something about popping pussies.

I don't know. Don't look at me.

I didn't pick it.

The crowd is thin at this hour (or really, *most* hours...) and the women are weary, counting down the seconds until four o'clock strikes so they can put their clothes back on and vacate the premises. Go home to their lives, where they're mothers, and wives, and sisters, where they run errands and take classes until it's time to come back to this hellhole.

It's exhausting, you know, *entertaining* and *satisfying*. People turn their noses up at the business, judging, like snobby little fucksticks, but it's a decent job, and nobody will ever convince me otherwise. It's honest work... not like, well, *pickpocketing*.

Whatever.

I head through the place, not stopping to acknowledge anyone. They all tower over me, the women wearing six-inch heels to keep eye-level with the men, while I'm currently barefoot.

Barefoot.

In a strip club.

Yeah, I haven't seen my dignity in a *long* time.

The office is in the corner, near the front entrance, tucked in beneath the DJ booth. I approach the closed door, hesitating, before tapping on it.

The door opens a crack, and I slip in right away, hearing it close behind me, locks securing. It makes my skin crawl. Locks are the sound of imprisonment.

Two young guys sit along the side of the room, attention fixed to a wall full of surveillance monitors. I avert my eyes, not wanting to see. It's easier to pretend nobody is watching those things. They say it's for our safety, that they watch us to keep us from harm, but I'd wager the thousand bucks I'm holding that if someone started mutilating any of those women, those two dickwads would just sit here and jerk off.

"I'm surprised to see you," a voice says behind me. "Figured you had other plans this weekend, since you said you weren't coming in."

"I did," I say, turning to face him. *George Amello.* He's in his late fifties, a clean-shaven Italian man with a wide smile and thinning hair. "I made some money."

"You *made* money," he says, sitting down behind his desk, his dark eyes on me. "How?"

"Does it matter?"

He laughs, a big, boisterous kind of laugh that makes people uncomfortable. "No, I guess it doesn't. How much you got for me?"

I step around the side of his desk, over to where he is, and pull myself onto it, sitting on the corner, facing him. My dress rides up, the tops of my lacy thigh-highs visible. I hand him the stack of cash, and he takes it, his gaze lingering on my thighs for a moment before he starts counting.

When he finishes, he opens a desk drawer and tosses the cash into it. He says nothing, just takes it. Not long ago, he used to offer promises, words of encouragement, but these days his brand of *help* is more like extortion, like I'm paying for his silence.

Well, I kind of am, but that's beside the point here...

His hand finds its way to my knee before running up my thigh, slipping beneath the bottom hem of my dress, his calloused fingertips caressing my skin. He's handsy, sometimes copping a feel—*inspecting the goods*, he calls it—but he never tries to take it any further. Some might say he's a decent human being for it. I say he's just embarrassingly impotent.

No amount of little blue pills will get *that* gearshift out of park, if you know what I'm saying.

So I tolerate it... for now... until the day comes when I don't need this place or his help anymore.

There's another knock on the door, and George gets up with a sigh, pulling his hand away as he struts to the door, unlocking it and yanking it open.

"Boss," a quiet male voice says as someone walks in. I look that way, tensing when I see a vaguely familiar guy. Young, with a buzzed head and soft hazel-colored eyes. He was at the bar tonight, the one a few blocks away.

He'd been with *that* guy, the one with the scar on his face and a lot of money in his wallet, the one drinking cheap rum straight from the bottle.

Oh shit.

I turn away, my back to the guy as he sits behind me, on the other side of the desk, hoping like hell he didn't notice me tonight. George retakes his seat, his hand right back on my thigh, tracing the lace with his fingertips.

"So?" George says. "How did it go with Scar?"

Scar? *Seriously*? How cliché can someone be?

The guy clears his throat. "He says he has nothing to do with what's been happening."

"Horse shit," George says. "It's gotta be him. Who else would have the balls to steal from me?"

Everyone, I think, keeping that to myself, pretending I'm not listening so George won't kick me out. Hell, *I'd* steal from him if I didn't count on his generosity to stay afloat. It wouldn't exactly be hard. He doesn't even lock the drawer he tosses his cash into.

"I don't know," the guy says, "but he was insistent, even got mad at the insinuation that he was a thief."

"He *is* a thief!" George says, raising his voice, his hand stilling on my knee. "He extorts half this fucking city!"

"But he says he didn't steal from *you*," the guy says. "I still presented your offer, though, that you'd be willing to cut him in if he'd knock it off, and he told me, well... he told me to bring you his counter offer, instead."

"Which is, what? Fifteen percent? Twenty? I'm not going over twenty-five, there's no way."

"He doesn't want your money."

"What does he want?"

"An apology, I'm guessing."

"*What*? Is that what he said?"

"Well, no." The guy pauses. "He said for you to suck his cock, but I'm pretty sure an apology was the sentiment he was going for."

My lips twitch as I force back a smile. *Oh god, don't laugh.* I seem to be the only one in the room that finds it funny. George's nostrils flare as he grips my knee, squeezing it.

"He said that?" George asks, his voice a low growl. "For me to suck his *cock*?"

"Yes," the guy says. "Said he won't kill you if you do a good enough job."

Oh, *wow*, this just keeps on getting better. I bite my cheek, hard, trying to keep a straight face, but I'm finding that hard at the moment. George's cheeks glow bright red, his eyes bugging out of their sockets, like those words have him so messed up he's about to blow a gasket.

George, he isn't exactly the *scariest* guy on the planet, but he certainly intimidates a lot of people, with his in-your-face attitude and his fiery temper. Oh, and he's also got one hell of an inflated ego, like he's invincible, which I guess compensates for the whole flaccid penis deal. I don't know. Who do I look like, Dr. Phil?

The point is, George struggles to keep his cool, which is showing at the moment, as his grip on my leg starts to hurt, like he's about to rip off my kneecap.

"The son of a bitch thinks he can *threaten* me?" George spats. "He thinks I'm afraid of him, that I'm going to apologize to him? He thinks this is all a joke? That *I'm* a joke?"

The guy doesn't answer. Maybe it's rhetorical, I don't know. But it's damn sure got me curious—*does* he? I know nothing about him, except he carries a lot of cash and he caught onto *my* game pretty fast.

"I'll kill him," George continues, standing up, finally letting go of my leg so he can pace around the small office. "Suck his cock? I'll cut it off! I'll cut it off and shove it down his throat, make him choke on it for talking like that! The nerve!"

The guy is still quiet. I turn my head, chancing a peek at him, and see he's staring at me. *Shit.* I don't know who he is. I stay far away from that side of George's business for good reason. One of his little thug henchmen, I'm guessing.

"Go back to him," George says. "You go back to that motherfucker, and you give him a message."

"What kind of message?" the guy asks, finally looking away.

"The kind that comes with a bullet, Ricardo. *That* kind."

Ricardo—as his name seems to be—lets out the quietest sigh before saying, "I hear you."

"Go on." George waves toward the door as he throws himself back down in his chair. "Get the hell out of here."

Ricardo leaves without another word, closing the door behind him. I sit here, not moving, waiting for George to calm down. Move too fast and I might spook him; linger too long and he might think I'm eavesdropping.

Well, I mean, I kind of *am*, but raising his suspicion isn't my intention. I'm trying to lay low these days, just squeak by under the radar.

George runs his hands down his face in frustration, grumbling under his breath, before his eyes settle on me. "Is there something you need?"

"Nope," I say, offering him a smile, one he doesn't return. "Just taking care of business. I'll get out of your hair now."

"You do that," he says.

Shoving off the desk, I tug my dress down, covering myself up before walking out. The music is still going strong, the bass vibrating the floor as I head through the club, navigating the dark hallway to the back door.

A cloud of smoke greets me as I step outside, the kind that makes my eyes burn and my nose twitch. Ricardo lurks there, right outside the door, frantically puffing on a cigarette, lips wrapped around the end of it like a porn star sucking dick. He turns when he hears me, tensing, *alarmed*, and lets out a stream of smoke my direction.

I wave it away, grimacing. *Gross.*

"Sorry," he mutters, puffing on the thing a few more times, back-to-back, before throwing it down and stomping it out, twisting his boot-clad foot on it so feverishly that he tears it to shreds.

Sorry isn't a word I hear often, especially not from any of the men I encounter in life. I kind of feel bad for the guy. Something's got him frazzled, and really, who am I to judge someone's vices?

"It's okay," I say. "Rough night?"

"You could say that," he says, eyeing me warily. "You one of Amello's girls?"

"You could say that," I tell him, repeating his words.

He nods. "How much?"

"How much *what?*"

"How much do you go for? How much to take you in one of

those back rooms right now and turn you out for an hour?"

The sympathy I felt just a second ago? Gone. "I'm not one of *those* girls."

He laughs dryly. "Come on, name your price."

"Not happening," I repeat. "So if you're looking for pussy, look somewhere else, buddy."

I go to walk around him, but he grabs my wrist to stop me. I snatch my arm away, scowling, and turn to him, stepping right up to him. "Don't touch me."

"Sorry," he says again, this apology not at all genuine, a small smile tugging his lips, like I amuse him. Like me being upset that he touched me is in some way *funny*. I want to smack that look off his face, but it wouldn't make a difference.

Wouldn't change what I know he's thinking.

Would probably get my ass locked up on an assault and battery charge tonight, really, which would lead to a whole host of other problems for me.

Big problems.

Can't risk it.

I take a few steps away when I hear him chuckling under his breath, mumbling, "Pussy probably isn't even *that* good, lady."

"Nice one, Slick Rick," I call back at him as I keep walking. "Your bitterness isn't showing at *all* there."

"Fuck you," he says.

"Yeah, you *wish,* asshole."

I hear the music in Mystic cut off, the DJ's incoherent mumbling replacing it. Closing time. Four o'clock. Shoving my icy hands in my pockets, I walk away, my feet painfully tingling, in that place right before numbness where everything just *stings*.

It's only a few blocks back to my apartment building, on the same street as the cheap bar, Whistle Binkie. My footsteps are hurried as I watch over my shoulder, making sure I'm not being followed. My shoes are gone when I reach the corner, no longer were I kicked them off. *Figures.*

What the hell have I gotten myself into this time?

4

"There's no place like home."

The little girl swung her feet as she whispered those words, tapping her bare heels together, but it wasn't working. Maybe she needed a pair of Ruby Slippers, like Dorothy. The house was big like a palace, so it might've been Oz, even though the road hadn't been yellow bricks leading to it. No, they had been normal streets, with so many cars, and so many people, none of them Munchkins singing songs, not even a pretty pink witch in a bubble.

Just a bunch of flying monkeys.

They belonged to the Tin Man. He didn't have the monkeys in the story, but he did in real life. Her mother called them that sometimes, which confused the little girl, since they didn't have wings. But whatever they were, she didn't like them. They were all loud, and they laughed like everything was *so* funny, but it was the kind of laughing that sounded mean. They said ugly words and called people bad names, and they didn't like girls, although they claimed they did. They kissed them on the mouth, like the Tin Man had kissed her mother, but then they pushed them around like they meant nothing.

The little girl didn't like it there, in that big palace, sitting on the stool at the bar in the kitchen, her legs so short they just dangled.

"There's no place like home," she whispered again, barely hearing herself over the loud chatter, knocking her feet together.

Still not working.

"What are you doing, kitten?"

The little girl raised her head, eyes lifting from her lap, meeting the Tin Man's gaze across from her, the only other person sitting down. His eyes were like metal, cold and gray like clouds.

"I wanna go home," she whispered.

He stared at her. "You are home."

She shook her head.

"You are," he said again. "This is your home, kitten. This is where you belong."

"I don't like it."

"You will get used to it."

"I want Mommy."

"*No.*"

His voice was sharp as he barked that word, silencing everyone in the room. *No one* liked the sound of it, not even the flying monkeys, who didn't think it was funny when the Tin Man got angry.

Tears stung the little girl's eyes, her gaze on her lap again as her bottom lip trembled. "Please."

She could feel so many eyes on her, everyone watching, waiting to see what would happen. A moment passed, where nobody reacted, before the Tin Man crooked his pointer finger beneath her chin, raising her head up with it to make her look at him.

"You do not need her," he said, not a hint of emotion in his words. "I am all you need."

"But—"

Before she could argue, his hand enclosed around her chin, palming her face, his strong, inked fingers digging into her cheeks, squishing them.

He gripped her tightly, leaning closer. "You will *not* speak of her to me again. Do I make myself clear?"

The little girl nodded, tears streaming from her eyes.

He shoved her face away, nearly knocking her from the stool.

"And stop crying," he demanded, standing up to walk away. "She is worth your heartache no more than she was worth mine. We will *both* get over it."

The little girl didn't believe that. She couldn't. *Wouldn't.* She might face her fears and wipe her tears, like her mother had taught her, but she would *never* get over it.

5

Lorenzo

A white split-level house in south Queens.

There's even a picket fence surrounding it.

It's fit for a picture-perfect family: Mom, Dad, two-point-five kids and a golden retriever, living happily in quiet suburbia. Four bedrooms. Three bathrooms. There's a library downstairs. It's in a neighborhood typically free of crime.

No murders.

No robberies.

No fun at all, quite frankly.

Just call me Ward Cleaver. *Leave it to* fucking *Beaver.* The house is all mine. I've found the American Dream.

I've got to say... the shit isn't all it's cracked up to be.

Snow covers the sidewalk that runs along the front of the house. The streets have been plowed since it started snowing, but everything else is doused in a layer of stark white. Standing at the foggy front window of the house, I stare out into the cold morning, watching thick flakes fall from the cloudy sky.

The monochrome tone is pretty consistent with how I'm feeling.

Monotonous. Drab. Tedious.

Fifty other fucking words you'll find in a thesaurus.

I've only lived here for a few months but I'm already itching to move again. Since coming to New York just a few years ago, I've stayed in eleven different places, most of which I hadn't exactly had permission to move into. I see an opportunity and I take it, whether it's acquiring a house or, well, a job position.

What can I say? I'm resourceful.

Can't fault me for that, can you?

"Is it still snowing?"

I turn at the sound of the voice behind me, watching as my little brother steps into the living room. Leo—or Pretty Boy, as I've always called him—is sixteen years younger than me, in his early twenties, while the thirties knocked on my door long ago. We're nothing alike. He's young and hopeful. I grow bitter as I age. He's got a lot of heart. I've been told a time or two that I'm a bit of a callous prick.

He loves this house, this neighborhood, and this dream...

The only thing I love is, well, maybe him.

Everything else is just a fickle fondness that I tend to grow tired of real fucking quick.

"Of course it's snowing," I say, strolling over to the black leather couch to sit down. "I've got things to take care of, so naturally it's going to snow all damn day and make everything as difficult as possible."

Leo steps by me to take the spot in front of the window. "Such optimism."

"Yeah, well, not all of us can be sunshiny all of the goddamn time."

Truthfully? I'm in a pissy mood. I've been home for hours, long enough to witness the sunrise, but that's nothing new. I've been an insomniac most of my life, which is probably why I'm so paranoid. Sleep evades me and people aggravate me, making my trigger finger a little twitchy, if you know what I'm saying.

Usually, I handle it better, the lack of sleep, but today it has me on edge for some reason.

My attention shifts to the coffee table in front of me. The red high heels sit in the center of it, side-by-side. I pick one up, running my fingertips along the red sole. The heel is long and thin, curved a bit, maybe six inches, and sharp enough that, in a pinch, she could've easily taken my good eye out with it.

After all, everything's a weapon if you look at it the right way, and I'm the MacGyver of murder. I could kill a man with a shoe like this. Wouldn't even faze me to have to do it, either.

"Do I even want to know why you've got those?" Leo asks.

I glance at him. "Long story."

"Does it end with your feet shoved into a pair of red pumps? Because if so, I'd really like to hear it."

"I'm afraid it's not nearly that interesting," I say. "Met a woman who was wearing these. She got away, left her shoes behind."

"How very *Cinderella*." He shakes his head. "And what, you're going to try them on every woman in the kingdom until you find her again?"

"If I have to," I say, setting the shoe back down beside the other one. Before I can elaborate, there's a noise upstairs, a loud thump above my head. My gaze drifts toward the ceiling as my back stiffens.

"It's fine," Leo says. "Just Mel."

"Who?"

"Mel," he says again. "You know… my girlfriend?"

"Ah, Firecracker."

He lets out a dramatic sigh. "We've been dating for over a year… you'd think my own brother would remember her name by now."

"Please," I say. "I barely remember *your* name, Pretty Boy. Names mean nothing to me. They're irrelevant. They don't define a person. They just label them. And well, if I'm going to label people, I'm going to label them in a way that defines them to me. Like… Firecracker."

"And how exactly does Firecracker define her?"

"She's loud," I say as feet stomp across the floor above my head, heading for the stairs. "She's kind of bangin'."

He lets out a sharp bark of laughter as he moves away from the window, stepping toward. "Are you hitting on my girlfriend?"

"Wouldn't dream of it," I say. "She's not my type."

"Could've fooled me," Leo says. "Thought your type was *breathing*."

43

"Ha-ha. I'll have you know I've got standards."

"Like?"

"Like a woman that doesn't expect me to have a conversation."

He laughs again, like he finds that genuinely funny. "Oh, the *horror* of having to talk to a female like she's actually a person and not just a warm body."

"Are you mocking me, Pretty Boy?"

"What do you think?"

"I think I've shot people for less attitude."

"Doesn't surprise me," he says. "Sounds like something someone allergic to feelings would do."

"I'm not allergic to feelings. I've got them."

"Do you?"

"Yeah, and right now I'm feeling pretty fucking annoyed by this conversation, so I'd rather we didn't have it."

"Oh, so it's not females you avoid talking to... it's really *feelings* you don't want to talk about. Got it."

He's pushing my buttons.

Leo might be the only person around who isn't afraid to do that. He looks me in the face without hesitation, never balking at what he sees, and he calls me on my shit, like a parent lecturing a child... which is kind of funny, you know, since I raised that little son of a bitch.

I'm supposed to be the mature one, the role model, but instead I think he might be the only thing stopping me from blowing up the whole goddamn world and everyone in it.

You see, I learned long ago that the most valuable thing you have is your reputation. It gets you things money can't buy, opening up doors that are usually sealed tight. Don't listen to that '*fuck what people think*' Sesame Street bullshit they spoon-fed you as a kid. You *should* care what people say about you.

Rumor and gossip... it matters. Because while you might be proud of your character, while you might be the kind of person who doesn't yield, it doesn't mean a damn thing if the jackass coming up behind you believes you're getting out of his way, because he's just going to run you over.

If my stepfather taught me anything, it was that the key to survival is *mimicry*. You be what you need to be for somebody. Wear the skin of a rattlesnake even if there's not a single drop of venom inside of you, because if you make them believe, they won't come close enough to get bit. They won't get close enough to see that maybe it's a disguise; maybe you're not as dangerous as they think. And if they do get that close, well, then you've got a choice: you either surrender or you become the thing they fear most.

I don't surrender.

But not everyone needs the same thing, and that's the trick. You can't just be all *one* thing. If you've gotta be a monster, you be a fucking *shapeshifter*.

And my brother? He's not a predator, so I don't have to be one with him. What Leo needs is someone to depend on, someone to believe in, someone who will protect him, so that's what I am. I'm his family. I'm his friend. I'm a harmless gopher snake without a rattle in my tail.

Who am I *really*? I like to think I'm somewhere in between. Maybe deep down I don't *want* to hurt you, but goddamn it, I will, and I'll destroy myself doing it if I have to. I'll get you even if it kills me. I'm like a honeybee.

I'm also apparently someone who likes animal metaphors when I need some damn sleep.

So blah blah blah, whatever whatever, the point here is *fuck feelings*, they get you nowhere.

"I'm going to bed. If you want someone to talk to, Pretty Boy, your girlfriend will be interrupting in about three seconds. Talk to *her*."

"About what?"

The bubbly voice chimes in right at the three-second mark as Leo's girlfriend waltzes in. Melody Carmichael. Leo calls her *Mel*. Of course I know her name. I made a point to learn it when I realized he was serious about her. Young, blonde, and good-looking, sure, but the girl has a mouth on her. Sometimes she talks so much I wonder how she's breathing, how she's not suffocating on all the words she insists on speaking.

And she cries. Jesus fuck, the girl *cries*. She sat right here on my couch and sobbed two nights ago while watching some movie about a man dying. Leo consoled her, holding her, while I stood in the doorway, wishing it were me that was dead. *Me*, just so I wouldn't have to listen to her blubbering for one more second.

"About Lorenzo's lack of feeling for females," Leo tells her.

Melody laughs. "I don't know... based on the noises coming out of his bedroom at around midnight last night, I'd say he was feeling *something* with a woman."

"He was making *her* feel something. Big difference." Leo turns back to me, cocking an eyebrow. "What was this one's name?"

"Barbie," I say.

"And is Barbie her real name?" Leo asks. "Or is that just what you're calling her, since she was platinum blonde and plastic?"

Okay, he's got me there...

"That's what I thought," he continues when I don't answer. No point wasting my breath. He knows. "Bet you probably don't even remember her real name."

"It was Tina."

"Really?"

"No, I don't know," I say, standing up. "I didn't pay attention to a word she said."

His laughter follows me as I snatch up the pair of heels and stroll toward the doorway. Melody eyes me cautiously as I pass her. She doesn't flinch away... *anymore*... but I wouldn't exactly say she lets her guard down around me, either. Her gaze shifts to the shoes, her brow furrowing. "Are those Loubitons?"

"That's what they say."

"Why do you have them?"

"Why do you ask so many questions?"

She has no comeback for that, which is for the best, considering Leo probably will hold it against me if I sucker punch his girlfriend for meddling in my business. I hear Leo chime in, explaining to her about Cinderella, but I just walk away. Prince

Charming, I am not, nor will I ever be. No, you see, people call me *Scar* for a reason, and it doesn't entirely have to do with the fact that my face got fucked up. I'm the villain; I'm the lion that swooped on in, destroying their pride lands. I killed the king and sent Simba packing. But unlike the fictional Scar from the cartoon, I don't intend to lose at the end of my story. Everything the light touches in this city belongs to me. *I'm* the fucking Lion King.

I know, I know… another animal metaphor.

Man, I need some sleep.

Trudging upstairs, I make my way down the hall, to the bedroom in the far back. Everything about it is impersonal, no distractions—plain white walls and a California king bed with the best mattress money can buy, the kind of memory foam that just cradles you, that embraces you like it *loves* you, cloaked in expensive Egyptian cotton, but none of that makes a bit of difference when it comes time to fall asleep.

After setting the shoes down on top of the only dresser, I peel off all of my clothes, discarding them on the floor, and fall right into the bed on my back, naked. The ceiling fan above me lightly spins around and around and around. I track it with my gaze. It helps me relax, like some strange version of counting sheep, or maybe I just get so dizzy that I eventually pass out, but regardless, I usually catch some sleep that way.

But not today.

No, even as I watch the spinning blades, instead of shutting down, my mind starts to wander, thoughts of a petite brunette with wild hair creeping in. The smirk on her red lips right before she ran that last time, the smug '*I got you, motherfucker*' smile, like she was gloating, invades every part of me, like an infection settling in, eating away at my insides. She has no idea who she's messing with, but she's going to learn. Little Miss Scarlet Letter robbed the wrong motherfucker. I'm getting my money back, every single penny of it, and she'll be damn lucky if I don't take her last breath as interest.

I wonder if she'll smile then, with me pinning her down, my body on top of hers, keeping her locked in place. I wonder if she'll smile when I wrap my hands around her throat, squeezing, pressing against the carotid artery, making her look me in the face as I wring her neck. I wonder if she'll smile as the color drains from her cheeks, as the spark diminishes in her eyes, because I sure as fuck will.

I get hard just thinking about it.

Nothing turns me on more than seeing someone struggle, fighting for survival. It's feral, instincts kicking in. They give it all they've got, because they know if they don't, there will be nothing left. I'll take it all. I'll take their dignity. I'll take their money. I'll take their family, too, if I want it. I'll take their life in every sense of the word. Desperation at its core, exposing those raw nerves of self-preservation. There's nothing more powerful than holding someone's life in your hands, knowing they're not strong enough to overpower you... knowing their only hope is *you* being merciful.

Closing my eyes, I grab my cock, roughly stroking it. Hard and fast, not trying to savor it, needing the release to ease my tension, hoping like hell it'll put me to sleep. It takes less than thirty seconds before my abs clench, my cock pulsating as the orgasm strikes me like a punch to the chest. Gritting my teeth, stifling the groan, I feel it as cum spurts out, hitting my stomach and the bed sheets. Warmth spreads all through my body, tingles coating my skin as my cock twitches. I stroke a few more times, breathing deeply as my muscles relax.

Finally.

Sighing, I let go, keeping my eyes closed, not bothering to clean up the mess. Heaviness settles into my limbs, numbness spreading.

But still... *still*... sleep won't take over.

"Fuck this," I grumble, climbing back out of bed, staggering, swaying, as I head for the shower. "Another day awaits."

* * *

"I thought you were going to bed?"

My brother's still in the living room.

His girlfriend is still with him, too, the two of them on the couch together, cuddling. That's all they ever seem to do. Kiss, and cuddle, and whisper, and fuck, a lovey-dovey cycle, day in and day out, like an old married couple.

"I did," I say, stalling in the doorway.

He blinks at me. "You did?"

"Yes."

"It's only been an hour, bro," he says, "if even *that* long. There's no way you went to sleep."

"I didn't say I went to sleep," I point out. "I said I went to bed."

"What's the point of going to bed if you don't sleep?" As soon as he asks that, he shakes his head. "Never mind."

"Never mind what?" Melody asks, glancing between us. *Nosey as shit.*

"Don't even ask," Leo grumbles.

Her brow furrows. "Don't ask what?"

"He doesn't want you to ask about me tugging one out upstairs."

"Tugging one—*oh*!" Her eyes widen. "Geez."

Leo groans. "I told you not to ask."

Shaking my head, I lean against the doorframe, my gaze going to the window. In the past hour, as I showered and dressed, waking up again, the snow slowed to a barely-present flurry, the conditions much more manageable. "So, how long do you think it should take to find someone in the city?"

"Uh, I don't know," Leo says. "Couple of days... weeks... maybe. How long did it take Ignazio to find who he was looking for?"

"Damn near twenty years," I say.

"Well, there you go," Leo says. "Two decades."

Two decades.

In case you don't know who Ignazio is, let me give you the *Cliff Notes* version of him: guy with a gun and a grudge looking for a girl to make him feel better. Took him way too long to catch up to her, and when he finally did, nothing went according to plan, which is reason number one-hundred and sixty-nine why I tend to work on the fly. I'm the kind of guy who will run into a burning building without thinking of the flames... especially since, you know, chances are *I* set the fire to begin with.

Am I making sense here?

I don't know.

I'm still kind of tired.

Point being, I don't have twenty years to wait. "I'll give it twenty more minutes."

Leo gives me a peculiar look as I pull out my car keys. "You're not driving today, are you?"

"Yes."

"Seriously? You? Driving?"

"Yes."

"With everything being all white and icy?"

"Yes."

"Are you feeling suicidal?"

I laugh at that question. He doesn't want me to answer it. I seem to forever exist in a gray area of life, caught in a web somewhere between homicidal and suicidal, and he knows it, no matter how much I try to shove rose-colored glasses over the boy's eyes. He's not blind to reality.

"As titillating as this conversation has been, Pretty Boy, I've got to go," I say, turning away. "Things won't do themselves, you know."

There's a sex joke in there somewhere, I know, but get your mind out of the gutter. There's still work to do.

"Good luck finding... whoever she is," Leo calls out. "Don't kill yourself! Or anybody else..."

He doesn't mean that in the intentional sense. Don't get it twisted. He just doesn't want me to skid off the road or plow into somebody.

I'm already shivering by the time I make it to my car in the driveway. I start it up, cranking the heat full blast, before reaching into the glove box, where I stash a spare pair of glasses.

The drive into northern Brooklyn should take fifteen minutes, but damn near half an hour passes before I pull up in front of the brick townhouse. Strolling to the front door, I bang on it. I bang… and bang… and bang…

Why the hell isn't anybody answering?

It takes a few minutes before the door is pulled open. Seven stands there, half asleep, dark hair a mess, wearing only a pair of red boxer shorts with elves on them.

Elves, Christmas ones, the pointy-eared little fuckers that work for Santa. He's got elves on his shorts, holding little packages, the words 'Merry Elfin Christmas' written all around them. I tilt my head to the side, staring at them.

Have I mentioned it's nearing the end of January?

Seven blinks rapidly. "Boss? What's going on?"

My gaze flickers to meet his as I shake it off. "Have you found her?"

His brow furrows. "Who?"

"The woman I told you to find."

"I, uh… what?"

"Have you found the woman?" I ask again. "How much more clear do I need to make that?"

"Uh, no, not yet."

"What's taking so long?"

He gapes at me like maybe he thinks I'm crazy, but I'm not the one wearing elf boxers a month after Christmas. "It's only been a few hours."

"So?"

"So… I haven't even had the chance to *look* yet."

"You've had the chance to sleep, though," I point out, gaze drifting back to his boxers. "At least I'm *thinking* you were sleeping, unless the missus has a little people fetish you haven't mentioned."

He seems to just now realize what he's wearing, because he makes a feeble attempt to cover up. "Sorry, boss. Yeah, we were sleeping. Actually, just dozed off a bit ago… figured I'd get right on it after catching a few hours of sleep, but if you need me *now*—"

"Don't worry about it."

"You sure?"

"Positive," I say. "Take your little Keeblers there and go on back to bed."

He hesitantly goes back inside, too tired and cold to insist otherwise. I guess if I want this done before I grow old and die, I'm going to have to do it myself.

Heading back to my car, I again crank up the heat before pulling out my phone, going right down the line, calling every damn number in it.

You know a brunette with a red S tattooed on her wrist?

No. Nope. Not ringing a bell, sorry.

Same conversation, again and again and again.

The day is long, *so goddamn long*, and I spend every waking second of it trying to track down the little thief. Nobody in *my* circles will acknowledge knowing her, at least. It's dusk already, as I sit in my car not far from the bar, just feet from where she robbed me, when my phone rings.

Seven.

"Gambini," I say as I answer it.

"I've got nothing, boss," he says. "I've tried every connection I've got and the description is just too vague. I even got up with Amello, since he runs his games out of that neighborhood, and he said she didn't sound like any girl he's ever come across."

"Figures," I mutter. "Thanks."

"Anytime. I'll keep digging, see what I can stir up."

"You do that."

Hanging up, I slip my phone into my pocket before strolling into Whistle Binkie, taking a seat right at the bar, encountering the same bartender from last night. Once again, he eyes me with alarm.

"Rum," I tell him. "Just give me the bottle."

He obliges, shoving a half-empty cheap bottle onto the bar in front of me. I'm not even going to pretend tonight, ripping the spout right out and tipping it back.

There aren't many other people here at this hour. I look around curiously, thinking maybe she might show up again, but I'm not that lucky. I gaze at the empty stool, where she sat less than twenty-four hours ago, staring at it for a moment before something strikes me.

"Hey, you wouldn't by chance remember a woman that was in here last night, would you?" I ask the bartender. "Young, brunette, red dress, sat *right there*..."

The bartender's attention shifts to the stool I point at before he looks at me again. "Morgan, you mean?"

I raise an eyebrow. "Maybe, if the Morgan you're talking about has a tattoo on her wrist."

"Cursive S," the bartender says.

Son of a bitch. "That's the one."

"I've always wondered what it stood for," he says. "She comes in sometimes, sits by herself, orders something cheap, flirts a bit then jets back out. I asked her once, you know, about the tattoo."

"What did she tell you?"

"She said it stood for '*stay out of my fucking business*'."

Okay, that makes me laugh. It probably shouldn't. She's got a mouth on her, that's for sure. "So, Morgan, you say?"

"Yep."

Morgan. I don't like it.

"Tell me something, Bar Boy. You wouldn't happen to know where I could find this Morgan, would you?"

He hesitates, like he doesn't want to answer that. *Ding, ding, ding...* there it is. I pull out my wallet, figuring cash always loosens lips, and tense when I open it.

Shit. Still empty.

Almost forgot she *robbed* me.

Once again, I laugh, even though I shouldn't find it funny. I don't even have anything on me to pay for the liquor I'm drinking. *Unbelievable.*

The woman is starting to be a thorn in my side, but I have to admit, as frustrating as it's been, I haven't had a dull moment in the past twenty-four hours.

I shove my wallet back away, standing up from the bar. "Tell me where to find her."

"I only know where she works," he says. "Will that help?"

6
Morgan

"Morgan... oh God, Morgan, baby... you're so *tight*."

His voice is nasally. So damn nasally. He sounds like a character off of *South Park*. Everything dries up at the mere sound of it, all desire withering away, dying an unfortunate death.

Why does he always have to *talk*?

Grimacing, I shove my face into the black leather couch cushion, unable to stop the cry that escapes my throat. *Ugh*, it hurts, like being fucked with a knife, pain stabbing at my insides. He probably doesn't hear the sound I make, though.

The music is too loud.

"You love that, don't you?" he asks, his hands grasping my hips as he thrusts, leaning over and shouting so I'll hear him. "Love the way my cock feels?"

"You know I do," I grind out, nearly choking on the lie. I hope he makes this fast.

He won't, though. No, I'm not that lucky. He'll savor every second of ignorant bliss, oblivious to the fact that I'm not into it. Stubby fingers explore, searching for a sweet spot he'll never find. I could draw him a map and it would still evade him, like the Holy Grail exists somewhere between my thighs.

Squeezing my eyes shut, I try to detach, try to not think about the fact that a sleazy middle-aged jackass in a cheap suit is pounding into me from behind, sweating and panting and having the time of his life, while I'm just desperately waiting him out.

Waiting... and waiting... and waiting...

A red glow covers everything. *The red room*. It's a cliché, I think, but it's a favorite here at Mystic for some reason. It feels like an eternity passes, each slam of his hips driving my face further into the couch. His overpowering cologne clings to the air, smelling sickeningly like pine, swaddling my senses until I gag. *Gross.* It's stifling. It's suffocating. I just can't seem to *breathe.* My chest aches for a deep breath I haven't taken in a long time, my heart locked in a steady, dull rhythm.

His grip on me tightens. I open my eyes when I feel it, knowing he's close to finishing. *Finally.* A few more hard thrusts before he grunts, stilling, dropping his body weight over on top of me. An exhilarated laugh escapes him, his warm breath ghosting across my skin. I shiver from disgust when his lips find my neck, his tongue drawing a path toward my ear, before he whispers, "I wish I could fuck you all night long."

"Me, too," I say, another lie, because *hell no.* I can hardly stomach a fifteen-minute rendezvous.

"Maybe next time," he whispers before moving away to stand up.

Exhaling, I slide down flat against the couch, relieved to have him not touching me. *For now.*

I watch as he gathers his clothes to get dressed. He's classically handsome, I suppose, if you like that sort of thing—dark hair, bronzed skin, eyes the color of an afternoon sky, deep dimples and perfect teeth. He's even got the most adorable freckles.

His phone rings as he pulls himself together, discarding the condom in the small trashcan behind a small bar on the left side. Pulling his phone out, he frowns. "Sorry, hate to cut this short, but I have to take this call."

Sorry? *I'm* not sorry. *Pfft, bye.*

He jets out into the hall, heading for the back exit. As soon as he's out of sight, I breathe a sigh of relief and get up. My pussy throbs but not in the good way, not in that thoroughly fucked, fully satiated way. No, it screams angrily at me for allowing the intrusion (I know, I know… ugh, ick, *gross…*). I'm pretty sure the man doesn't know the definition of foreplay, and quite frankly, the thought of his mouth on me, the thought of him caressing my body just makes me queasy, so painfully dry it will forever be.

I make my way to the changing room, the last door at the end of the hall by the exit. It looks like a middle school locker room. Smells like one, too. Hell, even *feels* like one sometimes. *Uncomfortable.* It's empty, all of the women working, but I've had my fill of this place for the night.

I'm getting out of here.

I go straight to my locker on the end, opening it and grabbing my black duffel bag to gather my things. I strip out of the skimpy black lingerie, changing into a pair of yoga pants and tank top, putting my coat on over it. Running my fingers through my hair, I pull it back into a ponytail as tingles creep along my spine, an unsettling feeling in the pit of my stomach.

I glance around the vacant locker room.

It's strange, the sensation that flows through me. It's one I'm all too familiar with. It's the feeling of being watched, the feeling that I'm not alone, even when I know I am.

Paranoia is a bitch.

Grabbing my bag, I slide my feet back into a pair of cheap black heels before leaving. My footsteps stall outside, and I glower. I hoped I could skedaddle out of here without enduring an awkward goodbye, but no such luck.

He's hanging up from his call when I appear.

"Sorry again," he mumbles, shoving the phone away as he eyes me. "You off work now?"

Technically, I had the entire night off, but this is the only place I'm willing to meet up with him. "Yep, heading out early."

"You, uh... want me to walk you home?"

I force a smile. "Nice try."

"It's just an offer," he says, raising his hands defensively. "Just looking out for you. It's late, and dark, and—"

"And I can take care of myself, thanks," I say, cutting him off.

"You ever going to trust me, Morgan?" he asks. "I'm here to *help* you."

"I know," I say. "But trust, well... it's not easy for me. And

57

it's not that I don't trust *you*. I just don't trust anything. You know how it is."

"I do," he admits, frowning. "Anyway, I should go. You okay? You need some money or, uh…?"

He goes to reach for his wallet.

I want to hit him in the nose for it.

"I don't want your money," I say. "I'm not a prostitute."

"Of course," he says. "I just figured…"

"That I needed money," I say, finishing his thought, "but I don't need *money* from you. What I need is for you to actually do your job, detective."

He grimaces. He doesn't seem to ever like that reminder.

Detective Gabriel Jones with the 60th precinct.

"Look, I'm going to talk to them again," he says. "First thing tomorrow, I promise."

"Thank you."

Gabe leaves, getting in his unmarked black Ford with tinted windows. I wait until he's gone before I start walking, keeping my head down, my steps hurried. My gaze flickers along the road, making sure he isn't circling and following.

He's done it before.

I've caught him every time.

There's no sign of the black Ford, but I still can't shake that feeling, the one that tells me something is *off*. I run the last block to my building, darting inside and pausing by the entrance, staring out the square glass window, waiting for *somebody*.

Nobody's around.

"I'm losing my mind," I grumble, padding up the stairs to my top floor apartment.

First order of business is a hot shower. I scrub every inch of my body, washing it all away. Every touch, every kiss, and every thrust—I purge it from my memory as if it never happened. Afterward, I dry my hair and grab a too-big, plain white t-shirt from my closet, not bothering with any other clothes.

I head for the steep winding metal steps in the corner of the tiny living room. Scaling them quickly, I push the door open at the top and step out onto the rooftop.

The frigid winter air slaps me, stinging my face and assaulting my bare legs, but I ignore it. Pulling myself up onto the concrete ledge along the side, I peer out into the city. Nine, maybe ten o'clock at night, a Sunday in the Lower East Side of Manhattan, not far from the East River. I can see for blocks, a bustle all around me as cars fill the streets and people walk along the sidewalks.

I'm barely out here for a minute before that feeling rolls through me again, so intense my stomach clenches.

I hate the sensation.

It's like being haunted, like there's always a ghost around me, following me, taunting me, not ever letting me be in peace.

I don't move, don't bother to look, as a chill ripples down my spine. Despite my best effort to stay composed, I tremble, goose bumps erupting along my skin as my hair stands on end, my reaction having little to do with the coldness outside.

"What do you want from me?" I whisper, staring out at the city.

"My money."

The voice rings out behind me, so close... *too close*. The gravelly deep tone hits me like a punch to the chest as it unexpectedly answers my question.

Someone's here. *Oh god.*

A shaky breath escapes me as I turn to look behind me on the roof.

The second I see the face, every muscle inside of me seizes, my heart even skipping a beat, hesitating, like it hasn't in a long time. My eyes scan him in the darkness—sharp features, strong jawline, sturdy build and a long scar that cuts through the side of his face, the jagged groove glowing in the moonlight. His eyes are opposite shades of blue—one damn near midnight, while the other is more of an early morning skyline.

Classically handsome, maybe not, but something about him is mesmerizing, like watching him is hypnotizing. It's not enough to overshadow my fear, though, because he's just as alarming as he is alluring, maybe even more so.

Scratch that. Definitely more so.

He stares at me, not a flicker of emotion showing on his face. There's almost something inhuman about it.

I'm not sure what to say or what to do, so I just stare back, but he doesn't seem to like that. No, his cheek twitches, his eyes narrowing, so I avert my gaze, scanning the rooftop around us.

Think. Think. Think.

He's blocking the way back inside, so I glance behind me, over the ledge, at the busy city street below.

Ugh, that drop would hurt like a son of a bitch.

"I don't recommend jumping," he says, "unless you want to go *splat.*"

I turn back to him. He's right. The odds of surviving that fall aren't in my favor. "What do you want?"

"I just told you what I want." He takes another step toward me, and another, and another, until he's close enough to reach out and shove me, if he wants, since I'm still sitting on the ledge. "I want my money."

"What mon—?"

His hand darts out, snatching ahold of my throat, long fingers wrapping around and squeezing, literally cutting off my words, silencing my plea of ignorance. I gasp, startled, panic flowing through me as the force of the blow thrusts me back.

I damn near lose my balance.

The only thing keeping me from tipping over the edge is his strong grasp, but it's also cutting off my flow of air, so...

Reaching up, I clutch tight to his wrist, but I don't fight. If I fight him he's liable to throw me right over the side, so I just hold on, clinging like he's my life raft, because if I go over, I'm taking him, too, not a shred of doubt about it in my mind.

"Don't act like you don't know what I'm talking about," he says. "If you had enough balls to steal from me, you shouldn't have a problem owning up to it."

He jerks me toward him, yanking me onto my feet on the roof. I inhale sharply when his hand leaves my throat, my knees weak, dizziness obscuring my vision. I'm half a second away from collapsing, my legs buckling, when he moves closer, pressing into me, pinning me against the concrete ledge, keeping me upright. He wedges between my legs, prying them apart, trapping me in place with his body. I'm hyper-aware of the fact that I'm nearly naked, damn near straddling his leg right now. I'm not sure if he realizes it, if he knows his knee is pressing into my crotch, but I hope not, because *ugh*... let me find some dignity here, will you?

"Let's try this again," he says, staring me in the face. "I say I want my money, and you say…?"

"Okay," I whisper.

He cocks his left eyebrow, like he finds my answer curious. "Okay?"

"I don't know what you want me to say."

"I want you to say you'll give me my money." His hand grasps my chin, tilting my face further toward him. "And then I want those pretty lips of yours to beg me for mercy, because depending on how fast you pay me back, I might be inclined to take it easy on you if you ask."

Before I can say anything, much less what he *wants* me to say, the man steps back, removing himself from my personal space, like just expects me to comply.

I suspect he's used to getting his way.

"I'll give you your money," I say quietly, taking a deep breath.

He nods. "Good girl."

I cringe at those words as I shove past him, heading for the rooftop door leading to my apartment. I don't exactly know who he is, or what he's capable of, but if he's ballsy enough to threaten George, I can't rule out him being some kind of monster. My mind's a flurry of thoughts, none I can seem to get a firm grasp on. *Scar*, they called him. I don't even know how he found me, which is most concerning of all.

How the hell did he get here?

The man walks in step with me, not letting me out of arm's reach. It isn't until I hit the warmth of my apartment, heading back down those metal steps, that I realize how cold the outside is. My teeth chatter, my skin flushed, body trembling. My hands are like blocks of ice, and I flex my fingers, trying to loosen them up again.

I head for the kitchen, having only a few seconds to pull myself together and *do something*.

He steps into the room behind me.

The moment he does, I lunge.

Throwing my body against his, I knock him back a few steps, catching him off guard with the force of the hit. His shock buys me enough time to put up a fight, to swing and kick and flail, kneeing him in the nuts.

BAM.

He flinches, hunching over from the low blow, giving me the chance to shove him into the stove. Reaching into the sink, I frantically feel around, blindly snatching up a dirty steak knife. I hold it up to his neck when he comes at me, the jagged blade pressing against his Adam's apple, digging into the skin.

"I'll slit your throat," I tell him, my voice steady, even though my hand is shaking so hard I almost *accidentally* cut him. "I swear, I'll—"

He reacts fast, so fast I don't anticipate it. Grabbing my wrist, he twists my arm, gripping tight, damn near pulling my shoulder out of socket. I grit my teeth to stifle a cry, pain ripping up my arm. His fingers dig into the underside of my wrist, jagged nails tearing at the skin as he presses against the pressure point, forcing me to loosen my hold. He rips the knife away with ease, still clutching my wrist, staring at my tattoo.

Which he scratched.

Which is now bleeding.

Ugh.

"Morgan," he says, his face contorting. "I was surprised to hear that was your name. I expected it to start with an 'S'. Makes me curious what *this* thing stands for."

He shoves my wrist into my face, making me hit myself. I scowl, trying to yank free from his grasp. "I'd rather die than tell you about it."

"That can be arranged," he says, letting go of my arm before tossing the knife back in the sink. "I want my money, Scarlet. I'm not going to tell you again."

I clutch my wrist, frowning, and stalk away from him, my heart viciously pounding in my chest as I head for the bedroom, not surprised that he follows.

He's not going to let me out of his sight.

A few crumpled bills lay on top of the stand beside the bed. I grab them, my stomach gurgling. I feel around in my coat pockets before scouring through my duffle bag, grabbing every cent I have left to my name before turning to him. "I've got three-hundred dollars."

He stares at me. "Three hundred."

"Well, more like two-ninety-four, but close enough."

"There was a thousand dollars in my wallet. Where is it?"

"I don't have it."

"What did you do with it?"

I don't answer that, biting my cheek. I'm not telling him. It's none of his business, and I need him far away from my situation. Far away from *me*.

"Look, can't we just...?" I motion to the bed, bile burning my chest as it forces its way up my throat, punishing me for making this suggestion. "You know."

"Fuck?" he guesses.

I swallow thickly, nodding.

He steps closer, invading my personal space once more. I have room to move away but I stand my ground, not wanting to recoil from his advances. I don't look him in the face, keeping my head down, but I feel his breath against my cheek as he leans over, whispering, "We can fuck, absolutely, if that's what you want. But you'll still owe me afterward, because I don't pay for pussy, especially pussy that has a habit of whoring itself out to *cops*."

A shiver rips through me.

My knees go weak.

That weird feeling still lingers inside of me, and I realize, the whole time, it was him. He was there. He followed me. I don't know how, but my gut says he did.

"I don't—" I almost say I don't whore myself out, *period*, but that's a lie, technically. I've done it before out of desperation. Besides, life fucks me every single day, and I just bend over and take it. I whore myself out to life in an attempt to keep breathing. "I don't know what else I can give you. So either fuck me or kill me, because I've got nothing left to offer beyond that."

He stares at me as I drop down on the edge of the messy bed. He's contemplating it. I know he is. I know his type. He's debating whether or not that will be adequate payment, if I'm even worth the thousand dollars I stole from him.

"You don't look like a junkie, so I'm assuming it's not drugs," he says. "Although, that would explain the prostitution."

I grimace. "I'm not a prostitute."

"You just offered to fuck me for money."

"Well, yeah, technically, but…"

I don't finish that because I'm not sure how I'm supposed to, if it'll even make sense to him. *Unlikely.*

"Beg for your life," he says after a moment.

I shake my head.

"Beg me," he demands. "Get on your knees."

I shake my head again.

Reaching beneath his coat, inside his shirt, he whips out a black gun, pointing it at me, pressing the muzzle against my forehead. "*Beg.*"

"No."

The word sounds weak, but I know he hears it. I cut my eyes at him, everything inside of me taut, like a string close to snapping from being pulled in different directions, already threadbare.

He stares at me, his expression blank, his finger on the trigger.

Slowly, something in him shifts, the corner of his mouth twitching, the slightest hint of a smirk tugging his lips. The sight of it makes my heart pause for the second time tonight, losing rhythm for just a moment. I don't know what to make of it. Why the hell is he *smiling*?

"You're going to pay back every penny," he says, "*plus*

interest. An extra hundred for every day it takes you. You got me?"

"Yes."

He lowers the gun, tucking it away, before snatching the money out of my hand. He turns then, like he plans to just leave, but my voice calls out, stopping him. "Wait."

"What?"

"I don't even know who you are. How am I supposed to pay you if I can't find you?"

He shrugs. "Figure it out, Scarlet."

* * *

"Figure it out, Scarlet," I grumble mockingly as I shove the door away from the cinderblock at Mystic, back here for the second time tonight.

At work. On my day off. Again. *Bullshit.*

I keep to myself, not bothering with anyone, until I reach the office and tap on the door, hoping George is around. I hear shuffling inside, breathing a sigh of relief until it opens and I come face-to-face with somebody who isn't who I want to see. *Ugh.*

Slick Rick, the asshole named Ricardo, the one who clearly hasn't yet succeeded in *sending a message* to the guy they call Scar.

"You need something, cupcake?" he asks, eyes scanning me. I'm wearing the equivalent of pajamas, yet he still gawks at me like I'm indecent or something.

"I need to see the boss," I say, pushing past him.

I don't make it far before he grabs my arm to stop me.

"He's busy," he says. "Come back later."

I yank away from him. "I can wait."

George is sitting at his desk, on the phone. His raised voice echoes through the room, so enraged it keeps me from approaching. Instead, I linger by the entrance as Ricardo shuts the door and takes a seat, rubbing his hands along the thighs of his black slacks, like his palms might be sweaty. *Not good.*

"What the fuck do you mean they said *nothing?*" George yells. "How do you get robbed when they say nothing? Huh? What, they walk in and you just hand over the money, they don't even have to *ask*?"

He pauses long enough to take a deep breath, long enough for whoever's on the line to try to explain, but it does nothing to calm George down.

"I don't care!" he yells. "There's no excuse! Do something about it! Nobody steals from me!"

He doesn't bother hanging up, instead slamming his phone down on the desk, over and over and over, shattering the screen. I don't even think he notices me here, tunnel vision sending his attention straight to Ricardo. "Why hasn't that thieving son of a bitch been *dealt* with?"

"I'm working on it," Ricardo says. "I called him, trying to get another meeting, and his lackey said he was *busy*."

"Busy robbing me!"

I'm almost inclined to chime in, to ask if they're talking about Scar... because if so, he was actually busy stalking me to my apartment, but I remain silent instead. *Not my problem.*

"I'll try again," Ricardo says, "right now."

Ricardo gets up, slipping out of the office. George's gaze trails him but stalls on me. *Shit.* "You need something, Morgan?"

"I, uh... was just trying to see about maybe picking up some more work this week?"

That's not what I wanted.

I wanted to get some information about Scar, but I'm pretty sure that's a topic I shouldn't bring up at the moment.

"Come back tomorrow," he says, shoving out of his chair. "I don't have time to deal with your schedule right now."

"Oh-kay," I mumble as he storms past me, leaving me in the office alone. I glance around. No cameras in here. I don't know how long he's going to be gone, so I make it fast, scooping up his discarded, shattered phone, muttering, "Please work."

Ding. Ding. Ding.

It works.

Screen lights up, asking for the security code. *Shit.* I immediately try the usual combinations, repeating numbers and birthdays, before hitting *1-2-3-4* and rolling my eyes when it opens. I scroll through his contacts, finding a number listed under Scar. Opening the top desk drawer, I pull out a pen, jotting the number down on my hand before returning the phone to how I found it. I drop the pen back into the drawer, seeing the cash still just lying there that I gave him.

Fuck.

Fuck.

Fuck it.

I snatch it up, shoving it in my pocket, before shutting the drawer again and heading for the door, running right into someone as soon as I step out.

"Whoa buddy," I say as Ricardo appears in front of me.

That was close.

He narrows his eyes at me. "What are you doing?"

"Leaving," I say, trying to move when he grabs my arm for the second time tonight.

"What *were* you doing?"

"Pretty sure I don't answer to you," I say, yanking away, "so keep your hands to yourself, *cupcake.*"

I leave, because there's no way I'm hanging around here. The money feels like it's burning a hole in my pocket, glowing like a beacon, screaming thief... thief... thief...

Once back in my apartment, I head for my black duffel bag, scouring through it to pull out my cheap little cell phone, flipping it open. *Dead.* Plugging it into the charger, I wait until it comes alive before punching in the numbers scribbled on my palm, calling Scar.

It rings... and rings... and rings.

Voicemail picks up.

"It's, uh... me... *whatever.* I'm sure you know who I am. I've got your money, so come get it, I guess."

I flip the phone closed, staring at it for a moment before tossing it back in the bag. I'm not sure how long it'll take him to show up, but I hope he makes it quick.

I want to be done with this.

I have more important things to deal with.

7

"Where is she?"

The Tin Man's voice was angrier than the little girl had ever heard it, laced with bitter venom as he hissed every syllable. She trembled, hiding in the bottom of the kitchen pantry, tucked behind some boxes.

One week.

She'd been at that house for seven long days, and every minute that passed made her hate it more and more. It made her hate *him*. She hated him more than she'd ever hated anybody, more than Buzz and Woody hated Sid from next door.

He was *horrible*.

Her stomach growled as she chewed on a piece of dry bread that she'd stolen from the counter, hoping it would soak up all of her queasiness, but it wasn't working.

"I don't know," another man said, one of the flying monkeys, the one who stuck closest to the Tin Man. He was more like the Cowardly Lion, she thought, because he was big, and looked mean, but maybe he was more of a softie, because the Tin Man spooked him sometimes.

But then again, the Tin Man spooked *everybody*.

"Unacceptable," the Tin Man growled. "Find her! You hear me? I will not do this again. I want to know where she went and what she is doing. *Now!*"

"Yes, *Vor*," the Cowardly Lion muttered, stomping out of the kitchen as the Tin Man lost his temper, glass shattering against the wall near the pantry. The little girl whimpered, nearly choking on the bread, and tried to crawl further back into the shadows as footsteps came her way.

The door opened, light blasting her. Those cold gray eyes met her gaze, a frown on his face. *Guess he found me.* He stared at her in strained silence before crouching down, getting on her level. "What are you doing in there?"

She shrugged.

He scanned her, pursing his lips. The Tin Man wore a fresh, crisp suit the same color as his eyes. It made him look even more robotic, like he really had on armor. His gaze shifted to the hunk of bread she clutched as he scrunched up his nose. "You stink."

Her brow furrowed.

"You have become feral," he said, his lips twitching before a small laugh escaped, light and amused, his anger gone, just like that. *Scary.* "You have not bathed all week. You are filthy. You still have on the same nightgown and your hair has not been brushed."

She scowled, knowing that was true. She was dirty, and she probably *did* stink, but it didn't matter. She was just waiting for her mother to come. She promised she would find her.

"I have been patient with you," he said. "You hide from me. You avoid me. I have not punished you for breaking the rules. You leave your room when I tell you not to, you snub my kindness, refuse to eat what I have sent up and instead choose to steal from my kitchen. You *steal.* I understand you are upset, kitten. Your mother has hurt you. She hurt me, too."

"You hurt *her,*" the little girl said. "You made Mommy cry."

"I know I did," he said, not denying that, "but she gave me no choice."

"Why?"

"That is not a question we ask. It does not matter. But we are here now, you and I, and she is not, so we must learn to live without her... *together.*"

The little girl shook her head.

"You will obey me," he said.

She shook her head again.

He didn't like that answer.

Reaching into the pantry, he grabbed her arm, yanking her

out of it and throwing her across the room. She skidded along the kitchen floor, dropping her bread, stunned, and started to cower, knocking a stool out of the way as she pressed back against the bar.

The Tin Man moved toward her.

"You *will* obey me," he said again, the anger returning to his voice. "You can either cooperate and be happy here, or I can make every moment torture for you. Understand?"

She nodded slowly.

"Use your words," he demanded.

"Yes," she whispered.

"Yes *what?*"

"Yes, sir."

He crouched down, reaching for her, ignoring the fact that she flinched. He grasped her chin, his touch firm as he pulled her face toward him, mere inches of space between them. It made her heart race and her body shake and not in a good way.

"Yes, *Papa*," he said, "or Daddy, if you prefer. Your choice, but choose one, because you will call me as I am."

She said nothing, trying to hold her breath, wishing he would let go, but he waited... and waited... and waited, staring at her.

He didn't even *blink*.

"Yes...?" he prompted. "Use your words."

"Yes, Daddy."

His expression softened as he pressed his lips to her forehead, kissing the spot her mother had last kissed, taking it for himself. Tears filled the little girl's eyes, but she held them back, knowing crying would make it worse.

"Good little kitten," he said, standing back up, turning away without another look. "Go clean yourself up. I have something to do. I want you bathed by the time I return, and I want that nightgown *burned*. If you still stink when I get back, I will hose you off in the backyard."

The little girl may not have known much, but she knew enough to believe him. He *meant* those words.

8

Lorenzo

Picking up the cheap square coaster from the bar, I set it on its corner and attempt to spin it, watching as it wobbles and falls right over. A cliché in a kilt grins up at me from it, discolored, parts flaked off from a splash of rum destroying the pulp board.

Whistle Binkie.

It's Scottish, obviously, but who the hell knows what it means? Probably something as horribly stereotypical as the rest of the place. *As fucking formulaic as my life is becoming.* I think about asking the bartender, figuring if anyone knows, it would be him, but that would mean interrupting the babbling blonde sitting to my left, and that's not happening, considering I'm supposed to be listening to whatever she's going on about—puppies or kittens or rainbows, I don't know.

Besides, I don't *really* give a shit. I'm just trying to distract myself until Blondie's good and lit and willing to bend over for me in the bathroom.

Which, judging from the slurred giggling that reaches my ears as a hand slides along my thigh, is probably soon…

I shift toward her, just enough to see her, but not enough to give her a full-on view of my scar. She knows it's there, of course— she saw it when I walked in after ten o'clock tonight, and she's spent the past two hours just barely stopping herself from asking me how I got it. Women like a bad boy with a tragic backstory. Maybe it's the thrill of it, the excitement of being with someone dangerous, or maybe it's biological, something rooted deep within them, those mothering genes that makes women want to nurture those the world turns its back on.

You see, men and women, we're wired differently. Women look at me and think, 'poor baby, he just needs some love', whereas men? Men take one look at my face and think, 'stay away from that motherfucker'. But go ahead and tell a woman that. Tell her I'm dangerous. Tell her to stay away.

It'll just make her want me more.

"You're beautiful, you know," I say when Blondie stops chattering long enough for me to chime in. It's not a lie. She is beautiful, but *all* women are in their own way, aren't they?

Well, all of them except for my mother, but I don't know if *woman* is the word I would use to describe her. She was more of a raging bitch.

Blondie's cheeks tinge pink, a grin on her gloss-coated lips. Her posture loosens more as she leans into me, giving me a whiff of her strong, flowery perfume.

My nose twitches.

"Can I ask you something?" she asks, her voice dropping low, the syllables lazily tumbling from her tongue. "Your, uh... scar." She waves her finger in the direction of my face. "How did that happen?"

I start to answer, concocting a bullshit sob story to avoid spilling my truth to someone I don't know, someone I'll *never* know beyond what her pussy feels like, when the stool on the other side of me jerks out, the wooden legs scratching against the floor.

The noise is irritating.

I *cringe*.

Something slaps down on the bar in front of me, on top of the coaster, covering the little Scottish man.

"He pissed off the wrong woman, I'm guessing," a sugary voice interrupts, so close it's like she's speaking right in my ear. "He's got the kind of face you can't help but want to fuck up."

Blondie's eyes widen, like she's horrified someone would say something so cruel, like *she's* offended, but all I feel is a slight stirring, a battle inside of me between amusement and annoyance.

I'm not sure which sensation is going to win that war.

74

"Well, she's not *entirely* wrong," I say, glancing at the bar, a thick stack of cash greeting me. "It was a man, though."

She scoffs. "Some floozy's husband, then."

I pick the money up, shifting away from Blondie to relax back against the stool. My eyes flit to the right, to the exasperated brunette, her eyes not so doe-like anymore. They're narrowed, aimed at me, her arms folded across her chest.

Scarlet.

Her guarded stance only entertains me more, a smirk tugging my lips as I sort through the cash, counting it. It's been almost a week since I confronted her, which means the interest racked up quickly. A few hundreds, some twenties, and a shitload of ones... more ones than I've ever held at one time before.

"It's all there," she says, her voice turning as defensive as her presence.

I ignore that and keep counting, absently running through numbers as my gaze trails her. Her flimsy coat covers most of what she's wearing, leaving only black fishnets visible. Black high heels peek out of a bag hanging from her shoulder, instead of being on her feet where they belong. Thick, dark makeup surrounds her eyes as a golden glow radiates from her cheeks. Some of it is smudged, like she's been wearing it for a while, but her deep red lipstick looks fresh.

She shifts position when my gaze lingers on her mouth, like she's uncomfortable with my attention, her skin shimmering under the dim bar lights, flecks of glitter coating her.

I turn back to the money, saying nothing until I finish counting. "There's only thirteen hundred here."

"I already gave you three hundred," she says. "That makes sixteen hundred... the thousand I took, plus an extra six hundred, since it took me six days."

"Seven days," I say, glancing at my watch. "You missed midnight by about twenty minutes."

She blanches, jaw going slack. "That's *bullshit*. I've been trying to get ahold of you for a week! You haven't answered any of my calls!"

Huh. "You called me?"

"Yes!"

I pull my phone from my pocket, opening my call list.

Missed call.

Missed call.

Missed call.

All blocked numbers.

"See?" she says. "Look at all those missed calls!"

"Number's blocked," I say, putting the phone away.

"So?"

"So, I don't take calls from cowards."

She blinks rapidly. "Coward? I left you voicemails!"

"I don't listen to those. And before you even say it, I don't text, either."

"That's just *stupid*," she says. "You've been nowhere. I've looked. And people know who you are, sure, but nobody *knows* you. They don't know where to find you. All they have is this stupid phone number that you never seem to answer. How is that *my* fault?"

"Tough break," I say as I pull my wallet out of the back pocket of my jeans. I shove the wad of cash in, barely able to fold it before putting it away. "You should get better friends."

"That is... *wow*." She laughs, not a stitch of humor to the sound. "I don't know what I did to deserve this, but I must be the *worst* person in the world to have stumbled upon *you*."

I don't respond to that, watching her posture change, outrage washing away all restraint. She yanks her coat open, a little black dress greeting me beneath. She pats herself down, reaching into her bra and yanking out a stack of bills. More singles. She counts them, flicking through the money so heatedly I'm expecting her to rip a few.

Shaking her head, she tosses the cash on the bar in front of me. "Twenty-nine dollars. Oh, and..." She reaches into the bag on her shoulder, pulling out a small zippered pouch. She holds it upside down above the bar, a few coins spilling out of it. She scowls. "Like, sixty-six cents."

"Look at that," I say, snatching up the money—even the change—and shoving it in my pocket, not bothering to put it in my wallet this time. "Only seventy dollars and thirty-four cents to go."

She storms away, nearly knocking over the stool as she goes, charging through the bar and disappearing outside into the cold night. I turn in my seat again, facing Blondie, not surprised to see she's watching me warily, no doubt trying to make sense of that exchange in her drunken state.

"Where were we?" I brush a curl from Blondie's face, my fingertips grazing her warm cheek, making the blush return. "Oh, right… my scar."

I launch into a story about a doomed afternoon in Central Park with my family, how we witnessed a mob hit and became collateral damage in the process. *Leave no witnesses behind.* I survived, vowing vengeance on those that attacked us. I've got her eating out of the palm of my hand, more hero than villain in her mind, as I place a hand on her knee and slowly run it up her thigh. I'm about to take it further when the door bursts open. Coldness sweeps through the bar, footsteps loud as they stomp my way, even though the woman is in her bare feet for some reason. *She's fucking crazy.*

Scarlet shoves in beside me again, holding a black leather wallet. She flips it open, the driver's license of some middle-aged white guy greeting me from the plastic window inside. She raids it for cash, counting out loud.

"Twenty… thirty… forty… fifty… fifty-five… sixty… sixty, uh, seven." She groans. "You've gotta be kidding me."

"Did you just pickpocket someone else to pay me?"

She shoves the money my way. "Save your self-righteous pandering for the floozy over there. I'm three-dollars short."

"And thirty-four cents," I point out, taking the cash.

"And thirty-four cents," she mocks. "Unbelievable."

"I'll give it to you," I say. "The few dollars you're missing."

"Really?"

"It'll cost a hundred dollars for every day it takes you to pay me back, of course, but sure…"

She groans. "*Of course.*"

Her gaze scans the bar, settling on the bartender as he heads our general direction. It's the same one from every other time. He gave me a bottle of rum as soon as I sat down again. He's learning.

I watch as Scarlet's expression shifts, a flit of a smile on her lips. She shoves the stool further away to get closer to the bar, reaching up on her tiptoes to lean across it, gathering his attention. He approaches, looking at me warily, like he's assessing whether or not she's *with* me right now, before focusing his attention on her. There's a glint in his eyes, apparently deciding she's fair game.

He smiles. "Hey, Morgan."

She arches an eyebrow, her face lighting up. "You remember."

Her voice changes when she says that, growing sweeter. She's exaggerating every syllable, blatantly flirting.

I wonder if she'd be doing that if she knew he was the one who ratted her out to me.

"Of course," he says. "What can I get for you?"

"Well, uh, actually..." Her smile grows sheepish as she gently bites down on her bottom lip, a moment of silence passing before she whispers, "I was kind of hoping you'd do me a favor. It's totally okay if you can't, I completely understand, and I really hate to ask..."

"What do you need?"

"To borrow four dollars," she says. "Like I said, you can tell me no, but it's just that, you know, it's been a long night, and..."

"Oh, don't worry about it," he says, pulling a wad of crumpled cash from his pocket. *Tips.* He wades through it, handing over four singles. He doesn't question it, just dishes out what she asks for.

She takes the money, beaming at the guy. "Oh my god, you're my hero. Thank you, thank you, thank you!"

Heat rushes up his neck, flushing his face as he laughs a bit. "It's just a couple bucks, no big deal."

He wanders off to help another customer. The second he turns the other direction, Scarlet's smile dims. She shoves the money at me. "Now *that* guy is a gentleman."

I grab it. "He's a doormat. A pussy. A *parasite*."

"Says the asshole who just bled me dry."

"I didn't," I say, looking her in the eyes, my voice low. "I could've, though. I could've slit your throat and took your life instead… could've turned that red room just a little bit redder while your little cop friend took you from behind, if you would've preferred it that way."

The color drains from Scarlet's cheeks as the spark dims in her eyes. It's fleeting, a flash of emptiness, like she's nothing more than a shell of a human. *Cold.* I don't have to wrap my hands around her throat to kill her, no… those words take the life right out of her.

She knows I watched them.

Seems they were too preoccupied to notice my presence as I lurked around that night. And the look that passes across her face right now? She wore it then, too. She wore it as he fucked her. Not a stitch of enjoyment. Not a stitch of *anything*. It was as if a switch got flipped inside of her, shutting off her humanity, turning her into a puppet with strings. He fucked her, yeah, but he didn't fuck *her*. Whatever made up who she is vanished the moment the man put his filthy hands on her.

The look is short-lived, though, life rushing right back into her. Her nostrils flare, hands clenching into tight fists, like maybe she wants to hit me, like maybe she's considering clocking me right in the eye for having the nerve to witness something she wanted to go unseen. She shoves closer, brazenly pressing up against me, her voice barely a whisper as she says, "You probably *should've* killed me."

"And why's that, Scarlet?"

She hesitates, like she doesn't know how to answer my question, and turns to leave as she says, "You wouldn't understand."

I snatch ahold of her arm, keeping her there.

I'm not done.

Her eyes shoot daggers my way, her hands still balled into fists as she tries to yank away, but my grip is firm. Heat radiates off of her, like anger is literally burning up her core, an explosion imminent. It might be fun to watch her go *kaboom*.

"Let go of me," she says, her gaze on my hand. *"Now."*

"Sit down," I tell her as I nod to the empty stool, loosening my hold on her arm.

She pulls away. "Why the hell would I do that?"

"Because I told you to."

She scoffs, dramatically rolling her eyes. It strikes me as wrong. *Childish.* The woman has a spark in her, a fire running wild, but that kind of immaturity seems beneath someone with brass balls of her caliber. Sure, I don't *know* her, so maybe she really is just a brat. I've met my fair share of those since coming to New York. Hell, I've *fucked* my fair share of them. But my intuition tells me something different.

Besides, I've seen her innocent act. She plays people like they're a piano and she's Chopin, pounding away at their keys, and the ignorant fools don't even hear her music. I hear it, though. It's pretty goddamn loud to my ears, the kind of music that resonates with the deepest, darkest parts of the soul... or whatever bit of it you might have left. Her own little *Funeral March.* Dun, dun, da-dun...

"Sit down," I say again, this time shoving the stool toward the bar, damn near pinning her with it. "You look like you could use a drink."

"Do I look like someone who can *afford* a drink?"

My eyes scan her when she asks that, knowing she doesn't have a penny to her name at the moment. It's curious, though, why she does what she does if she's not rolling in money...

"Sit down," I say for the third time, "before I make you."

"I'd seriously like to see you try," she says, but despite those words, she slips up onto the stool beside me, not putting up nearly as much of a fight as I expected. While I tend to appreciate people surrendering, it's a pity, because I probably would've enjoyed making her.

I lean her way, my mouth near her ear. "Good girl."

"I'm not sitting here because you told me to," she says

angrily. "I've just had a really shitty night, yeah, a really shitty *life*, so I could use a drink. But don't think this means I'm staying here for you, or *because* of you, or that I'm interested in having a threesome with you and Goldilocks over there, because that's not happening."

"Not a fan of threesomes?"

"Not a fan of *you*."

"Ah, that's crazy," I say, snatching up the empty shot glass the bartender gave me earlier tonight. I pour some rum into it before shoving it Scarlet's way. "Everyone likes me."

She picks it up. "Nobody likes you."

I grin as I turn back to Blondie. Even *she* doesn't seem to be fond of me at the moment, annoyance crossing her face as she glares in Scarlet's general direction. "You like me, don't you, beautiful?"

Her sky-blue eyes turn my way, no longer cloudy from the alcohol haze. No, that window of opportunity has passed. Her expression is guarded, like maybe she's seeing me for the first time, self-preservation rearing its ugly head. You see, while women like bad boys, they don't *really* like them. They want a bad boy in reputation, not one in execution. They don't want to see it. They don't want to be reminded we're not good people, that it's not a role we're playing.

It happens time and time again.

You shoot *one* scumbag in front of a pretty little blonde and suddenly you go from being James Dean to Charlie Manson.

Women don't like Charlie Manson.

Well, those with any *sense* don't...

Blondie shoves her stool back and mutters, "I need to use the restroom," before walking off, grabbing her coat and carrying her purse along with her. She's not coming back. That much is obvious.

"Huh." I turn back around. "Guess nobody does like me."

"Told you," Scarlet says.

"Ah, well, that was for the best," I say as Scarlet brings the shot to her lips. "I probably would've shoved her head in the toilet when I fucked her in the bathroom. Might've drowned her by accident."

Those words come from my lips when Scarlet tries to swallow the liquor, catching her off guard, it seems, because she chokes. Rum spews out as she coughs, her eyes watering. Her face would be bright red if it weren't for all the makeup. She grabs her chest, trying to take a deep breath, as the bartender rushes over. "Morgan? Are you okay?"

"I'm fine," she wheezes, not sounding fine at all, which makes the guy panic. He's three seconds away from jumping over the bar, from attempting CPR, and I'm not the only one who sees it. Scarlet holds up her hands in front of her, shaking her head. "Really, seriously, I'm fine. Just went down the wrong hole."

Grabbing a rag, he wipes down the bar in front of her, still making a fuss. "Are you sure? Can I do anything?"

"The woman said she's fine," I chime in, slapping her on the back a few times. "Run along now, Bar Boy."

He doesn't argue, frowning as he walks off, offering only a brief look back at her. Scarlet catches her breath and scrubs her hands over her face as she mutters, "I'm starting to understand what everyone says about you."

"And what, pray tell, *do* they say? Don't leave me in suspense here."

"That there's something seriously wrong with you."

"Oh, well, I could've told you that. There's a lot wrong with me."

"Is that right?"

"Absolutely," I say. "For one, it doesn't look like I'll be getting my dick wet tonight, thanks to you, which I'd say is certainly a problem, don't you think?"

"Tragic," she says, looking at me, her makeup smudged even more now. It almost looks like bruises under her bloodshot eyes. *Tragic.* Her voice was tinged with bitterness, sarcasm, clearly a defense mechanism, because those eyes that regard me silently scream tragedy, the kind that isn't to be made light of. The kind of tragedy that breaks bodies and steals souls. The kind that twists decent people into sociopathic assholes.

The kind that turns beautiful women into ghosts.

Someone once told me that evil can sense itself inside of others, our hearts beating in a different rhythm than most, playing a morbid song that only other evil knows. And while I'm not saying she's evil, and I'm not sure I'd call myself it, either, I know I've got demons, and those demons are sniffing all around her right now, recognizing something within her, something not-very-good.

"Who broke you?" I ask, genuinely curious.

Who desecrated something meant to be so pure?

She regards me, not reacting to that question, not denying it in the least or pretending to still be in one piece, as she sits beside me, thinking it over. Eventually, she turns away, grabbing my bottle of rum and helping herself to a double shot, which she swallows without hesitation. She shudders, closing her eyes and tilting her head back, her expression damn near erotic.

She likes it, I realize.

She enjoys the burn.

Can't say I'm surprised.

You burn a little witch at the stake and she'll laugh in your face.

That shouldn't turn me on, I know, but fuck if it doesn't.

She'd smile, without a doubt. I know it now. If I wrapped my hands around her throat, if I strangled the life right out of her, she'd look me in the eyes and smile. It almost makes me want to do it. Almost makes me want to kill her, just to get the chance to watch her die. Most people go out on their knees, whimpering, begging, pissing their pants and snot-sobbing, like they've got no control over their bodies, leaky fucking faucets of disgrace. It's repulsive. But she's got a backbone, one I'd get a hell of a lot of pleasure out of bending.

"Who says I'm broken?" she asks, opening up her eyes again, her expression calm, like the fire smothered whatever emotions she might've been contending with.

"I do," I say. "I can tell just by looking at you."

"And what, you think you can fix me?" she asks, turning in her stool to face me, shifting her body closer, so close I can smell the liquor on her warm breath as she whispers, "Think you can make me whole again? Save me from the world? Save me from myself? Fill me up, maybe fuck the *feeling* back into me, like the big, strong, man you are? Make me a real woman, instead of a broken little girl?"

There's a sickening sweetness to her voice that sends a chill down my spine. If I never heard a thinly veiled '*fuck you*' before, that was certainly one for the books. I move closer to her, uncomfortably so, cocking my head slightly as I lean in, watching as her body tenses. She thinks I'm about to kiss her, my mouth just inches from hers, before I stop, my voice gritty as I say, "On the contrary, Scarlet, I don't think you need to be fixed *at all.*"

"No?"

"No," I say. "I think you're perfect the way you are."

She stares at me again, not moving.

This woman, she does a lot of staring.

I don't like it.

Her gaze claws at my skin, like she's trying to peel away layers and find what might exist beneath whatever she sees when she looks at me. I'm used to the horrified looks. I tolerate the pity fucks. Men, they lower their eyes, they never look at my face for too long, but her? This little thief, barely five and a half feet of battered flesh and bone, stares me right in the eyes like she has not a fear in the world.

But it's an act, I know, because everyone is afraid of something. *Everyone.* Even the most courageous man in the world fears cowardice. Hell, even *I* have fears, but I'm not telling you what they are, so don't even ask me.

"You don't have to tell me," I say, "but I bet I can guess."

She arches an eyebrow. It looks a lot like a challenge.

"I'm guessing it was a man," I say, "a man who swore he would save you from the world but one that ended up destroying your world instead."

Her cheek twitches.

That's all the confirmation I need.

Without responding, she shoves her stool back, away from the bar, and stands up. She pauses there, between us, looking me in the face again. "Sixty-six cents."

"What?"

"You owe me sixty-six cents," she says, matter-of-fact.

I turn around in my stool, watching as she walks away, leaving me with those words. *Sixty-six cents.* The corners of my lips twitch, amusement finally winning the battle, wiping away all annoyance for the moment. She heads for the door just as it opens, a blast of cold air rushing through the bar, carried inside with a group of loud guys. White, every single one of them, the blond-haired, blue-eyed frat boy variety, three-sheets to the wind. Scarlet slams right into one of the guys so hard she nearly knocks him on his ass.

BAM.

He staggers as she grabs ahold of him, like she's attempting to keep the guy upright. Her hand slips into his pocket, yanking out a wallet, as she says, "Oh my god, I'm so sorry!"

He gets his wits about him and drunkenly grins at her like she's the prettiest thing in the world, throwing an arm around her shoulder. "Nah, it's okay, babe! Don't tell me you're leaving? Come on, let me buy you a drink!"

"Wish I could," she says, "maybe next time."

She slips under his arm, skirting around him, pushing him toward his friends, the whole group laughing as they stagger toward the other side of the bar. Scarlet glances inside the wallet, scowling, before tossing it on a table nearby as she walks out.

No cash.

Shaking my head, I turn back to the bar. The bartender's standing in front of me, staring past me, his eyes fixed to the abandoned wallet by the door. He blinks a few times as he seems to put the pieces together, turning toward the group of guys, his lips parting, barely a sound escaping before I grab his arm. I drag him across the bar, yanking so hard that his head almost slams into mine.

"Mind your own business," I say, "if you know what's good for you."

I shove him, and he stumbles, letting out a shaky breath. He doesn't utter a single word about the wallet, heeding my warning.

Pity, really.

Since it seems there's no fucking happening tonight, I probably would've enjoyed splitting his head wide open.

9
Morgan

They say Disney World is the happiest place on earth.

I can't attest to that, since I've never been, but I'm pretty sure I *do* know where the most miserable place is: the 60th precinct in Brooklyn.

"Detective Gabriel Jones, please."

The woman sitting at the front desk, Officer Josephine Rimmel, leans back in her chair, the receiver of the ancient switchboard phone tucked in the crook of her chubby neck. She greets me revulsion, like I'm a skunk stinking up her lobby, spraying my funk all over the place, her muddy brown eyes picking me apart as she glowers, like she's contemplating calling pest control to ask them to exterminate the vermin scurrying around her precinct.

"Hold, please." Her long pink-painted fingernail hits a button on the switchboard, cutting off the call, before barking a lone word at me: "Name."

She should know my name.

I've told her it thirty-nine times. Not once. Not twice. Not even a dozen times. Thirty-nine. As often as we've seen each other, starting on my first visit to this brick and concrete hellhole nine months ago, you'd think we'd be best friends by now. I certainly remember her name. I remember every excruciating detail I've been forced to learn about her over time—like how she can't go a week without a fresh manicure, picking out a new pink polish every time, which means I've seen thirty-fucking-nine different shades of pussy pink coating her nails, but yet she can't be bothered with something as simple as my name.

"Morgan," I say. "Morgan Myers."

Officer Rimmel grabs the phone again, dialing the extension for Gabe's third-floor office. I drum my chipped red-painted nails on the top of the counter as I wait, my stomach twisted in tight knots, the only thing keeping my sickness at bay. It rings a few times before I can faintly hear his voice through the line.

"Uh, yeah, that woman's here... yeah, yeah... okay, sure thing." Officer Rimmel hangs up, glaring at me. It didn't escape my notice that she didn't even have to *use* my name. "He'll be down when he gets the chance."

Sighing, I walk over and plop down in the first cheap blue plastic chair I come to in the cramped lobby, angling my body to where I can see the entrance, making sure nobody walks in that I recognize. I shouldn't be here. This is arguably the most dangerous place for me to show my face. I shouldn't even be in *Brooklyn*.

My gaze scans the others waiting in the lobby, skimming along faces I've never seen before, unguarded eyes that aren't the least bit worried about my presence, forever in suspense as I wait for that singular moment where recognition sparks. It's bound to happen someday. Millions of people might live in New York City, but the circles most of us run in are small. It's inevitable, I think, that someday, I'm going walk in here and somebody is going to take one look at me and know exactly who I am. They're going to know my story. They're going to know my history.

Unlike Officer Rimmel, they're going to remember my name, and then what?

The elevator past the front desk dings, opening, before I have to think about those potential consequences. *Death, if I'm lucky.* Gabe steps halfway out, grasping the elevator door, holding it open and blocking it with his body as his stern eyes seek me out. He motions with a sharp nod of his head for me to join him, and I stand up, grateful today isn't the day I'm going to be spotted. I slip past him, onto the elevator, my sneakers quiet against the floor. Gabe joins me, pressing the number '3' before repeatedly hitting the 'door close' button, pounding against it, as if that'll make it work any faster. As soon as the door finally closes, the elevator moving, he leans back against the wall.

He says nothing, but his eyes speak volumes as they scan me. Up. Down. Up. Down. It's only a few seconds as the old creaky elevator takes us up two floors, but it's an eternity under his scrutiny, as he eye-fucks me from across the stifling confined space. Even wearing layer upon layer of clothes, dressed down in sweats and a thermal long-sleeved shirt covered with a hoodie, a black knit hat pulled down low, over my ears, he has a way of making me feel exposed. He reminds me of someone else… someone I once knew, a long time ago.

He reminds me of the man who stole my innocence.

He looks at me like I'm some*thing* and not some*body*.

The elevator dings, opening again, and Gabe steps off without acknowledging me, knowing I'll follow. I keep my head down as I trail him to his office in the back corner, glass walls surrounding it, leaving the space exposed. *Transparency*, they boast, but it doesn't make a difference, not when they give them blinds to shut out the world if they choose to. And the moment we're inside, Gabe closes the vertical blind. *Of course.*

"Did you talk to them?" I ask.

"Who?"

"Whoever you needed to talk to. You promised you'd talk to them about me again."

"Oh, yeah… I did."

"You did?"

"Yep." He offers a small smile as he pulls me around so my back is to him. His arms wind around me, his hands grasping my breasts over my clothes, roughly kneading them through the thick fabric. "I talked to my Sarge just this morning about you."

"Really? You did?"

"Of course," he says, leaning down, forcing my head to the side as his lips find my neck, kissing and licking, nothing gentle about it. He sucks on the skin, sending small bites of pain through me. "I told you I would, didn't I?"

"Yes."

Sickness still brews inside of me, but all I can do is swallow it back and hope it stays down. Gabe's hands are all over me, groping and tugging fabric, yanking my pants down as he shoves me flat against the thick cherry wood desk that takes up most of the office space, right on top of stacks of case files.

Inhaling deeply, I turn toward the door. He's wasting no time today. As Gabe unbuckles his pants, I reach down and touch myself, trying to get aroused. Pain, to me, usually means pleasure, but there's a fine line there, one Gabe falls on the wrong side of.

People walk by, ignoring what's happening, as Gabe thrusts inside of me, banging against the desk, not bothering to keep the noise down. They all know what's happening but nobody looks. Nobody *cares*. Not a single one of them pay a bit of attention as he loudly grunts, getting his rocks off.

I just lay here and take it, not bothering to touch myself anymore. It's a waste of time. A waste of energy. I'm not going to enjoy it. My body goes limp, my mind wandering as people stroll past, going about their business. Just once, I'd like someone to peek inside, even just a flickering glance, a moment of curiosity that forces their eyes to acknowledge me.

Do you know what it's like to be invisible? Do you know what it's like to have the world turn its back on you, to turn a blind eye to your existence, like you never even mattered? Do you know what it's like to scream until your throat is raw only to realize everyone tuned you out long ago and nobody heard a single word?

Because I do. *I know.*

It only takes a few minutes for Gabe to finish, slumping over, panting. "You working tonight?"

"I have the night off," I say.

"That's a shame," he says. "I was going to come by. You would've liked that, wouldn't you have?"

"You know I would've," I lie, because *no thanks*.

He moves away from me, flippantly discarding his used condom in the recycling bin. I stare at it as I pull my pants up.

Is latex recyclable?

I don't think so.

Shaking it off, I watch Gabe as he zips his pants back up.

"So, what's the plan?"

He plops down in the office chair behind the desk and starts shifting through the files he just fucked me on top of. "The plan?"

"Yeah, the plan," I say. "What did they say? What are they going to do about the situation?"

"Nothing."

"Nothing?"

"Nothing."

I blink a few times, that word like a weight pressing against my chest, cutting off the air in my lungs. *Nothing.* "What do you mean *nothing*? You told me—"

"I told you I'd talk to them," he says, "and I did."

"But that's not right. It's not fair. It's not *enough*!"

He cuts his eyes at me. "I'm doing all I can."

"But you've done nothing! You keep promising me you'll do something, that you're working on it, that if I trust you, it'll all work out, but nothing is happening!"

"These things take time."

"It's been nine months, Gabe. Nine fucking *months*."

"What do you expect me to do, Morgan? Huh?"

"Something," I say. "Anything."

"I told you—I'm doing all I can. And if you want me to *keep* doing that, it's in your best interest to watch how you talk to me, because I can stop. I can turn it over to another detective, maybe even pass it to the squad at headquarters, where they'll *really* do nothing, if that's what you want."

"What I want is for you to help me, like you promised!"

"You want some help, Morgan?"

"Yes!"

"Then how about I give you some advice," he says. "You dug yourself a hole, sweetheart, a hole so big it might as well be a grave. And they're going to bury you in it, first chance they get, unless you get out. But all this you keep doing? All this *noise* you keep making? You're just making it all worse. The hole just keeps getting bigger and bigger."

"What else am I supposed to do?"

He shrugs. "Forget about it."

Those words are a slap to the face. I *flinch*.

"You're still young," he continues. "Start over, move on, build a new life. People do it all the time."

Those are probably the cruelest words that have ever been spoken to me, and that's saying something, considering the world I live in. Life stopped playing nice with me when I was just a kid, and I grew up fast after that... faster than a kid should *ever* grow up. But I never let it stop me, I never gave up, fighting to make a life for myself, a life of my own, building sand castles out of nothing that I could call home. It was all stolen from me, though, in the midst of a storm, and he tells me just to start over? To give up? To move on?

I don't want to react. I don't want him to know he's getting to me. I'm not going to cry, that's for sure, because Gabriel Jones isn't worth a *single* fucking tear. But the lump in my throat keeps growing and growing, my eyes stinging, and I know I need to go before he realizes he got to me.

I walk away, grabbing the office door and yanking it open, slamming it against the wall as I storm out. People stop what they're doing, eyes flickering my direction, like the floor comes to a standstill at the commotion. I head for the elevator, slapping the button as I hazard a glance back at the judgmental faces.

"Oh, *now* you all want to look?" I shout as the elevator dings, opening. "You want me to bend over so the rest of you can take turns, let all of you brave boys in blue *fuck* me a bit more?"

I step into the elevator and hit the button for the first floor, but before the door can close, whisking me away from this hellhole, Gabe steps in. The second we start moving, he slams his palm against the stop button, the elevator screeching to a halt. A loud buzzer goes off. I know they can hear it on all the floors. I can only imagine what they're all thinking.

Probably that he's fucking me some more.

I reach past him, attempting to grab the button so we'll start moving, but he blocks my hand, shoving me back against the side of the elevator.

"Pull the button back out," I growl. "Now."

92

"You need to calm down," he says. "You're making a scene."

"Says the guy holding me hostage in an elevator."

"Look, I know you're upset, but you're acting irrational."

"Irrational?" I shove against him, trying to force him away from me. "Fuck you!"

He narrows his eyes when I kick him, since shoving him isn't working. Okay, maybe *that* was irrational, assaulting a police officer, but whatever. He deserves it.

"We're building a case," he says. "You know that. We've been building a case for *decades*, Morgan. Yeah, you're waiting, but it's nothing compared to the time this department has put into this case. So I sympathize, I do, but we can't jeopardize everything because of what amounts to a fucking *civil* dispute!"

I blink a few times. I don't even know what to say. He calls it a civil dispute, like it's nothing more than a petty little squabble. I stay quiet, refusing to let him see how much that hurt me, and he pulls the button out so the elevator can move again.

Officer Rimmel looks up when I step into the lobby, her gaze flickering to where Gabe lingers. A look crosses her face, her eyes narrowing as they again seek me out, watching me pass. Jealousy, or maybe just disgust... I don't know. Does it matter? She doesn't know what it's like to be me. She could never understand, so she can take that look and shove it up her snobbish ass.

It's early evening, the air blistering as it approaches dusk. I pull my hood up before shoving my hands in my pockets. Keeping my head down, I cut around the side of the precinct, heading for the subway.

I slip through the small gathered crowd, squeezing into a spot along the back. The F train approaches after a few minutes and I step onto it, finding an empty seat toward the middle of the car.

The sun is setting by the time I make it back into the city, the train taking me straight to the Lower East Side. I walk the few blocks to my building, my head still lowered, despite no longer being in Brooklyn.

Because, when it comes down to it, nowhere is safe for me anymore... if I was ever really safe anywhere to begin with. I used to think I was, but then again, I used to believe a lot of things that were never true.

Like, that Santa Claus brought Christmas presents, and fairy godmothers were real, and good things happened to good people, and love was something everyone deserved.

I used to believe in big houses with white picket fences, in perfect families and happy endings. I used to think what was meant to be would inevitably find a way, but as the days go by, I start to wonder if maybe I'm just delusional. Maybe things only happen if you force life's hand. You call life's bluff and go all in, risking losing everything on the off chance that maybe you'll *win*.

My stomach is twisted in knots and my lungs burn, every breath a chore. Physical pain has *nothing* on emotional torment. And at least once a week—once a fucking week for the past nine months—I get that feeling in my chest, the feeling that tells me I'm somehow still alive, that my heart still exists, somewhere, continuing to beat, despite the fact that it had been brutally ripped out, *stolen*. Every time I go to Brooklyn, I'm reminded of the life I lost, and I hate it... I hate the feeling of helplessness, the reminder of the void, but I keep going, I keep enduring, I keep living... because the only thing worse than going to Brooklyn is me *not* going there.

I head into my building, trekking up to my apartment, every one of those one-hundred and eighty-six steps feeling like torture, darkness setting in by the time I reach the top. The dim lights in the halls flicker, only half of them lit. I open my apartment door and step inside, shutting it behind me, and am about to hit the light switch when movement in my peripheral stops me. It's subtle, just a shadow shifting, not making a sound at all, but I know enough to know it's the silent ones that are the most terrifying.

Death doesn't always come with a scream and a bang, no... death, when premature, usually comes like a whisper on the wind, quietly stalking you until it can rob you of your last breath.

The shadow moves closer and my heart stalls a beat before

frantically pounding, echoing in my ears. I react fast, reaching under my hoodie, my hand slipping beneath the band of my bra and grabbing the small butterfly knife tucked there. Whipping it out, I flick the lock off and flip it open as I swing toward the shadow, not giving it a second thought. I thrust the blade at the form lurking in the darkness, swinging and slashing, hitting *something*. A loud curse carries through the apartment in a gritty male voice—not the voice I *expected*, but son of a bitch, it's too late to stop, because I've already cut him.

No turning back now.

He grabs me when I jab the blade at him again, grasping my right hand and squeezing hard to disarm me. Shit. Shit. *Shit*. Before he can do anything, before he can stab me with my own knife, I thrust my left hand at him, slamming the heel of my palm into his nose with every bit of strength I've got.

BAM.

It's enough to get him to let go, catching him off guard, his hands protectively shielding his face as he curses again. *Fuck*. I've got ten seconds to get myself out of this before he recovers.

Ten… nine… eight…

Turning, I move toward the door to run out, the seconds ticking away.

Seven… six… five…

I grasp the knob when he grabs me, his grip strong. Fuck, make that only *five* seconds. He bounced back way too fast, like it didn't even faze him. I spin his way and try to hit him again, flailing my arms, when he shoves me, throwing me against the apartment door.

His body slams into mine, forcing the air from my lungs, the knife suddenly pressing against my throat. I blink a few times, otherwise not moving, not wanting him to have some knee-jerk reaction and slit my throat on accident.

Or intentionally, either.

Jesus Christ, he could…

He *might*.

Although my vision is hazy and it's pretty damn dark, I easily make out his face, my eyes scanning his features with caution, lingering on the scar. It glows in the night, like a jagged lightning bolt, the same shade as the evening moonlight streaming through the bare windows.

Scar. I still don't know his real name. The man's like Beetlejuice... or hell, maybe he's Voldemort. He's fucking Bloody Mary. *Don't dare say his name or he might show up.* I get why, too. He's not the devil you want to conjure. But I've dealt with a lot of evil in my short life, and this motherfucker is the *least* of my problems.

Or, well, he *was.* He's just made his way right to the top of the list of people who want to hurt me, and he's certainly in the position to do it. Blood streams from his nose, but he either doesn't notice or doesn't care about it, too fixated on staring me in the eyes, not a hint of anything in his expression.

Blank.

My eyelids flutter as he draws the slick blade along my skin, just hard enough for me to feel it, before he presses the tip of the knife against a spot on the side of my neck. I wince. Stinging pain ripples from the spot as the sharp point of the blade breaks the skin, drawing blood.

He *cuts* me.

"That's twice now," he says, leaning close to whisper those words in my ear, pinning my body against the door. The heat radiating off of him swaddles me. "Twice you've come at me with a knife. There won't be a third time, Scarlet. You ever try it again, I'll kill you. I'll cut you to pieces while you beg me to stop."

He turns his head, his nose brushing against my cheek, smearing his blood on me... blood I drew hitting him. I close my eyes, still not moving, the knife against my neck. It wouldn't take more than a flick of his wrist to shove the blade in. He lingers there, the rusty copper odor of blood greeting my nostrils as it mixes with his scent. I don't know if it's soap or cologne or something else entirely, but the man smells citrusy, fresh and vibrant. *Blood orange.*

Warm breath ghosts across my skin, and I exhale shakily the second I feel his tongue. It runs along my cheek, tasting my skin, licking his blood right back off. The knots in my stomach tighten as my knees weaken, an onslaught of tingles coursing through me, assaulting my senses.

Jesus Christ, he's demented. There's something seriously wrong with this guy. I should be repulsed, and part of me is terrified, but that's the part that once used to be an innocent little girl.

That's not me anymore.

Reaching around him, I fist the hair on the back of his head, weaving my fingers through the locks and yanking hard, pulling his mouth away from my cheek. A grimace twists his expression as a flare of rage burns in his eyes. That was either a grave mistake I just made or one of the best ideas I've ever had in my life. Passion emanates from him like heat from a fire, warming the air between us so much I damn near start sweating as he growls.

Oh god, he *growls*.

The sound pulses through me, like electricity to my soul. I don't know what the hell I've gotten myself into, but when he slams his body against mine again, shoving me back into the door, instinct takes over. I go with it, grabbing onto him, wrapping my arms around him as he drops the knife. It clatters to the floor between us, and I consider, for a split second, diving for it, but the thought is wiped away when he kicks it, sending the damn thing sliding across the living room. *Smart.*

"What turns you on more?" he asks, his hands grasping my thighs as he pulls me up. "The fighting or the fucking?"

I wrap my legs around his waist, bracing myself, clinging to him as he thrusts, the force of his hips slamming me into the shaky door. Sparks ignite inside of me as something hard rubs that sweet spot between my thighs, hitting my clit despite all of the fabric, sending jolts through my body.

Oh fuck.

"What makes you think I'm turned on?" I ask, my voice breathless, earning a chuckle from him, the sound spawning goose bumps across my skin.

"Call it a hunch."

A gasp escapes my throat when he thrusts, again and again, like he's fucking me with our clothes on, slamming into me with so much vigor I can barely think. I grind against him, desperate for friction, banging my head against the door as I tilt my chin, his mouth again finding my flushed skin.

His teeth nip along my jawline, biting, scraping, nothing loving about his lips, nothing sweet about his tongue, as he makes his way to my ear and whispers, "I would *destroy* that pussy."

"You think so?" I ask, those words making parts of me tingle that haven't come alive in quite a while, like a match being struck and *finally* finding a flame.

"Without a doubt," he says, not letting up. Pressure builds inside of me as I run my fingers through his thick hair. "I'd wreck you for any man that came along after me, put them all to shame, because I'd give you *exactly* what you wanted."

"How could you possibly know what I want?"

"Because," he says, grabbing a fistful of my hair and twisting my head, forcing me to turn away from him. "Looking at you is like looking in a mirror, Scarlet."

He keeps his grip on my hair, holding my head there, pinning me to the door with his body as his other hand slides between us, slipping down the front of my pants. Rough fingertips rub my clit, and I let out a cry at the jarring sensation.

Holy fuck, I'm *close*.

I can feel it in every inch of my body, all the way down to my bones—the tension, the tightening, the desperate need for unraveling as it builds and builds and builds. He yanks my head further to the side, pain creeping across my scalp. His lips are on my throat, his tongue swiping across the small cut from the knife. The stinging sensation shoves me over the edge as he brings me to orgasm. Pleasure rushes through me. I squeeze my eyes shut, my lips parting, noise catching in my throat as my body convulses.

Uhhhhh...

"Fuck," I gasp. "Uhhh... *fuck*."

As soon as it fades, he stops, letting go of my hair, letting me look at him again as he removes his hand from my pants. I damn near fall, my legs dropping down, feet hitting the floor again as he pulls away. I stay pressed up against the door, keeping my distance, even as he retreats a few steps, giving me space. He retrieves my knife from the floor, regarding it in the darkness. Four-inch blade, iridescent rainbow coloring, the dark handle etched with spiders.

My heart pounds hard, making my vision hazy as he strolls toward me with it.

His eyes flicker from the knife to me, as a small smile twists his lips. Locking the blade away, he holds it out. I take it carefully, surprised that he's returning it. He seems like the type to confiscate people's possessions and call them his own. Not that I have room to talk or anything, considering stealing from him is what got me in this mess in the first place, but still... I don't know what to make of it.

I don't know what to make of *any* of it.

I slip the knife away, eyeing him. "Why are you here?"

"Sixty-six cents," he says, reaching into his pocket and pulling out a few coins, tossing them at me. I don't try to catch them. There's no point. They hit the floor and scatter, rolling around, a discolored quarter coming to rest near my foot. "Figured I'd pay you back before midnight struck and interest kicked in."

I stare at it. "Well, I guess we're even now, huh?"

"Seems that way."

Pushing away from the door, I move past him through the apartment. I'm still fully clothed, but I feel completely exposed in front of that man right now. *Way* too exposed. "I'm sure you can let yourself out, you know, since you had no problem letting yourself *in.*"

I make my way up to the roof. My hands are shaking and I need fresh air. I need the hell out of there. The place is a stifling cubbyhole made of splintering wood and crumbling brick, not much of an apartment, much less a *home*. Even most prison cells have four walls and a ceiling, a place to lay your head while cut off from society.

I've lived worse places, though. *A lot* worse.

Try sleeping chained up in a concrete dungeon, and then

we'll talk about living in hell, because I've been there.

A cloud of breath surrounds me, my teeth chattering, as I step out onto the roof, strolling over to the ledge and sitting down on it. The wind is bitter cold, slicing against my skin like razor blades, but I welcome the sensation, letting it cool my feverish skin.

It's nice just to feel *something*, even if that something is pain.

My gaze drifts out toward the river just a handful of blocks away. Massive housing projects block most of the view from here, but sitting on the ledge, right in this spot, I can see a sliver of the dark water between the buildings, and beyond that, the skyline of Brooklyn.

Just a moment passes before I hear the noise coming from my apartment, the sound of footsteps on the ladder leading to the roof behind me. I don't turn to look, listening as he comes near. He's not trying to go unnoticed, not sneaking around, but his approach is reserved, more casual than determined.

I don't know what he wants.

I don't know why he's still here.

But I don't have it in me to ask, either.

What does it matter?

The icy wild blasts me with his unique scent as he props himself against the ledge beside me. I cut my eyes his way when he sniffles, rubbing his busted nose with the back of his hand, the bleeding stopped for the most part. He says nothing at first as he looks out at the city, but his silence isn't some form of punishment he's forcing upon me.

No, it's a rare solace, one I find I'm grateful for.

Eventually, though, he finds his voice. "You should go for the eyes, you know."

"The eyes?"

He nods. "You break a nose, they'll recover once the adrenaline kicks in, but you take an eye out and they're fucked. They can't catch you if they can't find you."

Huh. "I'll have to remember that."

10

The pink nightgown had always been the little girl's favorite. Ruffled short sleeves, soft cotton, with a big bow on the front of it. Her mother told her she was a beautiful princess whenever she wore it, and she had felt that way.

But as the little girl sat in the Tin Man's den, perched in a black leather chair way too big for her small body, she felt kind of like Cinderella *before* she went to the ball, the one with the wicked stepmother, except the little girl had a *Papa*.

She didn't like the new nightgown he'd given her. It was white and made her skin itchy. She kept scratching... and scratching... and scratching. *Ugh*. She stared at the flickering flames in the fireplace as it ate up what was left of the pink fabric.

"Why couldn't I keep it?" she asked quietly, looking to the Tin Man sitting in the identical chair beside her, a small table separating the two of them.

He plucked a glass off of that table, filled almost to the top with a clear liquid. It looked like water, but he grimaced when he drank it, which told the little girl it might've been something different.

"It stunk," he said, his voice lazy, words slurring. He slouched, long legs spread out, his knee constantly moving.

"You couldn't clean it?" she asked.

He took another drink before casting a flat look her way, no humor in his watery, bloodshot eyes. "It stunk like your *mother*."

The little girl still didn't understand. Her mother always smelled so pretty.

"But if we washed it—"

"*Enough!*" His voice was sharp as he slammed the glass down on the table, spilling some out, sloshing it onto his skin. He shook his hand angrily, a sprinkle splashing the little girl as he waved toward the fire. "It is gone, kitten. *Ash.* You cannot have it back. It is not worth your tears and neither is *she,* so stop crying. Do you hear me? *Stop crying!*"

She wasn't crying, not right then, but as he screamed those words, tears streamed down *his* cheeks. Picking up the glass again, he hauled his arm back, flinging it across the room, shattering it in the fireplace.

The little girl tried to slink away as the flames roared. The Tin Man ran his hands down his face, wiping away his tears. Growling, he stood, his hands clenched. In a rage, he beat himself in the chest with his fist as he snarled, "Stop this, right now! Stop it!"

She whimpered, his anger scaring her, the sound drawing his attention. The Tin Man turned her way, flexing his fingers. "Go to your room. I cannot deal with you... not while I am still grieving *her.*"

The little girl got up, running from the room, wanting out of his sight before her own tears started to fall. As soon as she was in the hallway, she heard him scream, just like she'd heard that night a week ago. Except, he was alone now. Her mother wasn't there for him to turn his anger into pain.

Her mother was gone.

But where?

11

Lorenzo

My stepfather, Edoardo Accardi, ex-enforcer for the now extinct Genova crime family (you're welcome for that, by the way), had a certain flair for theatrics. The man had a way of talking, of saying things, like he was always standing on a stage in a one-man show of his own fucked-up production, and most of the time, only one person sat in his audience: *yours truly*. It wasn't voluntary, I can tell you that much. No, the man targeted his monologues right at me, assaulting me with the words just as hard as he used to batter me with his fists. *This is for your own good, Lorenzo*, he'd say. *Toughen up. Stop crying. Don't beg. Be a man, goddamn it. Be a fucking man!* Never mind the fact that I'd been just a boy at the time… a boy who couldn't understand how beating me unconscious was for my own good… a boy who heard nothing but riddles whenever the man spoke.

But he succeeded, because all these years later, I can still hear his voice. His words bounce around in my head, taunting me, turning me into the monster he'd tried—and failed—to put down so long ago. And while I can't exactly claim to be fond of his methods, I'll give credit where credit is due—the man certainly knew what he was doing.

The hardest part of the business is minding your own.

He used to say that all the time. I never really understood it until I came to New York.

And here on the rooftop of the rundown walk-up, tucked into a shitty-ass Lower East Side block, freezing my nutsack off as I sit on the cold concrete ledge beside a crazy pickpocket with red lips and watery eyes, I'm having a hell of a time minding my own business, because there's a big part of me itching to dig into hers.

Women are distractions and feelings are detrimental, but I'm finding myself feeling some type of way about this woman at the moment, and I don't appreciate it. There's voodoo in her blood, and it makes me want to slit her fucking throat so it'll all spill out, rain red down on the city beneath us before shoving her over the side.

Fly, little witch. Don't forget your fucking broom.

But I don't do it. I don't do anything. Because I try to not be that kind of person—the kind of person that beats others for their own good.

Edoardo Accardi might be in my head, but he's never been in my blood.

Scarlet stares off into the distance, like she's lost in a void somewhere along the edge of the neighborhood. I can see part of the river a few blocks away. Hell, from right here, I can just about see the dock I stood on in the darkness the night I first encountered Scarlet, when I met whatshisname to talk about his boss's problems.

Reaching into my pocket, I pull out my beat up old metal tin and flip it open, taking out a joint and the battered book of matches, ripping one off and striking it against the back of the pack, igniting the flame on the first try. Lighting the joint, I inhale deeply, taking the smoke in and holding it, before extinguishing the flame with the flick of my wrist and tossing the match over the side of the building.

"Did you fuck him?" I ask, slowly releasing the smoke from my lungs.

Scarlet's brow furrows as she turns my way, her eyes flickering to the tin as I close it. "Who?"

"Whoever put the hickey on your neck."

It takes her a moment before she lifts her hand, fingertips pressing against the side of her neck, surprise on her face. The patch is small, more red than purple, which means it's fresh. I took it as a thumbprint at first, like someone had choked her, but the more I looked, the more I saw the bruised lips forming on her skin. Someone marked her not long ago, probably while I was already here, waiting in her apartment. Chances are, whoever that is probably also fucked her, and while that might not be any of my business, I find it curious.

Curious, because of the hunger I saw in her eyes when I had her pinned against the door, as she ground against me, practically fucking the gun tucked in my waistband, desperate to satisfy an ache.

Which means they might've fucked her, sure, but they didn't do a goddamn thing for *her.*

She looks away again without answering.

"Figured," I say, taking another hit, letting the smoke burn my lungs as the sensations soothe my muscles, calming the storm in my mind. "Was it your little cop friend again?"

"Does it matter?"

"No, not really. I don't get down with the whole *sloppy seconds* thing, no matter who it is. Not in the business of picking up another man's slack."

"You can leave, you know," Scarlet says, her voice flat. "Really, you can go."

"Do you *want* me to leave?"

She doesn't answer again, acting as if I didn't ask that question, continuing to stare out into the city. Icy fog surrounds her with each shallow breath, but she doesn't otherwise seem bothered by the cold. It's strange to me, considering I'm finding it damn near intolerable. My asscheeks are like ice cubes.

"So, where are you from?" I ask.

A moment passes before Scarlet turns my way. "Really? You had your hand down my pants five minutes ago, a knife to my throat a minute before that, and you want to make small talk now? What's next... the weather?"

I shrug. "The cold doesn't seem to bother you."

She sighs loudly as she looks back away. "I was born and raised upstate. I'm used to the cold."

"How'd you end up here?"

"I saw a movie that made me want to see the city, so I ran away and never looked back."

"Ah, let me guess. *Breakfast at Tiffany's*? Oh, no, wait... *Westside Story*?"

She shakes her head. "*The Muppets Take Manhattan*."

Okay, that makes me laugh. "Sounds life-changing."

"You've never seen it?"

"Can't say I have."

"They come to the city to make it on Broadway, and I figured, you know, what was stopping *me* from doing that?"

"Can you sing?"

"Nope."

"Dance?"

"Not the kind of dancing they're looking for."

"Hate to break it to you, Scarlet, but that's probably what was stopping you."

"Yeah, well, in my defense, I was only fourteen at the time, so I had no idea what I was getting into. I was convinced that all I needed was a ticket to New York City and everything would work out, that someone would take one look at me and think, '*yep, she's the one*,' and my life would be perfect."

"You've been on your own since you were fourteen?"

"I ran away when I was fourteen, but I was on my own long before that. I didn't really have anything here, you know, but I had even less *there*. At least here I had the freedom to do whatever I wanted to do, to be whoever I wanted to be. I figured whatever trouble I got into in the city would pale in comparison to what I went through before." Frowning, her voice is quiet as she adds, "Turns out I was wrong."

"What trouble did you get into?"

"A guy promised me the world only to destroy my world instead," she says, cutting her eyes my direction. "Or however you put it."

"Tough break."

"Yeah, well, it is what it is. So, what about you?"

"What about me?"

"What's your story?"

"I have no story."

"Everyone has a story."

I consider that, continuing to smoke, grateful when it starts to warm me up, fending off the bitter cold. The world always feels better when a haze covers it, hiding a little bit of the harsh reality. "I was just a normal guy... normal family, normal life. But I was at the wrong place, at the wrong time, and saw something I shouldn't have seen. The mob killed my family, tried to kill me, but I survived, and well... I've been gunning for them ever since. Doesn't matter what I have to do, who I have to kill. I'll get my revenge."

"A vigilante? That's what you're telling me? Just a guy trying to punish all the bad in the world?"

"Pretty much."

Rolling her eyes, she swings around, shoving away from the ledge as her feet hit the roof. She comes right at me, pressing up against me, as I let out a stream of smoke, blowing it right into her pale face.

She inhales slowly, glaring at me. "Bullshit."

I cock an eyebrow at her.

"That's the Punisher," she says, "so unless your real name is Frank Castle, that's not *your* story."

"You calling me a liar?"

"I'm calling you a *bullshitter.*"

A smile slowly spreads across my lips as she backs away, clearly done listening to my bullshit. She's right, of course. That's not my story at all, but my story isn't for the faint of heart, so I keep it to myself. "You're the first one to ever figure that out."

"No, I'm just the first one to call you out on it," she says. "They're all too afraid to call a spade a spade, but I've long ago moved past being *scared* of people like you. If you don't want to tell me, fine... don't tell me. But I don't have time to play games. You can't even give me the courtesy of a simple truth. Hell, I don't even know your *name*. All I know is that they call you Sc—"

"Don't say it." I cut her off, my voice sharp as I drop the

joint to the rooftop and smash it out before stepping toward her, surprised when she doesn't retreat. *Brave little soul.* "I know what they call me. I don't need you to remind me."

"Yeah, well, good for you, I guess," she says. "I'm glad at least *you* know who you are."

I watch her walk toward the entrance back to her apartment, itching to follow her, but my fingertips are tingling and there's a good chance I might strangle her if I get close enough. She's annoyed, and maybe she has reason to be, but that doesn't make her attitude any easier to deal with.

"Lorenzo," I call out.

Her footsteps falter as she looks back. "What?"

"My name," I say. "It's Lorenzo."

Her eyes scan my face in the darkness, like she's expecting some sign of deception, but she won't find it. A simple truth. That's what she asked for, so that's what I'm giving her.

"Your turn," I say. "I want a name."

"You know my name."

"Not *your* name. I want the name of the man who broke you."

Her gaze shifts to her feet as she kicks at the cold tar-covered rooftop, like she's avoiding having to answer, before her lips part with a long exhale. "I'm not broken."

"Save the theatrics, Scarlet. Just give me the man's name."

"Kassian Aristov."

Kassian Aristov.

She blurts it out like she hadn't meant to tell me, a pained expression crossing her face, full of regret right away. *Huh.*

The name isn't one I know, but then again, I don't make it a habit to remember names. It's familiar, though, like maybe I've heard it before, spoken in passing, and I think I might know why. "Russian, huh? He wouldn't happen to be one of *those* Russians, would he? The *Organizatsiya?*"

She doesn't answer.

I've come to learn lack of a response from her is as good as confirmation. The woman got mixed up with the Russian Mafia.

She walks away, going back down to her apartment. I should leave. *Mind your fucking business*, I know, but I can't help myself.

I follow her.

She's in the kitchen, searching through the fridge. There's not much in it—a jug of milk, a few takeout containers, some orange juice, and part of an old chocolate bar. It's kind of pathetic. Scowling, Scarlet grabs the chocolate and gnaws on it before sipping orange juice straight from the carton. It's some generic bullshit store brand juice, no pulp, watery. Smells sickeningly sweet. I know. I investigated before she got home. "How can you drink that?"

She shuts the fridge door and leans back against the counter, regarding me as she holds the carton. "This coming from a guy who drinks rum straight from the bottle?"

"Rum has its benefits. There's no benefit to what you're drinking. There's not even any pulp in it."

"What are you, the orange juice police?"

"Maybe."

"Well, Mister Minute Maid, this juice here only costs a dollar at the bodega on the corner. I'd certainly call *that* a benefit."

"Why don't you have more money?" I ask, glancing around the gutted apartment. It's barely livable, just the bare necessities. "You in debt to a loan shark or something? Is that the problem? The Aristotle asshole stealing *everything* from you?"

She glares at me, biting off a hard corner of the plain chocolate bar and chewing slowly. "Why are you still here?"

I shrug, knowing I'm striking a nerve. "I'm just saying... you're gorgeous. Selling pussy, you ought to be able to afford more than *this*. Fucking you should cost a pretty penny. God knows that pussy's probably worth it."

Her glare softens to just a stare. She's quiet, like she's getting her thoughts in order, before she says, "I'm not sure whether that's a compliment or an insult."

"It's whatever you make it, Scarlet," I say. "I don't pay to play, but my guys do, and you're higher caliber than the women they usually slide on into. So you living like *this* makes no sense."

"Yeah, well, it's really none of your business, is it?"

"No."

"There you go, then," she says, waving her juice at me before taking another swig. "Unless you're planning to lick it or stick it, Lorenzo, keep your nose out of my *business*."

A smile touches my lips. *Touché.*

Opening the fridge again, she shoves the carton back in, tossing what's left of the chocolate bar in a nearby trashcan. She strolls toward me, her eyes scanning my face. I grab her before she can walk out of the kitchen, pulling her to me, catching her off guard. She gasps softly, the sound rushing through me as I cup her chin, pulling her face up.

No hesitation, I press my lips to hers, kissing her hard. It's only a few seconds before I push her back away, breaking the kiss already. She inhales sharply, eyes wide as she regards me, like she isn't sure what the fuck to think about what just happened.

I lick my lips. "It *tastes* cheap."

She blinks, face contorting, like I've offended her. "What?"

"The orange juice," I say. "I can taste it on your lips."

"Oh, I, uh... *oh.*"

I sweep my thumb along her mouth as her lips part, like she wants me to kiss her again, even though we both know I'm not going to. "I prefer it with more of a *bite*. Maybe next time."

"Maybe," she whispers.

I pull my hand away and turn around. She says nothing as I leave.

Maybe that means she wants me gone, after all.

Or maybe she just knows she'll see me again eventually.

* * *

There's this place over in Brooklyn, a club called Limerence. On paper it's just another strip club, but in reality, it's the one of the biggest whorehouses around. A couple hundred bucks can get you the best half-hour of your life with a gorgeous bendy brunette who can take even the biggest sinner straight to heaven with just the flick of her tongue.

Or so I've heard...

The guys occasionally swing through when they're not otherwise occupied, splurging on the strongest liquor and the sweetest women money can buy. I've never been, since paying for pussy isn't my thing, and I'm certainly not there right now.

No, this place is the *opposite* of Limerence.

Mediocre building in a low-rate area near the river, skirting the slums, full of hoodlums with just a few bucks, shoving lone dollar bills in G-strings as they negotiate for a quick, cheap fuck.

Mystic.

Nothing mystical about the shithole.

As it turns out, George Amello owns the place. Who would've thought? That makes him Scarlet's *boss*, which is funny, you know, considering he told Seven he'd never heard of the woman.

"Can I help you?"

I turn toward the sound of that voice, to the guy standing right inside the main entrance at Mystic. Six feet tall, arms as thick as thighs, a dark bald head shining under the flickering colorful lights. He's scowling the kind of way that makes me think he doesn't know what it's like to smile—that all business, panties in a fucking twist kind of scowl. He probably thinks he's intimidating, but a knee in his shriveled nuts could easily take him down.

"I'm here to see your boss," I tell him, flicking my wrist, waving him away. "Run along and get him for me. Make it quick."

He stands there, raising his eyebrows, and hesitates a moment, delaying so long I'm close to losing my temper. Music is thumping wildly not far from my head, some eighties hair-band song, pouring sugar on a cherry pie or some equally metaphorical food-inspired bullshit.

"I think you ought to leave," the man says. "Amello doesn't entertain folks that don't have appointments."

"He'll make an exception for me."

"What makes you so sure?"

"Because he isn't going to like what happens if he doesn't."

It must sound like a threat, because the guy reacts as such, uncrossing his bulging arms as he takes a step toward me, like he expects me to balk. I raise an eyebrow, just daring him to lay a finger on me, when a voice cuts through the tension, shouting over the music. "Darrell, its fine. I'll see him."

Ah, ol' Mello Yello, the yellow-bellied motherfucker. I turn, seeing him standing in the doorway to an office beneath the DJ booth. He eyes me warily, probably wondering why I came here.

I waltz past him, right inside. Amello clears his throat, saying, "leave us," to a pair of guys. They vacate the office and Amello shuts the door, hesitating there, like he's nervous to be alone with me. *Probably ought to be.*

"Georgie Porgie, Puddin' and Pie," I mutter, strolling across the office, around his desk. There's a wall full of monitors broadcasting live, showing every nook and cranny of the club, women performing acts not meant for innocent eyes. "Kissed the girls and made them cry."

"What are you doing here?" he asks, sitting down behind his desk, ignoring my teasing. *Smart.*

"Why? Am I not welcome?"

"Didn't say that. I was just wondering what brought you here tonight."

"Good question," I say, my gaze scanning the monitors, stalling on one near the top, a view of a dim hallway. A woman saunters through it, leading a man toward an isolated back room. I can't see her face, but I recognize the rest of her.

"Well?" he asked. "What do you want, Scar?"

I kind of want to kill him. Not even going to lie. But at the moment I just want him to shut the fuck up so I can watch her in silence. That's not going to happen, though. No, he's too nervous. He fidgets and huffs and shifts around in his chair, waiting for an explanation for my presence.

"I think we got off on the wrong foot, Georgie," I say, watching as Scarlet leads the man out of the hallway. I scan the other screens until I find her again.

It's a perfectly square room, a small platform in the center, a pole jutting out of it and connecting to the ceiling. A deep leather lounging couch takes up the back as mirrors line the walls surrounding it. Besides that, a few wayward leather chairs are shoved aside, and a small bar runs along the left, red lighting consuming the room.

Scarlet glows... well... *scarlet*. There's no other way to describe how the color tints her skin. She's stunning, bathed in red, just like I knew she would be.

A smile lifts my lips as I turn to Amello. He's lucky, so damn lucky, and the son of a bitch doesn't even know it.

"I don't take well to being called names," I say. "Nor do I appreciate having my reputation called into question. I didn't rob you. Your money doesn't mean shit to me. So you can take your ten percent and shove it up your ass, because I've got no use for your measly pennies. But I like to think I'm a reasonable man, so I've decided to let it go this time, because I figure, you know, maybe you just don't know any better, but you'll learn, if you know what's good for you, and it won't happen again. You got me?"

He glares at me. He isn't happy, that's for damn sure, but he's got me. He's not a *complete* idiot.

"What would *you* think," he asks, "if you were me?"

"I'd think I had something somebody wanted," I say, my gaze flickering back to the surveillance monitor. How true that is... but it's not his money I'm after.

I find myself wanting the beautiful bendy brunette that's working in this shithole.

"We can be friends, you and I... but that's a choice only *you* can make," I tell him. "If you don't want to be my friend, you don't have to be. But I learned long ago there are only two kinds of people in this world, so if you're not my friend, Georgie? I guess I'll have to count you among my enemies."

I walk out, saying nothing else. He glares at me, having no rebuttal. What's there to say, anyway? *Nothing.*

The club is loud, the music still thumping, some techno bass bullshit without any words now. Blinding disco lights flash, the girl on the main stage swinging around a pole, wearing reflective material, like a cracked-out gymnast.

I've got nothing against strippers. Really, I don't.

I've got nothing against prostitutes, either. You do you.

But I do have something against people who can't even function without shooting something into a vein, without snorting something up their nostril. I spent the first half of my life under the care of someone more cocaine than woman. The agitation, the erratic behavior, the nosebleeds. My mother blew out her septum when I was just a kid, had plastic surgery more than once to try to hide the evidence. I can spot an addict a mile away thanks to her, and the woman on the stage? Cracked-out, without a doubt.

I avert my eyes as I stroll through the club. Instead of heading for the exit, where the bouncer still lurks, watching me, I veer toward the back of the place. Halfway down the hall, my footsteps falter, and I pause in an open doorway, the soft glow of red lights spilling out all around me.

I'm not supposed to be back here. The glares women give me as they strut past, leading guys to and from these rooms, tells me so. *No sex in the champagne room.* We've all heard it. They say it doesn't happen, but I know, in some places, in some situations, sex is negotiable.

Flash enough cash and pussy can be yours.

I know it happens here.

But Scarlet? She's not even naked.

Not right now, at least.

She's dancing. She looks so utterly bored. Does nobody else notice? Although she smiles, there's no fire in her eyes, her stare damn near vacant. I'll give her credit, though—she's got rhythm. Her hips sway perfectly in tune with the music, like her body is feeling it even if *she's* not.

The little red, lacy see-through get-up she's wearing leaves little to the imagination, even less as she slowly unfastens her top, teasing the guy as the straps fall down her arms.

She pulls it off after a moment, tossing it aside, exposing the most stunning set of tits I've ever laid my eyes on. They're small, barely a handful, but fuck if they're not perfect—perky, and natural, with the kind of nipples that beg to be tasted.

The man reaches for her when she turns toward him, his hands moving on their own, like it's instinct around a set of tits *that* beautiful, but she grabs his wrists without missing a beat, stopping him as she shakes her head. *No touching.*

He obliges, dropping his hands to his side, shoulders slumping with disappointment. Can't say I blame the guy. She teases him for a moment, shoving them in his face as she dances, straddling his lap and pushing him until he's lying on the lounge couch. His eyes drift closed, his hands linking together behind his head, as Scarlet turns around.

Her expression glazes over.

Bored. Bored. *So fucking bored.*

Her eyes are fixed to the ceiling, to the lights shining down on her, as she half-heartedly grinds her ass against his crotch. I watch her for a moment before taking a step into the room. She's quick to sense my movement. Her head lowers, and a hint of panic sparking in her eyes. *Alarmed.* Her gaze meets mine, the guy not noticing a difference, but I can sense it. I see the way her posture changes, her breathing labored, shaky exhales escaping her lungs as she watches me. I slowly approach, my footsteps undetectable over the sound of the music.

If she's truly bothered by my presence, she doesn't let it show, not missing a beat as she dry humps the guy. It's not like in her apartment, not like when I had her pinned to the door, thrusting against her, driving her to the brink.

No, she's getting nothing from this. No arousal. No excitement.

Fucking *boredom.*

I pause in front of her, cocking an eyebrow, as she continues going through the motions. A small smile twists her blood-red lips. It does something to me, that smile. I don't know how to explain it. People don't get to me the way a look from this woman claws its way under my skin.

Nudging her chin, I tilt her head up further, watching her throat flex as she swallows, like I might be making her nervous.

Good. Her lips are parted, her warm breath greeting me as I lean down toward her, tilting my head. My thumb slowly swipes along her bottom lip, smearing her lipstick, just a breath away from her mouth, when she whispers, oh-so-shakily, "Kissing is gonna cost you."

I laugh under my breath and press my lips to hers—once, twice, three times—soft, barely a peck, but she bites my bottom lip the last time, sending a sharp stab of pain through it. I wince, licking my lip as I stand back up, a slight copper taste on my tongue. She drew blood.

She knows it, too.

There's the spark.

It lights up her eyes.

Squeezing her chin, I lean down again, kissing her once more, rougher this time, before whispering, "You taste better now."

She still hasn't missed a beat.

The woman is good at what she does, that's for damn sure.

Letting go, I retreat a few steps, my eyes scanning her, my gaze lingering on those tits. There's more I'd like to stick around and do, but I know damn well Amello is watching my every move.

I'm going to have her, though.

No doubt about it. I've made up my mind.

Men like Amello get their panties in a twist when you steal from them. He called me a thief, so that's what I'll be. Like I said, if you don't appreciate what you've got, someone like me will be more than happy to take it.

Scarlet's cheeks flush, visible even through the thick layers of makeup, her eyes twinkling, every ounce of boredom gone in a blink.

Definitely not the only one getting a thrill out of this.

I stroll toward the doorway just as the song changes. It's barely a second of silence before the music starts up again, but something happens in that moment, a shift in the air when someone off in the distance screams. My footsteps falter. Turning my head, glancing back, I watch Scarlet come to a stop. She springs to her feet, alarmed, snatching her top off of the floor and fumbling with it, desperately trying to put it back on, but there's no time.

No time.

Chaos erupts. More screaming. Running. Voices shout over the music, incoherent words I don't understand, but Scarlet seems to. Eyes wide, her body trembles as she mouths something, but her voice doesn't seem to work right now.

Uh-oh.

The guy she'd been straddling sits straight up, realizing his lap dance is over, in a drunken stupor as his bloodshot eyes narrow at me.

"Who the fuck are you?" he asks, but I don't have a chance to answer before a distinct rat-ta-tat-tat sound echoes through the club, the harrowing rattle of incessant gunfire.

AR-15, I'm guessing. My chest tightens. *Son of a bitch.* Is he being robbed? *Again?*

"Oh god," Scarlet says, finally finding her voice. "No, no, no…"

There's a tremor to those words. Terror coats every syllable. Never took her for the kind to buckle in the face of danger. She sure as fuck didn't balk when it came to *me*. The commotion gets louder, people fleeing from the club, racing down the hall toward the back exit before doubling back, like that way is blocked.

Whoever it is has the place surrounded.

Sitting ducks.

Scarlet retreats deeper into the room. It's only seconds. That's it. Mere seconds of pandemonium. She jumps behind the bar to the far left of the room, cowering there, shielding herself from view. I take a few steps that way, not completely approaching, just coming close enough that I can see her.

No, it's not a robbery, and it's clear she senses it, too

It's more like a massacre.

I know a thing or two about those.

I stand there, shoving my hands in my pockets, staring at the doorway as someone bursts in. A man dressed in all black, wearing a ski mask. *Huh.* The drunk from the lap dance freaks out, yelling, "Who the fuck are *you*?"

Unlike when he asked me, this guy is kind enough to respond. He answers right away with a bullet to the face, no hesitation.

Who the fuck are you?

BANG.

Scarlet doesn't move at all, doesn't make a sound, as the gunshot echoes through the room, a big, burly motherfucker pulling the trigger, dropping the scumbag with a single shot.

He turns to me next, pointing the gun, finger still on the trigger, but this time, he pauses. Eyes narrowing, he studies my face before shouting something out in a foreign language, a single word sticking out of the gibberish: *Scar.*

My hands clench into fists in my pockets as I force myself not to go for my gun. "I guess my reputation precedes me, huh?"

He looks like a bear, I think, the burly motherfucker, as he shoves the ski mask up, offering me a glimpse of his face. He doesn't respond with words *or* a bullet, which I think is answer enough.

Someone else joins us, a bit shorter and smaller, otherwise similar in features. No ski mask, this one. No gun. He's not even dressed in all black, instead wearing a dark gray suit. He carries himself differently, too, an air of confidence surrounding him, much of his skin covered in dark tattoos.

That would make him the leader.

That's pretty easy to see.

It's peculiar, though, almost surreal, a strange sense of déjà vu assaulting me. If I weren't witness to this, I swear to fuck, I'd probably suspect myself, too. It feels too familiar, like watching a cheap reboot of a classic. Either this is a case of great minds thinking alike, or this guy has been studying my playbook.

The moment the newcomer yells, spouting off something foreign to his guys, Scarlet reacts. I see her tense from the corner of my good eye. She presses against the bar, trying to fade into the shadows, as she mouths something to herself, over and over and over, still not making a sound.

Look, it doesn't take a genius to put four and six together

and come up with ten, you get what I'm saying? Cowering woman. Foreign McFuckFace with his own little massacre squad. It's like I'm in the midst of yet another *Die Hard* sequel.

Does that make me Bruce Willis? I don't know.

But I am willing to bet that makes ol' Bebop and Rocksteady here our dastardly villains. And doing that basic math in my head, I'm saying it all adds up to the *Russians*.

The men chatter back and forth as I observe them before someone says that damn word again. *Scar.*

He turns to me then—their leader, ol' Bebop—and stares me down as he steps closer. "The notorious *Scar*. I have heard much about you."

"Good things?"

"Horrific things. Murder. Mayhem."

"So... *good* things," I say again.

He laughs. "The best things."

"Good to know," I say. "I'm not sure I can say the same about you, though."

"You have not heard of me?"

I was going for I hadn't heard any *good* things, but we'll go with that. "Afraid not."

"Oh, but I am sure you have," he says as he smiles. "You just do not know it was *me* they spoke of. Reputation is not important to me. I do not care what anyone thinks as long as I get what I want."

"And what is it you want?"

"Depends on which day it is." He laughs again. "Today, like most days, I am looking for a girl. Maybe you have seen her?"

"Maybe," I say. "Does she have a name?"

"Morgan," he says. "She is a very pretty girl. You would not forget her if you saw her. She has the sweetest smile."

That she does.

"Doesn't ring a bell," I tell him.

"That is a shame," he says as he glances around the room. He can't see behind the bar from there, but if he comes any closer, Scarlet is *fucked*.

His gaze shifts that way, and he seems to consider it, before gunshots erupt in the hallway, a man shouting, *"Vor!"*

It captures Bebop's attention, and he glances that way, muttering under his breath before turning back to me. "I have respect for you, Mister Scar. I admire a man who takes what he wants, because I do the same. So I will leave you in peace, since my fight is not with you."

He walks out with that, leaving the room, but Rocksteady lingers behind, his gun still aimed at me. He only lowers it when someone shouts from the hallway. "Markel!"

I'm guessing that's his name, since he reacts to it. Not that it matters. Nothing about them matters to me, personally, but it clearly matters to Scarlet.

Rocksteady vacates the room. The chaos in the club dies down as the intruders leave. Everyone else has fled, or hell, maybe they're all dead. Again, not that it matters, but I just stand here, hands still fisted in my pockets.

"Don't move," I say, knowing Scarlet can hear me. "I'll let you know when it's clear."

I quietly stroll from the red-tinted room, crunching on glass as I walk down the hall, passing bullet-ridden walls. It's not the worst scene I've ever been involved in, but it's not exactly pretty, either. I make my way through the main club, looking around, eyes skittering past the bouncer at the front door, dead in a pool of blood.

Calling that one karma.

I stall in the doorway to the office, looking at the wall of monitors, most of them destroyed by the AR-15. Amello is nowhere to be found, probably the first to run like a little bitch when the bullets started flying.

"When the boys came out to play," I mumble, "Georgie Porgie ran away."

After checking the rest of the club, I make my way back to Scarlet. The police won't be far behind, which means I need to get the hell out of here. Scarlet is still in the same spot, behind the bar, knees pulled up to her chest, arms wrapped around them.

I pause, regarding her as I pull my coat off. She's wearing very little, still topless, trying hard to cover herself—not out of some sense of propriety. She's just nervous. I wordlessly hold the coat out to her and she takes it, slipping it on, zipping it up. She's so petite it almost goes to her knees, longer than the dresses I've seen her wear.

"Come on," I say. "I'll walk you home."

I hold my hand out to her. She looks at it, like she isn't sure if she wants to touch me, but she concedes after a moment.

She's rattled. I can tell. Her knees are practically knocking together, her hand shaking in mine as I help her to her feet. She pulls away from me as soon as she's upright, shoving her hands in the pockets of my coat.

Scarlet keeps her head down as she quickly walks down the hall, toward the back exit, but instead of going outside, she veers to the locker room.

"Whoa, where are you going?" I ask, grabbing her arm to stop her. "We need to go."

She yanks away from my clutch. "I need my stuff."

"Just leave it," I say. "Fuck it."

"You don't understand," she mutters, ignoring me as she goes about her business, heading over to a locker to pull out a duffel bag. It only takes her a few seconds, doesn't slow us down much, so I drop it, even though it's absurd.

It's just *stuff*.

She hurries out the back door of the club, eyes surveying the neighborhood, on guard, like she fully expects the boogeyman to leap out at her from somewhere in the darkness.

My cock is an icicle within minutes of stepping outside. Every inch of me is frozen solid except my feet… my feet keep on moving, keeping up with Scarlet. She only lives a few blocks away, so it doesn't take us long to get there. Nobody followed us that I could tell, and I'm pretty damn good at gauging when someone is watching, so I think she'll be safe for now.

But still, there's some part of me not yet okay with letting her out of my sight.

Curiosity, maybe.

Mind your own business and you'll live a hundred years. Problem is, you know, a hundred years is a long time. Do I *really* want to live that long?

My curiosity says, 'I don't think so'.

So I follow her inside, and I trail her up the stairs, watching as she turns the knob to her apartment and walks right in. The place hadn't been locked any of the times I've shown up.

"Locks broken?" I ask curiously, stepping into the apartment as she leaves the door wide open behind her, probably the closest thing to an invitation I'm going to get from the woman. I linger there, flicking the deadbolt, watching as it slides out just fine.

She doesn't respond, which doesn't surprise me, since she hasn't said a single word since back at the club. She kicks her shoes off, leaving them lying in the middle of the floor on her way to the bedroom. She doesn't shut herself in there, doesn't even attempt any privacy as she unzips the coat and takes it off, snatching up a wrinkled plain white t-shirt from on top of the messy unmade bed and pulling it on, covering herself. She walks back out, lugging the coat along, and shoves it at me, punching me in the chest with the damn thing. She lets go of it and turns, heading into the kitchen.

If she comes back with a knife, I swear to fuck, I'm going to slaughter the woman...

"You're welcome," I call out, putting my coat back on. It smells like her, and I turn my head, inhaling along the collar. *Huh.*

"Thank you," she says quietly as she reappears in the doorway, clutching a clear bottle of something. Rum... vodka... *something.* She takes a drink of it, lingering there, leaning against the doorframe, her eyes questioning as they regard me... as they watch me smelling my coat, like some panty-sniffing pervert.

I shrug, zipping it up. "It smells like you."

"What do I smell like?"

"Like sex and shame," I say, smirking at the scowl she directs my way as I inhale again. "And something distinctly vanilla."

"It'll fade." She takes another large swig of the liquor, grimacing, before continuing. "It's just my lotion... vanilla orchid.

The sex, well, I'm afraid you'll have to wash that off."

"And the shame?" I ask, strolling toward her. "How long until that fades?"

She laughs dryly. "I'll let you know if it ever happens."

I take the liquor from her, glancing at the label. *Rum.* The bottle's made of flimsy plastic, utterly cheap, the kind of rum that puts hair on chests and can put a motherfucker through puberty again. It's not for the faint of heart, no, but neither is *she*.

She's gritty and raw, but goddamn, the woman is beautiful. The more I look at her, the more I see it.

I take a swig, not reacting to the bitterness, and hand it back as I stare down at her. "Why don't you lock your door, Scarlet?"

"No point," she says. "Locks won't stop someone determined to get in."

"So you make it easy for them?"

"I'm just realistic. I could seal myself up in here tight, with a hundred locks on the windows and doors, but all that'll do is trap me, like some caged animal, and I refuse to do it. Besides, you know, all of this?" She waves around the apartment. "None of it means anything to me. If people want to help themselves to it, so be it... they can have it all."

She takes another swig before pushing away from the doorframe. Shoving by me, she strolls across the room, that vanilla scent wafting toward me.

"I hate to break it to you," I say, glancing around, "but I don't think you could give half of this shit away. No offense, but it all kind of looks like, well... *shit.*"

"That's because it is," she says, pausing at the window to look out. "Most of it I found or stole."

"What do you do with all of your money?"

"Is that your business now?"

"No."

"So why are you asking?"

Why am I asking? I don't know. I don't even know why I'm here, why I'm bothering with this woman at all. "Just trying to riddle you out."

"Don't bother," she mutters as I stroll closer, pausing behind her. "My problems are my own."

"Ah, come on. You can spill all your secrets to me, Scarlet. I'm good at pretending to listen."

She laughs, a genuine kind of laugh, as she tilts her head, regarding my reflection in the grimy, cracked glass of the living room window. "I'm sure you are, but I learned long ago not to bare my soul to just anyone. It seems to make people think they're entitled to *every* part of me, like I owe them everything and can keep nothing for myself."

"Yeah, well, I'm not just anyone," I tell her. "Besides, it's a little late to try to keep everything under lock and key, considering what went down tonight. So how about you show me yours and I'll show you mine?"

She turns around, eyebrow raised as she leans back against the cold glass. It's chilly in the apartment, the heat barely working, but that doesn't seem to bother her. Not much does.

"Go on," she says. "You first."

"Me first?"

She nods. "Excuse me if I don't trust you to live up to your end of it, considering the bullshit you tried to feed me last time. So yeah, you first."

"Fair enough." I pause, trying to think of something to tell her, something dark enough to entice her own little demons to want to peek out and join me today. "I've killed people."

"You've killed people."

"Yes."

She stares at me. *Hard.* She doesn't look horrified. Hell, she kind of looks bored again. "That's your big, dark secret? That you're a murderer?"

I shrug a shoulder. "Not dark enough?"

"It's plenty dark," she says. "It's just not exactly a *secret.*"

Well, damn.

"I lie, cheat, steal, rob, pillage, plunder, slaughter... seventy-five other fucking words you find in a dictionary associated with the word 'criminal'."

"That's nice, that you know how one of those works," she says. "That's kind of vague, though."

"You want details?"

"I want something I don't already know."

Pressing my hands to the windowpane on either side of her, I lean closer. Her breath hitches, her eyes fixed to mine, back flat against the glass. She's flustered, having me so close.

"I wanted to kill your boss tonight," I tell her. "I showed up, walked into his office, wanting to end his life, but then I saw you were working. You were on one of the screens, leading that man into the back, and just like that, I changed my mind. Because while killing him would've been a thrill, it wasn't nearly as enticing as *you*. He lived to see another day thanks to the little hero in red fishnet thigh-highs."

She blinks a few times. "Did he?"

"Did he *what*?"

"Live?"

It takes a second for me to realize she's asking if the Russians got him after I left him alive. "I didn't see him lying around anywhere, so I'm assuming he's fine."

She nods slightly, like that doesn't surprise her. "You should've killed him."

"Why's that?"

"Because he ordered someone to kill *you*."

"Did he?"

She nods again.

Huh.

Maybe I'm supposed to be worried about that, but I let out a light laugh, amused that he had the guts. If the rat bastard wanted me dead, he had ample opportunity to try it himself tonight.

"I'll have to remember that," I say. "Your turn, Scarlet. Tell me something I don't know."

"I just did."

"Something about *you*."

She hesitates.

She hesitates so long I know she's not going to say a word.

I lean down, sliding my nose along her skin, inhaling that warm vanilla scent, before saying, "Come on, I showed you mine, didn't I?"

"You don't understand," she whispers.

"Then make me."

As soon as I say that, she pushes away from the glass, shoving against me, forcing me to take a step back, but I resist, refusing to move. We had a deal, goddamn it, and if she didn't want to make it, well, then she should've thought about that before I told her something.

I step to the side, in front of her, when she tries to go around, blocking her path once again when she dodges the other way, pinning her there by the window.

Frustration clouds her face, and I half expect her to hit me, to swing that fist she clenches and punch me right in the jaw, but instead she comes at me, shoving against me, before thrusting up on her tiptoes. Her mouth is on mine, those red lips forceful as they kiss me hard, furiously moving, like maybe she couldn't find the words to speak so she's trying to steal them from me.

Figures.

Fucking thief.

A chill runs down my spine as I roughly grasp the back of her neck, holding her there, and kiss her back. My tongue slides into her mouth, meeting hers. The woman tastes as good as she smells, so fucking good that I groan. My other hand slides up beneath the edge of her white shirt, grabbing her hip, yanking her closer.

"This is how you want it?" I ask between kisses. "You'd rather fuck than talk?"

"Shut up," she growls, making me stumble back as she shoves me toward the bedroom, dropping the bottle of liquor to the floor, discarding it, not giving a shit as it splashes out, pooling along the wood and splattering the two of us. Frenzied hands unzip my coat, tugging at it. "Just… *shut up.*"

I oblige—for the moment, at least—and let her push me toward the bedroom, kissing her the whole way there, even letting her tear at my clothes. Every second that passes, her frustration seems to grow, the woman close to Hulking-out and just smashing every goddamn thing. She yanks at fabric, like she thinks she's strong enough to rip it apart, so I help her out, tossing my coat aside and breaking the kiss so I can pull my shirt off.

Her hands tremble as they fumble with my pants, like she's nervous, or excited, or fuck, maybe *both*. I'm having a hard time getting a read on her, especially when I reach for her shirt and she blocks my attempt to strip her. A voice deep in the recess of my mind screams something about this is *off*, but that voice is snuffed out quicker than a gunshot to the temple when her hand slips into my boxers and grabs my cock.

BAM, all pussyfooting gone.

"Fuck," I groan, my voice gritty, my eyes closing as I tilt my head back. Her hand is warm, her skin velvety soft, but her touch is firm as she strokes, hitting just the right places to set me off. Her thumb massages the sweet spot on the underside of my cock, the sensitive outer ridges of the head, right where those nerve endings are bundled.

Jesus, this woman knows her anatomy.

A+

Top marks.

Summa cum laude.

Valedictorian of her motherfucking class.

I could stand here and feel it forever, just get lost in the sensations rolling through my body, but if she's *this* good at a hand job, her pussy will without a doubt blow my mind. My pants slide down my legs, dropping to my ankles, and I try to kick my boots off, but they're not budging, and you know what?

Fuck this.

I can fuck her with my clothes on.

Grabbing her wrist, I pull her hand away before I explode already. Wouldn't take long, that's for sure, not with the way she's touching me. I pull her onto her bed, damn near falling from my shackling pants, my hand still clutching her wrist. My thumb presses against her pulse point, feeling the thump-thump-thumping from her heart racing.

Twisting around, she uses her free hand to reach over to a bedside stand, yanking a drawer open to retrieve a condom. She rips the golden foil wrapper with her teeth, and I let go of her wrist, watching as she rolls the condom on me.

I don't undress her. If she doesn't want me to, hell, I *won't*. Shoving her legs apart, I settle between them, hitching her knees up. Her thong is barely a piece of string, easy to shove aside as I reach between us, caressing her bare pussy.

Her mouth falls open, a soft sigh escaping, when I push my middle finger inside of her, pumping it in and out. My thumb roughly rubs her clit, the simple touch making her moan. It doesn't take long until she's soaking wet, writhing beneath me.

Grasping my cock, I rub the head along her warm pussy, stroking her clit with the tip, before lining up and pushing in. Fuck, she fits perfectly, like a leather glove. Her breath hitches, and she clutches a hold of me, wrapping her arms around me, her red-painted nails digging into the skin of my back.

I pound into her, on top of her, covering her with my body, digging my boots into the cheap mattress for traction with each hard thrust. Those nails rake across my skin, leaving stinging trails as she claws her way through me with each whimper, and moan, and cry, her legs wrapping around my waist, welcoming me inside.

Fuck, this woman...

Yeah, I'm actually *fucking* this woman.

She grows quiet, her grip loosening, scratches becoming barely-there touches, her body shifting every time I thrust into her.

She's limp in the bed.

Pulling back, I look down at her tucked beneath me. She's staring off into the distance, gaze fixed to a nearby wall. Dazed. Zoned out. *Gone*.

"Oh, no, no..." Grasping her chin, I turn her head, forcing her to look at me. "You're not doing that blank slate shit with *me*."

She blinks a few times before her eyes narrow.

"Go ahead, get mad," I say, continuing to thrust. "But when *I'm* inside of you, Scarlet, you don't get to fade."

"I'm not," she says defensively.

"Liar, liar, pants on fire..."

She growls, hands running up my back before she fists my hair, tugging on it, yanking me back down toward her. "I'm not *fading*."

"Damn right you're not," I say, brushing my nose against hers before I kiss her.

She doesn't fade again, those moans returning, turning to sharp cries as I stroke her clit, bringing her to orgasm.

Again.

And again.

And again.

I hold myself back for as long as I can, watching her as she comes apart at the seams, the sounds escaping her primal, like a wild animal, before my body just can't take anymore. If I don't come soon, my balls are going to *revolt*. They're seriously going to close up shop and go the fuck home. Grunting, I thrust hard, knocking the flimsy bed into the wall, as a swell of pleasure runs through me.

"Fuck," I groan, gripping her tightly, fishnet-covered legs still wound around me as I spill into the condom. Stilling, I press my forehead to hers, catching my breath, inhaling her scent. The vanilla is still there, yeah, but the smell of sex overshadows it now, and the shame?

Yeah, that's *still* all over her.

"Satiated," I say, still balls-deep inside of her. "Is that what your Scarlet Letter stands for?"

She shoves me when I ask that, pushing me off of her. "Stupid."

I pull out with a groan. "Stupid?"

"That's what yours would stand for," she says. "Stupid. And *smug*."

"Satiated," I say again, standing up, finding myself in quite the predicament, considering my pants are wound around my ankles like shackles and I need to make my way to the bathroom to dispose of the condom. My ass is on full display, and I'm not exactly modest, you know, but I'm kind of hoping I don't fall flat on my face.

It's possible.

Plausible.

Probably going to happen.

So I sit back down on the edge of the bed and untie my boots, yanking them off. After dropping them to the floor, I pull off my pants, wearing nothing but my socks as I seek out her bathroom.

It's small.

I'm talking *tiny*.

Fucking minuscule.

I have to be careful taking a piss, my dick practically bigger than the width of the room. A can't-walk-into-the-shit closet. A hole in the damn wall. It's completely ridiculous.

When I'm finished, I go back to her bedroom. It's late, and I'm exhausted, which means I probably ought to give Seven a call to come pick me up so I can try to get some sleep tonight, get my head back on right. Maybe now that I've been inside of *her*, it'll purge all these goddamn thoughts of her from inside of *me*.

Scarlet is sitting on her bed, her knees pulled up to her chest, her shirt stretched around them as she huddles beneath it. Not for warmth, no… more like trying to shield herself from the world around her. *Nervous again.* I sit down on the edge of the bed, eyeing my discarded clothes on the floor.

"It's been nine months," she says quietly.

"Nine months since what?"

"Since I last came face-to-face with Kassian."

Ah. "I'm assuming that was him tonight?"

"Yes."

"And you've been hiding from him for nine months?"

She laughs dryly. "I've been hiding from him *a lot* longer than that, but it's been nine months since he last found me. I've managed to evade him for forty long weeks."

"Almost broke your streak tonight."

"Almost," she agrees.

"What does he want from you?"

She shrugs. It's not an evasion. I can tell the reaction is genuine. She doesn't put it in words, but I know what she's saying... she doesn't understand what he wants. Maybe she knows, in her head, but she's listening with her heart, a dangerous path to go down.

"Whatever it is he wants, you probably should give it to him so he'll go away."

"But what if he won't?" she asks. "What if *this* is what he wants?"

"What, mayhem?"

"Yes."

"Well, then, you get rid of him a different way."

I draw a line along my throat with my fingers, making my point, as I lay back on the bed. It's uncomfortable, but I'm exhausted, too lazy to put on my pants yet. *Shit*. My eyes are burning, my head starting to pound with the beginning of a headache, thanks to the adrenaline rush finally fading, mediocrity creeping back in.

"That's not an option," she says quietly. "Murder isn't always the answer."

Laughing, I close my eyes, covering my forearm with them. "Hell, and here I thought it *was*..."

12
Morgan

The sun rises in the east.

I'm not sure how old I was when I learned that. To this day, I'm not even sure why it happens that way. Although, it doesn't really matter, does it? It's just an undeniable fact, one I think about those mornings when I sit up here, on this rooftop and watch the sun peeking out over the Brooklyn skyline, bathing the borough in an orange glow, like the streets are on fire.

Some days, it feels like they might be.

It feels like Brooklyn is burning and I'm just here, sitting, watching it disintegrate as I breathe in the smoky air, my lungs scorching and chest aching, not doing a goddamn thing to stop it. Because, seriously, what the hell am I supposed to do? Huh? I've yelled 'fire' so many times that nobody even looks my way anymore when they hear me screaming, like I've become nothing but white noise in a crowded city full of overpowering voices.

I'm probably not making any sense to you. It's okay. I don't understand myself anymore most days. I just sit on this ledge and stare out at the fiery horizon as another day dawns, too strong-willed to ever fling myself off the side of this building but yet too damn powerless to ward off my inevitable fall. So I sit, and stare, and wait, and cling to the little bit of hope I wake up with every day, but I don't stop doing it, I don't just give up, because maybe— goddamn it, *maybe*—I'll find my wings again and get to *soar*.

Fly the fuck away from all of this.

But until then, I'm just grounded.

Tagged and tracked.

My wings got clipped.

I'm a little caged birdie.

Sighing, I bring the joint to my lips and inhale, taking a puff of scorching smoke into my lungs, holding it, letting it soothe the pain away as it makes my head just a bit more foggy so I stop agonizing about a life on the other side of that too-deep river that I'm never supposed to cross.

"You know, I didn't kill you when you stole my wallet. Didn't kill you when you stole my *money*. But my medicine? That's crossing a fucking line, Scarlet. I might throw you off the roof for that."

That voice makes my skin prickle, places inside of me tingle, as it calls out behind me on the roof. *Lorenzo*. The tiny hairs covering my body stand on end, like sparked by electricity, as I hear his footsteps. I wouldn't classify myself as 'frightened', because I'm pretty sure he's not really going to kill me, but I would say it's kind of alarming, because, well... I'm only *pretty* sure. There's still that chance he might actually throw me off the roof and make me go *splat*.

"Your medicine, huh?" I glance at the horribly rolled joint I got from the repurposed Altoids tin I swiped from his pocket while he snoozed in my bed.

"Yes," he says, pulling himself up on the ledge beside me, swinging around so his feet are dangling over the edge. He's dressed now, from head-to-toe, like he took a nice little nap so he's ready to go. "It's medicinal."

I take another hit of it, holding the smoke for a second as I offer the joint to him. Or, well, relinquish it, I guess. Not really mine to *offer*.

Letting out the smoke, I playfully ask, "So what's your ailment, huh? Glaucoma?"

Wordlessly, he takes it from me. "Close."

Close.

My stomach drops when I see he's staring at me peculiarly. He motions toward his injured eye. *Shit*. He's being serious?

"I, uh... I didn't realize..."

"You didn't realize my eye was all fucked up?" he asks, taking a hit, letting the smoke filter right back out as he says, "Kind of hard to miss, Scarlet."

"No, I mean, I know it's messed up. I'm not blind, I can *see*, but I just didn't realize..." I trail off as he curves an eyebrow, continuing to stare at me. *I'm not blind. I can see.* Did I seriously just say that shit? "Wow, I should probably stop talking."

"Might be a good idea," he says, taking another hit before holding the joint my way, like he's actually offering it to me. I take it from him, watching as he exhales slowly. He doesn't *look* offended, at least. "I used to be able to see shadows, make out shapes, but that kept getting worse, went away completely about a year ago. Total darkness now. I'll probably lose the eye eventually. Hell, I'm surprised it's survived this long. It's been dying one hell of a painful death for about twenty years now. Guess it's as stubborn as the rest of me."

"I didn't realize..."

"Yeah, I got that," he says. "Got it the two other times you said it. Don't go walking on eggshells around me over some perceived disability you're thinking I've got now. Don't pity me. I've learned how to compensate for what I'm missing. You don't need depth perception or pinpoint aim to throw a fucking grenade."

"I don't pity you," I say, because I don't... I don't pity him at all. I more so pity the people who cross his path, who incite his wrath, like I seem to be doing at the moment. *Getting on his nerves.* "So it hurts? Your eye? What does it feel like?"

I'm asking a lot of damn questions. That's what the look he gives me says. But I'm as high as a skyscraper, so high I'm almost convinced I can fly. His *medicinal* is the good shit, and yeah, maybe it's medicine to him, but it's also highly illegal, I know, because there's no way something that potent is government taxed.

"You trying to figure out my weaknesses?"

"I'll tell you mine if you tell me yours."

"Big words for a woman who would rather bare her pussy than bare a piece of her soul," he counters, his gaze trailing down my body. I'm still wearing what I put on last night, feeling filthy, the smell of sex still all over me. "Your pussy's nice, you know… *beautiful*… but I wouldn't exactly call it a secret, not when it's something a lot of people already know."

I cringe at his words, shoving the joint back at him, done with it.

He takes it, smoking the rest in silence, holding it in his lungs for long moments before exhaling slowly in my direction, his gaze still on me. I stare off into the distance, at the horizon, watching the orange hue surrounding Brooklyn fade to the typical dismal gray as the day goes on.

"I watch the sunrise every morning," I mumble. "I've never told anyone that before. I come up here and I sit and I watch as it rises over Brooklyn. The apartment is shitty, and the building smells like piss, but the view from up here is the best I've found, so I stay… I stay and I watch the sunrise. I look forward to it, every morning. Another day dawning, another chance for things to finally go right. It's the only time I feel hope anymore, the only time I feel *alive*. It's my favorite time of day."

Lorenzo stubs what's left of the joint out on the ledge, smashing the remnants into the concrete. "I see sunrise every day, too."

I look at him with surprise. "You do?"

He nods. "Except when I see it, you know, all I think is 'here comes another day of bullshit surrounded by all these idiots.' Doesn't really leave me feeling hopeful."

I laugh at that, although I can tell he's not joking. "That's about how I feel come sunset—another night in the trenches, trying to survive to see another sunrise. So far, I've got a pretty good record. A couple close calls, but I'm still undefeated, so that's gotta count for something."

"Why do you do it?"

"What else am I supposed to do?"

"*Anything*," he says. "Literally anything else has to be better than what you're doing."

"Do you know what it's like to try to get a job in this city? A legitimate job? I'm guessing you don't or you wouldn't be asking me that."

"On the contrary, Scarlet, I know *exactly* what it's like."

I roll my eyes, because *yeah, right.*

"I've got a brother," he says. "Good kid, tries to live on the straight and narrow. He doesn't have the heart for the business I'm in, wants nothing to do with it. I watched him bust his ass trying to find work with just a high school diploma."

"Yeah, well, I don't even have one of those," I say. "So I do what I have to do, I use what I have, and maybe that makes me a crappy person, whatever... maybe I'm ruined now, maybe I'm worthless..."

"I don't think you're any of that," he says. "I think you're worth a hell of a lot more than you realize. You want to take your clothes off for money? Do it. But there are better places out there, better ways to do it. You don't sell something for twenty bucks that's worth thousands. You're only fucking yourself."

"Nobody else will take a chance on me."

"That's ridiculous."

I shake my head at his flippant tone. "Have you forgotten about last night? People would have to be crazy to hire me. George was the only one with the guts to risk it, and God knows that's out of the question now. There's no way he'll want anything to do with me. I'm on my own." I run my hands down my face in frustration, closing my eyes. This *sucks.* "Selling pussy on city street corners... I'm sure *that'll* look great on my resume."

"You could come work for me."

"Yeah, right." I scoff at that. "No thanks."

"Why not?"

"Because I don't particularly *like* you."

"And, what, you *like* bending over and getting fucked for a few bucks? Money that you clearly don't get to *keep*, judging by what I've seen about your life."

"It's not like that."

"Then what's it like? Enlighten me."

"Have you ever had to do something you didn't particularly

want to do, but you did it because it was in your best interest just to go along with it?"

"No."

I roll my eyes. *Again.* "It must be nice, being you, being a man in a man's world. Trying being a woman sometime."

"I wish I could," he says. "I'd have a pussy to play with all day long, wouldn't have to comb the city looking for a woman with low standards and loose morals, since that woman would be *me*."

He laughs, but I don't find him funny. Not at all. He hasn't the faintest idea what it's like being a woman, especially one in *my* predicament. I try not to let his flippant reaction get to me, but it stirs up a hurt I sometimes have a hard time hiding.

"Oh, *woe-is-fucking-me.* Just the fact that you can make a joke about that tells me all I need to know about you and your privilege."

"My privilege? Does this look like a face that's privileged? '

He points to his face, to make his point, like he thinks maybe I haven't looked at him in the last twenty seconds, like maybe I forgot what he looks like, but he still doesn't get it.

"Yeah, it does," I say. "I hate to break it to you, but your face isn't a detriment. It's not. If anything, it helps you. People take you seriously, not only because you're a man but because you're a man who clearly went through hell. They don't look at you and see something broken. They see something strong, something that *won't* break, because you're still standing, despite everything. It intimidates them. They respect you for it. But if you were a woman? You'd be ruined. The world would look at you and think 'aw, poor thing, someone broke her, she must be so weak.' That's what they think about a woman who has been though hell. Believe me, I *know*."

"I don't think you're weak."

"But you think I'm broken," I say. "You asked me who broke me, like I'm made of glass and someone can just shatter me and scatter my pieces, like I'm *that* fragile. I might be hurt, I might be beat down, but I'll be goddamn if a man will ever break me, Lorenzo. But the world can't comprehend a woman being *that* strong. We're supposed to buckle and break, like the only time we can possibly have any strength is if there's someone with a dick standing by our side. It's like a penis is a prerequisite for an opinion, so if I don't *have* one myself, I've got to be *utilizing* someone else's in order to have any say-so in my own fucking life."

He stares at me like I'm speaking some foreign language that he's never heard before, and I'm suddenly wondering what kind of women this man spends his time with, because they certainly can't be the type to stand up to him. "I haven't the faintest fucking idea what to say right now, Scarlet."

"Of course you don't," I say. "You don't know what it's like to have to pretend to be helpless just to stay safe. There's a reason girls yell 'fire' instead of 'rape', why we lie and say we have boyfriends instead of just saying 'no' when we're not interested. Because a lot of men respect another man's property more than they respect a woman's right to her own body. So while I'm forced to live in a man's world, I do what I have to do. And if that means taking my clothes off for some schmuck with a few bucks, then by golly, I'll do it, no matter how *you* feel about it."

I get up, to leave, because he's really touching a nerve right now and I'm dangerously close to doing something insanely stupid, like trying to fling him off of the roof. Wrapping my arms around my chest, my fishnet-covered feet trudge a few steps toward the door back down to my apartment when his voice calls out. "I get it."

I stall, turning around. "Do you?"

"Mimicry," he says, swinging around to face me. "You be whoever they need you to be."

Exactly.

"And I didn't mean to hurt you when I said you were broken," he continues. "It's just a word, you know. Broken. Just a fucking word. Hell, you can call me broken if you want. You can call me anything."

"Except Scar?"

He reacts as soon as I say it, body tensing, hands clenching in his lap. "You can call me that, too, if that's what you really want.

Doesn't make a bit of damn difference."

"You say that as you make fists, like you want to punch me for it."

"Maybe I do," he says, standing up, strolling toward me. "Doesn't mean I'm going to, though. It's a free country, Scarlet. Choose your own adventure. If you'd rather keep bending over for with these yellow-bellied motherfuckers, I won't begrudge you for it. But if you want to try something else, I'm sure I can find a place for you."

"I won't fuck you."

"We've already fucked."

"I mean I won't be your whore," I say. "So don't think I'm some *thing* you can just have or use or pass around. Nobody touches me without my permission, so don't think—"

"I don't think it," he says, cutting me off. "Wasn't my intention. You've got other assets, you know... pussy isn't the only thing you've got going for you." He grabs my wrist, pulling my arm up, his thumb pressing against the pulse point beneath my tattoo. I can tell it annoys him, not knowing what it stands for. "You're smart... stealthy... sharp... am I even getting close?"

I shake my head.

His cheek twitches. "Regardless, you are. You're slick, Scarlet, and I don't mean that in the wet pussy kind of way, although, well..." He pauses as he looks me over, like he's lost his train of thought, before he shakes it off, letting go of my wrist. "I'm just saying sex isn't all you're good for. You don't want to fuck me? That's fine. Under no circumstances is fucking me a requirement. But I've seen what you're capable of. So maybe you're right, about being a woman. I don't know, because I'm not one. Maybe, to make it on these streets, you need someone in your corner. In that case, you need to reassess who that someone is, because if they're not taking you seriously, Scarlet? If they don't see you for the threat you are? They're doing you no goddamn good, because when trouble comes, they buckle, baby. They're the ones who aren't strong."

He stares at me, like he's awaiting some reaction, some sort of intelligent response to that declaration, but he's kind of rendered me speechless, so I just offer him his own words. "I haven't the faintest fucking idea what to say to that, Lorenzo."

A smile cracks his face as he grasps my chin, tilting my face up further, and holding me there. His touch sends sparks through my body, my heart racing in my chest. Working for him would be dangerous, very dangerous, in every conceivable way, and I'm just not sure if that's a risk I can take.

"You just think about it," he says. "Jamaica Estates over in Queens… it's a white house on Midland, not far from Grand Central Parkway. You want me, that's where you'll find me. My door's always open. Literally. I don't lock my doors, either."

His thumb lightly swipes across my bottom lip before he pulls away, letting go, his hand leaving my skin.

I just stand here as he leaves, waiting until he's gone before returning to my apartment. I shower and change clothes, grabbing my oversized black hoodie, tugging it on before leaving, too.

I need to clear my head. I need to make sense of this mess.

I need to make another trek to Brooklyn.

* * *

Dry heat billows from the vent in the ceiling right above me, ruffling my frizzy hair, blowing wayward strands into my face.

I don't bother pushing them away.

It feels like Death Valley in this glass cube they call an office, the fluorescent lights too bright and the air too warm. My palms are sweaty, hands shoved in the pocket of my hoodie. Every breath makes my lungs burn, stiff and achy in my chest, like smoke inhalation got the best of me this morning.

I'm still high.

I can feel it.

The blinds are up and the door is propped open, giving a clear view inside the office, so anyone walking past can see me sitting here. It's unnerving, but I'm grateful for the openness. It means the detective is too busy to think about hanky-panky right now.

He's been in and out of the office for the past thirty minutes, barely acknowledging my presence, shuffling through paperwork and muttering under his breath. I'm curious what he's working on, but if I ask he'll just say it isn't any of my business, even if it *is*... he doesn't tell me anything.

I stare past him, beyond him, out of the office window of the precinct, a stream of sunlight reflecting off the glass, reminding me of the orange glow this morning. "Two hundred and eighty sunrises."

Gabe shuffles through a few files as he says, "You shouldn't be here, Morgan."

That's what he always says.

You'd think he'd be tired of repeating himself.

"Yeah, well, here I am," I mumble as I toy with the edge of the sleeves of my hoodie. "Always exactly where I don't belong."

He lets out a deep, exaggerated sigh as he sits back in his chair. "The guys over at the seventh precinct are gonna want to interview you."

I nod, not surprised.

The police would be crawling all over Mystic. I'm not on record as working there, officially, but my name is bound to come up. The security monitors are nothing more than live feeds, so there won't be any recordings, which means they're going to be desperate for witnesses.

They'll find none.

Nobody's going to talk.

Certainly not me.

"Was it him?" Gabe asks.

"What do you think?"

"I think it certainly sounds like something he'd do."

"Well, there you go," I say.

"So you saw him?" Gabe asks. "Kassian?"

Kassian.

My gaze shifts to my lap at the sound of that name. Sweat rolls down my back. It feels even harder to breathe in here now. Why the hell is it so hot?

"I heard him talking," I say. "He was looking for me."

"Did he see you?"

"Would I be sitting here if he did?"

"No," he mutters. "Probably wouldn't."

I can't even begin to imagine what Kassian might've done had he found me hiding behind that bar, how he would've reacted to the sight of me cowering there without a top on. *Probably would've killed everyone.* We've been doing this dance for a long, long time, but these past nine months have been the worst. I'm *exhausted.* Most intense game of Hide & Seek ever played, except it's not a game. Not really. There's nothing fun about what we're doing. I want to quit, forfeit, call it a tie and walk away with my head held high, but Kassian Aristov plays to win.

There's no negotiating with that man.

It's his way or no way.

And I can't let him win this one. I *can't.* And he knows that. Him winning means the rest of us *lose.*

"Do you ever watch the sunrise, detective?"

Gabe sighs dramatically, ignoring my question, like maybe he thinks I'm being stupid. "Go home, Morgan. It's not safe for you here."

"Not safe in the 60th precinct?" I gasp with mock horror, clutching my chest. "Whatever do you mean?"

"You know exactly what I mean."

"Yeah, well, if I'm not safe surrounded by police, what makes you think I'll be safe anywhere out there?"

"He hasn't found you yet, has he?"

"Not yet," I say, *yet* being the operative word. If he figured out I was working at Mystic, it's only a matter of time until he traces me to the apartment, considering George owns the place.

He set me up there when I hit bottom, after I threw myself at his mercy, having nowhere else to turn for help. He hates the Russians with a fiery passion, and the enemy of my enemy, well... let's just say they're the only ones stupid enough to jump at that chance.

"Can I ask you something else, detective?"

"If I say no, will that make you leave?"

"No."

"Then fire away."

"What do you know about a guy they call *Scar*?"

Gabe stops what he's doing and looks at me. "I know anyone with a street name like Scar is probably going to be bad news. Other than that, nothing."

"Nothing?"

"Nothing," he says. "Why?"

"No particular reason."

"*Why*, Morgan?" he asks again, voice louder. "What have you gotten yourself into now?"

"Nothing."

"Nothing?"

"Nothing."

Man, this conversation is going *nowhere*.

"Go home," Gabe says, standing up, "and stay there. Stay off the radar. Stay out of trouble. Don't do anything *stupid*. Don't jeopardize what we're doing here."

"What *are* we doing here?" I ask. "Because I'm not really seeing anything being done."

He squeezes my shoulder. It's meant to be affectionate, I guess, but his touch makes my skin crawl. "I'm protecting you, Morgan, just like you need me to do."

After he walks out, I sit there, considering those words. Protecting me.

If this is how they protect people, I think I'd rather protect *myself*.

13

"I have something for you, kitten."

The little girl tensed at those words, at the Tin Man's voice in the doorway behind her. It had been two weeks since that night when she'd been woken from her sleep for Hide & Seek.

When would it be over?

The little girl turned around in the wooden desk chair, where she'd been drawing with a stubby little pencil in the bedroom he called *hers*. The Tin Man stood there, dressed in a black suit, hands hidden behind his back. She hadn't seen him much in days. She stayed in that room, avoiding him after he burned her favorite nightgown.

She didn't like being there, but she liked it a tiny bit more when he wasn't around. The Cowardly Lion watched her the nights the Tin Man didn't come home. He wasn't always nice, but he wasn't as mean. Sometimes, she thought she might like him.

Her stomach gurgled and her hands shook as she fisted the pencil. "What do you have?"

The Tin Man said nothing, did nothing, just staring at her, not moving from the doorway. After a moment, he pulled something from behind his back, his hand dwarfing a stuffed bear. Threadbare in some patches, its fluff kind of matted, the tan coloring filthy brown. An eye was gone and an ear was barely hanging on, but it was the most beautiful thing the little girl had ever seen, because it was hers. *Hers.*

Her mother had given it to her.

She hadn't seen it since the night she'd dropped it in the kitchen near where her mother slept. Her eyes widened, lips parting, heart beating wildly in her chest.

"For *me?*" she asked.

"It is yours, yes?" He looked at it, making a face. "Hideous thing. Do you even *want* it?"

She frantically nodded.

Of course she wanted it.

She wanted it *so bad.*

But she didn't dare move from the chair, didn't dare try to get it. Not yet.

He knelt down then, eye-level from the doorway, and held it out for her to take. The little girl was terrified it might be a trick, but she wanted it so much she had to try. Standing up, she approached him, reaching for it. He kept his grip on the bear, not yet releasing it. "Does it have a name?"

She nodded.

"Use your words."

"His name is Buster," she whispered.

"Buster," he repeated before finally letting go. The little girl snatched the bear to her chest, hugging it tightly.

The Tin Man stood back up, like he was just going to leave, like it hadn't been a trick at all. He really had something for her, something he would let her keep.

In a snap decision, the little girl flung herself at him, hugging his legs, squishing the teddy bear against his thigh. He froze, looking at her. She worried she'd made a mistake until his hand gently stroked her long brown hair and he hugged her back.

"Thank you, Daddy," she whispered.

His finger crooked beneath her chin, making her look up at him. "I would do anything for you, kitten."

She wasn't sure if she believed that, but his gentle tone made her smile. For the first time in fourteen long days, she *smiled* at him.

The Tin Man grinned down at her, again stroking her hair, his shoulders sagging, his posture less tense, like maybe he remembered his heart again. Maybe it was in his chest, beating all weirdly just like hers, kind of scared still, but almost a little bit happy, too. It didn't last long, though, as something happened to his smile, making it freeze on his face, like the smile her mother gave her the night when things went all wrong.

"You look like her," he said, his tone flat. "I pray you never *act* like her. I would not handle that well."

He pulled away, prying her off of him, leaving her standing there in a cloud of confusion. She shook it off, though, her smile only growing as she hugged Buster, holding him to her nose and inhaling deeply.

It was *almost* like hugging her mother.

14

Lorenzo

Puzzles.

Each piece perfectly cut, molded to fit the ones surrounding it, unique in its own right so it can't go anywhere else, only where it belongs. Alone, the piece means nothing, a flicker of a picture, like a story without an ending, just a random scene without any credibility. It's like getting your dick wet but never getting off, sticking it in but not fucking.

What's the point of *that?*

Puzzles demand follow-through. You can't just dick out in the middle of one.

Or, well, *I* can't.

It's kind of a metaphor for life. Moments are pieces, formed together and built upon, creating the bigger picture within the border of your world. My puzzle is full of deformed shapes and jagged edges, but it still all fits together in its own twisted way, making a hideous fucking picture of my reality.

I like puzzles.

That's probably not a surprise.

The library on the first floor of the house is mostly vacant, just like most of the other rooms. *Only own what you can use.* An oversized ebony veneer table spans the center of it, golden brown and stark black wood merging together, the kind of table you'd find in a boardroom surrounded by those expensive ass ergonomic chairs. There's a single black leather office chair in here somewhere, shoved aside, as I stand in front of the table, gazing down at it, tapping the corner of a puzzle piece against the shiny striped wood, thinking.

I've been working on this puzzle for a few months now, since the day we moved into this house, the border completed, taking up half of the table, sections pierced together inside of it with others just sitting around. Eight thousand pieces. A replica of Michelangelo's painting on the ceiling of the Sistine Chapel.

Sounds boring, I know.

Just stick with me here.

It'll get better.

I try the piece a few spots before snapping it into place near the border. I look around, seeking out another, when light tapping echoes through the library from the open doorway as knuckles rapt against the wooden paneling.

Seven stands there, not crossing the threshold, clutching his phone. Or well, *my* phone, actually. He tends to filter my calls for me whenever he's around, like some pseudo-secretary.

He doesn't come any closer, waiting for acknowledgment. Others move around the house, the rest of my little personal wrecking crew, seven of them in total. There used to be ten, a nice, round even number, but the other three? Well, they met unfortunate ends due to their own stupidity.

I don't have many rules. Do what you want. Screw who you want. Steal, and lie, and cheat, if you must, but when I tell you something, you listen, and it's in your best interest not to annoy me, because I can be a bit touchy.

Oh, and don't step foot in my library without my permission.

"What is it, Seven? I'm busy."

"That guy is calling again."

"Which guy?"

"Ricardo Conti."

"Who?"

"Amello's guy."

"Which guy?"

"The one we met out on the dock that night."

"Ah, *that* guy," I say, trying a piece in a few spots before discarding it, picking up another. "He doesn't look like a Ricardo."

"That's his name."

"I don't like it."

"I didn't imagine you would."

There's nothing spiteful about those words from Seven, so I take no offense to them.

The guy knows how I tick.

I try my next piece, finding its spot, and move on to yet another when Seven clears his throat. "Boss?"

I look at him again, growing impatient. "What?"

"Ricardo," he says, holding the phone up. "He's calling."

"Now?"

"Yes," he says. "Do you want me to tell him you're still busy?"

"Depends on what he wants."

"To meet up with you again."

"Oh, well, invite him over, then."

Seven's eyes widen. "Here?"

"Yeah, why not?" I shrug. "It's still cold as fuck. I'm not hanging out on some dock tonight, freezing my nuts off again. If he wants to see me, here I am."

"Yes, boss. I'll tell him."

Seven retreats as I continue working on my puzzle, trying to focus, but my vision is blurring and making it hard to see, the colors all merging together. I try for a bit longer before giving up, a headache setting in. Snatching the chair closer, I drop down in it, propping my feet up on the corner of the table as I close my eyes, draping my arm over my face, trying to block out all of the light.

God knows how long I sit here, zoning out, dozing off, before a throat clears. I open my eyes, alarmed, seeing a man stepping into the library. *Ricardo.* Sitting straight up, feet hitting the floor with a thud, I reach for my gun. I point it before he can come any closer, aiming center mass.

"One more step and I pull the trigger," I say as he comes to an abrupt stop, raising his hands, like surrendering might stop me from shooting. *Ha.* "Do you always make it a habit to enter someone's domain without knocking?"

"I was invited," he says. "And the door, you know, it's open, so I thought…"

Seven appears behind the guy as he trails off. Grabbing him, Seven roughly pats him down, snatching a small gun from a holster under his clothes. Seven quickly disassembles it, taking all the bullets, before handing the gun back to him. His brow furrows as he takes it."

"You can have the gun, but only once it's empty," I tell him, "Ammunition is a no-no in my house. You see, bullets don't come with names on them, which means anyone can catch one, if you pull the trigger, and I can't get down with that. You got me?"

He slowly nods as he eyes *my* gun.

I know what he's thinking.

"Rules don't apply to me," I say, "so don't get any stupid ideas. You want to kill me, Ricky, and you're going to have to get creative, because I'll shoot you in the fucking heart the second you start getting twitchy."

He slips his gun back into the holster, keeping his hands where I can see them after that.

"Now proper protocol is you *knock*," I tell him. "If the door is open, knock on the doorframe. It's not that hard. Go ahead, try it."

He still seems confused, like he's not grasping it, like maybe I assumed he had balls when the guy is just recklessly *stupid*. After a second, he raises his fist and taps on the wood beside him.

"Good boy," I say. "Now, what do you want?"

"You, uh… you told me to come."

"Because I assumed you wanted something."

"I delivered your counter offer to my boss," he says. "Figured you'd want to know."

"My counter offer? Refresh my memory…"

"You said for him to suck your cock."

"Oh." I laugh. I did, didn't I? *Huh*. Didn't expect him to actually relay that message. Amello still let him live after that? "And what did your boss have to say?"

"He declined."

"Figures," I say, spreading my legs out, slouching. "Pity, though. Bet he sucks good cock. Probably does it enough, you know, *practice makes perfect* and all that. Guess you'll just have to do it in his place. You spend much time on your knees for him, Ricky? Or do you prefer to just bend over and let him fuck you for a bit?"

Ricardo stands there, gaping at me, like he's trying to figure out whether or not I'm being serious. He swallows thickly, Adam's apple bobbing, and I cock at eyebrow, purposely being dramatic about it.

"I don't," he starts, pausing before saying, "I mean, I'm not..."

"Come on, spit it out."

"Or just swallow it," Seven jokes.

I laugh. "That's probably a better idea. You should be grateful for every drop."

Ricardo takes a deep breath. "I'm not gay."

"Neither am I," I say, "and neither is Seven, for that matter, but he'd suck it if I asked him. Wouldn't you, Seven?"

"Absolutely," Seven says. "Anything you ask."

Lucky for Seven, I respect him enough not to ever ask that of him. I respect his personal boundaries, because he *commands* it. He doesn't just demand it, like some whiny brat with a big mouth that needs something shoved in it. He carries himself like someone to respect. But still, he'd do it if I ever asked him to, because I command respect, too.

This guy, though, he's got balls, but they might be *too* big if instead of getting on his knees and saying 'yes, please' he's hesitating like a little bitch.

"Come in," I tell the guy. "Leave us, Seven."

Seven nods before walking off. Ricardo carefully steps into the library, his approach cautious, his gaze flickering all around. He pauses, maybe two feet in front of me, unsure of what to do.

"Tell me something," I say, too exhausted to prolong this, as much as frazzling him amuses me. "Did you come because your boss has another grievance he wants to air? Or are you looking for a new job, considering what happened to your boss's club, you know, since people went *bang-bang-bang*?"

"I guess you could say that."

"You guess? Do you? Because I don't. I don't *guess*. Either you do or you don't. Either you're looking for a job or you're not. If you don't understand your own motivations enough to not have to take a fucking *guess*, then we've got a problem."

He stares at me. "I'm sure."

"Well, then." I prop my feet up on the corner of the table, lacing my hands together at the back of my head. "Tell me about yourself, Ricky."

He starts babbling. I don't know. I'm not paying the words any attention. I really don't give a shit what the guy's saying, don't care how he's framing himself, but his body language tells me everything. When you spend your life tiptoeing around psychopaths, you learn to listen to what's going unspoken. He blinks too much, fidgeting, tinkering with the watch on his wrist, playing with the clasp. Not a Rolex, I notice, not that it makes a difference in this situation, but it means he's either tasteless or broke as fuck, and either way, it sucks for him. Whatever he's saying, he's lying. Everything about him screams *deception*.

Tapping echoes through the library just when I'm about to call him out on it. Seven stands there, yet again.

"I thought I told you to leave us," I say loudly, my voice cutting off Ricardo's blubbering.

"You did," Seven says, "but somebody's here."

"There are quite a few people here," I say. "Me, you, Ricky... Pretty Boy is upstairs with Firecracker... and the rest of the guys, you know, Two through Six and Nine, they're all around, but that doesn't mean you should interrupt me when I'm in the middle of something."

"I mean *somebody else*."

"Who?"

"A woman," Seven says. "Young, brunette... I think it might be the one you were looking for."

"She's *here*?"

Seven nods. "She's outside."

"Why haven't you let her in?"

"Because she hasn't knocked," he says. "She's kind of just

lurking, you know, looking around."

"Huh." Dropping my feet down again, I stand up, strolling toward the doorway. I slap Ricardo on the shoulder, squeezing, before pushing him toward my chair. "Have a seat, I'll be back."

Seven eyes the guy warily before following me into the hall. "I don't trust that guy, boss."

"You probably shouldn't," I say, turning to him. "Where'd you last see her?"

"She was out front," he says. "Saw her lingering near the gate."

"Good." I motion toward the library. "Keep an eye on him, will you? I'm going to go check on our other guest."

"Yes, boss."

Seven goes to the library as I make my way to the back of the house, opting to go out that way and make my way around. The air is frigid, dusk growing close. *Sunset.* My footsteps are silent, my combat boots squishing into the damp earth, the snow finally melting. I creep along the side of the house, pausing when I hit the front corner. I zero in on her, catching subtle movement in the bushes. She's squatting down beneath the living room window, completely cloaked in black—sweats, hoodie, and sneakers.

She's watching through the window, watching my men as they do what they do, so consumed by whatever she sees *inside* that she doesn't sense me approaching. I pause behind her, watching her as she watches them.

It's like the *Inception* of fucking spying here.

I try to wait her out, but she proves to be patient. Minutes tick away. *Tick. Tick. Tick.* As much as I'd love to stand here forever, it's getting dark, and it's too damn cold for this nonsense.

"Are you going to come inside or what?"

As soon as my voice rings out, she tries to turn, caught off guard, but she loses her balance, planting right into the bushes on her ass. "*Shit.*"

I laugh as she scrambles to get to her feet. She quickly moves away from the window, away from the house, keeping some distance between us. The woman is sly, without a doubt... so sly

Seven's the only one who noticed her, the rest of my men oblivious, but still, she's a bit wet behind the ears.

Eyeing me warily, she shoves her hands in her hoodie pocket and says nothing, not answering my question, like maybe she doesn't have a response for it.

"Well?"

Still no answer.

Just a blank stare.

"Fine." I turn to leave. "Stay out here."

I only make it a few steps before her quiet voice says, "You've got a white picket fence."

That stalls me. I'm not sure why. Maybe it's the words. Maybe it's her tone. Something about it makes me turn back around. She's still just standing there, eyes past me, gaze trailing the fence along the property.

"What did you expect, barbed wire?"

"I don't know," she admits, looking at me again. "Just not a picket fence."

She seems almost in awe about it, but it's a fence. Just a fucking *fence*. I get the feeling, at the moment, that it means something more to her. But it's too cold for me to riddle that out, too cold to be metaphorical.

"Come on." I don't ask this time. "Come inside with me."

I head for the front door. She hesitates, eyes trailing me, before she finally follows without argument. The moment I open the door, the noise inside grows quiet, the little party in the living room coming to an abrupt halt as my men are on guard. *Intruders*.

"Put your dicks away, fellas," I say when guns are drawn, aimed my way in alarm. The 'no bullets' rule doesn't apply to them, either, but times like this I think it ought to.

They lower them so fast it's damn near comical, eyes bugging out like it's the fucking *Looney Tunes*.

A haze of smoke lingers in the room, the woodsy, musky scent strong in the air. Half-empty bottles of liquor are scattered over the coffee table. Strolling over, I snatch up a bottle of rum, taking a swig straight from it before pointing to Scarlet.

156

"Fellas, this is Scarlet. Scarlet, this is Two through Six, and Nine."

She blinks a few times but says nothing as the men mumble awkward greetings, like the motherfuckers have never met a woman before.

I walk back out, still clutching the bottle, and Scarlet follows me into the hallway. "You *numbered* them?"

"Yes."

"Why?"

"I imagine the same reason the Cat in the Hat called his little friends Thing One and Thing Two."

"Which is *why*?"

I shrug. "Who knows? It sounded good."

"Oh-kay." She doesn't sound convinced. "But what happened to One? Or, like, Seven?"

I stall in front of Seven, who lurks in front of the library, perking up at the sound of his name.

"Seven," I tell her, pointing at Seven with my liquor bottle. "One is gone, as are Eight and Ten, but Seven here is worth a dozen men alone, so I haven't felt the need to replace them."

Scarlet gives me a peculiar look, like none of this is making sense to her.

"Is this some memory thing, like your brain is wired wrong?" she asks. "Or are you just *that* much of an asshole?"

That makes me laugh.

Seven, on the other hand, tenses.

Afraid I'm going to kill her, probably.

Mormon, remember?

He's still got a few morals left.

"Probably a bit of both," I admit, slapping Seven on the back, wordlessly telling him to relax. If I were going to kill her, I would've done it when she robbed me, or when she pulled a knife on me... *twice*. Sticks and stones. Words from her sleek lips, no matter how bitter, are definitely going to go down smoother.

Moving past him, I step into the library doorway, seeing Ricardo still sitting there, exactly where I left him.

"Up," I say, snapping my finger, motioning for him to vacate my chair. He springs to his feet, his gaze finding Scarlet.

She walks into the room right behind me, cursing under her breath. "*Shit.*"

She regards the guy like a deer caught in headlights and he looks at her like... well, like something he wants to eat. *Uh-oh.* I admit it, yeah, the woman is delectable, but I'm the big bad wolf in these woods, and he's going to leave my Red Riding Hood alone.

I motion between them as I drop back down in my chair. "I assume you two know each other."

"I've seen her around," Ricardo says. "One of Amello's whores."

Scarlet makes a face but says nothing, skirting around the guy, giving him a wide berth as she makes her way to where I'm sitting. She's uncomfortable around him, which means she's got decent intuition.

"You drink, Ricky?" I ask, motioning toward him with my liquor bottle. "Smoke a little bit, maybe?"

"A bit," he says.

"Go fix yourself a drink," I say. "Hang out a while, get to know my guys. They'll make you feel at home. I have some business to take care of here. I'll come for you when I'm done."

He nods in acknowledgment, casting Scarlet a look before disappearing into the hallway. He seems to want to gut her. *Huh.* Seven trails our visitor right away to the living room.

Scarlet watches them before turning to me. "What, Slick Rick doesn't get a number?"

"Slick Rick?" I laugh. "I'll have to remember that one."

"You know he works for George Amello, right?"

"Yep."

"He's the one George ordered to kill you," she says. "He's supposed to send a message by eliminating you."

"Yeah, I figured that much," I say, kicking my feet up on the table as I lounge back in the chair. She looks concerned, like she's worried for my well-being. It's cute. *Real* cute. "So tell me, Scarlet, you come here to kill me, too? Because if so, you might want to come back later, since he beat you to it tonight. You'll have to wait your turn."

She blinks at me like I've lost my mind. Hell, maybe I have. "Are you insane?"

"Potentially," I say. "You?"

"Am *I* insane?"

I nod.

"I'm starting to feel like it," she mutters, running her hands down her face. "The fact that I thought it was a good idea to come here tells me I probably am."

"You come to take me up on my offer?"

Hesitating, she approaches the table, glancing down at the puzzle. Her eyes meticulously scan the beginnings of the art, but she doesn't touch any of the pieces, keeping her hands to herself.

"Did you know Michelangelo never wanted to paint this?" she asks after a moment. "The pope didn't give him much of a choice. He spent so many hours on his back, struggling, suffering, the conditions so toxic it made him sick. He spent the rest of his life walking with a limp because of it."

"No, I didn't know that," I say, "but I did notice you're avoiding my question."

She smiles softly, still gazing at the puzzle. "I know how that feels, having someone powerful controlling you, dictating what you do. But Michelangelo, he got his revenge. The whole thing is filled with blasphemy."

"I bet," I say. "Now answer my question."

"Yes."

That's all she says. *Yes.*

"You're taking me up on my offer?"

"Pretty sure that's what *yes* means."

I grin. "So, what I'm hearing here is that you want revenge on the asshole who controlled you... although, I'm guessing the Aristotle prick didn't make you paint a church. What did he do?"

"He stole from me."

"Stole what?"

"Everything," she whispers, "but mostly my innocence. He

took away everything good in my world, he stole it from me, everything I loved, and he tried so hard to snuff out every bit of light in my life, to make sure I never felt the sunshine again, and he did it, he said, for my own good, like that was what it meant to love somebody."

She turns to me, her expression passive, as those words run through my mind. *For my own good.* Yeah, I've heard that before.

"That's what makes him so cruel," she continues. "I used to read all these fairy tales, and I just think about how fucked up it is to realize that heroes are make-believe but monsters are real. That's the world we live in. There's no knight in shining armor out there. It's just me, trapped in a world filled with fire-breathing dragons, and that man is determined to burn me to a crisp."

"I knew a man like that once."

"What happened?"

I drop my feet to the floor and stand up, studying her for a moment before saying, "My *face* happened."

I stroll over to the wall of bookshelves along the back of the room, mostly bare except a few scraggly books and some lock boxes. I pull out a set of keys from my pocket, wordlessly unlocking a small metal box, and grab the black silencer from inside. Pulling my gun from my waistband, I turn around.

Scarlet is leaning back against the table, her hands shoved in her hoodie pocket again. Her gaze trails me, on guard, as I screw the silencer onto the Colt M1911.

I check the gun, making sure it's loaded. "So you like fairy tales, huh? You ever hear the story of *The Juniper Tree*?"

"No."

"Stepmother doesn't like her stepson, because he's set to inherit the family fortune, so she beheads him and feeds him to his father before burying his bones beneath a juniper tree."

She stares at me. "And then what?"

"That's it."

"That can't be it."

"Sometimes the stories are horrific, Scarlet. Just because you haven't found some bullshit Prince Charming doesn't mean fairy tales aren't real. They're just not always pretty pictures."

I walk out of the library, making my way to the living room. Seven lingers in the doorway, keeping an eye on our guest like I knew he would. The others lurk inside the room, laughing, joking. Ricky sits dead center of the couch, drinking straight from a bottle, hazy smoke surrounding him.

Clearing my throat, I step into the room, drawing his attention. His smile quickly fades, something sparking in his eyes when he sees the gun in my hand.

BANG.

I don't give him the chance to acknowledge what's happening, don't give him time to plead for his life, to try to shovel some bullshit, thinking I'm going to buy it.

BANG.

BANG.

BANG.

Back to back, I unload the bullets into him, suppressed but still loud enough for the noise to echo, merging with the sharp sound of his gurgling scream. Bullets hit his chest, his stomach, and the couch beside him, nearly hitting one of my men before the final one slams the fucker right in the head.

BANG.

Blood splatters the white wall around the couch. Ricky slumps over onto Three, his body still twitching, heart no longer pumping. Three shoves him off, cursing, as he stands up, flailing his hands like a hysterical little bitch, his reaction making the others laugh.

They *laugh*.

Bunch of sick fucks, finding it funny that their friend is splattered with brain matter.

I shake my head, shoving the gun at Seven, who takes it without question. White smoke surrounds us from the lube I use in the tube of the suppressor.

I know there's one hell of a sex joke in there somewhere, just begging to be made, but I don't have time for it right now, because the air's so thick the damn smoke detector starts screeching in the hallway, as if I'm not drawing enough attention.

"Clean the gun," I tell Seven before waving toward the mess on the couch. "The rest of you, do something about this before Three shits his pants."

They laugh some more as Three grumbles under his breath, trying to pull himself together. He's the whitest white boy around, with shaggy blond hair and light green eyes, freckles on his button nose, his cheeks all rosy, like he's always blushing. He's a cross between a California surfer and little Bobby Brady with the personality of John Wayne Gacy... you know, a murderous *clown*.

"Lorenzo? Everything okay?"

My brother's voice rings out from upstairs. I turn, stepping back out into the hallway to respond, and come face-to-face with Scarlet. She stands there, eyes kind of wide as they regard me, a look in them that I recognize... a look that tells me she watched what I just did. It's not fear, no. I've seen her scared. I watched her cower behind a bar in terror, remember? This is more so surprise, like maybe she didn't think I had it in me, like maybe she hadn't been taking me seriously until now.

Like she didn't realize I lived up to my reputation.

"It's fine," I yell, waving toward the blaring smoke detector, fanning the haze away. "Stay upstairs."

"Planned on it," he yells back. "Just, can you keep it down? I have to work in the morning, bro."

The blaring silences as I laugh to myself.

I'll never get over the irony of *me* raising a straight-laced member of society.

"I need a drink," I grumble, scrubbing my hands down my face as I walk away, detouring to the library for the bottle of rum. Scarlet follows me. I don't see her, or hear her, so much as *sense* her. It's a feeling ghosting across my skin from her eyes studying me.

"There has to be more," she says finally.

"More what?" I ask.

"The Juniper Tree," she says. "It can't end like *that*."

Taking a swig of rum, I turn to her. "You're still going on about that?"

"Yes."

"It's just a story. Stories have to end sometime. Hell, did you watch *The Sopranos*? Sometimes stories just stop. Shit just goes black. Wham, bam, over. No more, nothing left, *the end*."

She makes a face. "That sucks."

"Yeah, well, *life* sucks, Scarlet," I say. "You know that as well as anyone. Sometimes beasts are just fucking beasts, no matter how much you love them, Belle. It's a fact. I've seen love bring a monster back to life before, but most of the time, the monster just loves you to *death*."

She shakes her head, looking away.

I take it she doesn't like what I'm saying.

For a woman who claims she doesn't believe in fairy tales anymore, unhappy endings are sure ruffling her feathers.

"A white picket fence," I say, something clicking after a moment. That's what she said outside. *You've got a white picket fence.* "Is that what you want? To be proven wrong? For some *happily ever after* to come along and sweep you off your feet? Take you away from this bullshit life and give you your picket fence?"

"You're an asshole, Lorenzo."

"That doesn't sound like a denial."

"Is it so wrong to want to be happy?"

"Is that what makes you happy? *Really*?"

She noncommittally shrugs a shoulder.

"Well, if it is, you're barking up the wrong tree," I say, "because I can't give you that. Don't let the fence out there fool you. Around here, it's just a fence. It came with a house that I bought because my brother liked it. Nothing more. But what I can offer, Scarlet, is to stand in your corner. You and I, we can be the best of friends, but don't expect to find your fairy tale under my roof. You got me?"

She stares me down.

I think maybe I offended her. Not that it matters, though, because it's the truth, and the last thing I want is for this woman to get it twisted and think I'm something I can't be: her *hero*.

After a moment, she cocks her head to the side and says,

"Are you for real?"

"As real as it gets."

"Why would you be my friend? What do you get out of it?"

I consider that question as I sip from the bottle of rum, sitting back down in my chair. "The truth?"

"Please."

"I'm bored," I admit. "I came to the city because of a movie, too. *The Godfather.* But reality? It's nothing like it is in the movies. Most days we just sit around, waiting for something to happen. It's monotonous. The world, it's all in black and white, but you? You're so many shades of red, woman, and color me curious, but I find myself not so bored with your bullshit around."

"You know, Kassian's not just cruel," she says, approaching. "He's callous... soulless... *vicious.*"

"Cold-blooded, hardhearted, and a dozen other synonyms that mean he's a real piece of shit?"

"Yes," she says. "He's not someone you mess with."

"Yeah, well, I'm not Mary Poppins, either."

She pauses right in front of me. "Yes, but—"

Before she can finish, before she can rattle off something that'll probably offend me, a hundred bullshit reasons why I shouldn't befriend her, I snatch ahold of the back of her neck, gripping it tightly as I yank her down, forcing her to look me in the eyes, so close my nose brushes against hers.

Her breath hitches.

"I will slit his fucking throat and drink his blood, Scarlet," I say, my voice gravelly, quiet, and goddamn serious. "He might scare *you*, and maybe it's for good reason, but he doesn't scare me. Because all those words you used to describe him? I've been called them, too. I've earned my distinction, I fought for my title, and whether or not he's worth the fear he incites? Well, I'm still deciding. You got me?"

She exhales shakily, but instead of acknowledging what I ask, she lets out a laugh. "You're *crazy*."

"Welcome to the madhouse. Feel free to stay as long as you'd like, but as long as you're here, there are rules to be followed."

"Like?"

"Like betray me and I kill you. Lie to me and I kill you. Ignore an order and I kill you. Otherwise, do whatever the hell you want. You think you can handle that?"

"As long as you don't talk down to me because I'm a woman. You pull some misogynistic shit and I'll kill *you*. We got a deal?"

Those words, they do something to me, hearing that threat come from her lips, so at odds with that low, sultry voice. It makes me hard in an instant.

"Depends," I say. "Is telling you that I'd really like to fuck your throat right now *misogynistic*?"

She blinks a few times, like she didn't expect me to say that. "Would you say that to your men?"

"If something they said turned me on, I would."

My hand shifts, from the back of her neck to the front of her throat, my thumb and forefinger against her carotid arteries. I don't press hard, just resting them there, faintly feeling the blood pulsing through her system. Her heart's racing.

"Is it even possible for them to turn you on?" she asks, swallowing thickly, her throat vibrating against my palm.

"Oh, without a doubt," I tell her. "Nothing is impossible. But those guys, you know, they're crude, kind of scuzzy, so they're more likely to disgust me than get me hard. Still, though... I don't like to rule anything out."

I let go of her, relaxing back in my chair, and expect her to pull away now that I'm no longer holding her there, but she keeps her position, her hands coming to rest on the arms of my chair as she leans over me.

"Then I wouldn't really call it misogynistic," she says. "You're more of an equal opportunity asshole."

"Well, then, I guess we've got a deal."

"Guess so," she whispers, tilting her head as she licks her lips. She leans closer, the tip of her nose brushing against mine, her mouth a breath away when tapping echoes through the library.

Fuck.

I press my pointer finger to her lips, stopping her, and get to my feet, the movement pushing her away from the chair. Seven lurks near the threshold, holding my gun, freshly cleaned. Scarlet stands up straight, frowning, and I pause in front of her, gaze scanning her, before I pull my hand away.

Nudging her chin, I lift her face up.

She looks almost disappointed.

"Business first," I say quietly. "Maybe afterward there will be time for some fun."

15
Morgan

The stench of bleach makes my nose twitch, thick in the air, burning my lungs as I inhale the odor. *Ugh.* The living room has been thoroughly scrubbed, faster than I thought humanly possible.

It's clear, as I watch from the doorway, that this isn't the first time this has happened. They seem more on top of things than the professional Crime Scene Clean-Up crews in the city, and those guys have *plenty* of experience.

Lorenzo stands just two feet or so in front of me, so close that I could touch him if I wanted. His plain white long sleeved shirt is all jacked up in the back from the gun he shoved behind him, right in his waistband. Freshly reloaded, I'm guessing. The silencer is no longer attached, fisted in his hand, as he stands there, staring at his black leather couch.

He's trusting. Or maybe just reckless. I could snatch the gun from his pants and shoot him in the back of the head before he even knew it was happening. I'm not going to, of course. I'm just making a point.

I *could.*

If I wanted.

But I don't.

"We could throw a blanket over it," one of the guys says, breaking the silence. I don't know his name. Hell, I don't know his *number.* He's just... one of them. Dark hair, dark eyes, dark features, dark voice. Everything about him is dark, down to his all black clothes.

They're *all* wearing black, I realize, as I glance around the packed living room, except for Lorenzo, who dresses more like some hoodlum/model hybrid. It's weird, right?

I don't know.

I'm still not even sure what I'm doing here.

"A blanket," Lorenzo says, not sounding convinced.

"Yeah, you know, or one of them covers," the guy says. "The ones they put on couches. What are they called? Uh..."

"Couch covers," Lorenzo says.

"That's it!" The guy snaps his finger, pointing at Lorenzo, looking damn proud like that was some big revelation. "A couch cover!"

"That could work," someone says—the oddball of the group, the lone blond guy in a room full of mostly Italians. "My granny has one of those on her couch, hiding this big ass wine stain. It's ugly, you know, but it could do the trick."

Lorenzo turns his head, regarding the blond, his expression as flat as his voice as he says, "You gonna go rob your granny of her couch cover?"

He shrugs. "Well, yeah, if you need it, sure."

Lorenzo stares at him for a moment before turning back to the couch. I shift to the side a bit, peeking around him. There's a bullet hole in the back of it, where the guy had been sitting. It's not *that* bad, but it's noticeable, which I guess is a problem.

"Just get rid of it," Lorenzo says, waving toward it. "I'll get a new one."

The guys jump into action, teaming up and grabbing the couch, picking it up to move it.

They barely get it away from the wall when Lorenzo yells, raising his voice, damn near growling. "Put it back!"

The men are confused. You can see it in their faces as they cast him concerned looks, but I know what the issue is. Behind it, a hole is blown into the wall, a hell of a lot bigger than the one on the couch. Which, again, I'm guessing is problem.

They drop it back into place, stepping away, giving the couch a wide berth like *it* might attack them.

"Find some fucking duct tape or something," Lorenzo says,

turning, storming past me. "Fucking *incompetence.*"

He makes his way back to the library, the door slamming so hard I flinch.

The men stream out of the room, moving past me, all of them except for Seven, who stands near the window in silence. It doesn't take half a dozen guys to find duct tape, but I'm guessing none of them want to be the one who ignore an order.

I head to the library to check on Lorenzo, my hand grasping the knob when Seven's voice calls out, "Don't do it."

I stall, glancing back, seeing he followed me out, his expression serious.

"If the door opens, he's liable to shoot," he says. "He probably won't even look to see who it is."

I slowly pull my hand away from the knob, casting the door a sidelong look, as the men filter back through the hallway, one of them carrying a roll of silver duct tape.

"Come on," Seven says, motioning to the living room where the men congregate. "Join us."

I hesitate before going back that way, giving the library door one more look. The guy with the darkest features layers duct tape over the hole before dropping the roll onto the coffee table in front of him. They all go back to hanging out, like nothing had happened, barely missing a beat as they pick up liquor bottles, someone rolling a blunt.

I don't know what they did with the body.

Someone took him out the back door before returning, empty-handed.

"Scarlet, right?" Seven asks, lingering by the door.

"That's what he calls me," I say, pausing beside him. "My name's actually Morgan."

Seven smiles, holding his hand out. "Pleasure to finally meet you. I'm Seven."

I shake his hand. "Do you have a real name?"

"Bruno," he says, "but you can just call me Seven. It makes things easier around here."

"Seven," I repeat. "It doesn't bother you that he refuses to call you by your name?"

"Why, does it bother *you*?"

"No," I say. "Not really."

I'm surprised by my own answer. It's true, it doesn't bother me that he doesn't call me Morgan, although the first time he called me Scarlet, it hit a nerve. Holding my arm up, I shove my hoodie sleeve up, glancing at the tattoo on my wrist. My *Scarlet Letter*, he calls it. If only he knew how close that was to reality...

"Is he okay?" I ask, dropping my arm again. "Lorenzo?"

"He'll be fine," Seven says. "He just loses his cool every now and then. When the door's closed, leave him alone. When he feels better, he'll come back out. His library is off limits so don't go in without permission. If the door's open and he's in there, consider whether or not you really need him, because he's just as liable to shoot you as he is to say 'come in'."

I blink at him. "I feel like I should be taking notes."

"Probably ought to," someone else says with a laugh. I glance over at the other guys. They're all looking at me, but it was the blond that spoke. "He's *Natural Selection*, live and in the flesh. If you want to make it, adapt, because it's survival of the fittest around here. He weeds out the weak."

Hence the missing numbers, I'm guessing, but I don't say that. I don't say *anything*.

Reintroductions are made by Seven. He calls me Morgan, giving the others the courtesy of their real names. Three, the blond guy, turns out to be Declan Jackson, while Five, the one with dark features, is named Frank Romano. The others, they all blend together, and I'm not trying to be an asshole about that, but they're just Italian guys with Americanized names. There's a Joey, a Johnny, something else... *whatever*.

There aren't any more chairs, so I end up sitting on the coffee table, ignoring the alcohol, passing on smoking, trying to keep a clear head, but I get a contact high pretty quickly. They're all nice, I guess... nicer than I'm used to. Time fades away as they kid around, and I laugh a bit at their antics. They're almost like young boys, telling fart jokes.

I never hear the door reopen, but eventually, he's just *there*. Frank's telling a story, I'm barely paying attention, when he suddenly says, "Ain't that right, boss?"

"You know it."

Lorenzo's voice is quiet, calling out from the doorway, looking like he might've been lurking awhile. His eyes are fixed on me, his expression unreadable. It's like the man is an open book but whatever his story is just happens to be written in a different language.

One I can't read at all.

It's there, but what does it mean?

"Why don't you fellas take off for the night?" he suggests, although it's pretty clear that's really an order, since they all immediately get to their feet, swiping the liquor bottles and carrying them along as they shuffle toward the front door. Mumbled goodbyes are cast my way from a few of them, but for the most part they just nod to Lorenzo before disappearing.

After the front door closes behind them, Lorenzo strolls my direction, stepping past me to survey the thick duct tape patch over the hole on the couch. "Which one of those jackasses...?"

"Frank," I say, earning a peculiar look from him, his brow creasing with confusion. I roll my eyes. Of course. Does he even *know* their names? "Five, I guess you call him. His real name's Frank."

"I know his name," Lorenzo says. "Just surprised you do."

"If you know their names, why don't you use them?"

"Same reason you don't name a puppy unless you know you're going to keep it."

"Which is...?"

"Gotta keep them at a distance. Don't want to get attached."

Unbelievable. "So you dehumanize them, make them things and not people, because things are replaceable but people are one of a kind?"

"People aren't one of a kind," he says. "Puppies, you know, they love you, they play fetch with you, because you take care of their needs. Dogs out on the street, they kill whatever moves, whatever's weak, whatever they're sure they can beat, in order to survive. Affection is the only thing that keeps Lassie from going all *Cujo*."

"I thought that was rabies."

He turns to me. "I'm speaking metaphorically."

"Yeah, well, you're doing a shit job of it."

Laughing, he steps over to me, cupping my chin and tilting my face up, his thumb gently stroking my cheek. "They're wild animals, Scarlet. I see to their needs and they stay loyal because of it. But sometimes, you know, something goes wrong, so you don't let yourself get attached, in case you have to put one of them down. You get me?"

Yeah, I get him.

I get him more than he could ever understand.

We're just on different ends of the spectrum, him and I, both waiting for it all to fall apart, except he'll kill someone when it happens to him, whereas I'm terrified of being the one to die. He's braced and ready, locked and loaded, and I'm just free falling, dodging the crumbling pieces of my life as they rain down on me like meteorites.

"They respect you. I don't think they'd ever turn on you."

"Betrayal comes in many forms," he says. "Sometimes it's unintentional. Even the best-trained dog might snap at your hand if you try to take his food away. What do you do then?"

"Give him his food back."

"Or... snap his neck."

I shake my head. "You're insane."

"So you keep saying."

He leans down, and I've got about a three second warning, long enough to inhale sharply, before he kisses me. His lips are the softest things about him, warm and gentle, like a slice of heaven wrapped in hell, so worth battling the flames to feel his fire.

My eyes close, and I kiss him back, grasping his forearm, like maybe touching him will keep me grounded. Touching him will keep me in the moment, will keep me from floating far, far away. My brain, it likes to disconnect, to send signals through my body to abort thinking, feeling, *being*, to just dissolve into nothing and reshape again when it's over, because you can't break what's not solid, but I don't want to fade away with him. He ignites something inside of me, stirring up these little sparks in my gut that send jolts through my body, like a defibrillator to the heart.

It's terrifying, but fuck, to feel alive again...

It's *nice.*

Lorenzo pulls away abruptly, breaking the kiss, his voice low and rough, like sandpaper, as he says, "You're doing it again."

I open my eyes, regarding him as he steps back, my hands leaving his skin. "Doing what?"

"Switching off."

I scoff. "Was not."

Was I?

"What were you thinking about?" he asks.

"About not switching off."

"Is that hard for you?"

"Harder than it probably should be."

He laughs lightly, stepping further away, and nods out of the room. "Come with me."

"Where to?"

"Upstairs."

"What's upstairs?"

"Salvation."

Salvation.

Never has a word ever sounded so beautiful.

Standing up, I follow him, trailing him up the staircase onto the darkened second floor of the house. We walk past rooms to a door in the very back, and Lorenzo pushes it open, stepping aside, motioning for me to go in.

A bedroom. It's probably the size of my entire apartment back in the city, but there's very little inside of it, just the basics. The bed, though—the bed is monstrous, so massive he could throw orgies in it and never encounter another pair of testicles.

Okay, I'm exaggerating. It's not *that* big. But still, half a dozen people could sleep comfortably.

Lorenzo steps into the room behind me. He doesn't turn on a light. It's dark and takes my eyes a moment to adjust as I glance around, my gaze settling on a pair of shoes sitting on top of a dresser.

My shoes, I realize. The red Louboutins I discarded in the street when I ran from him.

"Figured you'd want them back," he says, seeing me looking. "Heard they were expensive."

"You don't even know," I mumble. I paid *a lot* for those damn shoes, more than a person should ever pay, but it didn't cost me money.

Lorenzo steps behind me, grabbing my hoodie to take it off. I raise my hands up, letting him pull it over my head, my heart racing as he tosses it onto the dresser, on top of the red heels, covering them.

He sweeps my hair aside, pushing it over my shoulder, and I shiver when I feel his breath against the back of my neck, his lips brushing against my skin.

"Tell me a story," he says.

"What?"

"A story," he says again. "Doesn't even have to be *your* story. Hell, tell me your favorite fairy tale."

"I, uh..."

I don't know what to say. His arms wrap around me, his hands going straight to my breasts, yanking my black tank top down and shoving my plain white bra up, palming bare skin. His teeth graze the side of my neck as he kisses his way down to my shoulder blade.

"Go on," he says. "I'm waiting."

"There was a princess named Nella," I say quietly. "She had a love affair with a prince, but they kept it a secret."

"Why?"

Why?

Why? Why? Why?

Why is he asking me this, why am I telling him a story, when his hands are all over me, touching, caressing, his fingers tweaking

174

my nipples, sending shockwaves down my spine?

"Because Nella had two older sisters who were jealous of her and would ruin it if they found out."

His right hand drifts, running the length of my torso before slipping beneath the waistband of my sweatpants, no hesitation. He rubs me through the fabric of my plain white cotton underwear, fingertips roughly stroking my clit. *Holy fuck.* This man and those hands... he doesn't play fair. *At all.* He presses buttons he's got no business pressing.

"So what happened?" he asks, pushing against me, pressing *into* me. He's hard, so damn hard... I can feel his cock against the small of my back. He practically manhandles me, shoving me toward the oversized bed, hand still down my pants, not missing a beat.

His fingers move the cotton aside, and I gasp when he touches me without the fabric barrier. It takes me a moment to find my voice again, to come up with words, as he forces my legs apart further.

"They made an underground glass tunnel leading from the prince's castle straight to the princess's bedroom so they, uh..."

I lose my words again when he drags me onto the bed, laying me down in the center of it. My heart races, thumping furiously as he hovers over me, cocking an eyebrow, staring down. "So they could fuck?"

"Basically."

My voice sounds smaller than I want it to. I sound meek. *Ugh.* That's not *me.* He's still staring at me, but I think he hears my timid tone, too, because his expression shifts. "You're not nervous, are you?"

"Nope."

I answer way too fast, way too *loud.*

He smirks. He knows I'm lying.

"*Tsk, tsk,*" he says, his voice low, rough. "What did I say I did to people who lied to me?"

"You kill them," I whisper.

"You're goddamn right," he says, gaze moving from my face,

down to my chest before trailing even lower. "And what I'm about to do to you, Scarlet? If it doesn't *kill* you..."

He trails off with a laugh.

I'm not sure if I like the sound of that.

My body, though, is most definitely a fan, every syllable he speaks bringing it more to life, like being roused from a deep, dark sleeping curse. *That which does not kill me isn't trying hard enough.* He said that the first night we met.

Lorenzo strips me, tugging my pants down, taking the underwear with it, yanking the shoes from my feet and tossing them to the floor, the clothes following.

"So they built some magical tunnel to sneak around and fuck," he says, kissing down my stomach, his tongue swirling around my belly button, dipping inside of it. I squirm, shivering at the sensation, and unconsciously reach for him, but he grabs my wrists, stopping me, his gaze returning to my face, his expression dead serious. "I'm about to fuck you with my mouth like you've never been fucked before, and you're going to keep telling me that story. You got me?"

"I, uh..." *Wow.* "Okay."

"You stop, I stop," he says, his gaze flickering down, right between my legs. "And I'm not going to *want* to stop, so you better not make me."

I'm not sure how this is going to work, my nerves through the roof. He's right—it *might* kill me. Because yeah, I've slept around... I've been *passed* around, like a piece of meat... but men that go down for the fun of it are unicorns.

At least, among men in the business of sleeping with women like *me*.

Gripping my wrists, he pins them flat against the bed as he settles between my thighs. I look down at him, watching in the darkness, chest aching, heart racing, and adrenaline rushing through my veins, fueled by anticipation. He's just a breath away. He's *right there*. His eyes flicker up, a warning in them.

Oh, shit, right, I'm supposed to be talking.

"They made this glass tunnel so they could sneak off

together," I repeat, stalling again, gasping, the moment his mouth is on me. He starts slow, running light circles around my clit with his tongue, but it's enough to make me arch my back and squirm.

Wait, ugh, how does this story go?

"Every night, the prince would go see her, just run there, buck fucking naked, slip into her room and they'd, uh... *fuck*." I throw my head back, the curse damn near catching in my throat, when his lips encircle my clit and he sucks on it, sending pleasure through me. "Fuck, every night... he runs over there. But the sisters, they find out, and they decide, you know, they can't have that. They can't let them... *fuck*."

It's torture, what he's doing. I can't see. I don't know. But his mouth is fully on me now, tongue doing whatever it does, flicking and licking, sucking and fucking, completely devouring me, like he's *starving*. I try to yank my arms from his grasp, but he isn't budging, his grip damn tight. I want to grab him by the hair and pull him closer, desperate for more friction, but I think I'm just as likely to punch him if he frees me, because Jesus Christ, what is he doing to me?

"The prince, he doesn't know," I say breathlessly. "That night, he runs through the tunnel, no clothes on. The glass is smashed, he's cut up, blah blah blah, uhhh... he, uh... *Christ*, that feels good."

Lorenzo laughs. The asshole *laughs*. His mouth is on my pussy, my clit pulsating from the feeling, the sensation damn near shoving me over the edge, an orgasm building, because he's laughing.

Yeah, I'd punch him.

"He's cut up, bleeding out... I don't know... dying. It's killing him... fuck, it's killing *me*..." I swallow thickly, squeezing my eyes shut. "Don't stop."

He doesn't stop, but I know he will if I don't pull myself together. *Asshole*.

"The glass is magic. His cuts won't heal. He's still dying, so the King, *oh god*..." I shift my hips, my toes curling when he hits a spot that sends shockwaves rippling through me, my thighs trembling. *Oh god... oh god... oh god.* "The King promises whoever heals the Prince can marry him."

Lorenzo releases my wrists, and I'm grateful for a brief moment, instantly running my hands through his thick, dark hair. He pushes a finger inside of me, maybe two, I don't know, fucking me with them before abruptly pulling his mouth away. His gaze finds mine when I open my eyes, and I almost panic (did I pause too long?) before he speaks. "What if it's a guy?"

He curves his fingers, hitting that sweet spot deep inside. The unicorn found the fucking Holy Grail.

Didn't even need a map.

He navigated right there.

It feels so good I can't make sense of anything else. It takes me a moment to remember he even spoke. "Uh, what?"

"What if a guy heals him?"

"I, uh... he marries him?" Did he really stop for *that?* "Are you seriously asking questions?"

He shrugs. "I'm curious."

"It can't wait?"

He smirks. "I like watching you squirm."

His mouth is back on me after that, but I've lost my train of thought, because now that he's added fingers to the mix, well, I really am going to die.

The pressure is building, and I'm panting, spewing out words.

I don't know if they make sense.

"Nella, she goes to tell him goodbye, gonna die, no cure, I don't know, *holy fuck*. But an ogre, you kill it, you save him. Nella overhears. Jesus Christ, don't stop, *please...*" I fist his hair, my breath hitching. I'm thinking Lorenzo's mouth could've saved the prince, because I don't think there's anything this mouth couldn't do. "She murders the ogre, cures the prince, they marry... blah, blah, blah, oh god, I'm gonna... *uh, Lorenzo!*"

Orgasm tears through me. I gasp. My legs shake. He doesn't stop, even though I've run out of words, doesn't let up at all, his mouth working miracles as I buck my hips, practically fucking his face. Tingles engulf me, goose bumps coating my skin.

It's short lived, the sky-high euphoria, but worth every damn second of stumbling through that story.

As soon as it fades, I relax back into the bed, my eyes closed, my muscles needing a moment to work again. Lorenzo sits up, his voice serious, matter of fact, as he says, "That was a terrible story."

"You're an asshole," I mutter, peeking at him.

"Seriously, *that's* your favorite fairy tale?"

"At least it has a happy ending."

He shakes his head as he moves closer, climbing up the bed, hovering right over me again. He slowly licks his lips, making a shiver runs through me. "I might be an asshole, Scarlet, but that little game kept you from fading, didn't it?"

Yeah, I guess it did.

He leans down, kissing me, fumbling with his pants, unbuttoning them.

"I'm going to fuck you now," he says. "That okay with you?"

I nod. *More* than okay. I'm aching, my body on fire, desperate to feel him inside of me again. I hate that I want it so much, that I want *him*, but he's like a drug, I think, one of those potent, addictive drugs that alters your brain chemistry.

"Good," he says, retrieving a condom from the stand beside the bed. He hitches my legs up, settling between them, as he pulls his cock out, rolling the condom on.

He wastes no time thrusting inside.

I cry out as he fills me, tilting my head back, and barely have a chance to adjust before his body weight is pressing upon me, his hand around my throat. A chill of fear shoots down my spine, but he doesn't squeeze. He could, though. Instead, he looks me dead in the face and says, "You zone out, I choke you. Whether or not I let go is anybody's guess. You still okay with this?"

I nod, no hesitation.

I probably shouldn't.

Hell, I *know* I shouldn't.

Would he let go? I like to think so. But I'm not *sure*, and that's what causes the panic to trickle into my chest, spiking my system. It's sick. Maybe *I'm* sick, the fact that it excites me, that being just a breath away from death makes me feel alive again.

I shift my body beneath him until he slips out a bit before I buck my hips up, slamming into him so he fills me. He's thick, and rock hard, but I'm so slick he just slides right in, like he was made to be inside me. His expression goes slack. I can practically *see* the pleasure flow through him. The man is rough around the edges, something so primal about him, but there's something else there, something unexpected.

So much passion.

He moves then. He starts fucking me, just like he said he would, slamming hard, one hand still on my throat, the other digging into my hip as he pins me beneath him. Every thrust knocks the air from my lungs as I gasp, and whimper, and moan...

"You like that?" he asks, his voice low, barely a murmur against my lips before he kisses me so hard it hurts. "You like giving me this beautiful pussy? Like me taking it hard? Beating it? Fucking it? *Killing* it?"

"Yes," I whisper, chills coating me as I let out a shaky breath. "I love it."

"Love it, do you?" he asks with a little laugh, nudging my head aside to kiss along my jawline. "Savage little thing, aren't you? Is that what your Scarlet Letter stands for?"

"Not even close."

He bites my chin, and I hiss, flinching, before he pulls back to look at me. His movements slow a bit, but he's still hitting deep, hard, pain tickling my stomach with every thrust.

"Seductive," he says. "Submissive."

He's just spewing out S-words, I know, but that last one grates a nerve. My cheek twitches, and I tense, nails digging into his skin as I rake my hands along his shoulder blades. His eyes widen, the corner of his mouth lifting. *Amused.*

"Don't like that one, huh?"

"Fuck you."

The hand on my throat shifts up a bit, fingers pressing into the skin, not cutting off the air to my lungs, but it makes me lightheaded. He increases his pace, pounding into me, the room filled with the sound of skin slapping, cries escaping my throat. My vision blurs, my entire body tingling, but I keep my eyes fixed on him out of pure principle. He expects me to fade. He thinks I'm going to float away. But fuck him, if he thinks I'm submissive.

Fuck. Him.

I might love the way he makes me feel, but seriously, *fuck him.*

"You want to hurt me, don't you?" he asks as I claw his back so hard I have to be drawing blood. "Got a bit of a sadistic side, don't you, Scarlet? You like to give it as much as you *take* it, want to fuck up my face some more as I wreck this beautiful pussy of yours?"

He lets go of my throat, pulling away.

I don't respond, because what can I say?

He forces my knees up to my chest, my legs over his shoulders as he shifts position, driving deeper, harder, faster. *Oh god.* His fingers find my clit, rubbing, stroking, and I can do nothing but make noise as he makes me come, over and over.

I don't know how much I can take, and he's not letting up. I'm soaked with sweat, my body trembling, muscles aching... even my *fingers* hurt from clutching his back. Eventually, he starts to slow down, hitting a few deep strokes. His face is nuzzled into my neck, teeth nipping at the skin as he grunts.

He stills then, lying down, not even trying to keep his weight off of me. Fuck, he's *heavy.* I wrap my arms around him, too exhausted to fight it, and hear him muttering under his breath. "I feel like I could actually sleep tonight."

* * *

Lorenzo *does* sleep, it turns out.

Me? Not so much.

For someone with a talent for zoning out, I can't shut my mind off, lying next to him. I watch him sleep for a while, like a creep, staring at the steady rise and fall of his chest. Every time I move, he stirs a bit, and I feel guilty as hell, disturbing his slumber, so I just lay there in silence until I can't take it any longer.

Carefully, I climb out of the bed, pulling my clothes on and tiptoeing out of the room before making my way downstairs. It's still dark, but I can see where I'm going, in that space right before sunrise where the world is just starting to lighten.

I pause at the bottom of the staircase, my gaze drifting to the living room to the right of me, seeing someone standing in the doorway. A young guy, dressed in a black cable-knit sweater, wearing khakis and black boots. The younger brother, I'm guessing.

He shakes his head, staring into the living room. "Do I even want to know what happened to the couch?"

"It got a hole in it," I say vaguely, not sure how much Lorenzo would share with him.

The guy startles at the sound of my voice, turning around. "You're not Lorenzo."

"Well, that's something to be grateful for, huh?"

He seems to be about my age and looks just like Lorenzo... or well, how I imagine Lorenzo would look if the world hadn't hurt him. Fresh-faced, wide-eyed, and kind of *adorable*, frankly. How he keeps any sort of innocence living in the same house as the menace upstairs, I don't know, but I commend him for it.

Every moment I spend with the guy, I feel myself slipping further.

"I'm Leo," he says, holding his hand out. "You are?"

"Morgan," I say, shaking his hand lightly. Manners. *Huh.*

Someone's apple fell *far* from the family tree.

"I'd ask how you know my brother, but well, I'm sure I probably don't want to know."

"Probably not," I admit.

Before either of us can speak again, there's noise on the stairs, footsteps that aren't trying to tiptoe. Leo glances up, something akin to shock crossing his face before he spins around so fast it's like he's twirling. "Jesus, Lorenzo! Really, bro? *Really?*"

I glanced behind me, eyes widening. Lorenzo's buck-naked, like the prince running through the glass tunnel, waltzing down the stairs like he's not got a care in the world.

He's groggy, only half-awake, everything prominently on display.

"Don't act like you've never seen a dick before, Pretty Boy," Lorenzo says, skirting around me, brushing *against* me. "I know you've got one. I used to change your diapers, remember?"

"No, I don't *remember*," Leo says, "but you certainly remind me enough."

"That's because it earns me the right to do whatever I damn well please," Lorenzo says. "I wiped your ass, made your lunches, taught you how to treat a woman, and I let your girlfriend eat my groceries. Let me air my balls out without jumping my ass about it."

Leo turns around then, laughing, no longer seeming to care or notice his brother's not wearing clothes. "*You* taught me how to treat a woman?"

"I did," he says, strolling past us, heading down the hallway, calling back as he says, "Showed you exactly what *not* to do if you were trying to keep one."

Lorenzo disappears into the back of the house, past the library. Kitchen, I'm guessing. Process of elimination.

"Well, you certainly did that," Leo mutters, turning to me, his cheeks flushing. "Sorry about that. He's, uh… well, he's *him*."

Okay, that makes me laugh, which isn't the response Leo expects, based on the strange look he gives me, but he's apologizing for his brother—a *genuine* apology for Lorenzo's behavior.

I'm wondering how the hell that apple even came from the same tree at this point, frankly.

"He doesn't bother me," I say. "I mean, he's a pain in the ass, but him being naked is probably the *least* bothersome thing about him."

"Ah, yeah, guess it isn't the first time you've seen… *it*," he says, laughing awkwardly. "You know, since you're here at six in the morning. It's just, well, I usually don't see them, since they don't often stick around to chat."

He's flustered. There's no way this guy even came from the same orchard as Lorenzo, much less the same tree. "*They?*"

"Yeah, the ladies that my brother—"

"Fucks," Lorenzo says, stepping out from the kitchen, carrying an orange. "The women I fuck. They're usually out of here *before* Pretty Boy makes it out of bed, so he's not used to this whole 'morning after' thing."

Pretty Boy.

He doesn't even call his brother by his name?

"Oh, well then... my bad," I say as I give Leo a smile. "Next time I'll just have to skedaddle before you catch me, then."

Leo's eyes widen, those words shocking him for some reason—maybe even shocking him more than his brother waltzing between us naked again does. "*Next* time?"

Lorenzo stalls on the bottom step as he starts to peel his orange. His cock is like two feet to the left of me, and I'm trying damn hard not to look, to keep my eyes straight ahead, but it's shining like a beacon over there, trying to draw me in.

"You'll have to excuse my brother, Scarlet," Lorenzo says. "He thinks you're one of my *wham-bam's*. I tend to impose a 'one ride per person' rule, so *next time*s are pretty unheard of."

Ignoring how the mention of Lorenzo's stream of women makes my stomach coil, I nod. "Understandable."

"I didn't realize there was something *other* than that," Leo says, eyes narrowing as he looks at his brother, clearly completely over the fact that he's not wearing clothes. "Care to fill me in?"

"No, not really," Lorenzo says, starting up the stairs. "By the way, Scarlet, you forgot your shoes."

I look down at my feet before it strikes me—the Louboutins. "Oh, can you bring them to me?"

"Fuck do I look like, a delivery boy?"

Lorenzo doesn't say anything else, trekking up the stairs.

I scowl, keeping my eyes on Leo. "I should probably, you know..." I point up the stairs. "Go get them."

Before Leo can respond, a shrill scream pierces the air, loud enough to make my hair stand on end. Leo runs his hands down his face as Lorenzo's voice echoes from upstairs: "Oh, give me a break, I *know* you've seen a dick before, Firecracker. I hear my brother

184

fucking you all the time."

I head up the steps, passing a shell-shocked looking blonde along the way, but she barely notices me, zeroing in on Leo.

"I know, I know," Leo mutters when she approaches. "You saw my brother naked."

Shaking my head, I set off along the second floor, finding Lorenzo's bedroom door wide open. He sits on the edge of his bed, peeling his orange, still not wearing any clothes. I hesitate in front of him, eyes scanning him, unable to avoid ogling him any longer. I've seen it all, yes, but I haven't exactly taken a lot of time to *look*, if you know what I mean. I wouldn't call him ripped, but he's definitely *fit*, some definition to his muscles. And the cock? Yeah, okay, it's gorgeous… if you can call a cock gorgeous, which I can, because I don't know how else to describe it. He's definitely more of a show-er than a grower, eight and a half inches, thick and cut, veins running along the shaft, and Jesus Christ, okay… I've got to stop looking.

My eyes flicker to Lorenzo's face. He's watching me, taking a bite of an orange wedge.

"Came for my shoes," I say, nodding toward where they sit on the dresser.

He says nothing, chewing in silence.

"Figure I should take them back before one of those wham-bam's you parade through here tries to steal them."

"Yeah, I'm sure your clients tip extra for you to keep them on while they fuck you."

Ouch. "Touché."

"Anyway, before you run off again," he says, tearing off another wedge of orange, "we should talk about payment."

I cringe. *Payment.*

Ouch, for real this time.

"You know what? Fuck you, Lorenzo. Seriously, *fuck you*. I should've known you were completely full of shit when you said you'd respect me, that you wouldn't do *this*." I wave around us, like that'll help me make sense, as he just stares at me, still chewing. "You're an asshole. Seriously. I didn't fuck you last night for *money*.

That wasn't what it was to me, and maybe it's what it was for you, whatever, but just, ugh… *fuck you.*"

I snatch my shoes from the top of his dresser when his calm voice says, "You keep everything you make unless it's a job *I* ordered. In that case, I pay you a commission based on your contribution."

I stall at those words. "What?"

"You're working for me now, right? That was the deal? I'm just laying out the terms, letting you know how working for me is going to go. When I need you, be there, but otherwise you can do whatever you want. The world is yours, Scarlet."

"I, uh… *ugh.*" Payment. "I thought you meant…"

"I told you I don't pay for pussy."

"I know, I just thought…"

"Thought I was saying it to hurt you? Thought I was just getting a low blow in?"

"Yes."

He shakes his head, still eating the orange as he stands up.

I don't ogle this time.

I want to.

God, I really want to.

But I don't.

He approaches me slowly. "I like fucking and fighting, Scarlet. I won't lie about that. I like fucking *you.* I like fighting *you.* I'll push your buttons all goddamn night long and make you want to rip me apart, but I'm not in the business of hurting people for no reason. I don't get off on that."

"Sorry."

He makes a face of disgust at that word. "Don't apologize to me."

"You just touched a nerve, you know."

"Don't make excuses, either. Calm your tits and it'll be okay."

"Calm my tits."

"Yes." His eyes flicker to my chest, and I know he's imagining them. "As gorgeous as those tits are, calm them."

"Fine." I scowl. "You're still an asshole, you know."

"I know." He breaks off a wedge from the orange, holding it out to me. "Want some?"

I hesitate, staring at it in his hand. "Ugh, *no.*"

"I swear to fuck, Scarlet. I'll forgive a lot of things, but if you tell me you don't eat *oranges*, we're going to have a problem."

I roll my eyes. "I learned long ago not to take candy from strangers."

"We're not strangers," he says, motioning to himself. "You've seen me naked."

"I'm getting the feeling a lot of people have seen you naked."

"Not as many as have seen *you.*"

Ouch for the third time.

"I should go," I say.

"Where are you going?" he asks.

"Back to the apartment."

"Is it safe there?"

"Probably not."

He nods, popping the orange in his mouth, before turning away. "Do me a favor, will you?"

"What?"

"Don't get yourself killed."

"I'll do my best."

I walk out, leaving him there, with no clothes on.

I've done a lot of difficult things in my life. *A lot.* But that's ranking up there among some horrific things, because walking away from him right now is proving harder than I thought it would be. It's not even that I won't see him again, because I will. I have a sneaking suspicion I'm going to be seeing him quite often. But at the moment, something inside of me is tugging, trying to pull me back to him like we're magnets, but I need to put some space between us—at least until I figure things out.

Because Lorenzo?

He's not the kind of guy you get attached to.

Especially when you're *me.*

I can't let him get so far under my skin that I can't get him back out again.

I head downstairs, clutching the heels, and encounter Leo still standing in the doorway to the living room, the blonde beside him.

His girlfriend, I'm guessing.

She glances up at me, and I expect some level of bitchiness, because really, in my experience, most feel threatened by a strange woman suddenly appearing, but she smiles instead, full-blown grinning. "You must be Cinderella."

That slows my steps. "What?"

"Lorenzo had your shoes," Leo says. "He was looking for you, said you ran away from him. Kind of sounded like Cinderella."

I laugh, looking at the shoes.

Pretty sure Cinderella didn't rob the prince before making her escape.

Also pretty sure the prince didn't consider killing Cinderella whenever he found her.

"I knew you'd pop up eventually," the bubbly blonde says. "I mean, come on, any woman would come back for a pair of red patent leather Louboutins. I had a pair once... or well, my best friend did." She laughs. "You know when your best friend has something, you do, too."

I wish I could say I knew what that was like. People just seem to come in-and-out of my life. "You got a name? I think Lorenzo called you—"

"Firecracker." She rolls her eyes. "Name's Melody Carmichael."

"I'm Morgan," I say. "What size do you wear?"

"Uh, an eight... or well, a thirty-nine and a half."

I flip the shoes over, glancing at the thirty-nine on the sole as I hold the shoes out to her. "It's your lucky day, Melody Carmichael. They might be snug, but I'm sure you can make them work."

Her eyes widen. "Are you kidding me? No way, I can't take your shoes!"

"You can," I say. "I have to warn you, though. Those shoes were a gift I never asked for, a gift I never *wanted*, and ever since I got them, I've been plagued with terrible luck. I'm not exactly superstitious, but I'd rather not risk it anymore. So take them, if you want them, but just... don't say I didn't warn you."

She squeals, kicking her black flats off, and takes the red heels, slipping them on her feet. "You, Morgan, are totally my *new* best friend."

I laugh, shaking my head.

We'll see how long that lasts...

16

One month.

Four weeks.

The little girl still counted, waiting... waiting... waiting for something that didn't seem to be happening. She kept coming up with reasons why her mother hadn't shown up yet. Maybe it took a long time to fix the front door? Maybe she was still sleeping?

She didn't know. She was still only *four*. Nothing about it made any sense to her, but she was trying to listen, trying to be a good girl.

Sitting in the bedroom, at the desk against the wall, she clutched the light blue crayon as she colored all along the paper, making a sky. Other colors were scattered around in front of her, while most were still wedged into the box. The Cowardly Lion had given her one of those big packs of crayons, over a hundred colors, some even glittery. She spent most of her time drawing, Buster sitting on the desk in front of her, watching, also waiting.

Waiting to go home.

Grinning, she set the crayon down, admiring the paper. She'd drawn the Tin Man, but not *as* the Tin Man... she drew him like the person he looked like, although she wasn't really good at drawing people. He looked kind of like a balloon animal, but she had his eyes right—gray, like the rain clouds.

She didn't want him to be lonely, and she didn't like his flying monkeys, so she drew herself standing with him.

Besides, *she* was kind of lonely, too.

"Come on, Buster," she said, snatching up the bear, tucking it beneath her arm. "Lets go show him."

The little girl made the trek down the big, winding stairs, taking them one at a time. There were so many it always took *forever*. She was getting used to it, though.

Getting used to the palace.

Noise echoed out from the Tin Man's den. The flying monkeys were there tonight, and they'd brought along some women. The group was drinking from bottles of that clear liquid, the stuff that made the Tin Man make faces. Music played through the den, a woman singing foreign words the little girl didn't know.

The little girl strolled to the den, the double wooden doors hanging wide open. She paused there, eyes wide. People were kissing, some dancing really close.

The light was so dim.

Where was the Tin Man?

"*Vor*," a voice called out, using a word she recognized, one the monkeys called the Tin Man sometimes. *Vor*. She turned in the direction it came from, seeing the Cowardly Lion in the center of the crowd. He pointed her way, saying something she didn't understand to the man right beside him. *Tin Man*.

A woman with long brown hair sat on his lap, straddling him, wearing just a bra and a skirt, her other clothes missing. He pushed her aside, his bloodshot eyes darting to the little girl in the doorway.

"Ah, there's my kitten!" He grinned. "Do you need something? Come here."

His tone was off. Too nice. Not right. A voice in the back of her mind whispered for her to hide, a voice that sounded *just* like her mother's. It was too late, though, because she'd already been spotted, so she carefully approached him, trying to ignore the looks the others gave her.

The Tin Man sat up further, forcing the woman from his lap. She slid to the floor instead, sitting by his feet, not going far. The little girl looked at her. She was young, like the little girl's mother, while the Tin Man was kind of older. She wouldn't call him *old*, no. He had no gray hairs at all. But he had hands that weren't soft and eyes that sometimes crinkled.

Menace

The little girl paused in front of the Tin Man, her stomach feeling sick when she looked him in the eyes. They were black, like midnight, the gray all gone.

"I drew you a picture," she said, holding out the paper.

"How sweet." He took it, squinting. "Is this *me?*"

She nodded.

His eyes cut to her.

Use your words. He didn't say it, but she heard it.

"Yes, Daddy."

"And is this you with me?" he asked, holding it up, pointing at it.

Her cheeks grew warm as people all around them looked. She'd just meant to show *him*. "Yes."

He turned it back around, studying it, still grinning. "It is perfect, kitten. I need to have it framed."

Her eyes widened. "Really?"

"Of course," he said, setting it aside, on the table, before patting his knee. "Come, *sit.*"

She wanted to say no. She wanted to go back up to her room, away from all of those people, away from the woman giving her weird looks from where she sat on the floor, but his expression left no room for arguing. She sat down on his knee, facing the side, and he wrapped his left arm around her. She used to sit on her mother's lap all the time, but she didn't much like sitting on his, wearing the white nightgown that *still* itched.

He smacked the woman's shoulder, motioning for something with his hand, and she handed him a rolled up dollar. He gripped the little girl tightly, so she wouldn't fall to the floor, as he leaned the whole way forward, nearly face-planting the table, and snorted a line of white powder.

Letting out a deep sigh, he leaned back in the chair again, his smile glowing.

"Do you love your *Papa?*" he asked, rubbing her back.

The little girl tensed at that question.

His stark black eyes regarded her. "It is okay, you are allowed to love me, no matter what your mother may have said. I am your father; my blood is inside of you. You might look like the *suka*, but you are half of me."

Suka. The little girl knew that word.

It was one of the bad ones.

She still didn't answer. She didn't know *how*. What if she lied by mistake? Would he be mad?

After a moment, he laughed, hugging her to his thick chest as he ruffled her hair. "One day. Even your mother once loved me. It is inevitable."

The little girl relaxed, her nerves easing. She didn't know if she'd ever love him, honestly, but maybe, if her mother loved him and he found his heart, it could happen.

Everyone around them laughed and joked, growing louder as time wore on. The little girl watched them.

The Tin Man grabbed a bottle of that clear stuff, pouring some into his glass.

"What's that?" she asked.

He held out the bottle, bumping her arm. "Try it."

She just stared.

"Aw, my kitten is a scaredy-cat?"

People around them laughed, that ugly laugh, the mean one she didn't like. Her face turned red as she took the bottle and put it to her lips. The second it touched her tongue, she gagged, her mouth on fire. It *burned*. Coughing, she couldn't catch her breath, swallowing a mouthful before she dropped the bottle, spilling it all over herself. The Tin Man caught it, laughing, as he slapped her on the back.

"Breathe," he said, slipping out of the chair, shifting her onto it alone. "Vodka is not for the weak."

"You're so cruel," the brown-haired woman said, still sitting on the floor. "She's just a little girl. She shouldn't even be here."

"She is *my* little girl. I say where she should be. Besides, what do you know about being a parent?"

"Probably more than *you* ever will," the woman mumbled. "Poor girl."

The moment those words were out of her mouth, something

194

snapped. The Tin Man grabbed the woman, fisting her long locks, and yanked her away from the chair, her shriek loud.

The little girl tensed, tears in her eyes, as the Tin Man slammed the woman's head into the table in front of them, over and over, white powder flying like dust all around, coating her face, as blood poured from her nose and her mouth. She choked on it, begging, but he didn't stop.

BAM.

BAM.

BAM.

The woman went limp as he continued to grip her by the hair, raising her face up to look at her, whispering, "poor girl," before dropping her to the floor in front of the chair.

Everyone around them watched, the other women disturbed, but the men acted like it was normal. The little girl shook and sobbed, wetting her nightgown as she clutched Buster to her chest, staring down at the floor.

The woman's eyes were closed, as if she was sleeping, just like the little girl's mother had been.

She'd wake up, wouldn't she?

The Tin Man turned to her. His eyes were still black. He tipped back the bottle of vodka, taking a drink straight from it, before he pointed it at her. "Go back to your room, kitten. Be a good girl for *Papa*. Clean yourself up."

The little girl stood, running from the room, going up the stairs as fast as she could.

17

Lorenzo

I know what it's like to be a teenage mother.

Okay, fuck, hear me out before you string me up.

I was only eighteen years old when I took custody of my little brother. He was two at the time, still in diapers. He doesn't remember the *before*, doesn't remember life with our mother, *his* father, but I remember every harrowing second of it.

I especially remember the sickening relief I felt when I watched them both bleed out...

At eighteen, I didn't know shit. My mind had been warped, my face fucked up, and I might've given up on life if it weren't for him needing somebody. I was all he had left in the world, and I vowed I'd make it right. I potty-trained him, sent him off to school, and helped him with his homework. I was there when he started kindergarten, and I was *still* there the day he graduated from high school. I taught him manners, gave him medicine, and made him eat his vegetables. I made the boy a man... the man I wasn't. The one I'd never be.

So while I don't *really* know what it's like being a teenage mother, calling me his father isn't enough, because you'd be hard pressed to find another 'father' who did as much as I did for that little fucker. I poured what was left of my soul into him.

"Don't start with me," I say as soon as I step into the living room, coming face-to-face with Leo, who is sitting on the couch. The duct tape patch is beside his head, blatantly obvious. I know he saw it. He's smart, that kid. He can riddle out what happened while he was in bed, and I know he's going to give me shit about it. "I'm not in the mood."

"When are you *ever* in the mood?" he asks.

"Every other Friday and twice on Saturday."

"It's Saturday," he points out.

"Yeah, well, try again later," I say. "I'm not in the mood right now."

He laughs, glancing at the duct tape. The son of a bitch never listens. "So I hear you put a hole in the couch."

"Respect your elders," I say. "Didn't someone teach you that?"

"I vaguely remember my brother saying it," he says, "but I mostly remember him telling me never to bow down to anybody."

"Except for *me.*"

"I don't remember any exceptions."

"Your memory's shit."

"So is yours," he says, "in case you've forgotten."

He's being a smartass, intentionally pressing my buttons. He's the man I'm not, yeah, but there's still so much of *me* in him.

It's infuriating.

"I'll get a new couch," I tell him.

He sighs. "That's not the point."

The point being that I murdered a man right here in our living room. I told him I'd keep that part of my life as far away from him as possible. I didn't promise, because I don't make promises, but I said I'd make a conscious effort, and I have.

I used a suppressor, didn't I?

I had it all cleaned up before morning came.

"I'll get a new couch," I say again. "I'll patch the hole in the wall, too."

"There's a hole in the *wall?*"

"Yes," I say. "It doesn't count, though, because it's the same hole. Sort of a through-and-through."

He scrubs his hands over his face as he stands up. A stomping clinking noise echoes down the hallway, coming our direction. Melody, I'm guessing. She explodes her way into the room, *kaboom*, skidding to a stop when she spots me. "Whoa, Lorenzo. You, uh, I… *whoa.*"

She blushes.

"I've got clothes on, don't worry," I say, looking down at myself—black pants, black boots, white shirt, black coat. *Exciting*, I know. "I only rock out with my cock out when it's dark out."

"Well, that's nice to know," she says with a laugh, strutting over to my brother. I watch her, my gaze settling on her feet.

Red heels, damn familiar, because I've stared at them for a while on my dresser. "Are they Scarlet's shoes?"

"Who?"

"Morgan," Leo tells her. "He calls her Scarlet."

"Oh, yeah!" Melody kicks her leg out, admiring the shoe on her foot. "Aren't they gorgeous? She gave them to me before she left, said she never really wanted them, which is *crazy*. I mean, who wouldn't want a pair of..."

Blah. Blah. Blah.

She just keeps on talking, telling me shit I don't care about, answering questions I never asked.

"Well, then," I say loudly, interrupting. "This has been fun, but I have business to attend to."

I walk out. She's still talking.

Maybe Leo's listening, I don't know.

Seven stands in front of the house, hanging out on the porch, quietly waiting for me to surface. I nod to him when I step out, wordlessly greeting him as I relinquish my car keys.

Being as I'm blind on the right side, I'm lacking in the depth perception department. I can legally drive, of course—not that *legality* matters—but I choose not to, unless I have to, because I'm likely to run somebody over. Human lives don't exactly leave me feeling sentimental, but speeding cars are kind of like stray bullets in the sense that when your aim sucks, you might kill yourself by accident, and my aim is the *worst*.

Hence the hole in the couch.

And the wall.

And the annoyed little brother.

There's not a hole in the last one... well, not one *I* caused, but he's still a casualty to my disability.

Not that I'm *disabled*, because fuck you, I'm not. I like to think we're only really limited by our lack of creativity, and I can get pretty creative.

"So what do you know about the Russians?" I ask Seven, pulling out my battered tin for a joint, lighting it as I wait for his reaction. He hesitates, eyeing me warily, which is never a good sign, having him afraid to share. Seven's got knowledge, being as once upon a time, in a land far, far away (Staten Island), the man wore a different kind of uniform than his customary black get-up.

Seven was a cop.

He found himself on the wrong side of the law, serving time in Rikers for selling secrets to the devil. And prison, you see, it doesn't rehabilitate men like him. It just turns them into men like me... hardened beyond reasoning.

"The Bratva?" he asks, like he needs clarification.

"Whatever they're calling themselves over here," I say, exhaling, smoke surrounding me. "I sure don't mean the KGB."

"Actually, a lot of the guys are ex-KGB," Seven says. "Soviet collapsed, they had a certain skill set, so they moved to the private sector."

"I appreciate the history lesson, Seven, but I don't really give a shit. I want to know what you know about the Russians around *here*."

He exhales loudly. "They work out of Brighton Beach. Unlike the *Cosa Nostra*, which has weakened—"

"You're welcome for that," I say, taking another hit, holding it in my lungs as he continues.

"—the Russians keep getting stronger. Smuggling. Diamonds. Black market-level stuff. Insurance fraud. Healthcare fraud. Credit card fraud. These days, their biggest payday is probably trafficking."

"Drugs? Guns?"

"People."

Human trafficking.

"Prostitution? Or deeper?"

"Prostitution, certainly, but it goes about as deep as it can possibly go. We heard rumors, back when I was on the force, that they were kidnapping girls and selling them off to the highest bidder."

"Rumors, huh? Not really a fan of speculation, Seven. I heard a rumor once that I was trying to murder my own best friend, but that was complete bullshit."

"I'd say the odds of *this* being false are slim. The Russians, they run that club—Limerence. I've never gone, the wife would *kill* me, but the guys, you know they go, and they talk. The women there?" He lets out a low whistle. "A lot of them probably wouldn't be doing the things they do if they had other options."

I finish smoking in silence, thinking that over, putting together the pieces of the puzzle that are starting to make up Scarlet. *Mind your own business.* I know. I fucking know. But she's becoming my business. I'm making her my business, whether you like it or not.

"Well, then, Seven, I suppose that means a field trip is in order," I say, slapping him on the back before tossing the remnants of the joint down, stomping on it. "Gotta check it out, separate fact from fiction."

"Limerence?"

"Yeah, you need to get a permission slip signed by the wife or are we good?"

He doesn't look like we're *good*.

He's looking a little green, actually.

Guess he doesn't like my plan, huh?

"Do you think that's a good idea, boss?"

"A *good* idea? Not likely. But that's never stopped me before, has it?"

"No," he says, "it hasn't."

* * *

Limerence.

It doesn't look like much of anything from the outside, a nondescript dark building with the name written in red cursive on a sign above a tinted glass door. *Red cursive*. No flashing lights or neon signs. No promises of tits inside. No bullshit description like 'gentlemen's club'. It's open to the public, sure, but they've got a specific clientele. The wealthy. The depraved. The kind that'll pay a lot of damn money for a taste of their darkest fantasy.

No matter how *dark*, I'm hearing.

Enough cash, no questions asked...

Security stands guard at the entrance, dressed in black, wearing earpieces like they're Secret Service. I have no doubt they have a direct line to whoever's running things.

I stop on the sidewalk in front of the place, gaze scanning the *Limerence* sign in the darkness, softly illuminated from beneath. My guys, they filter past, moving around me, waltzing inside without missing a beat. Security doesn't pay them any attention, too busy staring at *me*. Seven lingers behind, standing along the curb. My shadow, as always. He's too damn scared of the missus to dare come any closer.

"You can wait out here," I say, looking back at him, "unless you're in the mood for a lap dance?"

He shakes his head. "I'll pass."

Figures.

I approach the building. Security eyes me warily, but no one says a word as I go in. Everything around me is golden with a red glow, the lighting dim and music soft, and slow, and surprisingly doesn't make my head want to explode. Men pack the club, gathered at small tables, lounging in deep leather chairs as women dance around them. It's tame out here. PG-13. Barely a hand job in a cesspool of insatiable fucking. Looking for anything more than the flash of a set of nipples and your ass better be shelling out enough cash to be escorted to a different room for a different experience.

My guys congregate in the far corner, away from others, attention already being showered on them. A pretty little brunette sits on Three's lap, arms wrapped around his neck as she whispers who-knows-what in his ear, tits all up in his face, teasing him. Five is chatting up a brunette waitress, while the others are already long gone, probably in the back.

Took all of thirty seconds.

I slide into a chair at their table, slouching, folding my hands together against my chest. I'm not interested in partaking so much as observing, but damn if I couldn't use a drink.

"Rum," I say loudly, interrupting Five's conversation with the waitress. "A whole bottle would be nice, but I'll settle for the biggest glass you've got in this place. Straight up, no bullshit... the rougher, the better."

Three mumbles some cliché *that's what she said* joke, which makes the brunette throw her head back and cackle.

I wonder how much he pays her to pretend he's funny.

The waitress stalks off, over to the bar, and returns with a glass of clear liquid, handing it straight to me before diving back into her conversation.

The glass is barely four fingers tall, but beggars can't be choosers.

Or more like patrons shouldn't kill waitresses.

Same difference.

I take a swig from the glass, grimacing, before interrupting them again. "This isn't rum."

The waitress looks at me. "What?"

"It's vodka," I say, setting the glass on the table, some of the liquor sloshing out as I shove it her way. "I asked for *rum*."

"Are you sure?" She picks up the glass. "I mean, it's *clear*."

"So is water, but that doesn't mean it's what I fucking asked for, is it?"

"Uh, no, I guess not."

"Rum. R-U-M. Say it with me. *Rum*."

"Rum," she says quietly, her voice trembling as her eyes widen a second before she averts them, looking at the floor. She seems pretty damn terrified all of a sudden as she scurries away, her reaction confusing until my men glance over, looking at me.

No, looking *behind* me...

"A man who knows what he likes and accepts nothing less," a strong voice says, the words twinned with a deep Russian accent.

"Cannot fault a man for that, can we?"

"No," I say, "sure can't."

He walks around the table, past us, strolling over to the bar. *Kassian Aristov.* He slides in beside the waitress just as the bartender hands her a new glass. Before she can walk away, Aristov's arm slips around her slim waist, securing her at his side, one hand on her hip as the other snatches the glass out of her grasp. Bringing it to his lips, he drinks every last drop, setting the glass down on the bar as he leans over, whispering something to her.

Her eyes are on the floor again, every inch of her rigid.

She's terrified.

His expression is relaxed, casual, a slight smile on his lips, like her fear amuses him. No idea what he could be saying. He's not *yelling*, but the longer this goes on, the more the woman looks like she might collapse under the weight of his words.

After a moment, Aristov flicks the woman's cheek so hard she winces, her head tilting up, her eyes meeting his. He says something else, and she nods, before he turns, motioning for the bartender to give him a golden-colored bottle from behind the bar.

Appleton Estates. Jamaica Rum. I can see the label as Aristov approaches, dragging the waitress along with him. He stops beside the table, in my line of sight, his hand shifting from the waitress's waist to clutch the back of her neck.

"I'm sorry," she says, forcing a smile, although tears brim her eyes. "I hope you can forgive me. It'll never happen again. I promise."

Promises. I hate promises.

People break them all the goddamn time.

I nod, because I'm not sure what to say to that. What I *want* to say will probably only make everything worse for her, and it seems like she's having a rough enough time without my help.

"Rum," Aristov says, holding the bottle out to me. The outside of it is dusty, the bottle still sealed. "I must confess, we do not sell much here. We specialize in vodka, only the best, straight from Russia."

I take the bottle from him.

Aristov leans over, pressing a kiss to the waitress's temple before whispering, "Go to my office, *suka*."

Her head lowers, and as soon as Aristov lets go of her neck, she scurries through the club, out of sight. Aristov lingers, his eyes on me as I crack open the bottle, bringing it to my lips.

"On the house, everything," Aristov says. "*All* of you. Enjoy."

My guys, they celebrate, but I just sit here, still sipping rum while they scatter, wasting no time now that it's free. *Cheapskates.*

"Join me for a drink in my office?" Aristov asks, raising his eyebrows.

I shrug as I stand up. *What the hell?* "Lead the way."

His office is toward the back of the club, a small room behind a two-way mirror. He can see out, watching everything, but nobody can see in. The waitress stands inside, in the center of the room, hands clasped together in front of her.

It's not an *office* in the traditional sense of the word. It looks more like a typical studio apartment in New York. Leather couches surround a square table, a small private bar opposite the door with liquor bottles on it. *Vodka.* Above that is a loft, a white ladder leading up to it. I don't even have to take a guess why there's a *bed* in his office.

The lighting is soft, the walls white, with a red Persian rug covering part of the marble floor.

After shutting the office door, Aristov snatches up one of the bottles. He guzzles some of the liquor as he approaches the waitress, eyes meticulously scanning her before looking at me. His free hand grasps the back of her neck again, yanking her by it, turning her my direction. She whimpers, closing her eyes. "She is stupid, this one, but she is pretty, and there is nothing she cannot handle, if you would like to try her."

"She's not really my type," I say.

"Oh? What *is* your type?"

"The type that doesn't cower from me in fear."

Aristov laughs. "Ah, do those type of women exist? Most are afraid of their own shadows."

I don't entertain that with an answer.

He drags the waitress over to one of the couches, sitting and tugging her in front of him, shoving her down on her knees. He unbuckles his pants, not saying a word, and grabs her by her hair, pulling her face onto his lap as he pulls his dick out right in front of me.

The woman takes him into her mouth without putting up any sort of fight, and he lets out an exaggerated sigh as he smiles lazily, seeming damn pleased with himself.

Look, I'm not an idiot. This isn't my first day on the job, if you know what I mean. I know he's asserting his dominance or spraying his territory or whatever alpha male bullshit move you want to chalk this up to, a figurative pissing contest because I'm a rival lion who entered *his* den. So I get it, but the thing is, he doesn't know me. He's thinking this show will get under my skin, that it'll make me uncomfortable, that *I'll* cower, but that's not happening.

I told Scarlet he didn't scare me.

I meant that shit.

I will whip my cock out and measure that son of a bitch, right here, right now, if he pushes me. In the figurative sense, of course. Literally, my cock is staying right where it is.

"You sure you do not want a taste?" he asks, nodding his head toward the waitress blowing him. "You could fuck her. I do not mind. She squeals like a little piggie when you fill her up."

"I appreciate it, but I'm not fucking any of your women."

Or, well, hell, I *might* be.

I don't know.

I'm still fuzzy on his history with Scarlet.

But regardless, as far as I'm concerned, she's not *his*. She's not Amello's, either. She doesn't belong to either of those assholes.

Strolling over to the couch across from him, I sit down, relaxing back, sipping straight from the bottle of rum, not bothering to avert my eyes. Looking away toes a lie of cowering that I'm not even coming close to crossing.

I think he realizes it, that I'm not like the others he deals with. He could slit that woman's throat and I wouldn't flinch. I don't have it *in* me to flinch. He stops prolonging things, gripping the back of her head and shoving her down, making her gag, as he bucks his hips a few times, fucking her face until he spills down her throat.

As soon as he's done, he yanks her away. "Get back to work."

She runs from the room, shutting the door behind her. Aristov tucks himself back away, narrowed eyes fixed on my face. If anything, I think I'm ruffling *him*.

"Is there a reason you have come here?" he asks. "Since it seems to not be the appeal of my women, it must be the appeal of *me*, no?"

"Don't flatter yourself. You're not my type, either."

He shrugs, chugging more vodka. "I do not cower."

"So I've heard."

"You have heard?" He raises his eyebrows. "Earlier this week, you said you did not know me."

"I didn't," I say. "Kinda got curious when you busted into the club, spewing bullets, so I asked around. Led me here."

"So it *was* the appeal of me." He laughs, drinking some more, damn near finishing off the entire bottle in just a few minutes. How the fuck does he still have a functioning liver?

Hell, maybe he doesn't.

Maybe that's why he's after Scarlet.

Maybe he needs a transplant.

Maybe they're compatible.

I shrug, because in a roundabout way, what he says is true. I came because I had a sneaking suspicion I'd find Scarlet's *problem* here. "Like you said, you don't cower. Most people do. I've been in the city for a while, and I keep finding little boys who only talk the talk. So when I encounter someone who walks the walk, well, it gets me interested."

He sits there, continuing to drink, as he thinks those words through. I can see as the liquor takes hold of him, his posture relaxing, eyelids drooping, and leg lazily moving.

"We used to do business with the Italians," he says. "The families would come to us when they wanted something done but were too chicken. They had so many silly rules. Do not kill women, do not kill bosses, do not kill officers, but we do not have those rules. We were the loophole that kept their hands clean."

"I don't need loopholes," I say, "nor do I care if my hands are clean."

"That *I* have heard," he says. "You have built a very big reputation in a very small time, Mister Scar."

Mister Scar.

I can feel my muscles twitch when he says that, my body unconsciously reacting. I'd like to hit him, but I'd also like to walk out of here, and with my guys preoccupied with pussy, well, I'm not sure that would turn out to my advantage.

"Go big or go home, right?"

"Right," he says. "Are you working with George Amello? Is that why you were at his club?"

I shake my head. "Someone has been robbing him. He accused me. I didn't appreciate the insinuation, so I made an appearance to tell him how I felt about his finger pointing."

He laughs. "I must confess—that is *my* fault."

"*You?* Figured you were above petty larceny."

"I am," he says. "It was personal."

"Personal? What did he do to you?"

"He has my girl."

"The one you were looking for? Morgan?"

I have to force myself to use her real name.

He nods, pointing his bottle at me. "That is the one."

"So he took a woman from you," I say, trying to riddle it out. "Seems to me, looking at this place, you're not exactly hurting. Is one woman really worth all that?"

He doesn't seem to like what I'm saying. His slack expression grows hard, his shoulders squaring. Yeah, she's worth it to him. She's worth more than I might've realized.

After guzzling the last of his liquor, he shoves to his feet and strolls back over to the bar. For getting drunk so fast, his walk is awfully steady. He exchanges his empty bottle for a full one as he says, "She is different."

Different. I can tell he means that. Hell, he almost sounds *sentimental* about it, like he might actually feel something for Scarlet.

"I do not like when people take what is mine," he says, turning back around. "She is very pretty, my Morgan, and she knows it. She uses it to her advantage. It makes men want to help her, as if she needs *help*." He laughs bitterly, cracking open the bottle. "She is like a siren of the sea, and the only thing that might be stronger than her call is my money. That is why I will give half a million dollars to whoever coughs her up."

"That's a lot of money."

"It is," he agrees. "It is also a lot of incentive."

That it is.

I know quite a few people who would sell out their own mother for that kind of cash. Scarlet doesn't stand a chance. They say you can't put a price tag on feelings, but I'm pretty fucking sure half a million is a big enough payday to wipe that away.

For most people.

"What are you going to do with her when you find her?" I ask, the irony of this whole moment not lost on me. It wasn't long ago I was looking for the same damn woman and Seven asked me this exact question. Because men like me... men like Aristov? We react on principle. It's *ego*. We'd pay half a million dollars to get our hands on someone just for the chance to watch them bleed out, and it would be worth every penny to us.

"That is my business," he says, that answer not a surprise. Pretty sure I said something similar. He walks toward me, setting his bottle down on the table before reaching into his back pocket for a wallet. Flipping it open, he pulls out something tucked in one of the pockets, shoved in behind credit cards and who knows what else.

A photo, I realize, when he holds it out to me.

I take it carefully.

It's worn and scratched up, the edges frayed, like he's pulled it out and shoved it back away hundreds of times. Brown hair is pulled up, messy on top of her head, some loose strands falling down around her face. It's Scarlet, without a doubt, but at the same time, it's not the Scarlet I know. The girl in the picture is young—fourteen, maybe fifteen. Still a teenager, her face slightly rounded, soft with a bit of innocence. Not a hell of a lot, but some. She's smiling her half-smile, like she's as happy as she could possibly be, which isn't really *happy* at all. More like not quite as beaten down.

"That was taken a few years ago," he says. "She is a bit older, but she is still the same pretty girl."

Before I can respond, there's a knock on the door to the office. Aristov folds his wallet up, shoving it in his pocket, and snatches up his liquor bottle as he yells, "Come in!"

The door opens, a man walking in. I saw him once, at Mystic—the guy that was with Aristov, the big burly motherfucker that looks a lot like him. He hesitates when he sees me, eyes narrowing.

"What are you doing here, Markel?" Aristov asks.

"Needed to talk to you about..." Markel trails off, staring at me, before he turns to Aristov. "Am I interrupting something?"

"I was just leaving," I say, standing up, waving my bottle of rum at Aristov. "Thanks for the drink."

"Anytime," he says.

I glance at the picture once more before holding it out to Aristov. He takes it back, gazing down at it in his hand as I walk away. I stroll past Markel, who watches me go.

Limerence is packed, my men nowhere in sight.

So I leave, because tonight's not the night to start trouble, even if trouble sounds like a lot of damn fun right now. Security at the door doesn't say a word as I leave, carrying the rum with me, because *fuck it*.

It's mine now.

Seven lingers by the curb, my shadow in the darkness. He hasn't even moved. He looks at me as I approach, assessing, like he's figuring out what happened without asking. I get in my car, not bothering with the seatbelt, taking a swig as Seven joins me.

"Find what you were looking for?" he asks.

"Even more."

"That's good," he says, hesitating before adding, "It *is* good, right?"

"I don't know." I glance at the club, my gaze skimming along the red cursive. "He wants her."

"Who?"

"Scarlet."

He lets out a low whistle. "What does he want with her?"

"Didn't say, but he's offering one hell of a reward to whoever hands her over."

He drives away from the club, merging into traffic. Not a word is spoken, but I can see him fidgeting, his fingers drumming against the steering wheel.

He's wondering if I'm going to take the offer.

He doesn't ask, though.

Maybe he's afraid of hearing my answer.

Maybe, deep down, he already knows.

18
Morgan

I don't have cable. Hell, there isn't even a television in this rundown apartment. No Wi-Fi. No computer.

I've got a cell phone, of course, one of those cheap prepaid burner ones, loaded with minutes in case of an emergency, but I usually forget to charge it, so a lot of good *that* does.

I used to have a stereo, but not anymore. Music surrounded me too many nights as it was and reminded me that I became *this* woman, the one who danced until her feet had blisters, the one who wore skimpy lingerie to work.

The woman I never wanted to be.

A woman I might never get away from.

I miss it all sometimes. I miss the noise. Movies. Music. Laughter. *Fun.* I miss dancing for the hell of it and playing games. The only time I run anymore is when I'm being chased.

Just once, I want to throw caution to the wind again, go where my heart leads me instead of always worrying, worrying, worrying. I want to laugh, and shout, and sing at the top of my lungs, dance in the moonlight and actually feel happy about it for once. *Yeah, right.* I want to hear birds chirping instead of men catcalling. I want to hear music playing that makes me smile instead of—

A doorknob turning.

Shit.

My head snaps up, eyes going straight to the apartment door. Even in the darkness, I can see it slowly opening.

Shit. Shit. Shit.

I move as silently as possible, running on my tiptoes, grateful the wooden floor doesn't squeak as I dart into the kitchen. Snatching a knife from the drawer, I slide into the small space beside the fridge, pressed up against the wall, my heart frantically racing. I try to hold my breath, straining my ears, listening for footsteps, or movement, or *something.* Maybe heavy breathing?

I hear nothing.

It's silent, and still, the air frigid in the apartment, so cold my teeth chatter as I shiver. *Or maybe that's from fear, dumbass.* I stay in place, hiding, waiting, but nothing's happening.

Minutes tick away.

Maybe I'm going insane.

It's dark. I could've imagined it, right?

Maybe I did.

I give it a few more minutes, the apartment remaining quiet, before I take a deep breath. *Face your fears...*

I peek around the fridge and step out, barely making it three steps through the kitchen when a shadow moves in the darkness, a figure stepping into the doorway. *Fuck.* It's like being punched in the chest, the air leaving my lungs, my vision blurring for half a second as I grip the handle of the knife tightly, ready to fight.

I raise my arm, but before I can lunge, bright light hits me, and I wince. *What the fuck?* It takes a few seconds for my brain to catch up, for my eyes to make out the sight of Lorenzo, his hand on the light switch right inside on the kitchen wall.

The asshole turned the light on.

He raises an eyebrow, not saying a word, as he casually leans against the doorframe, clutching a bottle of liquor, taking a drink, his eyes on my hand.

On the knife.

Shit.

Instinctively, I release my grip, letting it clatter to the floor by my bare feet. My hands are trembling. I clench them into fists, but it doesn't little to calm me down. "Jesus Christ, Lorenzo, you scared me!"

He meets my gaze, taking another drink, before waving the

bottle toward the knife. "Thought I told you not to pull another knife on me."

"I didn't know it was *you*," I say. "You didn't exactly announce yourself."

He says nothing, drinking some more, watching me as he does. His gaze crawls across my skin, giving me goose bumps. I shiver again, crossing my arms over my chest. I'm fully clothed, wearing pajamas—old gray sweats and a black t-shirt, my hair still wet from a shower, knotted on top of my head in a messy bun. I'm wearing not a stitch of makeup, my skin bare except for the lotion I always wear.

Shoving away from the doorframe, Lorenzo strolls through the kitchen, approaching. The closer he gets, the more my heart races, my stomach doing somersaults. He's not drunk, I don't think, the bottle in his hand only a quarter of the way gone, but there's something off about him. I can't put my finger on it. "What's wrong with you?"

He stops right in front of me. "What makes you think something's wrong?"

Even the way he says that feels wrong, but I can't exactly explain it. I don't know what it is. Besides, he just answered my question with a question, which is a giant red flag.

I don't answer him, since he didn't answer me. After a moment, he raises a hand, to touch me, but I take a step back, putting space between us. His brow furrows, and I try to go around him, to get out of the kitchen, but he grabs my arm, pulling me back toward him. "What's wrong with *you*?"

"I asked you first."

"I don't give a shit," he says. "Answer my question."

I want to tell him to fuck off, that I don't owe him any answers, but he'd probably just ask again and again until I caved and gave him what he wanted. "You're being weird."

"How?"

"Ugh, I don't know." I pull my arm from his grasp, and he lets go without a fight. "I can't explain it. It's just a feeling I've got."

He stares at me again, the corner of his mouth turning up

slightly with a hint of a smirk. He takes a swig of his liquor before walking over and picking up the discarded knife. It's small, with a blunt tip and a serrated blade, the first knife I came across and probably the worst one to try to attack somebody with.

Shaking his head, he tosses the knife onto the counter before turning back to me. "You're just being paranoid. There's nothing wrong with me, except maybe that it's cold as fuck in here. Does the heat not work?"

I relax a bit. Okay, that's plausible. I might be paranoid. "The heat works. It just, you know... sucks."

"Sucks," he repeats, walking back over to me. "I guess that's one way to keep warm."

"Is *that* why you showed up here? Think you can drop in any time you want and get your dick wet?"

"Can't I?"

I roll my eyes, starting to walk away again, when he laughs. He's *laughing*. The sound stalls me.

"I'm just fucking with you," he says, pausing before adding, "or well, *not* fucking with you. However you want it. Not a big deal."

He skirts past me, out of the kitchen, flicking the light off as he goes, leaving me standing in the dark alone. Brow furrowing, I follow him to the living room, thinking he's leaving. "Where are you going?"

"To smoke," he says, bypassing the front door, instead going to the ladder that leads to the roof. "Join me or not. Whatever you want."

Ugh. I scrub my hands over my face, groaning, as he makes his way up onto the roof. He's giving me whiplash. Dealing with him is the last thing I expected to be doing tonight, considering I just saw him this morning, but now he's here... well, he's *up there*... and it kind of just makes me want to be wherever he is.

I know he's just a man. A man with flaws. A man with his own problems. And I know he can't solve *my* problem. Not really. He can't fix what's wrong with me. Nobody can. They can't even understand. But being around him, it makes me feel things, things

I've missed just as much as the music and the laughter, things that make me feel alive again.

He's excitement. He's adrenaline.

He makes my heart do stupid shit.

Shit my heart shouldn't be doing.

Because everything that turns me on about him could also snuff me out. He's violent. He's temperamental. He's dangerous. *So dangerous.* Twenty-four hours ago, I watched him murder someone. He didn't even flinch as he pulled the trigger.

But then again, neither did I.

I watched him do it without reacting.

Maybe we're not that different.

It doesn't really matter, though, because the devil already took my soul. I have nothing to offer Lorenzo.

Not that he'd even *want* it.

Sighing, I stalk over to the ladder and climb up onto the roof. Lorenzo sits on the ledge, legs dangling over the side of the building, a cloud of smoke already surrounding him. I smell it as I approach and climb up on the ledge beside him, sitting down so close our arms touch.

Lorenzo turns to me and leans closer, like he might kiss me, but instead he lets out a stream of smoke. My lips part, and I inhale deeply, taking the remnants of the hazy air into my lungs, closing my eyes as I hold it, relishing the slight burn in my chest.

I exhale after a moment, reopening my eyes, and catch him staring at me, still just a breath away from my mouth.

I turn away, lowering my head, looking down over the side of the building, down at the chaotic city. My heart continues to batter my ribcage, chills covering every inch of my skin. I gently swing my legs, my bare foot grazing against his black combat boot. His boots are untied, loose on his feet, like at any moment they might fall off, but he doesn't seem to give a shit.

It's a long drop. I live on the sixth floor. From up here on the roof, it might as well be seven stories.

"Do you think it would hurt?" I ask, gazing down.

"What?"

"Falling."

He takes a hit of his joint before wordlessly offering it to me. I take it, bringing it to my lips and inhaling, as he glances down.

"Falling doesn't hurt," he says. "I imagine it feels nice those few seconds, soaring through the sky."

"Yeah, I guess it's hitting the ground that hurts."

"I wouldn't even say that. From this height? You've got about a ten-percent chance of surviving. The hit, it probably doesn't hurt. It'll either kill you or incapacitate you, and either way it'll be instant. Pain won't come until you wake up and realize you're not dead. So no, I don't think falling hurts, but living through it sure as hell would." He lets out a dry laugh, taking the joint back from me. "That's usually how it goes, you know... dying has *nothing* on the horrors of surviving."

How true that is...

"That doesn't sound so bad," I mumble. "Falling."

"I swear to fuck, Scarlet, if you jump off of this roof..."

"I'm not planning on it. I'm just saying, there are worse ways to go. And when death catches up to me, well, it won't be as instant as going *splat*. He'll make it much worse than that."

"By 'death' I'm assuming you mean Aristov," he says, passing the joint back. "When Aristov finally catches up to you."

"Yeah," I mumble, taking a hit, sucking deeply and holding it in my lungs until I start coughing. The smoke streams out of me, my eyes burning, *watering*. "His weapons of choice are his hands."

"So, strangulation, suffocation..."

"Worst way to go."

My throat feels raw, my chest tight. I can almost *feel* his thick hands wrapped around my neck, choking the life out of me, his face just inches from my own. I always just hoped I'd see a fleck of humanity, but there was never anything there. The man is a shell. He may as well be made of metal, whatever's inside of him short-circuiting. He's inhuman. Seeing him kill others desensitized me, but realizing he'd kill me, too? Realizing 'love' to him wasn't love at all, that it was obsession, that it was all about *possession*?

It almost broke me.

218

Almost.

"Old age."

Lorenzo's words draw my attention, pulling me out of memories that feel lifetimes ago. I take another hit of the joint, tingles running through my body, warming me from the inside, that floaty feeling starting to take over, before I hand it back. "Old age?"

"Worst way to go."

That makes me laugh harder than it should. "You're kidding, right? Of all the ways to die, you think *that's* the worst?"

He shrugs, stubbing the joint out, before picking up his Altoids tin from between us on the ledge and shoving it back in his pants pocket.

"I'd love to live long enough to die of natural causes," I say. "If only I could be so lucky..."

"Live for a century only to have your body shut down, your heart giving out, your brain disconnecting, forgetting everything you did and everyone you might've given a fuck about, suffering alone and terrified, shitting your pants, not even knowing your own name? I'd rather be doused in gasoline and set on fire."

I cringe. Jesus Christ.

"Besides," he continues, "would be bullshit, living the way I do, if I don't at least get the chance to go out in a blaze of glory while I can still enjoy it."

"That's no way to live."

"Says the woman thinking about *falling* off a roof while hiding from some jackass like a scared little punk bitch."

"You don't understand."

"You're right. I don't."

There's a part of me that wishes I could explain it to him, that wants to make him understand, but there's another part of me—the stubborn, hardhearted part—that can't risk fully confiding in this man.

Facts often change perception. Sometimes stories have plot twists that turn everything upside down. So I keep my secrets guarded closely to my chest, not cracking myself open, because there's a chance when he sees what's all inside of me, he might walk away and not even look back.

I don't know that he would, I don't even *think* he would, but he *might*, and I selfishly need him to stick around. I couldn't handle that rejection right now.

"It doesn't matter," I mumble, swinging around, pulling myself back onto the roof. "I'm going inside."

Before I can even take a step away, Lorenzo's hand shoots back, grabbing my arm. "Did you hear that?"

I glance at him. "Hear what?"

Just as I ask that, a faint thumping noise reaches my ears, like footsteps against metal rungs. *The ladder.* My eyes dart toward the opening on the roof, leading to my apartment, trembling when I hear it again from inside.

Someone else is here. *Fuck.*

I'm frozen solid, hoping it's my imagination, until I hear voices. *Accents.* Lorenzo swings around, getting to his feet. He doesn't say anything, dragging me across the roof, his hand gripping my arm so tightly it hurts. He takes me over to another ledge before letting go, hauling himself up on it, not even hesitating before dropping over the other side, *disappearing.*

"Lorenzo!" I call out, heart racing as I pull myself up onto the ledge, terrified, hearing a loud bang of metal, watching as he drops onto the old fire escape below, nearly losing his balance when he hits *hard.*

He recovers, staying on his feet, and looks up at me. "Now or never, Scarlet."

Now or never.

I glance behind me, back onto the roof, flexing my hands as they shake. *Now.*

I jump.

Or well, I fall.

I wish I can say I'm graceful about it, that I pirouette off the ledge and float on down, but I more like flail mid-air for a second, squeezing my eyes shut and holding my breath, before slamming right into Lorenzo. *BAM.* My bare foot catches on the edge of the fire escape, and I nearly slip through the opening, down another level, but Lorenzo grabs me, yanking me to him before I fall any further.

I wince, blood seeping out from a fresh cut on my foot, the metal edges of the fire escape jagged and rusty. *Awesome.* If Kassian doesn't get me tonight, tetanus certainly might.

Talk about some karma.

"Go," Lorenzo says, his voice firm as he nudges me, making me move. I'm still trying to get my bearings, but I hold onto the fire escape as I make my way down. I'm surprised I'm not yet caught when I get to the bottom, grabbing the ladder and shoving on it, but it only budges a little bit.

Ugh. George is a slumlord. Piece of shit building is a death trap.

"Jump," Lorenzo says impatiently, nudging me again. Sighing, I grab the ladder, climbing over, and dangle from the end of it before dropping to the sidewalk, right on my ass, with another wince.

Of course, this bastard lands beside me, jumping down, managing to stay upright. Grabbing my arm, he yanks me to my feet, nearly throwing me back down as he shoves me. *"Go."*

I take a few steps, because he gives me no choice, but then I stall. "Where?"

He shrugs.

The man fucking *shrugs.*

All casual and calm, just a flippant lift of his shoulders as he leans back against the building not far from the entrance.

What the hell?

"What are you doing?" I ask incredulously as he props his boot up against the building, his posture relaxed, hands shoved in his coat pockets. He's just standing there, like he's *waiting.*

"You'd rather fall than face him, so I got you down still alive," he says, "but I'm not afraid, Scarlet, and I've never run from anyone a day in my life."

"But—"

"Go," he says again, louder. "Quit pussyfooting."

He's insane, this man. Bona fide batshit crazy. Groaning, I run around the corner, into the alley, spotting the black Mercedes parked there. *Whoa.* I retreat, to go the other way, when there's noise in front of the building.

Voices, distinguishably Russian.

Out of time, I dodge behind a row of dumpsters, overflowing with trash, wedging myself between two of them and squatting down, gagging.

Maybe this makes me a coward, I don't know, but I'd rather be a breathing coward than a brave corpse.

"Where is she?"

Those are the first words I hear, as I strain my ears.

The voice is familiar. *Markel.*

"Who?" Lorenzo asks.

"You know who," Markel says. "Morgan."

"Oh, did you find her?" Lorenzo asks. "That was fast."

"Listen, you son of a bitch," Markel says, losing his temper. "You think you're funny, but I find *nothing* funny about you. You are involving yourself in business that has nothing to do with you."

"Business, is she?" Lorenzo's voice doesn't waver from its casual tone. "Thought it was personal."

"It's *both*," Markel says. "Either way, it has nothing to do with you. We don't want any problems. There doesn't need to be any. The girl, she is Kassian's. So stay away from her, leave her to *us*, and there will be no hard feelings. Just give her up."

"See, that's where you're wrong," Lorenzo says. "Because I'm already feeling like there *are* some hard feelings here, with the way you're all in my space right now. Your breath smells like ass and you just spit in my face while spewing your lies about not wanting problems, and there's nothing I hate more in this world than a liar, Pooh-Bear. *Nothing.* So run along and tell Christopher Robin that I said I've got a pair of nuts he can suck on, but otherwise, I've got nothing for him. You got me?"

I grimace. Kassian won't like that.

"You'll regret that," Markel says. "You're willing to give up your life for a dumb little *suka*?"

Menace

I squeeze my eyes shut, my stomach angrily churning.

"Oh, I'm not giving up anything," Lorenzo says. "All I'm saying is I don't have her. Hell, you can check my pockets if you want. Here, *look*. See, she's not here. Nope, not in my coat, either. I don't have her, and I don't appreciate the insinuation that I *do*."

"Then how did you know to come here?" Markel asks.

"I think the better question is how you knew where I went," Lorenzo says. "And be *very* careful how you answer that, Boo-Boo, because I don't take kindly to being tracked."

His voice finally raises an octave, the anger emanating from those words sending a chill through me.

"I did not follow you," Markel says. "It seems you and I just had the same destination."

"Bullshit."

It's silent for a moment—a very long moment—before Markel says, "Kassian will not let you keep her."

"That's funny," Lorenzo says, "because I don't recall asking him for his blessing... maybe because I don't give a fuck what he thinks."

I wait for a response, my heart hammering hard, but all I hear is footsteps after that, drawing closer, closer, closer...

I duck further into the shadows, watching as two guys strut past. Markel, Kassian's younger brother, but the other I don't know. One of his many minions.

It's funny, I think, as I watch them get in the Mercedes, squealing tires as they speed away, going back to Kassian empty-handed, that it's his brother he's sending, considering Markel had a soft spot for me. He was once the closest thing I had to an ally.

I stay in place after they're gone, not knowing if it's safe. A minute or so passes before footsteps quietly approach, a shadow moving in the alley, stalling in front of the dumpsters. "You gonna stay there all night?"

I peek out at Lorenzo, grimacing. "Maybe."

"Maybe," he repeats. "Well, if you want to stay there, so be it, but otherwise, let's get the hell out of here."

"And go where?"

"Home."

"Home," I mutter, stepping over the trash, gagging again. It *reeks*. "Don't really have one of those I can go to."

"I've got one I can share."

He turns to walk away, but I hesitate. "What?"

"You got anywhere else to go? Family? Friends?"

"No."

"Okay then, my house it is."

"Seriously?"

"Look, we're not picking out fucking drapes together, Scarlet, but you need a place to lay your head and I've got one of those. You can sleep on the couch if you want—just overlook the hole in it. Had a little accident."

I follow him out of the alley, slightly limping. My foot feels like it's on fire, the rest of me sore. "Accident-*schmaccident*."

He pauses, glancing up and down the block. "Don't like the couch? I've got a bed."

"A spare bed?"

"*My* bed."

"Won't me sleeping in your bed put a damper in your game?"

"No."

That's all he says. *No.*

"Where are you going to take your *wham-bam's*?"

He looks at me then, raising his eyebrows. "You really want to talk about this right now? *Here?*"

"Well, I mean, I'm just trying to figure things out, because as grateful as I am for the offer, I've yet to meet a person who didn't have ulterior motives. So I'm wondering what yours are, before this goes any further, because no offense, but I'm not interested in being your fluffernutter."

He grabs me by the waist, pulling me away from the alley. "My *fluffernutter?*"

"Yeah," I say. "I'm not fluffing your nuts while you fuck other women. That's not in my job description."

I'm dead serious about that, but he laughs. "That won't be a problem. Besides, I pretty much just declared war for you, Scarlet. At least if you're sleeping in *my* bed, I know I'm winning."

"Yeah," I mutter. "Hell of a prize you've won."

"Come on," he says, ignoring that. "Let's go."

"Wait, I need my bag," I say as he tries to pull me past my building. "It's upstairs."

"Again with that goddamn bag?"

"Yes."

He groans, and I expect him to fight me on it, because I know he's frustrated, but instead he lets go of my wrist. "You've got about two minutes, woman, so make it fast."

19

The little girl's drawing was on the refrigerator.

She sat on a stool at the bar in the kitchen, a bowl of fresh porridge in front of her, untouched. Her gaze was fixed on the drawing. It wasn't a frame, like he'd said, but it was still on display.

Her mother always covered their refrigerator with the little girl's art, layer after layer, heavy magnets holding it all up. The Tin Man had used a piece of duct tape to stick it there, dead center of the freezer door, not a magnet to be found anywhere.

"Why are you not eating your *kasha*?" the Tin Man asked, his voice low and gritty, kind of like sandpaper to the little girl's skin. His eyes were gray again, but they didn't appear very kind that morning.

"I don't like porridge," she said, looking down at the bowl. "I like Lucky Charms better."

"Lucky Charms? You like the marshmallows? You like all that sugar?"

"Yes."

"Too bad," he said. "We eat to live, kitten. We do not eat for fun. So eat your *kasha*. It is good for you."

Frowning, she took a bite, forcing it down. In the month she'd been there, she hadn't had any sweets. No cakes, no cookies, no candies, no *nothing*. It was all soups and stews and too much fish, which she hated, but if she didn't eat what he made her, she just went hungry. She missed ice cream, and pepperoni pizza, and even hot dogs. She missed Kool-Aide, and root beer, and chocolate milk. Tea or water was all he ever offered, except that bitter burning vodka. *Yuck*.

The little girl missed so much, but most of all, she missed her mother, who used to say life was too short to eat *yucky* stuff.

The little girl looked over at the Tin Man as he sat across from her, reading a newspaper. "Daddy?"

"Yes?"

"She woke up, didn't she?"

He didn't look up from the paper. "Sure, kitten. Woke up good as new. We had a laugh about it this morning before she went home."

He was lying. Nobody laughed that morning. The little girl had sat at the top of the stairs, afraid to come down, and watched the Cowardly Lion carry the woman outside wrapped up in a black tarp.

"I meant Mommy," she whispered, looking at her porridge, thinking she'd rather starve than force down any more of it.

She could feel his eyes then, regarding her in silence.

"Your mother is fine," he said finally. "We have not laughed about it yet, but we will, and everything will be as good as new when we do."

Her eyes lifted, meeting his stern gaze. "She woke up?"

"Of course," he said. "Does that surprise you?"

She slowly nodded.

"Words. Do not *mime* your answers."

"Yes," she said.

"Why?"

"Because she didn't find me yet."

He stared at her for a moment longer before his expression cracked. His lips twitched with a hint of a smile. "You think she is looking for you? That someday you will hear, '*Knock-knock, kitten, Mommy is here*'?"

The little girl nodded again, earning an annoyed growl, his fist slamming against the bar so hard her bowl bounced, some of the porridge splattering out.

"*Words.*"

"Yes, Daddy."

He laughed again, that mean laugh now.

"I hope you do hear it," he said. "I hope she crawls out of the Hell she is in and comes for you, kitten. I would enjoy watching

228

that happen."

He ruffled the top of her head, still laughing as he walked away, leaving her with the porridge she didn't want and an answer she couldn't understand.

Did that mean she wasn't coming?

20

Lorenzo

The first thing I hear, when I open my front door, is that fucking song from that goddamn movie.

You know what I'm talking about. You might have even guessed it already. The one about the big ass boat and the iceberg, with the rich bitch and gutter rat making googly eyes at each other. *Draw me like your French whores, asshole. I'll never let go. Blah blah blah.*

Yeah, that one.

Saturday night—or well, guess it's Sunday morning now, isn't it? A few minutes past midnight. Leo is here somewhere with Melody. I know this, because she's singing along, like this is Karaoke Hour on the RMS Titanic.

Sighing, I step out of the way for Scarlet to enter, wanting to smash my head into the wall in hopes that maybe I'll go unconscious and won't have to hear this for a second longer. Scarlet strolls right to the living room, stopping in the doorway, looking in.

After shutting the door, I join her.

They're cuddling on my couch, my brother and his girlfriend, all tangled up together with a big blanket covering them. I'm not sure if they're dressed, to be honest. Wouldn't be the first time they fucked on my couch, just like this, watching some sappy love story.

I think it's a kink.

Some people like spanking.

Others like voyeurism.

My brother likes to fuck his girlfriend as she sobs over fictional characters.

Me? I like a little bit of everything... with the exception of that last one. Stick a finger in my ass all you want, but the second you start boo-hoo'ing, I'm done.

They don't pay us any attention, and I'm not even trying to interrupt whatever that is. Nudging Scarlet for her to follow me, I head to my library. I walk right in, but she hesitates before crossing the threshold.

"Shut the door," I tell her, plopping down in my chair. "Maybe it'll muffle the sound of that dying cat out there."

Scarlet laughs, shutting the door. "You're such an asshole."

"Could be worse," I say. "I could muffle her with a pillow, but I won't. Don't I get credit for that?"

"Nice try, but no," she says, approaching. "You don't get points for *not* killing your brother's girlfriend when the only thing she's guilty of is being a terrible singer."

"She's so damn emotional, and she's always just... *peppy.*"

Scarlet gasps with mock horror. "How horrible!"

"Fuck you," I mutter. "It's exhausting to be around."

"She's still young."

"She's the same age as *you.*"

"Yeah, well, I'm not exactly normal," she says. "I was forced to grow up quick when I was just a kid. But her? I imagine she's had a normal life. Well, until *you* came into it, so cut her some slack."

"I do," I say. "She's still breathing, isn't she? Still out there singing. Still hanging around, eating my groceries, watching my television, getting her pussy played with in my house."

Scarlet leans against the table beside me, shaking her head as she crosses her arms over her chest. "You'll probably be saying all that about me... eating your food, using your electricity, showering with your hot water—"

"Getting your pussy played with?"

She rolls her eyes but doesn't deny it.

I grab her hips, pulling her between my legs. "Look, all I'm saying is if you're going to sing, do that shit silently so nobody has to listen to it."

She laughs, her hands on my shoulders. "Should we talk silently, too, so you don't have to listen to that, either?"

"Preferably," I say. "Unless it's dirty talk, in which case, I'm more than happy to hear you."

"*Wow*," she says, voice flat. "You keep being so charming and I might start catching feelings."

"I wouldn't blame you," I say. "Just, you know, keep them to yourself, in case they're contagious."

"Don't worry," she says. "I practice safe sentiment. I'll be sure to wrap it before I *yap* it."

I laugh at that. This goddamn woman. She's got a mouth on her, without a doubt, the kind of mouth that's destined to get her in *a lot* of trouble in life.

Already has, it seems.

Aristov, he's the kind of guy who likes to break wild horses, and Scarlet is one of the most strong-willed I've ever encountered. She might not be broken, but it wouldn't take much more, not with the way she buckles when it comes to him.

It's uncharacteristic.

Sure, I haven't known her long.

But she doesn't flinch from me.

I don't scare her.

So why does *he*?

My eyes narrow slightly, and damn if she doesn't notice, because I see her stiffen in response to it.

"Tell me about Aristov."

Her expression blanks. There she goes, trying to fade on me, shutting down.

"I've already told you about him," she says. "He's a cruel man."

"One that stole from you."

"Yes."

"He stole the light from your life," I say, recalling her words. "He stole your innocence."

Her eyes close. It's automatic. She can't even look at me when I say that. When she reopens them, they're glassy, but she doesn't shed a single tear.

I've yet to see her cry.

"Yes."

That's all she says.

Since she's not elaborating on her own, fuck it... I'm going to *ask*. "How?"

It's a simple question, but I know right away she's not going to answer it. Her hands leave my shoulders and she steps back, out of my grasp, as she forces a smile on her lips, the fakest smile I've ever seen.

"I stink," she says. "Do you mind if I take a shower?"

"Of course not," I say, waving her away. "Help yourself to whatever. It'll take me *at least* two weeks to start complaining about you, so make yourself at home."

"Thanks," she says, turning to walk out of the library. "I make no promises when it comes to singing in the shower, though. Sometimes I just can't help myself."

"Make that one week, then," I call after her. "I'll start complaining by next weekend, so enjoy these next few days."

She laughs, disappearing from the room.

I stare at the doorway once she's gone, drumming my fingers on the arm of the chair. She evaded like a motherfucker. She wasn't even trying to be sly about it. She just flat out wasn't answering.

Shoving up from the chair, I stroll out of the library, making my way into the kitchen for something to eat. There's not much in here, so I just grab two slices of bread, pull out some lunch meat, and slap that shit together with a dab of mustard. *Viola.*

I take a bite, chewing, as I grab a Capri Sun from the fridge and walk out. My sandwich gets smashed as I stroll back down the hall, so busy tearing the plastic off of the small yellow straw that I almost drop it all.

"Hey, bro."

I stop near the living room when Leo greets me. I look up at him before glancing into the room. Melody isn't singing anymore, *thank fuck.* "Hey."

"So that lady," Leo says. "Morgan."

"What about her?" I ask, fiddling with the straw, trying to poke it through the hole but I'm using the wrong end. *Goddamnit.*

"She's back already, huh? Saw her walk by a bit ago."

"She needs a place to stay," I tell him, flipping the straw around. "Figured I'd be nice for once. Got a problem with that?"

"Not at all."

I shove the straw in, impaling the fucking thing, putting it right through the other side of the little silver pouch, stabbing my hand. I'm three seconds away from just squeezing the damn thing and letting it squirt out, wherever the hell it wants to go, figuring at least *some* of it will make its way into my mouth, when Leo snatches it from me, fixing the straw before handing it back.

"Thanks," I mutter. "These things are bullshit."

Look, before you go thinking I'm incompetent, remember my world is two-dimensional. I've adapted to that, for the most part, but sometimes objects are *assholes.* I misjudge distances, can't catch a fucking thing, spill drinks and bump into door frames. I also can't seem to ever get a straw in a hole, which, as I'm sure you can imagine, makes sticking things in *other* holes a bit of a struggle.

Pussy is what I'm getting at, in case you didn't pick up on that. I aim and sometimes miss like a virginal teenage boy who has never used his dick.

I take a sip, sucking through the straw.

"I don't know why you keep buying those," Leo says. "They give you trouble every time."

"I like them," I say. "Besides, no bitch ass little juice pouch is going to best me, Pretty Boy."

I hit the stairs, making my way up them as I take another bite of my sandwich. It's dark on the second floor. I flip on the light in my bedroom just as the water shuts off in my bathroom.

I sit down on the edge of the bed, kicking my boots off as I eat. They're already untied, so it isn't that hard. I shove them aside with my foot just as the bathroom door opens. My gaze shifts that way as Scarlet steps out, nothing more than a gray towel wrapped around her. She pauses, looking at me, so I hold out my half-eaten sandwich. "Hungry?"

I expect her to scoff, maybe laugh, but she plucks the thing right from my grasp and takes a bite, mumbling, "*Starving.*"

Well damn. I hand her the Capri Sun. She sucks the rest of it down as she finishes the sandwich.

Pulling my shirt off, I toss it across the room. I miss the hamper, of course, but it doesn't matter. General vicinity. Scarlet watches me, tossing the empty pouch in the trashcan near my bed. She makes it. Doesn't even look.

I shake my head.

"So," she says, "I've got a problem."

"No shit."

She purses her lips. "I have no clothes."

"That doesn't sound like a *problem* to me."

I grab the towel, slowly pulling it away, taking it off and tossing it aside, again near the hamper. Scarlet doesn't move as my gaze trails her body.

I've seen this woman naked a few times now, but beyond the obvious, like those gorgeous perky tits, I've never really *looked.* You know what I'm saying? But I see it now, every inch of her petite body. Strong legs. Wide hips. Slim waist. My fingertips trail her collarbones before running down her chest, brushing across those pert nipples.

Scars pepper her skin. They're not blatant, little marks here and there, healed burns and cuts, the most noticeable scar below her belly button, dangerously close to the Promised Land.

"Do I pass inspection?" she asks. "Or are there some violations I need to work on?"

Glancing up, I meet her gaze. "You can work on that mouth of yours."

"What's wrong with it?"

"It's running a little rough. Nothing a face-fucking can't fix, though."

Her eyes widen. "Big words for a guy who drinks Capri Sun."

I try to keep a straight face, but I crack at that, letting out a laugh. "Got me there."

Grinning, she does some bullshit little bow before turning, like she thinks she's going to walk away from me. *Yeah, right.*

Before she can take even a step, I wrap my arms around her from behind, dragging her to the bed. I don't climb in it, just shoving her down on the edge of it, her top half pressed into the mattress, my left hand planted firmly on her back, along her spine. I lean over top of her, my mouth near her ear as I say, "We'll see how much shit you're still taking when I'm through."

Kicking her legs apart, forcing her wide open, my right hand slips down, stroking her bare pussy. There's nothing gentle about it. Nothing *tender.* I rub hard, not fucking around. It's mere seconds before she's drenched, soft moans escaping that she's trying to hold back. She doesn't want me to see how turned on she is by this.

I slide two fingers into her, going slow at first, before I start really fucking her with them. Her eyes close as she fists the comforter, letting out a whimper. She's trying so hard to be still, to not react, but pleasure is the most difficult thing to mask. You can bottle up your feelings and suck up your tears, put on a brave face instead of showing fear, but when that spine-tingling euphoria rolls through your system, there's no denying it.

Bodies are traitors.

They wave red flags.

And those slick juices coating my hand tell me everything. The way her thighs tremble, her back arching, her knuckles white with tension as she clings to the bed, holding on tight. Goose bumps coat her arms, the fine hairs bristling, her cheeks flushed, lips parting, throat flexing as she swallows, but her mouth is so damn dry it does nothing. Her voice is raw, strained from trying to force back noises, so much so that it sounds like she's growling, like she just wants to annihilate me, rip me to fucking pieces. I've got her eating straight out of my palm, but she's the kind to bite the hand that feeds her.

Fighting and fucking.

Fucking and fighting.

Emotions heighten sensations. We all know that. But she can't let herself be happy, she can't let that guard down, so she gets real goddamn angry. It fuels the fire inside of her until she's shooting off sparks.

So yeah, I don't need her to tell me how she's feeling, but fuck if I'm not still going to *ask*.

"That feel good?" I ask, my other hand sliding away from her back, around the curve of her ass, settling between her thighs. I start rubbing her clit again, and it throws my rhythm off, but not so much that I don't make it work. Fucking. Stroking. In, out, around, and around... "You love it, huh? Love to have that beautiful pussy played with, to have it worshiped, getting fucked *just right*."

She groans.

Her breathing is labored, the tension in her body growing as she shifts her hips, writhing. She's damn close to orgasm.

"Open your eyes," I say. "Look at me."

She obliges, turning her head more, her eyes meeting mine. I stare at her, saying nothing else, and she stares right back, unyielding. I keep doing what I'm doing, watching her unravel and come apart right in my hands.

Fuck.

Orgasm tears through her, muscles pulsating, her entire body shaking as her mouth falls open and a cry of pleasure escapes. It's beautiful, the way her face contorts, her eyes trying to close again, eyelids fluttering, but she keeps her gaze trained on mine. I ride her through it until she relaxes, the hand from her clit moving back to her ass as I pull my fingers out of her and pop them right in my mouth.

She makes a guttural noise.

I suck the taste of her off of me before pulling them back out, my wet fingertips tracing her lips. "You ever taste yourself?"

"Do *you*?"

I slip my fingers into her mouth and groan as she wraps her lips around them, sucking, her tongue caressing my fingertips. "All the time."

Her eyes widen as she releases my fingers, pulling her mouth away. "You're kidding."

"Do I look like I'm kidding?"

"No."

"Well, then, there you go."

I sit down beside her. Slowly, she rises up, pushing away from the bed, and drops down to the floor on her knees.

She sits there, looking up at me, but keeps her hands to herself.

"Is there something you want, Scarlet?"

"Do you like how it tastes?"

The question bursts out of her, like she's been dying to ask it. I laugh, taking a page from her book by flipping it around. "Do *you?*"

She shrugs, carefully reaching toward me, like she's afraid I might bite. She unbuttons my pants and pulls down the zipper, her hand slipping inside. I groan as she palms my cock, stroking a few times in the confinement of my pants, before she pulls it out.

"Condom?" she asks.

I nod my head toward the bedside stand, and she pulls the small drawer open, looking in. She keeps one hand on my cock, stroking, as she searches through my stash with the other, grabbing a plain condom. Nothing special about it. She uses her teeth, tearing the packet, and pulls out the condom, promptly popping it in her mouth.

In her fucking mouth.

The condom.

The entire thing.

Before I can say anything, she goes down on me, wrapping her lips around my cock, starting at the tip, and takes the entirety of it down her throat in one deep stroke, not stopping as she gags.

"Goddamn, woman," I groan, my hands grasping the back of her head, my gaze flickering to the ceiling fan above as tingles flow through me. Round and round it goes, as Scarlet's mouth works up and down a few strokes.

She pulls away then, *way* too soon, and I look down at the condom rolled on my cock.

She put the fucking thing on with her mouth.

Her *mouth*.

"Witchcraft," I say as she stands up, shoving against my chest, pushing me so she can climb onto my lap. She straddles me, as I lean back, propping up on my elbows on the bed.

She sinks down onto me—warm, and tight, and wet... *so fucking wet*. Where I'm sitting, she doesn't have much room, but she doesn't need it. She rolls her hips, arching her back, slowly moving, my cock sliding in and out just enough to drive me crazy. Parts of me are tingling that should never tingle as she teases me. *Teases* me.

The woman is giving me a lap dance while I'm balls-deep in her pussy.

I raise up a bit, reaching out, my fingertips brushing across a tit, circling a nipple. I'm about to pinch that son of a bitch when Scarlet slaps my hand. *SMACK*. "No touching."

The sharp blow stings, catching me off guard. I pull my hand back, stalling mid-air. She hit me. *Hit* me. And not just some love tap... a full on fucking slap. "Hit me again. I *dare* you."

"If you don't keep your hands to yourself, I will."

She sounds pretty damn sure of herself. I lower my hand, propping on my elbow again as I stare at her.

Look, let's be real here. It takes a lot of balls to lay a hand on me. I'll cut the damn thing off and beat you to death with it, let you die by your own hand, since you *must* be suicidal to try that shit. I'm not even going to sit here and pretend the urge to lash out didn't strike me the second I felt the sting, but being as my balls are aching for a release, that's not really in my best interest.

So I do some meditative *woosah* bullshit and calm the hell down, since I'm not into necrophilia, and I'd rather be fucking her than killing her at the moment. I might be a bit screwed up in the head, but I'm not *that* far gone.

"I'm not paying for this shit," I tell her.

A smirk turns the corners of her lips as she says, "Didn't think you would."

Scarlet fucks around for a little while longer, tits tauntingly in my face, slowly riding me. She's trying to get a rise out of me. Figuratively, that is. I'm already as hard as a rock, but it's the rest of me she wants heated.

I'm going to tell you a secret.

A *big* secret.

It's working.

What she's doing, the way she moves? The way her body fits on top of mine, forming to me, *warming* me? It's got me feeling some type of way. I want to throw her off and pin her down, fuck her until she can't even walk and then make her crawl out of my goddamn house. But then I'd just want to drag her right back, because she's under my skin, and what she's doing? It's *hot.*

I can think of a lot worse ways to spend my time.

So I wait her out.

Eventually, she sighs, leaning down over me, bringing her face just inches from mine, as she whispers, "You're good at this."

"At what?"

"At being a fucking jackass."

Laughing, I grab her, yanking her off and throwing her over on the bed before she can stop me. She lets out a loud squeal, startled, before she starts giggling.

She's fucking *giggling.*

I crawl on top of her, shoving my way between her legs, forcing her knees up to her chest with my weight pressing against them, pinning her there. She reaches for me, but I grab her wrists, holding them as she struggles. "Wait! This isn't fair!"

"You want me to let you go?" I ask, leaning down, pausing just shy of her lips.

"Yes."

"Ask nicely," I tell her. "Say 'Lorenzo Gambini, I beg of you, please, let me go and I'll suck your dick.'"

She laughs again, harder. "You wish."

"I do," I say. "No doubt about it."

Her struggling is pathetic. She could break free if she really wanted to, but she's barely even fighting.

I close the rest of the distance, kissing her lips, as I grind my cock against her, the tip of it rubbing her clit. She moans into my mouth as she stops struggling, relaxing into the bed.

Surrendering.

"Lorenzo Gambini," she whispers between kisses, "I beg of you, please... *fuck me*."

I kiss her once more before pulling back, shifting position, smirking. "Well, since you asked so nicely..."

I thrust hard, sliding right in first goddamn try.

BAM.

21
Morgan

You know that dream people have where they're out somewhere—school, work, *somewhere*—only to realize they forgot to put clothes on that morning and everybody is staring at them?

I think I might know what that feels like.

The kitchen is quiet, strangely so, considering there are five of us packed in the room. I'm sitting at a round table, in a matching wooden chair, across from Leo and Melody. She's playing on a cell phone, cutting her eyes at me every now and then, her expression full of curiosity, while Leo isn't even pretending to be interested in anything else. He's just blatantly staring.

And he's not the only one.

Seven stands across the room, leaning against the counter. I can feel his eyes watching me, too.

Yep, I showed up naked to class.

It's funny, really, because I've been naked in public, around plenty of people, and it wasn't always pleasant for me, but it rarely felt this awkward.

I've got clothes on, although they're obviously not mine—black long sleeved shirt that could pass for a little dress with a pair of blue shorts underneath. Or well, okay, they're really boxers. Boxers with alligators all over them. *Florida Gators.*

I didn't know Lorenzo liked sports.

There's *a lot* I didn't know, I think, as I glance across the room at him, and it smacked me right in the face just a bit ago when I walked in here. Lorenzo's facing away from me, barefoot, shirtless, dressed only in low-slung black pajama pants and a pair of glasses. *Glasses*. Black frames, square, thin—not showy, barely even noticeable, but I see them. He moves around, alternating between sorting through paperwork spread out along the counter and tending to whatever's cooking on the stove.

Yes, you heard me right.

He's *cooking*.

And I don't mean Pop-Tart in the toaster level cooking. The man, who fed me half of a crappy sandwich and a juice pouch last night, has bacon sizzling as he flips pancakes and sips fresh-squeezed orange juice.

Seriously. I watched him squeeze it.

He even poured me some.

I glance down at the glass in my hand, at the pulpy juice, biting the inside of my cheek. No ninety-nine cent generic bodega juice for *this* family. They all keep looking at me like I'm peculiar, yet they're acting as if *that* is normal.

Lorenzo turns around, and I look up as he steps toward the table, half-expecting him to give me weird looks, too, but no, he's glaring at his brother. Swinging a spatula, he smacks Leo in the head, the loud *thwack* echoing through the kitchen.

"Shit!" Leo winced, the hit pulling him out of his trance as he rubs the back of his head. "What the hell was that for?"

"The table isn't set," Lorenzo says. "What are we, *animals*?"

Leo stands up, dramatically rolling his eyes, and Lorenzo swings the spatula again, barely grazing his shoulder with it as he jumps out of the way. "Okay, okay, I'm doing it! *Geez*..."

"You're not too old for me to take over my knee, Pretty Boy," Lorenzo said, pointing the spatula. "You weren't raised in a fucking barn."

"No, but I was raised on a farm," Leo says, grabbing some plates from a cabinet.

"It's an orange grove," Lorenzo says, "not a farm."

Orange grove.

I glance at my orange juice again, bringing it to my lips for a sip. This is all starting to feel very TV-sitcom, like Lassie is about to run in and tell us Timmy fell down the well.

Lorenzo tosses the spatula in the sink and brings platters of food over as Leo sets the table. I look at the empty plate in front of where I'm sitting and go to leave when Lorenzo slides into the chair beside me, gripping my thigh, forcing my ass back into the seat.

"Help yourself, Seven," Lorenzo calls over to the guy, still leaning against the counter. "You know how it goes."

"I appreciate it, boss," Seven says, "but the wife made omelets this morning, so I couldn't eat another bite even if I wanted to."

"I figured," Lorenzo says. "The woman feeds you morning, noon, and night."

"And packs me snacks in between," Seven says, and I think he's joking until he pulls a protein bar from one coat pocket and a little Ziplock bag of carrots from the other. *Wow.*

"You're married?" I ask.

"Twenty-five years next month," he says with a smile. Married longer than I've been alive. "She was my high school sweetheart. Married her right after graduation."

"Regrets that shit every day," Lorenzo says as he dishes out food onto plates.

"I've never once regretted it," Seven says, "not even when she rides my ass about the company I keep."

Lorenzo finds that funny, while I'm too busy doing math in my head. That means Seven is about forty-three years old... same age as Kassian.

I glance at Lorenzo, suddenly curious. "How old are you?"

Leo laughs at my question. "He's older than sin."

Lorenzo shoots him a look as he says, "Pretty much forever sixteen."

"He's pushing thirty-seven," Seven chimes in.

Thirty-seven.

I look at Leo. "And you're twenty-one?"

He nods. "Yep."

Sixteen year age difference. Lorenzo mentioned he started taking care of his brother when he was around two, which would've made Lorenzo—

"I was eighteen," Lorenzo says, and my eyes widen, wondering if I was doing the math out loud, but he just cuts his eyes at me with a slight smile, like he'd read my damn mind. "I know the look."

"What look?"

"The *trying to riddle shit out* look," he says, grabbing the plate in front of me, shoving it closer. "Eat your breakfast, Scarlet. I'm not opposed to taking *you* over my knee, either."

"I'd like to see you try," I mutter, grabbing a fork and stabbing the pancake on my plate. Before I even have to ask, Lorenzo picks up a thing of syrup and passes it to me, like he read my mind yet again. *Weird.*

I eat in silence. It's good. *Really* good.

He didn't burn any of it.

I always burned everything when I tried to cook.

Melody starts chattering, talking Leo's ear off, while Seven remains in spot, waiting for whatever.

A phone rings eventually, coming from the corner. Seven pulls one out of his pocket, holding it up. "It's yours, boss."

"Who is it?"

"Blocked number."

"I don't talk to cowards," Lorenzo says, pushing his chair back and standing up. He puts his hand on my shoulder as I set my fork down, my plate empty. "Sun's up, which means the trucks will be here soon. You coming, Scarlet?"

I have no idea what that means, which means I don't know how to answer, but Lorenzo doesn't wait for a response, so I'm taking that as a rhetorical question.

"Clear the table when you're finished, Pretty Boy," Lorenzo calls back as he walks out. "Don't forget to do the dishes."

Leo rolls his eyes. "I *really* need to get my own place."

Seven walks by the table and says, "Don't let your brother hear that. He'll catch a case of *empty nest syndrome*."

"On the bright side," Leo says, "he could put as many holes in the couch as he wanted, not having to worry about me being around."

"That's not a bright side, kid," Seven says, laughing. "Without you around, keeping him straight, there's no telling what he might do. Besides, you're his saving grace. That'll never change. No matter where you go, that man is a part of you, just like you'll always be a part of him. That's how it goes."

Seven walks out, and I get up from the chair, following him as Leo mumbles something about *cutting the cord.*

I smile softly, shaking my head as I make my way upstairs. Lorenzo is in his bedroom, his clothes already changed, sitting on the end of the bed to put on his boots. He glances up as I stall in the doorway and says, "That what you're wearing today?"

I look down at myself.

"To each their own and all that," he continues, "but you might freeze your nipples off."

"My problem, remember? I'm temporarily clothes-less as well as homeless."

He looks me over before getting up and waltzing past, stopping at the top of the stairs. "Firecracker! Come here!"

It takes Melody maybe thirty seconds to appear on the stairs. "Yes?"

"Most of your shit is here, right?" he asks. "I mean, you pretty much live in my damn house..."

"Right," she agrees, looking nervous. "Is that a problem?"

"It's actually looking like a solution," he says. "You got an outfit Scarlet can borrow?"

I can see the relief on her face as she smiles, trudging up to the second floor. "Of course."

"There you go," Lorenzo says. "Problem solved."

Temporarily, I think. I can only survive borrowing off of others for so long before I have to get my own stuff.

I follow Melody down the hallway, to another bedroom on the opposite end. It's a complete and utter mess, piles of clothes strewn everywhere, all of it *hers.* I can hardly tell a guy even sleeps in there. Melody wades through it all, chattering away, talking color schemes and fabric choices and body types, sizing me up. She rattles off a whole slew of questions that I have no idea how to answer, making this 'putting on clothes' endeavor feel more like an interview process.

I mean, yeah, don't get me wrong here—I'm not a t-shirt and jeans gal by any means. I love pretty clothes and putting on makeup, and if I had to list my greatest talents, there's a good chance 'walking in high heels' would be up there. But at the moment, brand names are the least of my priorities.

"Something comfortable," I say. "Warm, preferably."

"Comfortable and warm," she mumbles, scouring through the closet and dresser for what feels like forever before picking out an outfit. "Ha!"

Black fleece-lined leggings and a red slouchy sweater. *Nice.* I take it from her. "Thanks."

"Oh, wait!" she says. "You can't go barefoot!"

I scowl at my bare feet just as she steers toward a terribly familiar pair of red heels. "Oh, Jesus, no. *Anything* but those. I've had a rough enough week, I don't need to invite that negativity into my life."

Melody laughs, like that's funny, but I'm serious. Every time I wore those shoes, I ended up *running*. And that wouldn't be a problem, but like I've said, I only ever run when being chased by somebody, and that's not any fun.

Melody tosses me a pair of black boots. "How about those?"

"They'll work," I say. "Thanks again."

I turn to leave but come to an abrupt stop, damn near running into Lorenzo lurking in the hallway. He scans me, making a face. "You're not dressed yet? Why do you women take so long to get ready?"

I roll my eyes, pushing past him. "Why are you men such assholes?"

I hear his laughter as I go into his room, followed by his answer: "Probably because you're so fucking slow."

* * *

An old warehouse in the Greenpoint neighborhood of Brooklyn, just across the border from the borough of Queens. It looks like the kind of abandoned building that you'd see as the setting of some low-budget horror movie, broken glass and crumbling bricks, a faded sign barely clinging to the structure, covered in graffiti. People probably cross the street to avoid even walking near it, whereas it looks a lot like the places I slept in after running away so many years ago.

Hell, I might've slept *here*. Who knows?

Trucks idle in the alley beside the place. Three of them, to be exact, identical white box trucks, each backed right up to rusted metal dock doors along the side.

I walk slightly behind Lorenzo and Seven, letting them take the lead since I have no idea what any of this is. The closer we get, the more peculiar it all appears. Metal bars cover the shattered windows, heavy chains and locks on all the entrances, making it damn hard to get inside. It's *eerie*. A few guys are already here, gathered in the alley, looking haggard, one of the men even propping himself up against the building, dry-heaving.

"Long night, fellas?" Lorenzo asks. "You look like shit."

They try to perk up, reacting to his presence, like soldiers being called to attention, but they do a crap job of it. Instead, they end up just grumbling in response, grunting and groaning, as if that's answer enough. *Longest night ever.*

Lorenzo shakes his head, walking through the group, his expression hard as he says, "Somebody's missing."

"Yeah, uh, De—, uh, *Three*," one of the guys says. *Four.* "Must've slept in."

"Or he hasn't even gone to bed yet," Seven says, skirting past everyone as he pulls a set of keys from his pocket and starts unlocking the warehouse.

Three. The blond. Declan.

"Have you tried to get ahold of him?" Lorenzo asks.

"Yeah, got his voicemail," Four says. "Didn't even ring. Phone must be dead."

Four. Jimmy? Johnny? Joey? I don't know.

"Well, then, *he* better be dead along with it," Lorenzo says, "because *no longer breathing* is the only justification for blowing me off this morning. I don't care how long your night was, don't care how drunk you got, don't care how much pussy you fucked... I say be here, you show up."

He doesn't even raise his voice, but there's a subtle rage there, in the quiet evenness of his tone, that makes everyone stiffen with alarm.

"Why are the rest of you just standing here?" Lorenzo asks. "Think because Three is off, doing God knows what, that it gives you all a pass to just hang around with your thumbs up your asses? Get to work. *Now.*"

They scatter, not needing anymore incentive, heading into the warehouse and shoving the dock doors up. The churning screech of metal makes me cringe. Lorenzo approaches the back of the trucks one-by-one, greeting each driver before handing over envelopes he pulls from inside his coat in exchange for paperwork. His men start to unload the trucks. Seven takes on more of a supervising role, while I linger in the alley, pretty damn confused.

I feel like my teacher just announced a pop quiz when I don't know the material. *Shit.*

Totally bombing this.

They're halfway through the first truck, pulling out big wooden crates and hauling them into the warehouse, when I approach Lorenzo, who is flipping through paperwork, squinting, like he's struggling to read it.

"Forgot your glasses?" I guess.

His gaze flickers to meet mine. "I only wear them when I need them."

I'm almost inclined to point out that he's looking like he might need them *now*, but his expression keeps me from verbalizing that. I touched a nerve.

"So, what should I do?" I ask.

"Do whatever you want, Scarlet."

"I need to make money," I say, because what I *want* is sort of irrelevant. "So am I getting paid for this?"

"Depends."

"Depends on what?"

"On if you do any work," he says, scanning me slowly. "You're not really built for manual labor."

"I'm stronger than I look."

"I know," he says, looking back away. "Didn't say you couldn't do it, just that you weren't *built* for it."

Before I can tell him how full of shit he sounds, he shoves his paperwork at me, forcing it in my hands, letting go so fast half of it clatters to the ground.

"Inventory," he says. "Three usually does it, but he's not here, so congratulations... the job is now *yours*. Go through the crates and make sure it's all accounted for. Seven can help you."

"I, uh, okay."

That wasn't what I expected.

"When you're finished, you get paid. Don't fuck it up."

"Yes, sir," I mumble, mock saluting him, before gathering the papers I dropped and heading for the crates. The paperwork is sort of a mess, just a jumble of words that make little sense. The crates, though, have random letters stamped into them, like the wood has been branded, corresponding with letters on the top of the papers, followed simply by numbers.

GCD: 1205

HMX: 78

QPY: 9

Two dozen crates total. No mention of what's inside.

I look around for Lorenzo, hoping for some clarification, but he's nowhere to be found.

After the trucks are emptied, they drive away, the dock doors again lowered before the men disappear, leaving only Seven.

"Is this some kind of code?" I ask him, waving the papers. "Like some made up language or something? *Ullshitbay.*"

Seven laughs. "*Afraidyay otnay.*"

Afraid not.

"You know Pig Latin?" I ask, surprised. What are the odds?

He shrugs a shoulder. "I've got kids who used to think they were sneaky."

Kids.

The man has *kids*?

"You're kidding," I say. "You're a dad?"

"Twice over," he says. "Two boys."

Huh. "How old?"

"About your age," he says, grinning. "One's eighteen, just started at NYU... the other's twenty-one, finishing up at Columbia."

I gape at him. The man not only has a wife that packs him healthy snacks, but he has kids that attend prestigious universities. "Wow, that's..." *Wow.* "Can I ask you something? Without offending you?"

"Sure," he says.

"Why the hell do you work for *Lorenzo*?"

His eyes widen.

"Nothing against Lorenzo, of course," I say. "You just don't seem like the kind of guy who would ever even cross paths with him."

"Ah, well, you see, I made a career out of crossing paths with men like him when I worked for the department."

"You were a police officer?"

"Yes."

"What happened?"

"Money happened," he says. "You don't make much with the force, and the mob offered me one hell of a deal that came with quite a few zeros attached to it. All I had to do was look the other way a few times and slip them a bit of information, you know, so they could stay one step ahead. I had a family to take care of, a mortgage, private school to pay for, and I thought, hell, wouldn't it be nice to be able to afford a vacation? So I did it. And then I did it again. And the next thing I knew, I was so deep in their payroll there was no separating me from them."

"So you quit the force?"

"More like they fired me." He laughs dryly. "Got locked up six years for bribery. Came out, had nowhere to go, but I needed money, so I had to do something. My wife was working herself half to death trying to stay afloat, and with college tuition, well... there never seems to be *enough* money. Life is expensive."

"That it is," I mumble, turning back to the paperwork, feeling bad for the guy. He's just doing whatever he has to so he can take care of his family. "So, inventory..."

"Self-explanatory. Number beside it is the quantity of whatever's inside."

"What *is* inside?"

He grabs a crowbar, waving it. "Open them and find out."

One at a time, Seven pops open the crates, exposing layers of straw with all sorts of stuff tucked between. Guns, ammunition, liquor... *a lot* of damn liquor. A hundred and seven bottles of Cuban rum.

Not to mention the crate full of cigars.

Cuban, too, I'm guessing.

We make it through most of the crates in about two hours before he pops the second to last one open and pauses. "You'll want to be careful with this one."

"Why? What is it? Bombs?"

I laugh as I walk over to it, while Seven sort of just shrugs, not laughing. What the hell? The list says there are fifty of whatever it is, but all that's in the crate are two more small wooden crates with metal latches on them.

Carefully, I brush some of the straw away before picking up the first crate, damn near dropping it when I catch sight of what's stamped into the side.

"Grenades?" I hiss. "Seriously?"

Fucking *grenades*.

Seven shrugs again as a loud ring cuts through the air, startling me. I jump, jarring the box, but I keep a tight grip on it. Seven pulls out a cell phone, glancing at the screen with a sigh before shoving it back away.

"Just flip the lid and make sure there are twenty-five tubes in each," he says.

I set the crate down, opening it to count. I check the other crate before putting them away, grateful to be done with those.

"So, okay, the guns I understand," I say. "But what the hell does he need with *grenades?*"

"He says it's because he's got terrible aim, but truthfully? He likes to be dramatic."

"Well, then," I mumble, waving toward the last crate. "What's next?"

"Probably the most valuable thing of all."

I can't even imagine what that might be.

Grenade *launchers?*

Seven pops the lid, and I laugh. No straw in this one. Nope, nothing but oranges. *A lot* of oranges.

"You're kidding me, right?" I pick one up, eyeing it. "What, are they filled with cyanide or something?"

"No, they're one-hundred percent authentic Florida oranges, straight off the Gambini groves."

"What does he do with all of them?"

"Eat them, squeeze them and drink them... most get sent out to market, but the rest he keeps."

I glance at the paperwork. *953.*

"Get to counting," Seven says. "The sooner you finish, the sooner we can leave."

Counting oranges, it turns out, is harder than you'd think. I pull them all out, a few at a time, trying to divide them into smaller piles to count, but the sons of bitches want to roll all over the place. I try three times, losing track and miscounting, ending up so far off the mark I have to start over. *Ugh.*

It takes me two hours.

Two hours to count nine-hundred and fifty-three oranges, clutching the last one in my palm as I motion toward Seven, who opted more so to take the supervising role than *help* with me, also. "All there."

I tear at the orange peel, piercing it with my thumb and pulling it apart. Seven watches me warily. "What are you doing?"

"Eating a damn orange," I mutter. "I think I've earned it."

Seven doesn't look like he agrees with me on that, but he says nothing as he shoves the lid back onto the crate. I stroll out of the warehouse and down the alley as Seven locks everything back up. He joins me on the corner, hands shoved in his pockets.

Again, he says nothing.

I follow Seven down the street, to where the car is parked, and tear the orange apart, tossing the scraps on the sidewalk.

I look up as we approach, seeing Lorenzo perched on the hood of the car, waiting.

"Boss," Seven says, nodding in greeting.

"Took you long enough," Lorenzo says, pulling an envelope from his coat and handing it to him.

"She's not the fastest," Seven says. "Felt like I was dealing with the Count from Sesame Street."

I scowl. "Fuck you, Snuffleupagus."

Lorenzo waves toward us. "Go home, Seven."

Seven hesitates. "You sure you don't need me to drive you, boss?"

"I'm sure," Lorenzo says, his eyes fixed on me, watching as I pull a piece of orange off and pop it in my mouth. "I've got it covered."

Seven surrenders the car keys as well as a cell phone, turning it over to Lorenzo before walking down the block, casting a worried glance back at us.

The concern on his face makes my skin prickle.

Lorenzo sits there, clutching both objects in his grasp, his eyes fixed to me so intently I can feel his gaze burrowing *through* me, crawling under my flushed skin.

"You're making him walk?" I ask.

"He lives nearby. It's not an inconvenience."

"Oh."

That's all I say. *Oh.*

This is starting to feel awkward.

He's still staring at me.

"What? You look like there's something you want to say."

"There's *a lot* I want to say. Just debating how much to keep to myself."

"Oh."

Again, that's all I say. *Oh.*

Wow, he sure brings out the eloquence in me, doesn't he?

I just stand there, eating the orange, not sure what else to do. It's sweet, really juicy, and I can tell it's fresh.

Lorenzo waits until I finish before shoving off of the car and approaching me on the sidewalk. I stand still, sucking the juice off of my fingers, as he pauses in front of me, standing toe-to-toe.

"Did you enjoy that?" he asks, his voice low.

"The orange?"

"Stealing from me again," he clarifies. "Did it give you a thrill taking what wasn't yours?"

His question makes my heart pick up pace. "Well, the orange was delicious."

He doesn't react to that. After a moment, he pulls an envelope from his coat. "Your payment."

My fingertips barely graze the thing before he yanks it back away.

"A thousand dollars," he says.

"You're paying me a thousand dollars?"

"No," he says, handing the envelope to me, this time letting me grab it. "That's how much you're paying *me* for that orange you just ate."

"Wait, seriously? An orange costs like a dollar at the store."

"Well, then, you should've gotten one from the store instead of helping yourself to *mine*, huh?" He takes a step back, tossing his keys at me. "You're driving."

I try to catch them but miss, the keys clattering to the sidewalk. As I pick them up, Lorenzo climbs into the passenger seat to wait for me.

This is a terrible idea.

The worst, really.

"In the interest of full disclosure," I say as I climb behind the wheel. "I don't have a driver's license."

"Have you ever driven before?"

"Yes, but..."

Lorenzo waves me off, silencing me with the flick of his wrist, before saying, "I'm sure you can handle it."

Sighing, I start the car, hesitating again. "Out of curiosity, on a scale of one-to-ten, how much are you going to want to kill me if I hit something?"

"Just drive the damn car, Scarlet."

Putting it in gear, I pull away from the curb. It's not far, from Greenpoint to Lorenzo's house, but it's a long enough drive to have me on edge, wound tight by the time I'm parked safely in his driveway.

"For the record, I wouldn't kill you for crashing my car," he says, leaning closer to whisper, "I'd just bill you instead."

Lorenzo goes inside, leaving his phone lying there, not bothering to take the car key back. I sit there for a moment, staring at the steering wheel, before grabbing my envelope, tearing it open.

A stack of cash. I count it, stunned that he's paying me three thousand dollars. I count back through it again, shoving most of it in my pocket, leaving the last thousand in the envelope. I go inside then, the house silent, no sign of Leo or Melody.

Lorenzo is in his library. I almost walk right in but hesitate. He's standing beside the table, staring down at the puzzle spread out along it. After a moment, he picks up a piece, trying it a few places before it snaps right in.

I tap on the doorframe.

His eyes flicker my way, but he says nothing, so I don't move, not going any closer.

Lorenzo tries a few more puzzles pieces in silence, finally getting one into place before saying, "I inherited the orange grove from my father."

"Oh," I say, for the third time in an hour.

"I was young, around four, when he died. My mother hired a hitman. I don't remember much, but I was there when it happened. My mother wanted him dead so she'd inherit everything, not knowing he left it all to *me* instead."

"Ouch."

"She managed to get control of the property while I was still a minor, but I was growing up too fast, and she knew they were running out of time."

I expect him to continue his story, but he grows quiet, simply working on his puzzle. "So what happened?"

"The same guy who killed my father beat me half to death with a shovel before trying to bury me alive. I was sixteen at the time."

I gape at him. "Your mother hired the hitman to kill you?"

"Didn't have to hire him," he says. "She'd married the motherfucker, so getting rid of the stepson was more like an anniversary present."

"I, uh… *fuck*."

"Together, they had Pretty Boy, the picture perfect little family with only one thing still standing in their way: *me*. My eighteenth birthday was approaching, so I knew, sooner or later, he was going to try to kill me again."

"Did he?"

"Never got the chance. They died on the grove they tried to *steal* from me, so I guess that means I got the last laugh."

I'm not sure what to say, so I just blurt out the first word that comes to my mind: "Sorry."

"Don't apologize to me."

"Fine," I say. "I'm *not* sorry."

He laughs to himself, plopping down in his chair as he regards me. "You can come in."

Slowly, I stroll into the library, approaching where he's sitting. I drop the envelope onto his lap. "A thousand bucks."

He picks it up, pulling out the cash, and shoves it right into his pocket without counting. Crumpling the envelope, he tosses it aside before pulling me down to him.

His lips are soft as he presses them to mine, kissing me gently, sweetly, his tongue exploring my mouth and caressing mine. It doesn't last long before he's pushing me back away, creating some distance between us.

"You taste like oranges," he says, licking his lips. "Good oranges. Not that cheap watery shit from a box."

"Does that make you want to ravish me?"

"Or else strangle you," he says. "You walk a thin line."

258

I laugh at that as I turn to walk out, not wanting to press my luck any more tonight, and make it to the doorway when his voice calls out.

"Scarlet?"

I glance back at him. "Yes?"

"I should've killed you."

He says that matter-of-fact. There's no threat to the words, no anger in his voice, just a stark reality that sounds almost sorrowful. He should've killed me.

I've stolen from him, used what belongs to him without permission, taking what I have no right to take. But yet I'm still alive, he's kept me breathing, long after he would've killed others for doing what I did. I'm not sure why that is, why he grants me leniency that he doesn't give others, and judging by his expression, I'd wager a guess that he doesn't know why he does it, either.

I nod. "You should've."

22

Three months.

Ninety days.

The little girl couldn't count that high. She tried to keep track, but she lost her way somewhere in the middle, the days blurring together.

She hadn't left the palace at all. She'd missed three months of sunshine, missed running barefoot in the grass and soaring high on a swing, chasing butterflies and picking flowers for her mother to keep.

The Tin Man wouldn't let her go outside. All the doors were full of locks and armed with an alarm. So most days, when she got tired of drawing, she just stood at the window with Buster and stared out, remembering how her mother used to take her to the park every weekend and push her so high on the swings she thought she could *fly*.

"What are you doing, kitten?"

The little girl turned away from the window, looking to the Tin Man in the doorway of the bedroom. He didn't look like himself today, not wearing a suit, dressed down in a pair of black shorts and a plain white t-shirt with white sneakers. Tattoos *covered* him. She never got to see most of them. They weren't colorful pictures, like some people had, just weird drawings and words in dark ink, like he forgot a piece of paper and wanted to doodle one day.

"Nothing," she said, because it was true.

She wasn't doing anything.

Just more waiting.

"Then come on," he said, nodding his head. "You can come with me to the beach tonight."

Her eyes widened. The *beach*? "Can I go swimming?"

"If you can find something to wear to swim. You have five minutes. Be downstairs."

He walked away. He didn't have to tell her twice. She tore the bedroom apart, finding a pair of black cotton shorts and a yellow tank top, yanking it on. It wasn't a swimsuit, but that didn't matter. She'd swim in a dress if she had to.

She met him downstairs five minutes later, finding him in the foyer, holding a duffel bag with a towel draped over it.

He barely even looked at her before opening the front door, ordering her to go ahead of him. The warm air blasted her when she stepped outside, and she smiled, feeling the last bit of the day's sun on her face. It was already so late. Did people go swimming at nighttime?

She didn't ask, not wanting him to change his mind. They drove about ten minutes in his black car before parking near the shoreline. She could see the sand, could smell the water, could feel the breeze on her face as it rustled her messy hair. It was the best feeling *ever*.

They walked out onto the beach just as the sun set. Nobody was in the water, few people even near the sand. It was closed, she realized. Everything around them was closed, even the amusement park in the distance. Off-season. *Coney Island.*

"Go on," he said, "but stay where I can see you."

"Won't I get in trouble?"

He scoffed. "From *who*?"

"The police?"

The Tin Man laughed, like he found the police funny, before waving toward the water. "Go swim. I will keep you out of trouble."

She didn't know how he could do that, if swimming was illegal, but she wasn't going to pass up the chance. She ran off, the sand soft against her bare feet, the water warm as she crashed right into it.

It didn't matter that she had no one to play with. It didn't matter that she was out there on her own. After three months of only really having Buster, she was kind of used to being alone.

She laughed, and splashed, soaked from head to toe, sand clinging to every part of her. Her attention drifted to the Tin Man every so often, making sure he could see her, and watched as a group of guys joined him. They stood in the darkness, talking, exchanging things, none of them looking like they were having fun out there on the beach. *Flying monkeys.* They weren't like the others, though. These guys were new. They didn't have tattoos. The Tin Man turned away from them eventually, his attention on her. He waved, motioning for her to come to him.

Time to go.

The little girl ran out of the water, heading straight for him, flinging water everywhere. She skidded to a stop near the group, her stomach queasy.

One man let out a low whistle, a guy with freckles like polka dots and eyes like seaweed. "Man, she looks *just* like her, doesn't she?"

The Tin Man made a face as he shoved the towel around the little girl, covering even her head so she could barely see anyone. He pushed her behind him, away from the group, as he took a step toward the man, standing right up against him, his voice gravely serious as he said, "I let you have the *suka,* I let you stick your cock in her, and I did not kill you for it, but if you so much as ever *ask* about my daughter again, *svinya,* I will cut off your balls. I do not care what leverage you think you hold over me."

The Tin Man shoved against him, making the man retreat a few steps, and stood there, holding his ground, as the group left. Once they were alone, he turned back to the little girl, drying her hair as he crouched down before wrapping the towel around her properly and securing it under her arm.

"Are you hungry, kitten? You must be starving. I have been so busy today I have not fed you."

He didn't wait for her response before standing back up and grabbing her hand. She looked at his inked fingers in surprise as he pulled her along.

He'd never held her hand before.

"What do you like?" he asked, looking down at her. "You do not like *my* food, so tonight I will treat you to yours."

Her eyes widened. "Really?"

"Yes," he said. "Take a pick."

"Peanut butter and grape jelly!"

He laughed. "I do not think we will find that here."

She ended up with hot dogs, eating two whole ones by herself, and he even bought her a chocolate ice cream cone before they returned to the car to make the trip back to the palace. She smiled as they drove along, watching out the window, sitting in the front seat of his car, where she wasn't *supposed* to sit.

"Thank you, Daddy," she said quietly when they parked.

It had been a good day. She felt *happy*. Maybe the Tin Man wasn't so bad. Maybe she should think of him as something else, maybe something like Daddy.

Just Daddy.

He cupped her chin and pressed a kiss to her forehead, lingering for a moment, before whispering, "If only you were not so much like the *suka*."

23

Lorenzo

Three injured. Three dead.

That's what all the news reports said.

Six people caught bullets that night at Mystic—half of them died, while the other half lived.

The neurotic asshole that exists inside of me loves the symmetry of it. Three has always been my favorite number. Three books in a trilogy. Three sheets to the wind. They say the third time is the charm. Three strikes and you're out. Rock, paper, scissors... Beetlejuice, Beetlejuice, Beetlejuice... the good, the bad, and the ugly... need I go on?

Hell, there are three good *Star Wars* movies. I'll leave it up to you to figure out which ones I'm talking about.

They say deaths come in threes, too.

I don't know who *they* are, but they're on the mark in this case. Three dead because a madman burst into a club, hunting for Scarlet.

That's one hell of a burden to carry.

"Sorrowful."

Scarlet turns to me when I say that word.

"That's how you look," I tell her, grabbing her wrist, my fingers pressing into the 'S' tattoo. "Sorrowful."

She glances down at where I'm touching her, giving a small half-smile, before looking back at the club in front of us. "That's not what it stands for."

"I'm starting to think it doesn't stand for a damn thing," I say. "*Sucker.* Me. For fucking thinking it had any meaning. Maybe you just like the letter S."

"Maybe."

"Maybe it's not even an S at all," I say, examining it. "Maybe you got fucked up one night and woke up the next morning and there it was, and even *you* don't know what it stands for."

"Maybe."

"Or maybe you're just being salty as hell."

She pulls her arm from my grasp. "Or maybe it doesn't involve you, so it shouldn't concern you. You ever think about that?"

"Smart ass."

She laughs, the sorrowful look fading. "Shut up."

"Make me, slut."

She gasps, shoving me so hard I stumble a step. "You *asshole*."

"What? It starts with an 's'."

"Such a shithead," she says. "Can't you just... be *nice* for once? People died here, Lorenzo. I'm trying to, you know..."

"Be sorrowful?"

"Be *respectful*."

"Oh." I make a face, waving that off. "Fuck them."

"What?"

"Fuck them," I say again. "You think a single one of them would've mourned *you*, Scarlet? You think they'd be respectful if *you* died?"

She's quiet, staring at the club, not answering that.

"So fuck them," I say for the third time. "You have to be careful who you give pieces of yourself to, because even a little bit here and there adds up to a hell of a lot eventually, and it's not worth it, losing yourself to them, giving yourself to people who don't give a fuck about you. You keep pouring yourself into other people and you'll just wind up empty."

She sighs. "You're—"

"An asshole, I know."

She cuts her eyes at me. "I was going to say you're right."

I cock an eyebrow at her. "I'm *what*?"

"You're right."

"Well, I'll be damned. She's learning."

"Kiss my ass."

"Maybe later," I say, stepping away from the curb to approach the club. "Other things to do first."

"Wait, what? Where are you going?"

"Inside."

"Why?"

"Figured I'd send my condolences to Georgie Porgie while I'm here."

"How do you even know he's here?"

"I don't," I say, glancing back at her. "You coming?"

She scoffs. "No way."

"Suit yourself, then." I wave her off. "Do whatever you want, Scarlet."

The door is unlocked, so I walk right in. Everything has been cleaned up, the floors scrubbed, bloodstains covered, holes patched, all evidence of what happened wiped away. I hear voices coming from the office so I head that way, turning the corner and startling the men inside.

No hesitation, guns are pulled, aimed my direction.

"Hello to you all, too."

Amello stands at his desk, surrounded by mounds of paperwork, sorting through all of it, shredding *a lot* of shit. "What do you want, Scar?"

"A friendlier greeting would be nice," I say. "So would a pepperoni slice. Kind of hungry. Thirsty, too, so maybe a drink. Wouldn't say *no* to having my dick sucked, either."

He raises his gaze, meeting mine. "What do you want from *me?*"

I step into the office, moving past the armed men, and take a seat in a chair across from Amello at the desk. "You could tell these buffoons to do something about their guns. Use them or lose them, if you know what I'm saying."

Amello motions for them to lower their weapons.

"No offense, Scar, but..."

He pauses.

Hesitates.

I learned long ago that when someone says 'no offense' there's about a seventy-six percent chance they're about to offend the fuck out of you. They think those bullshit words will help them get away with it, but that doesn't work with me. I know it, and he knows it, because it's clearly written in the deep lines of his troubled face.

"But? Go on, I'm listening."

"I can't do this right now," he grumbles, plopping down in his chair, running his hands down his face. "I've got the cops riding my ass, my business is in shambles... nobody wants to work with someone facing all this *heat*... and the Russians... the fucking Russians!" He lets out a manic laugh that sounds strained, like he's damn close to shedding tears. "They shoot up my place, they attack me, my business, all because of that little *bitch*! If I knew where she was right now, I'd wring her fucking neck!"

"That's a bit harsh, don't you think?"

"Harsh? Three of my guys are *dead*."

"I don't see how that's her fault."

"They were after *her*!"

"But you knew that, didn't you? You knew the Russians wanted her, and you used that to your advantage."

"I *helped* her," he says, his back straightening, a hint of anger in his voice. "She had nowhere to go, no one to turn to, so I took pity on her. I gave her a job. I gave her a place to live. And look where it got me. I'm *fucked*. I should've turned the little bitch over to Aristov the second I realized who she was. She's not worth the trouble. He can have her."

"I beg to differ," I say. "He wants her, he's going to have to go through me first."

"You?" His expression flickers with surprise before he lets out another laugh. "She got you, huh? Charmed the pants right off of you, did she? Got you thinking she's some damsel in distress that you can save? You know nothing about her. You want my advice? Wash your hands of it. Toss her out on his front porch, be done with the bitch."

Before he can say another word, I spring out of the seat, grabbing him by the hair on the back of his head and slamming his face against the top of the desk. *BAM.* He cries out, blood spewing out onto the paperwork, streaming from his busted nose. Yanking his head back up, I whip out the gun from my waistband, pointing it at his neck, pressing right where the carotid is.

His men react, drawing their weapons once more, shouting, panicked, their hands shaking hard.

Makes me wonder if they've ever shot anyone.

"They got their guns back out, Georgie," I say. "Are we using them this time? Because I'm not opposed to pulling the trigger if that's where we're going with this. Just say the word and I'll blow this artery apart."

He swallows thickly, raising his hands up as if in surrender, his voice again strained as he says, "Put down the guns."

Nobody moves.

"Uh-oh, they're not listening."

"Drop the fucking guns," Amello growls. "Get out of here! All of you! Leave us!"

It takes them a moment before they lower their weapons and retreat from the office, backing up into the club, leaving us alone. Amello glares at me, blood streaked all over his face, his eyes glassy. He's scared, yeah, but he's furious, too. I think he might be the kind to cry when he's angry, because he looks damn close to boo-hoo'ing.

"You owe me a couch, Georgie," I say, letting go of him. "I came here to collect."

"What the hell are you talking about?"

"A couch," I say. "*My* couch. You see, it got fucked up when I blew holes in that incompetent little asshole you sent to kill me."

"I don't know what you're talking about."

"Sure you don't." I pull the gun away, backing up a step, but I keep it trained on him, just in case... *just in case I decide to blow his head off for the hell of it.* "You owe me a couch, so my guys will be here in about three minutes to collect."

He winces, clutching the bridge of his nose.

"Nothing to say? Speak now or forever shut your mouth."

Nothing.

The door to the club opens on the three-minute mark, noise filtering in, familiar voices greeting my ears. My men are here. Amello grows even tenser, his shoulders squaring as he holds his head up. His men are outnumbered now, so I know *they're* not going to try shit.

"So, nice talk," I say, lowering my gun, aiming it at the floor. "My condolences on your club, but it wasn't her fault. It was *yours.* Maybe if you weren't so fucking weak, Georgie, people wouldn't do this shit to you all the time."

I turn, walking to the doorway, glancing at my guys. Amello's men are still lurking, off to the side, watching.

"Which one, boss?" Seven asks, looking around.

I point to a black leather couch nearby, one with gold accents. "That one will work."

A few of my guys pick it up, moving it out to a truck outside, one of their personal vehicles, I'm guessing. I don't know the specifics. I don't micromanage shit. I just give the orders. It's up to them to figure out the rest.

Seven lingers, playing my shadow as usual.

I'm about to tuck my gun back into my waistband when I hear a voice behind me in the office, Amello muttering under his breath, "Bitch is lucky I didn't turn her over to them sooner."

Uh-oh.

I turn to the side, aiming the gun back into the office, but I don't even look, because frankly, it wouldn't matter. Shooting blindly, it's kind of like Russian Roulette. If the bullets all miss him, well, hell, guess it's his lucky day.

BANG.

BANG.

BANG.

I unload the gun, bullet after bullet, pulling the trigger in rapid succession until it does nothing but click.

CLICK.

CLICK.

CLICK.

His men react, going for weapons, but my men are around, so well, they punk out, as expected. Seven draws his gun as the others rush in, the group locked in a showdown as I slowly turn the rest of the way around.

"Aw, look at that…" Amello's slumped in his chair with a hole in his face, damn near right between his eyes. Couldn't have been more perfect if I tried. "Bullseye."

I slide my gun in my waistband, turning back to the others, zeroing in on Amello's men. "You've got two choices, fellas. Either man-up and pull the trigger or put the guns down and get out of here. You've got about, oh, thirty seconds before *I* decide whether you live or die, so choose quickly." I glance at my watch. "Tick… tick… tick…"

They run. I'm not surprised. Scatter like cockroaches when a light flicks on. My guys, they leave once the others flee, all except Seven, who waits for me to go before him.

"How'd you get here, boss?" Seven asks when we step outside. "Do you need a ride?"

"No, Scarlet's…" I look around, up and down the block. She's not here. The BMW isn't parked where it had been, some piece of shit Honda now there, and it doesn't take a genius to riddle this one out. The woman took off in my car. *Goddamn it, Scarlet.* "Actually, make that a *yes.*"

* * *

I've been told a time or two that I spiral.

Zero to sixty in the blink of an eye.

One second, I'm perfectly fine, laughing, smiling. The next, I've got my hands around someone's throat, choking the life out of them.

There's probably a name for whatever's wrong with me, but I've got no interest in a diagnosis. I don't need treatment. Until people stop being ignorant, I'm going to keep on getting pissed. No little mood-stabilizing pill can stop that from happening.

But still, sometimes, I can feel it. I feel myself spiraling hard, and falling far, making mountains out of molehills that even *I* struggle to climb.

And today? I'm feeling it.

My hands shake.

I can hardly see straight.

Shaky fingers reach down, picking up a puzzle piece, and I try it in a few places before giving up, moving to another, and another, and yet a-fucking-nother, before finally snapping one in. Adrenaline still surges through my veins, not yet faded. I'm trying to calm down, focusing on my puzzle in the dim library, and it's helping a bit to keep me from lashing out but it's doing a shit job of clearing my mind of all the chaos.

"Boss?" Seven calls out, tapping on the doorframe from out in the hallway. "Your gun."

I glance at him. He cleaned it for me, reloading the thing. I've come to trust him a lot, I realize. If he makes a mistake, next time I pull that trigger something might not happen, and where's the fun in *that?*

I hold my hand out. "Give it here."

He steps into the library, approaching, slipping the gun into my palm. I grip it tightly, not putting it away yet, just feeling it in my hand.

"The guys switched the couches out," Seven says. "What do you want to be done with the old one?"

"Just throw it out by the curb."

He nods. "Yes, boss."

Seven lingers. I can feel his gaze. Setting the gun on the corner of the table, letting go of it, I turn to him. "Something you care to talk about?"

"I'm surprised you let those guys go this afternoon," he says. "You let them live."

"So?"

"So you've been giving a lot of second chances lately."

"Is that a problem for you?" I ask. "Figured you'd be happy

to have less dead bodies around, since I'm pretty sure murder is a sin in *every* religion, including yours."

"It's not a problem for me," he says. "I just want to be sure it won't lead to a problem for *you.*"

I stare at him. "You think I'm getting soft?"

"Not at all," he says. "But every second chance you give is just another opportunity for that person to harm you again."

"Yeah, well, that sure keeps things interesting, doesn't it? A win was always a win to me, no matter how it came about, but where's the fun in winning if it's always by default? If I'm the only man left in the race, does it even really matter if I cross the finish line? Because I'm not entirely sure that's a win for me anymore, Seven. I think everyone else just *lost.*"

He doesn't seem to get the distinction. In fact, he's looking at me like I might be going crazy. I've done *a lot* in the presence of this man. I've slit throats, stolen money, fucked women, and blown up stuff, and he never once looked at me like he's looking at me right now.

Like I'm making no goddamn sense.

Like maybe it's his right to question me.

Nuh-uh, 'fraid not.

I snatch the gun from the corner of the table, switching the safety off before cocking it, pointing it at his feet.

BANG.

BANG.

BANG.

He jumps back, out of the way, his reflexes fast, as three shots tear through the floor of the house, right where he was standing. The bewilderment leaves his face real fucking quick, replaced with one I'm used to seeing aimed at me: *fear.*

Just like that, he's sweating profusely, eyes wide, stance guarded, like he wants to get the hell away from me but he knows he can't go, not like *this.*

I have a lot of respect for Seven, respect others didn't seem to have for him. *Once a cop, always a cop.* That's what they say. NYPD gets in their blood and the only way to get it out is to spill every last drop. But I've always *liked* that about him. He is who he is. He's a man that would do anything for his family, and I mean *anything*, and I've been able to use that loyalty to my advantage.

But don't think he's indispensable.

Don't think I *need* him.

Don't think I won't shoot him in the fucking foot if he's not smart enough to jump out of the way of the bullet flying toward him.

I'm not training monkeys here. This isn't a three-ring circus. The man's gotta be able to follow his gut.

"What gets you out of bed in the morning, Seven?"

"My family," he says quietly. "They have needs. It's my responsibility to make sure they're taken care of, no matter what."

That's the answer I expected.

"Do you know what gets *me* out of bed in the morning?"

He doesn't even hesitate before saying, "Leo."

I laugh and set the gun back down, seeing him visibly relax once it's out of my hand. "I wish I could agree with that. I wish I could say he gets me out of bed. He used to, you know, but he's grown up, and when it comes down to it, he doesn't need me. Not like he used to. He keeps me grounded, keeps me from doing a lot of things I shouldn't, but that's not because he needs me, Seven. It's because I raised him right, and if I become a danger to him, he knows to cut his losses. *Snip, snip.*"

"So what gets you out of bed?"

I sit down, not sure how to answer that, so I just go with the word that makes the most sense: "Hope."

Surprise flickers across his face.

That, he didn't expect.

"Hope," he repeats.

"Hope that maybe today will be exciting," I say. "Maybe today I won't be so goddamn *bored*. Maybe, if I get my ass out of bed, something will actually happen. Maybe something will get my blood pumping and I'll *feel* things instead of wasting away in tedium. Maybe, just maybe, today will be different and I'll finally find a *real* reason to get out of bed in the morning. I don't begrudge you your purpose, Seven. I respect it. You do what you have to. But don't walk in my house, questioning what *I'm* doing, because if you step on my toes, I'll shoot yours off. You got me?"

"Yes, boss."

Just as he says that, a ringing shatters the silence. Sighing, I pull the phone from my pocket. *Blocked caller.* I toss it at Seven, annoyed. "Take this fucking thing before I break it."

He catches it, nodding in acknowledgement, before leaving the library.

I sit there once he's gone, listening as the guys move around the house, making themselves at home as usual, as I stare at the fresh holes in the floor. It's funny, I think, how looks can be so deceiving. Here we are in suburbia, with picket fences and big backyards, perfection from the outside, yet nobody knows what goes on within the walls.

I work on my puzzle some more, trying to distract myself, and hear the front door open after a while. I figure it's Leo getting home from work, so I'm surprised when tapping echoes through the library, followed by the soft feminine voice. "Knock, knock..."

Scarlet.

I don't acknowledge her, and she stands there, quietly waiting, and waiting, and waiting, until her patience grows thin. Groaning, she shoves away from the doorframe and takes a single step closer, right over the threshold.

Grabbing the gun, I cock it, aiming it her direction, my finger on the trigger, ready to pull it when she takes an immediate step back.

"Whoa, buddy," she says, raising her hands defensively. "Testy today."

"You stole my car."

"I *borrowed* it," she says, pulling the keys from her pocket and holding them up. "It's right outside."

I look at her, raising my eyebrows, voice dead serious as I repeat myself. "You stole my car."

"No," she says. "I didn't. You told me to do whatever I wanted. Those were your exact words. *Do whatever you want to do,*

Scarlet."

"I didn't mean take my car!"

"Yeah, well, you really didn't specify, did you? 'Do whatever you want to do' means I could do whatever I wanted to do."

"And what, you wanted to steal my car?"

"I wanted to drive it," she says, "so I borrowed it."

My fingertips are tingling, my heart pounding hard. The adrenaline, as it merges with the anger, is one hell of a rush. It almost makes me sick to my stomach, the way it takes over my insides.

God, I want to shoot this woman…

"So you borrowed it," I say, repeating her words.

"Got you on a technicality, huh?" she says as she leans against the doorframe, like she's not worried at all.

"You think I won't kill you? Do you honestly think I won't pull this trigger, technicality or not?"

"I think you might," she says.

"That doesn't scare you?"

"Should it?"

She sounds genuine, asking that, like she really wants to know if she *should* be scared. I want to say yes, it should terrify her, because it terrifies damn near everybody else, but I don't know… would *I* be scared? I don't think so. The fear of dying left me long ago, the first time death knocked at my door. I don't know exactly what she's been through, but being as the head of the Russian mob is currently hunting her, I'm thinking shooting her in the face would be merciful compared to what he might want her for.

But mercy killings aren't really my thing.

"Where'd you go?" I ask, lowering the gun, setting it back down on the table.

"Home," she says.

"Home?"

"Yes."

I motion for her to come in, and she strolls closer as I say, "I wasn't aware you had one of those."

She pauses in front of me. "Doesn't everybody?"

She's not making much sense at the moment.

She seems almost... *dazed*.

I grasp her chin, tilting her head as I pull her face closer to me. Her eyes are bloodshot, glassy. "Are you high?"

She laughs bitterly at my question. "No."

"There's something *off* about you."

Scarlet clutches my wrist, trying to pry my hand away. "I've had a rough day, so excuse me for not being my bright-eyed, bushy-tailed self, Lorenzo."

I let go when she averts her gaze.

She's been crying, I realize. She sucked it the fuck up before walking in here, but there's no doubt she was crying.

I look at my puzzle, grabbing a piece, trying it in a few places. "Where's *home*, Scarlet? With the Russian asshole?"

She laughs bitterly again as she takes a step over, helping herself to my chair. Tilting her head back, she scrubs her hands over her face. "No, *not* with him."

"Good," I say, "because if I find out you took my car for a rendezvous with that jackass, I *will* shoot you, technicality or not."

"You think I'd...? That I would really... with *him*?" She blinks rapidly, staring at me, looking like she might try to cry again, this time in front of me. "That's just... *wow*. You don't understand. You just don't get it. If you did, you wouldn't think... *ugh!*"

She throws her hands up, shaking her head. Okay, she didn't cry, but I definitely offended her.

"So, tell me about home."

"Do you really give a shit?"

"Maybe."

She's quiet for a moment.

I continue working on my puzzle.

"It's a white house with a bright red door and wooden floors. It's small, I guess, but it's two stories tall, two bedrooms, one bathroom, you know, with everything else that comes in a house. It has a lot of little spaces, cabinets and closets and cubby holes."

"And that's home?"

"Yes."

"So why are you *here*?"

"Because home is where the heart is, I guess," she says.

"And what, your heart's *here*? I need some elaboration. You're weirding me the fuck out with this."

She laughs at that. "No, but it's not there, either. Not anymore. It's just... it's hard to explain. I wish it was still there, and seeing the place, well, it just reminds me that it's gone."

"So why go there?"

"Because I need to remember."

"Remember what?"

"That I have a heart still out there somewhere."

I don't know what to say to that.

Anything I do say will probably make me sound like an asshole.

Because it's easier, you know, to forget the heart exists at all.

But I'm getting the idea that her heart may be what gets her out of bed in the morning, so I won't begrudge her that. To each their own.

The front door to the house opens again. I hear a commotion, something getting the guys riled up, voices loud.

I pick up the gun again, thinking I probably ought to just glue the fucking thing in my hand with the way today is going, and step out of the library, pausing in the hallway, glancing toward the front door, straight to someone I quite frankly didn't expect to ever see again.

Three.

He looks at me as soon as I aim the gun. Fear flashes in his eyes as he raises his hands. "No, no, wait! *Please!*"

"A week," I say. "You've been gone for *seven* days."

"I know," he says, "but it wasn't my fault!"

He looks pretty damn rough. Someone worked him over good. Fresh bruises. Old bruises. He's filthy. He *stinks*. I can smell him the whole way down the hall. It makes my nose twitch. "Whose fault is it?"

"The Russian," he says. "Aristov."

Huh.

"He snatched me that night at Limerence. Me and this girl, we were going at it, next thing I know I wake up in some fucking basement, chained up like a dog."

"So, what, you got roofied? Kept as a pet for the Russians? What did they want?"

"Her."

Three's gaze flickers past me. I don't have to turn around to know Scarlet will be standing there.

Of course he wants her.

"He just kept saying she was his," Three continues. "He wanted to find her. He wanted me to help."

"And did you?"

Shock passes across his face. "What? *Fuck no!* I told him to fuck off. He said he just needed an address, that he'd do the rest, that I didn't have to get my hands dirty, but I wasn't telling him shit."

"So how'd you get out of there?"

"I guess after a week, he realized I wasn't cracking, so he let me go."

"He *let* you go," I say with disbelief. "Which means he probably *followed* you."

He shakes his head adamantly. "He didn't, I swear. Nobody did, I made sure of it! I took five trains and three cabs, even rerouted into the city, just in case. He was going to kill me, I think, but he decided to have me bring you a message. He said—"

Ringing cuts him off. He falters.

Seven pulls my phone from his pocket, glancing at the screen, shaking his head.

Three's voice chimes back in. "He said to answer the phone when he calls you. He's tired of getting your voicemail."

Son of a bitch.

Guess the mystery of the *blocked number* has been solved. I'm still not answering it.

The ringing stops.

I lower the gun, shoving it in my waistband.

"Well, then, who's up for making a trip to Limerence?" I ask. "There's a lot of money in it for you."

Hands shoot up.

Every single one of them volunteers—even Three, as fucked up as he already is, and Seven, whose wife would kill him if he stepped foot in that place. My guys, they don't back down from a challenge, especially where cold hard cash is involved.

"Go tell that Russian bastard I'll think about accepting his call when he grows some balls and unblocks his number, because pussies don't get talked to, they only get *fucked.*"

I turn, to go back into the library, catching Scarlet's concerned gaze.

"Oh, and say it just like that, word-for-word," I say, glancing back at the guys. "And if you survive, when you come back here for payment, don't let him follow you. I mean it. You endanger my brother, I'll kill you all myself."

24
Morgan

Is a library still a library if there aren't any books?

Wouldn't it be more of a study?

That's what I'm thinking about, as I sit on the floor in the library right beside the door, knees pulled up to my chest, arms wrapped around them, back against the wall. I mean, he's got a handful of books, maybe a dozen, but the shelves are pretty much barren. Are twelve books enough to push it into library territory?

I don't know.

Don't really care, either.

But I've got to think about something or else my mind will just drift to thoughts I'm trying desperately not to have, so I'm thinking about him, and his room, and his *life*...

Lorenzo.

He's working on the puzzle. I've seen him do it before in little spurts, but he's been at it now for hours consistently, making quite a bit of progress as I watch. He's methodical, the whole process clearly serious to him, but at the same time I think he's actually enjoying himself. It's *strange*. Every now and then he'll get this look on his face, like contentment and relief and pride all rolled into one.

I've seen the man in the throes of passion. I've seen him excited, and agitated, and dangerously cold. I've watched his emotions fluctuate the spectrum, but I think this is the first time I've ever seen him *calm*.

Like, this is the guy who raised his little brother to be the responsible, respectful guy Leo is. *This* is the guy who could actually have a library and not just a barren room with bullet holes littering the floor.

Yeah, I noticed them...

He's wearing his glasses, a light illuminating the area around the table, although the rest of the room is dark. Night fell hours ago. We're the only ones here. None of his guys have come back yet.

He doesn't seem worried, but *I* am.

Knowing Kassian, they could all be dead.

And I kind of like the guys, you know, what I know of them. Not a single one has ever made a pass at me, thinking because I've done certain things obviously that's all I am. Men that treat me like a *person*... what a concept. So I'd rather them not lose their lives because I'm here.

"I'm going to bed," I say quietly, pushing up from the floor. I know Lorenzo hears me, because he glances my way, but he says nothing.

I make it down the hall, toward the stairs, when the front door shoves open. My heart stalls a beat, thinking finally *maybe* one of them is back, but Leo walks in, along with Melody.

"Hey, Morgan!" Melody says. "I love the color of that top!"

I glance down. It's some watercolor-looking mash-up. I took the money Lorenzo paid me and invested in some new clothes of my own. "Thanks."

Leo smiles in greeting, and I return his smile, but jet out of there before any further conversation happens. Trekking upstairs, I kick my shoes off, pulling off my jeans and unhooking my bra before climbing into the bed, snuggling up with a pillow.

I'm not tired.

Hell, I can't even sleep.

I lay here, listening to the sounds from downstairs.

Maybe another hour passes, I don't know, before the front door opens, voices rushing through the house. Carefully, I climb out of the bed, creeping out into the hall, pausing as I lean against the banister at the top of the stairs. They're all here, gathering in the hallway, Declan and Frank even sharing a laugh about something. I can't hear much of what they're saying, but they survived, so I guess that's something.

I make my way back to the bed, curling up on my side, hugging the pillow again. Relieved. *For now.* Barely a minute passes before I hear noise, and I peek over just as Lorenzo walks into the room. He meets my eyes, so he knows I'm awake, but he says nothing, tugging off his shirt, stripping down to nothing before climbing into the bed beside me.

His arms snake around me, pulling me back into him, his lips going right to my neck, leaving a trail of kisses along the sliver of exposed skin.

"Tell me a story," he says, hand sliding beneath my shirt to palm a breast.

I smile to myself. That's his not-so-subtle way of telling me he wants to stick it in. "Why don't you tell *me* one?"

"You didn't like the last one I told you," he says, tugging at my underwear, pushing it down to my knees, just enough for his other hand to slide between my thighs. A soft moan escapes me when his fingertips graze my clit, and I shove the underwear the rest of the way down, kicking them off to spread my legs, so he can reach better.

"I'm sure you can come up with a better one."

"True story or fairy tale?"

"Hmmm... both."

I yelp, surprised, when he yanks me around, over on top of him. He lays flat on his back as I straddle his waist, his cock *right there*, hard, pressing against me. I shift my hips, rubbing against him, my hands flat against his bare chest. My shirt is long enough to cover everything so he can't see, but I know he feels it. He lets out a low groan, wrapping his arms around me, pulling me down for a kiss.

I lose myself for a moment, kissing him deeply, roughly, groaning as he nips at my lips, tingles flowing through my body when he grasps my hips, pulling me up. I feel it, his cock pressing into me, slowly slipping inside as he teases me with the tip. My head goes fuzzy, warmth consuming me.

It isn't until he thrusts up, hard, filling me completely, that it knocks some sense back into my brain. I pull from his lips, barely able to get the word out. "Condom."

He looks at me, his hands moving, running along the curve of my ass before he grabs my shirt, pulling it off and tossing it over the edge of the bed. His gaze scans me, from the top of my head to where we're connected as he reaches over and starts rubbing my clit. "Do I need one?"

"I, uh... I mean..."

What kind of question is that?

"I'll pull out," he says, shifting his hips, pulling out just a bit before pushing back in. "If that's what you're worried about."

"I, uh... *Christ*... I can't get pregnant."

"You physically can't, or you mean getting pregnant is the worst thing that could happen?"

"Uh, I mean..." Fuck, he feels good, deep inside of me, nothing between us. "Both."

I start moving, rolling my hips, sliding up and down slowly on him. My brain is still trying to argue a point, chanting, '*condom, condom, condom*,' like a twelve-year-old boy, but the haze is taking it over, the tingles blocking it out. '*Fuck it*,' my heart frantically beats. '*Just let him fuck you, you know you want it.*'

Closing my eyes, I gasp as he thrusts up into me, meeting my rhythm. His fingers steadily stroke my clit, rubbing circles, sending jolts of pleasure along my spine, stronger and stronger, until the explosion hits.

My muscles seize up, my toes curling as he rides me through a strong orgasm. As soon as it starts to fade, he grabs me by the back of my neck, pulling me down closer to him, making me look him in the face.

I brace myself, hands flat against his chest, holding on as he bucks hard, fucking me, gripping tighter every time my eyelids start to flutter, parts of me trying to drift away.

Another orgasm hits, and I cry out, my breaths strained, but before I can recover, Lorenzo throws me off of him, catching me off guard as he pins me to the bed.

"What—?"

Before I can get anything else out, Lorenzo covers my mouth with his hand, squeezing my face, silencing my words. Shoving my legs apart, hitching my knees up, he thrusts inside of me, barely giving me a second to adjust before he starts to fuck me.

Hard.

Deep.

Fast.

BAM

BAM

BAM

I scream into his palm as sensations flow through me. Pleasure and pain warps every inch of me as he rests his body weight on top of me, making my chest ache, my muscles clenching. My fingers dig into his back, scratching at the skin, as he brings his mouth to my ear, his voice low and gritty.

"Once upon a time, there was a woman—a woman with a gorgeous little body and a mouth made of *sin*. The only thing sweeter than this woman's pussy was the thirst she had inside of her, a thirst for fucking and fighting, for tempting fate," he says, and I let out a whimper, gripping to him tightly, as another orgasm starts to take over. *Fuck*.

It hits me so intense I buck against him, my fingernails tearing skin as I bite his palm.

"Jesus Christ," he growls, yanking his hand away from my mouth, griping instead to my jaw, shoving my head away, forcing the side of my face into the mattress. His mouth is back on my ear, tongue swirling around it before he says, "This woman, she tempted fate so much it was a goddamn miracle she wasn't dead, but she was lucky, I think, because fate brought her a man, one who would kill for a sip of the thirst inside of her, who would start a war over that sweet, *sweet* pussy."

His words send a chill through me as I close my eyes. He fucks and threatens, kisses and caresses, grabs and bites, over and over and over again, until my body starts to give out. Groaning, he pulls away from me, shoving my legs further apart as he pulls out.

Opening my eyes, I watch in the darkness, breathing heavily, as he strokes himself, coming *right there*, between my thighs. He rubs it in then, gently stroking my clit with his fingertips, before leaning down, kissing along my stomach, his tongue circling my belly button, before moving down even further, his mouth on my pussy.

"Oh God," I whisper, my toes curling. I don't know how the hell he does it, bringing my body right back to life again with nothing more than the tip of his tongue.

He's gentle, so fucking gentle, almost painfully so as he brings me to yet another orgasm. I gasp, grabbing ahold of his hair, arching my back as the pleasure ripples through my trembling thighs. As soon as I collapse back onto the bed, he makes his way back up, kissing along my stomach, before his mouth finds mine.

I kiss him, tasting myself on his lips, but more than that, I can taste *him*. Every inch of my body flushes at that realization.

"I think you're trying to kill me," I whisper.

He laughs into my mouth, nipping at my bottom lip. "If I was really trying to kill you, Scarlet, you'd be dead."

* * *

The sun's starting to rise outside, but you can't tell it looking at the horizon. Thick gray clouds cover every inch of sky, blocking the warm orange glow from appearing. Everything just seems to gradually get lighter, like a veil is being lifted, exposing what was already hidden beneath.

Sunrise, it always makes me feel hope, another day dawning, another chance at things turning around for me, but today?

It all just felt so horribly *bleak*.

"Ten months," I say. "Before we know it, it'll be a year."

An entire *year*. I can't even fathom it.

Detective Jones lets out an exasperated sigh as he scrubs his hands over his bleary face, rubbing the overgrown scruff along his jaw. He looks like *shit*. His suit is rumpled. There's a stain on his white shirt. He's in need of a trim, his hair sticking up in a few places, and his socks, well… they don't even match.

He's a *mess.*

But I have no sympathy for him.

Maybe that makes me a bitch.

I used to come here, begging, pleading, feeling like a burden for needing his help, but those feelings faded as I became more jaded. The first few months were the worst, though. Back then, I didn't think the tears would ever stop. But at some point along the way, my anger surfaced when I realized I was on my own, that nobody could help me. I had to help myself.

And here we are, ten months in, and I'm still treading water, closer to sinking than I am to swimming. I'm slowly *drowning.*

Gabe picks up his coffee mug, gently blowing into it, steam rising out, surrounding his face like a cloud. I got here before him this morning, was waiting in the lobby when he eventually wandered in, fifteen minutes late for his usual shift, which is fifteen minutes he could've spent working on *my* case.

Yeah, right... like that would ever happen.

"You shouldn't be here," he mutters, sipping his coffee.

"Yeah, well, where else am I supposed to go?"

"Wherever you've been these past few weeks," he says. "Where *have* you been, anyway?"

"Around."

He casts an annoyed look my way, not liking my evasive answer, but I'm not telling him where I've been staying. That information is *classified.*

"After the attack at the club, I figured you'd be laying low, maybe *finally* getting the hell out of the city," he says. "Especially with George Amello being dead."

I gape at him. "He's *dead?*"

He nods, swirling his chair back and forth, still sipping his coffee... *still not doing any work.* "Someone shot him."

I sigh, looking away from him to glance out the window.

It's silent for a few minutes.

George is dead, and it's probably my fault.

"I went to the house the other day," I say quietly. "I haven't gone there since everything happened."

He mutters something under his breath. I don't catch it all, just a few words here and there, notably '*stupid*' and '*death wish*'.

"It looks the same," I tell him. "It was strange. Seeing it, being there... it felt like just yesterday, like no time at all has passed. I didn't expect that. I didn't expect it to still feel so *raw*."

He doesn't say anything, but the look he gives me says enough: 'get over it'. He's never uttered those words directly, but I know he means them, I know he *thinks* them, every single time he looks at me this way. *Pity*. He pities me. Not enough, obviously, or else he'd actually do something about my situation, but just enough for him to humor me, for him to pretend to want to help.

"Maybe you should talk to someone," he suggests.

"I am. I'm talking to you."

"I mean somebody who might be able to help you."

"Again, I thought I was."

He sighs, setting his coffee down. "I mean a therapist, Morgan. Maybe a grief counselor."

"I don't need a shrink. I just need someone to give a fuck about me."

"Come on, don't be that way," he says, shoving out of his chair to step closer, pausing in front of me. "You *know* I care. I'm doing everything I can. I'm monitoring the situation."

"Monitoring the situation." I shake my head. "That sounds a hell of a lot like you're just sitting back, watching it happen."

He grasps my chin, his thumb stroking along my jawline as he tilts my head his way. "It's going to be okay. I swear it. You just need to be patient for a little while longer. You want the case to stick, don't you? When we take him down, you want him to *stay* down, right?"

"Of course."

"Then it's going to take time. We can't rush this. We're not stopping, we're not giving up... we're just taking the time to get it right so what happened before doesn't happen again. Okay?"

I used to buy his bullshit. Used to hang on to every syllable, believing he meant every word. And maybe some part of him is genuine, but that doesn't mean he's being *honest*.

Menace

I sometimes say I'm fine when I'm not. I say nothing's bothering me when I'm distraught.

Little white lies to keep harmony. And I can tell, by that 'get over it' look Gabe gives me, that he doesn't think they'll ever nail him.

I say nothing, which the detective assumes means I've been placated, judging by the way he visibly relaxes, his thumb swiping across my bottom lip.

This son of a bitch…

He smiles, a smug little smile, as he tugs the zipper of his pants down. His free hand snakes inside his boxers, stroking himself beneath the material as he says, "It's been too long, babe. I've missed seeing you."

Before he can whip it out, I smack his hand away from my face. "You bring that thing anywhere near me, Detective Jones, and you'll never use it again."

His eyes widen. "What's gotten into you?"

"I don't know," I say, "but I know what's never getting into me again, and that's *you*. I'm not your little fucktoy. Your job isn't to use me as you see fit. Your job is to serve and *protect*. So do your goddamn job, detective, and keep your dick in your pants, because I've been waiting for ten fucking *months*, and I'm running out of patience."

I got no sleep last night, none at all, every inch of me exhausted and sore. I haven't even showered yet, leaving when it was still dark, while Lorenzo soundly slept. I didn't want to wake him. He looked so peaceful. So I just threw on the first clothes I saw, pulled my hair back in a sloppy bun and headed out, remnants of the man all over me. I can smell him on my skin.

Gabe just stares at me with disbelief, hand still in his pants, clutching his dick, but he makes no move to whip it out, lucky for him.

After a moment, a series of beeps ring out, sucking away some of the awkwardness infiltrating the office. He unclips the department-issued cell phone from his belt, glancing at it before fixing his pants.

289

"Got something I need to deal with," he grumbles, waving the phone in my face before heading for the door. "Show yourself out, Miss Myers."

I sit here, even after he's gone, staring across the office out the window. Nobody says a word about me being here, nobody bothering me.

It's like I'm invisible.

Eventually, my eyes wander to the messy desk, to the stacks of files covering the top of it. It blows my mind how outdated things are here, case files kept as actual files, folders full of papers instead of being stored digitally.

Not really *secure*, is it?

I glance behind me, out of the office, double-checking nobody is paying me any attention, before shoving out of the chair and slipping around the side of the desk. The files have names scribbled on them in pen. I shift through them quickly, glancing at the handwriting. Blah. Blah. Blah. *Bingo.*

Aristov.

I bring the file to the top of the stack. It's thick, bursting at the seams with paperwork. Flipping it open, I scan through some of it, skimming paragraphs and pages, glossing over most of it.

Drugs. Guns. Fraud. *Murder.*

A lot of allegedly this and allegedly that, he said/she said bullshit, but not much in the way of *evidence*. No ballistics, no fingerprints, no forensics. A stack of witness statements, each one wrecked with writing, covered in black marker: retracted... missing... deceased... uncooperative... unreliable...

I stall at the last one, blinking a few times at the name on the top of it: Morgan Olivia Myers. *Unreliable.*

"Whatever," I grumble as I flip the page.

I skim through the rest. Blah. Blah. Blah. *Nothing.*

"You have to be kidding me." I shove it all aside as I scan through files again. There has to be another one somewhere. There has to be *more*. Besides my original witness statement, there's very little about my history with Kassian and not a goddamn peep about the pain of the past ten months. "Mother*fuckers.*"

I shove a stack of files, sending them scattering along the desk as anger runs through me. Have they even done *anything?*

Shaking my head, my eyes scan the desk again, and I'm about to walk away when a name catches my eye. *Gambini.* It's sloppily scribbled on a fresh folder.

I know that name.

I pick it up, and am about to scan through it when the phone on the desk lights up and starts to ring. *Shit.* I jump, caught off guard, and shove the file beneath my hoodie, securing it with the waistband of my pants as I get the hell out of there.

I keep my head down as I make my way to the elevator, heading down to the first floor. As soon as it dings, the doors opening, I step off and freeze, hearing the unmistakable sound of a familiar booming laugh echoing through the lobby.

Oh my fucking—

My head snaps up, my eyes going straight to a man just ten feet from me. I catch a glimpse of his profile as he stands there, elbows against the front desk, leaning over to talk to Officer Rimmel working the command center. *Markel.* He's laughing, flirting, and she's smiling at him. *Smiling.*

The woman, with her neon pink nails, has never smiled at me. Not once, in ten months.

As the elevator doors behind me close, my eyes bounce from Markel to the exit. Shoving my hands in the pocket of my black hoodie, I lower my head, my eyes on the checkered linoleum.

I hope like hell I stay invisible as I force my feet to move.

You can do this. You can do this. You can do—

Shit.

I'm yanked to an abrupt stop as a hand wraps around my bicep. Turning my head, I catch his eyes, piercing through me as I'm pulled toward him so fast I damn near lose my balance.

"*Suka,*" he says, grinning, using that word so casually, as if it's my real name. *Bitch.*

My heart pounds furiously.

My head is swimming.

I'm in deep shit.

Deep, deep shit.

'*Let go of me.*' Those words damn near come from my lips, but I know it's a lost cause, pleading at this point. He's not going to just let me leave. So I've got about five seconds to save myself, to find a way out of this, because being in a police precinct won't be enough to stop him from throwing me over his shoulder and dragging me out of here.

One. Two. Three. Four.

"Pussycat got your tongue, *suka*?" he asks, letting out a laugh. "Haven't you missed me?"

Five.

I don't think. I just react.

Pulling my hand from my pocket, I point a finger at his face, poking him right in the eye, jabbing hard. BAM. He flinches, letting out one hell of a sound, the shriek so loud everyone turns our way in alarm.

"You *bitch*!" Markel shouts, covering his eye with his free hand. I know he's pissed when he says it in English. His hold on my arm loosens in reaction to the sharp pain, letting me slip from his grip and move away.

He tries to recover, realizing he doesn't have his hands on me anymore, lunging my direction but he's too slow. Chaos erupts, the command officer calling for help, the police trying to intervene, but it's too late for that.

I scream at the top of my lungs, scream so loud my voice cracks. "He's got a gun!"

Does he? I don't know. Probably not. But who gives a fuck? It does exactly what I need it to do, inciting panic all around us. People try to flee the precinct, the police frenzied, as I run for the exit, shoving through the crowd.

I damn near make it out before someone else grabs me. *Ugh, please don't be Kassian.* Turning, reacting, I swing blindly, striking *something.*

"Jesus, what the hell, Morgan?"

Detective Jones.

Fuck.

He rubs his shoulder, where I punched him, looking around in confusion, but I don't have time to explain. I push him off, heading out the door as Markel shouts something in Russian.

I shove past people, moving as fast as my feet will go. It's not safe here. I need to get off of the street. I need to get out of Brooklyn, but the subway isn't an option right now. Markel is probably already sounding the alarms. They'll be watching, swarming the area, trying to smoke me out.

Shit. Shit. *Shit.*

I run a few blocks, cutting down some alleys, heading the direction of Coney Island. I know these streets well. I've run them before. I've hidden in the abandoned buildings in the neighborhood.

But Kassian knows that.

He knows all of my old haunts.

It's the first place he'll check.

So fuck it, I instead swing right into a busy coffee shop. It's not a Starbucks, but close to it, some mass-produced franchise full of hipsters wearing bow ties and suspenders. I get in line, nervously looking around, making sure the coast stays clear, not really caring to actually order anything.

I don't even *like* coffee.

Yeah, yeah, I know. There's something wrong with me.

"I'll have whatever she ordered," I say when it's my turn, motioning to the girl who went before me, some young blonde that reminds me a bit of Melody. I dig some cash from my pocket, paying the astronomical fee for the drink.

"Name?" the cashier asks, grabbing a cup and a marker.

"Scarlet," I tell him.

I wait some more then, waiting for my drink, still looking around, observing everybody.

I zero in on a guy working alone at a small table near the door, his gaze fixed to his laptop, stickers covering the front of it. Bands, I'm guessing. Music. He's wearing a black t-shirt with a drummer on it. Scattered along the table are papers, a cell phone sitting on top of a closed textbook.

"Scarlet?" a barista calls, shoving a caramel-colored frozen drink up onto the pass. Guess that's mine. I snatch it up, sticking in a straw, as I head for the door.

"What's your favorite *Avenged Sevenfold* song?" I ask, pausing beside the guy alone at the table, trying to turn on the charm and act interested.

He looks up at the sound of my voice as I lean over, against the table, all up in his space. "Nightmare."

"No shit?" I smirk, straw against my lips. "That's mine, too!"

He grins at my response and seems to be at a momentary loss, which is for the best, because I don't even know who *Avenged Sevenfold* is. I just saw the sticker on his laptop and rolled with it. *Poor guy.* I grab the cell phone while he's distracted, trying to come up with something witty to say, slipping it up the sleeve of my hoodie before pushing away from the table and walking out.

I go another block, passing an apartment building just as someone is leaving. Darting over, I grab the door before it closes, slipping inside as I take a sip of the drink.

I expect it to be bitter and gross, but it's actually light and sweet. *Huh.* I pull out the stolen cell phone as I lean back against the wall near the mailboxes, pressing a button, breathing a sigh of relief when it comes to life. *No security code needed.*

So, okay, I don't exactly have any *friends.*

I used to call George in a pinch, but I don't foresee him coming back to life to help me.

I've turned to Gabe before, but seeing how I just assaulted him, he's out of the question.

So that leaves me with one person. *Lorenzo.*

Other than 911, it's really the only number I know.

Or, well, I hope I know it. I memorized it, weeks ago, when I tried to call him to pay back the money I stole, but my memory's a bit shaky, so...

I dial it, bringing the phone to my ear, as sirens wail in the distance, flying by. The phone rings and rings and rings, and I'm about to give up, when the line finally clicks and a voice greets me. "Gambini."

I pause. It's not *Gambini*. Not technically. Seven answers. It catches me off guard.

"Hey, Seven... it's, uh, Morgan."

"Morgan," he says. "Everything okay?"

Nope. "Yep."

"That's good," he says. "Did you need something?"

Yep. "Nope."

He's quiet for a second before saying, "Tell me what's wrong."

"I don't know that I'd say anything's *wrong...*"

"But?"

"I kind of got myself into a bit of a pickle. Not sure how to get back out."

"A bit of a pickle, huh? Where are you?"

"Coney Island," I say. "There's this apartment building right on west 17th. Big ugly brick one. I'm kind of, you know, hanging out."

"Hiding out, you mean?"

"Pretty much."

He laughs. "So Brooklyn, huh?"

"Yep."

"I'll be there in twenty."

He hangs up before I can say anything to him, but I respond anyway. "*Thank God.*"

* * *

I got stuck on a Ferris wheel once.

I think I was five or six at the time.

Something shorted, the operator screwed up, and there I was, stuck in a bucket thirty feet in the sky. Instead of being scared, though, I found it almost calming, being so high up, where nobody could reach me and nothing could touch me.

I still feel that way most of the time.

Like right now, as I sit here, legs stretched out along gray asphalt shingles on the sloped roof of the house in Queens, surrounded by the kind of quiet suburban neighborhood where carpool and playdates are things that exist, I feel *okay*.

That's saying something, you know, after the day I've had. It seems almost surreal, and I'd think it didn't really happen, except the file in my lap tells me differently. *Gambini*.

I've read it already.

Actually, okay, I've read it a few times.

Can you blame me? Pretty damn sure *you* would read it, too, if you could.

Sighing, I suck down the last of my frozen sugary coffee when I hear a door open nearby. Glancing down, I watch as Lorenzo steps out of the house, a cloud of musky smoke surrounding him, a joint between his lips.

It's the first I've seen him today. After Seven valiantly rescued me, bringing me back here, I discovered the library door closed for only the second time since I started coming around.

He's got a headache today, Seven explained. Might not see him.

Yet, there he is...

His hair is unkempt, all over the place, like he hasn't done a damn thing to it since I wound my fingers through it last. The rest of him, though, seems to be put together—white shirt, dark jeans, black boots. He smokes quietly, alone, watching the neighborhood, before Seven joins him.

"I'm heading home, boss," Seven says. "Wife is making lasagna for dinner, if you want me to bring you some."

"I appreciate it," Lorenzo says, "but I can fend for myself."

Pfftt, fuck that.

"You can bring *me* some," I call down. "I'm not dumb enough to pass up home cooking."

Seven laughs, waving toward me. "I think I've done enough for you today, Morgan."

I make a face at him.

Seven pulls out Lorenzo's keys and phone, passing them over before departing. Lorenzo shoves it all in his pocket, continuing to smoke in silence, watching as Seven drives off, leaving us alone.

Lorenzo tosses what's left of the joint down, smashing it with his boot as he turns slowly, his gaze flickering up to where I'm sitting.

He goes back inside, not saying a word.

I figure he went back to his library, but after a moment, the window from his bedroom shoves open and he climbs out onto the ledge before maneuvering around and pulling himself up onto the roof.

I wish I could say I got up here that smoothly, or that I even considered doing it that way.

I stole a ladder from a neighbor's backyard.

It's propped up against the side of the house. *Oops.*

He sits down beside me, knees bent, elbows leaning against them, his gaze surveying the neighborhood for a moment before he looks my way. He scans me slowly, his attention drifting to the file on my lap.

I know he can see his last name on it. It's written clear as day.

"You got a file on me, Scarlet?" he asks, his voice casual, nothing accusatory in his tone.

"No," I say, looking down at it. "Well, I guess I technically *do* now. It's your police file."

"My police file."

"Yeah, it's everything they know about you," I explain. "I kind of stole it from the detective's office."

"You stole it."

"Yes."

"Takes balls to break the law in a police precinct."

"Yeah, well, just add it to the list of other laws I broke. I probably have warrants out for me right now. Disorderly conduct. Criminal nuisance. Assault on a police officer. It all adds up."

"Sounds like you had an interesting day."

"Very."

"Kind of jealous," he says, eyeing me for a moment before turning away. "So, what's the file say?"

"What makes you think I've read it?"

"You wouldn't go through the trouble of stealing it if you weren't nosey as shit about what's inside."

Rolling my eyes, I pick up the folder and flip it open. There isn't much to it, just a few papers.

"Lorenzo Oliver Gambini," I say, reading the top sheet before cutting my eyes at him, watching as he whips out an orange, like he carries them around in his pocket. "Oliver? *Really?*"

"I distinctly remember your middle name being Olivia," he says, "which isn't much different."

"Yeah, but that's me," I say. "You're *you.*"

"We're a lot alike, you and I."

He says that casually, and I'm not sure how to take it, because my brain suddenly gets hung up on something else. "Wait, you know my middle name?"

Shrugging a shoulder, he starts to peel his orange, like him knowing my middle name doesn't mean anything, like him remembering *any* part of my name isn't a big deal. But it is, so I just gape at him, trying to make sense of that.

"What's the file say, Scarlet?" he asks again. "Less staring, more spilling."

"It, uh…" I look away from him, back at the papers. "Born and raised in Kissimmee, Florida. Your father was murdered when you were four. Your mother and stepfather disappeared about fourteen years after that. You officially became legal custodian of one Leonardo Michael Accardi on your nineteenth birthday, although you'd been taking care of him for a year by that point."

"You already knew all of that," he points out, seeming rather bored by my facts.

"You inherited an almost 200-acre orange grove that has more than doubled in size and profit under your control. Your business seems on the up and up, so no Al Capone level take down in your future, although they suspect you've got something hinky going on down there."

"Something *hinky,*" he says with a laugh. "What, like we're running guns through the grove? Because they'd be right."

"They seem more concerned about Cuban imports."

"Ah, yes, *priorities*. The rum."

"They don't have any evidence, though."

"Of course not."

"They do, however, have a shitload of stories about you. You're kind of like *Bigfoot*."

"Bigfoot?"

"Yeah, everyone's heard about him, most people think he's a myth, with nothing more than a couple blurry pictures and unreliable first-hand accounts as proof of his existence. Most of this file isn't even about *you*. It's a bunch of scary stories about a guy with a scar. Half this shit isn't even *believable*."

"Like?"

"Like you lit a building on fire in Manhattan with a bunch of men inside of it."

"I gave them a chance to get out," he says. "Not my fault they didn't take me seriously."

"You blew up a storage building in a public park."

"I just flicked a lighter," he says. "I'm not the one who made the place explosive."

"You detonated a grenade, killing most of the mob bosses in the city."

"See, okay, that's bullshit. They were already dead by the time that grenade went off."

"I, uh... *wow*."

I don't know what to say.

"In my defense," he says, not sounding like he really cares to defend himself, "they were all terrible people, so it's not like they didn't *deserve* it."

"So you've never hurt an innocent person?"

A smile touches his lips. "Do they exist?"

"What?"

"Innocent people."

"Children," I say. "Your brother."

I almost say *me*, but well, I think I've crossed too many lines to ever qualify as *innocent*.

"I would never hurt a kid," he says. "I guarantee there's

299

nothing in that file that says I would."

I look down at it, frowning, pulling out a scrap piece of paper with the detective's handwriting on it and holding it out to Lorenzo.

Suspected to have been involved in the death of 14-year-old Sally Walters in Kissimmee.

He takes the piece of paper from me, looking at it for a few seconds before balling it up, crushing it in his palm. He tosses it behind him, onto the roof, and goes back to peeling his orange.

The fact that he's not refuting it bothers me. My stomach gets tied up in knots.

"Is her autopsy report in there?" he asks after a moment.

"No."

"So you don't know she was strangled?" he asks. "Don't know she was brutally raped before being put out of her misery?"

"No."

But *he* does, and the fact that he knows it makes my head dizzy, bile burning the back of my throat. I don't want to think he's capable of such a thing. No, scratch that. I *don't* think he is. Killing people, yes, I've seen him do it, but rape is different. It's another level of cruelty inflicted by a different type of monster. I've met many of those monsters in my life, but he's not one of them.

"For the record, I didn't do it," he says. "She was my first girlfriend. *Only* girlfriend. I didn't hurt her. I just got lucky and stumbled upon her after my stepfather was through."

"Oh."

"Oh," he repeats as he stands up. "Anything else in the book of bullshit that I should know about?"

"No," I say, closing the file and holding it out to him. "You can have it, if you want."

"How nice of you," he says, snatching it from my hand, clutching so tightly the folder bends, as he leaves, slipping back down off of the roof, into the bedroom, slamming the window closed.

I touched a nerve. A *bad* one. And I know he's just going to go back downstairs now, into his library, and I won't see him again tonight. Ugh, I don't like it. My stomach is still in knots.

I didn't think it was possible, but... I might've hurt his feelings. *Ugh. Ugh. Ugh.*

Pushing to my feet, I quickly make my way across the roof. I scurry down the ladder, jogging around, and shove through the front door just as Lorenzo steps back into the library.

Fuck.

"Hey, hold on," I say, running toward him, skidding to a stop in front of the library just as the door is about to shut. Reaching out, I push it, shoving it back open before it can latch. "Ugh, Lorenzo, *wait.*"

He turns to me, still clutching the door. He looks like he wants to slam it in my face... or maybe, like, *punch* me. I don't know.

"You've got ten seconds," he says.

I take a deep breath, not sure what to say.

"Nine... eight... seven..."

"I didn't think you did that to that girl," I blurt out, because fuck it, he's counting, and I know when he reaches *'one'* I'll have missed my chance. "I know that's not the kind of man you are. I know you wouldn't have done that to her. I know you're better than that."

He lets out a bitter laugh. "Yeah, right."

He's about to slam the door for real this time so I shove my way inside the room. There's a flash of something in his expression. Anger. *Something.* I don't know. I can't pay it any mind. I've already crossed that threshold. No going back now.

"I swear to *fuck*, Scarlet, if you don't watch yourself..."

"Yeah, you'll kill me," I mutter, grabbing ahold of him, my hands framing his face, trying to force him to look at me but he's stubborn as shit and goes to pull away instead. "I'm serious, Lorenzo. Stop being so fucking pigheaded and just *look* at me."

He looks at me when I say that. *Whoa.* He actually *listens.*

I'm caught so much off guard by it that I don't say anything right away, just staring him in the eyes.

"Times up, Scarlet," he says quietly.

Before he can try to push me away, make me leave, I reach

up on my tiptoes and press my lips to his. I kiss him, softly, slowly, my palms gently against his cheeks, holding his face there.

He doesn't kiss me back. At least, not right away. But I can feel him relaxing more and more each time our lips touch, his anger waning.

He tastes like oranges, sweet and tangy.

My hands shift, grasping the side of his head, as I kiss down along his jawline, brushing against the scruff on his chin. I move to the other side, kissing the corner of his mouth before my lips graze against the scar slicing through his cheek.

The second I do that, he pulls his head back. He shoots me a strange look, I can't really read it, before he moves away from the door, away from *me*. He strolls across the room, tossing his case file onto the corner of the table near his puzzle, before sitting down in his chair

He goes back to eating his orange as if none of that even happened. The door stays open, and I'm already halfway in the room, so I take that as invitation to come the rest of the way in.

"Senile," he says, shaking his head. "I know that's not what your Scarlet Letter stands for, but it sure as fuck *ought* to."

I approach him. "I'm not old enough to be senile. Besides, you know, I think I'm pretty clear-headed."

"You're softhearted, Scarlet. Soft in the fucking head, too. It's dangerous. *You're* dangerous."

I laugh at that, pausing in front of him, pushing his hands out of the way and shoving him further back into the chair as I climb onto his lap, straddling him. He lets out an exasperated sigh, like I'm bothering him, but I wouldn't really call him angry anymore, so I'm chalking that up to a win.

Nuzzling into his neck, I kiss and nip at the skin, trailing my tongue along his throat, feeling it as he swallows thickly.

He tries like hell to ignore me, cocking his head away, finishing his orange in silence. As soon as he's done, though, I pull back, grabbing his hand, wrapping my lips around two of his fingers, lapping the remnants of juice from his fingertips with my tongue. I suck on them slowly as he watches me, cocking an eyebrow, not saying a word, but I can feel him as he grows hard.

I pull his fingers from my mouth and start to say something, to tease him, but I don't get the chance to say a word. He grabs me by the back of the head, pulling me to him, kissing me roughly.

I eagerly kiss him back.

Hands shove at clothes, pushing and tugging, doing just enough to free him as my pants are pulled down to my thighs. He strokes himself a few times before I sink down onto him, groaning into his mouth as he fills me.

He grasps me by the ass, squeezing, but his hands just rest there, not trying to take control, letting me lead. I ride him slowly, not breaking the kiss, goose bumps coating every inch of my skin.

Jesus Christ, he feels so good.

His hands start roaming, squeezing and scratching, his fingers raking along the small of my back.

"Fuck," he growls, pulling from my mouth, but it's only long enough to shed me of some clothes. He yanks off my hoodie, taking off my shirt, and I unhook my bra, letting it drop to the floor.

He kisses me again, a few small pecks, before his mouth moves, leaving a trail down to my collarbones. I wrap my arms around him, lacing my hands through his hair as he buries his face into my chest, his tongue exploring.

I hiss at a jolt of pain as he bites down on a nipple, closing my eyes, my toes curling. Tingles consume me, from head to toe, and I increase my pace, fucking him faster, coming down on him harder, feeling an orgasm stirring. He alternates between bites and licks, kissing and sucking at my breasts. I know he's leaving marks. I can feel them. They *sting*. My skin is raw, but I pull him to me tighter, wanting it rougher, wanting to feel every part of him inside every part of me.

"Fuck me," I whisper breathlessly, scratching at his scalp as I tilt my head back. "Fuck me until I forget everything."

He pulls back, and I loosen my grip, realizing right away that might've been the wrong thing to say. There's a sinister twist to his lips that sends a chill down my spine. Before I can say another word, he shoves up out of the chair, pulling out as he drops me onto my feet. Yanking me over to the table, he turns me around, shoving me flat down against it, right on top of his puzzle. My pants are forced the rest of the way down, shackling my ankles, as he kicks my legs apart as far as they'll go.

"Be very still," he says, a slight edge to his voice. "Try not to fuck up my puzzle."

"No promises," I whisper.

He braces himself, his hand gripping my shoulder, and thrusts inside of me. I let out a deep groan as my eyelids flutter. Fuck. He wastes no time, doing exactly what I asked.

He fucks me. It's powerful. *Brutal.* Hips slam into me from behind as he fills me deeply, over and over. Skin slapping noises echo through the room as he drives me into the table so hard it starts to move. I grip onto the edge of it, trying to hold on, trying to stay still, but he makes it impossible. Pain and pleasure merge inside of me, *consuming* me, and it doesn't take long before I start to grow numb. Tingles encompass me. My mind blanks out. Nothing exists except his cock inside of me, him on top of me, slamming into me from behind. I cry out with every deep thrust, incoherent noises, like everything inside of me is being purged.

Fuck.

Fuck.

Fuck.

Orgasm rips through me more than once. I lose track of time. I lose track of everything but *him*. An hour, or a minute, who knows?

He bites down on my shoulder when he finally comes. It brings me back around, my eyes opening, and I blink slowly, feeling him spilling deep inside of me. He doesn't pull out. Warmth flows through me, my muscles twitching, my pussy throbbing.

I don't know that I could ever get enough of this.

He pulls out, but I stay there, lying against the table, watching him. He pulls his pants up, buttoning and zipping them, before plopping back down in his chair. Exhaling loudly, he scrubs his hands down his face before pulling out his Altoids tin, retrieving a joint and lighting it.

"If you're hoping for another round, you'll be waiting awhile," he says. "My head is fucking *killing* me today."

I smile softly. "I'm good, thanks."

He smokes in silence for a moment, his gaze scanning me before he asks, "Were you serious about what you said?"

"Yes," I answer.

"Do you even know what I'm talking about?"

"No, but if I said it, I meant it."

He starts to say something when ringing cuts through the room. Pulling his phone from his pocket, he glances at it, brow furrowing.

His eyes flicker back to me as he presses a button, bringing it to his ear. "Gambini."

There's a brief moment where Lorenzo doesn't speak.

"Ah, Aristotle," he says, sounding amused. "I see you finally grew a sack and unblocked your number. Good for you. I'm proud."

My smile falls. *Kassian.*

I can't see the man. I can't even hear his voice. Miles separate us, as do thousands of people, but knowing he's just a breath away on the phone makes it feel like he's right in front of me again.

My insides coil.

My knees, they go weak. I desperately wish they wouldn't. But Kassian is like poison. Just a tiny taste on my tongue is enough to take me down. I hate it, reacting to him, but I can't help it. It ignites a spark, flooding me with memories, a flip-book of all the cruel things he's done, the ways he's single-handedly broken my reality.

Lorenzo's eyes stay fixed on me as he sits there, listening to Kassian. I wish I knew what he was saying, but at the same time, I'm terrified to hear what might come from his mouth.

"That doesn't work for me," Lorenzo responds. "Why don't I come to you instead?"

My stomach sinks.

"Got it," Lorenzo says.

He hangs up, slipping the phone back into his pocket, before standing up from his chair.

"What are you doing?" I ask. "What does he want?"

Pausing behind me, Lorenzo's hand brushes against my ass, before sliding further down, between my thighs, caressing me. My question goes unanswered, unsurprisingly. He slips a single finger inside, carefully sliding it in and out, as he leans down, trailing kisses along my shoulder blade. I'm sore, but he's so gentle.

I *moan*.

"You're insatiable," he says, his mouth trailing along my spine.

"You're just addictive," I whisper, "and I'm turning into a junkie."

He slides another in.

I close my eyes as he finger-fucks me.

I whimper, groaning his name. "Lorenzo."

Everything else is incoherent as an orgasm stirs. My body locks up, my muscles contracting at the swell of pleasure that fades away all too fast again.

Pulling his hand away, he reaches for me, and I open my eyes in just enough time to see it as his fingers brush against my mouth. My lips part, and he pushes his fingers in, the taste of both of us on my tongue.

He watches me, smiling.

"He wants to have a conversation," Lorenzo says, pulling his fingers from my mouth as he starts to walk away. "So I'm going to humor him, you know, for the moment, just to hear what he has to say."

I shove away from the table when he says that, moving so fast it tears apart a section of his puzzle, pieces sticking to the sweaty skin of my stomach. *Ugh*. I rip them off, tossing them onto the table, as I yank my pants up.

"You can't," I say. "You can't just *go* to him."

"Why not?"

"Because it doesn't work that way."

He stalls in the doorway. "And what way *does* it work, Scarlet?"

"I don't know," I say, "but not like this. Not on *his* terms. He's not someone you can just talk to. He's not someone you can rationalize with. I *know*. Don't you think I've tried? He manipulates people, and he twists things, and he uses it to his advantage, and he doesn't take no for an answer. *Ever*. When he makes up his mind, that's it. You can't appeal to his humanity because there *is* none."

"Well it's a good thing that's not what I'm doing."

"What *are* you doing?"

"I'm going to kill him."

Those words knock the breath from my lungs.

I gasp.

"Wait, you can't!" I shout as he walks out, running after him. "Please, Lorenzo. You can't just kill him!"

He's got his phone to his ear, calling somebody, as he reaches the front door of the house, looking back at me. That wounded look flashes in his face, like I again offended him, as he grinds out, "Don't tell me you care what happens to the bastard."

"No, but—"

"But," he says, cutting me off. "There's always a *but*, isn't there?"

"You don't understand."

"You're right," he says. "I don't. The guy terrifies you, and for the love of fuck, I don't know *why*. What's he got on you, huh? What is it about him that has you wound so tight that you're standing in my hallway, half naked, shaking, not wanting me to go blow his brains out so you'll stop? I mean, do you *like* this? Is that it? Are you having the time of your life pissing your pants over this asshole? Because if that's the case, carry on, baby. Don't let me stop this game you're playing."

I can feel tears welling in my eyes, my voice cracking as I say, "It's not like that."

He senses it, I think, because his expression hardens, that anger rushing back into him. "So you're just a pussy, huh? Maybe that's what your Scarlet Letter stands for. Just a fucking *scaredy-cat*.

But I'm not putting up with that shit. It makes no sense."

Lorenzo walks out, slamming the front door behind him, and I close my eyes, trying to keep tears from falling.

Face your fears and wipe your tears.

"Sasha," I whisper, even though he's gone, wrapping a hand around my wrist tightly, my palm covering the tattoo. "It's all for *Sasha.*"

25

The dice clattered along the kitchen bar top, coming to a stop in the center of it. The little girl stood up on the stool, practically climbing on top of the bar, crawling across it.

"One... two... three..."

She pointed, counting the dots, as a loud huff sounded out across from her, so close she could smell the stale stench of breath. *Vodka*. She scrunched her nose up at the Cowardly Lion. *Yuck*.

He stared at her impatiently. "Well? What is it?"

"I'm counting them," she said, looking back at the dice.

"Hurry it up," he said. "I don't have all day."

The little girl was pretty sure he *did* have all day, since all he ever seemed to do most days was hang around there, but she didn't say that, counting the dots.

Six on one; five on the other.

"Six and five," she said.

"Which is...?"

She hesitated, counting the dots all together. "Eleven."

"Eleven," he agreed, snatching up the dice to roll them again, looking at her pointedly. "Well? What is it?"

Around and around, again and again, he kept rolling and she kept counting. *Learning*.

Footsteps headed their way, the Tin Man strolling into the kitchen, his brow furrowing as he glared at her sprawled out across the bar. "What are you doing?"

"Counting," she said.

"I'm teaching her how to add," the Cowardly Lion chimed in, taking a drink from his bottle. "She's terrible at it."

The little girl groaned, sitting back on the stool. "It's no fun!"

"*Life* isn't fun," the Cowardly Lion said, pointing his bottle at her. "You don't want to be dumb, do you, little girl?"

"I'm not dumb," she said, crossing her arms over her chest. "My mommy—"

"Mommy or *dummy*?" he asked, laughing that mean way he sometimes did. "Like mother, like daughter, eh?"

"*Enough*," the Tin Man said as he approached, snatching the little girl off the stool and setting her on her feet. "Run along, kitten."

She stomped off, heading upstairs, and plopped down at the desk in the bedroom, crayons and paper scattered all around in front of her. Her chest felt all tight, like her heart was sad tonight.

Six months. Half a year.

The little girl didn't know how many weeks that was, much less how many *days*. But she did know it was the end of December, which meant Christmas was coming.

Grabbing a fresh piece of paper, she started drawing, as the first bit of winter snow fell outside her window. She drew until the sun set over the city, until darkness crept in.

When she finished her first picture, she moved on to another, not stopping until that one was done, too.

"Perfect," she said, holding them up, grinning, before snatching up Buster from the corner of the desk and making her way back downstairs. It was getting late, really late, and all the winged monkeys were gone.

She wondered if the Tin Man was sleeping, with how quiet it was, but flickering light filtered out from the den. The doors were cracked open, so she slipped between them.

The Tin Man sat in his chair near the fire, holding a bottle of vodka, his suit all rumpled.

"Daddy?" she whispered, carefully approaching.

"I thought I told you to run along."

He didn't even look up as he said that, legs spread out, his body slouched. His voice was low, like sandpaper again.

"I did," she said, "but..."

His eyes rose, bloodshot but gray. *Not all black today.* "But?"

"I drew you a picture," she said, holding up one of her drawings.

He regarded her in silence for a moment before motioning for her to approach. She walked up to him, holding the drawing out, standing still as he took it. It was a picture of the beach, the one he'd taken her to months ago. She'd even drawn the rides that had been nearby, like the Ferris wheel. She'd hoped he'd take her back there, maybe when it was open, but he hadn't let her leave the house since then.

After looking at the picture, he set it on the table. "What else do you have?"

The little girl looked at the second drawing, her heart racing. "A picture of Mommy."

"A picture," he repeated, "of your mother."

She nodded before reminding herself: *use your words.* "I drew it for her for Christmas. I didn't know how to draw her, really, I didn't know if her hair got long or what she wore or maybe she got taller, but I drew her like I remember, and maybe I can see her on Christmas, or you can give it to her?"

He frowned and held his hand out. "Give it here."

She handed it to him.

He clutched the sides of the paper, his knee moving, rocking back and forth, as he stared at the picture in silence.

"I didn't know if you had wrapping paper," she continued. "Can we get a tree now? I can decorate it and put the picture under it. Mommy liked the star on top."

He sighed. "We are not getting a tree, kitten."

"We're not?"

"What is the point? So you can climb it?"

"It's Christmas," she said. "Santa Claus brings presents."

"We do not celebrate Christmas." He set the picture down in his lap. "We are not religious."

"But Santa—"

"Is not real."

She gasped. It felt like he *hit* her. "You're lying!"

"No, your mother lied," he said. "She lied to me. She lied to you. That is all she ever did. Lie, lie, lie, lie, *lie!*"

He shouted the word '*lie*' so loud that she flinched, taking a step back, tears stinging her eyes.

"No!" She shook her head, clutching Buster tightly. "Why are you saying that stuff?"

"Because it is true," he said, snatching up her drawing, crumpling it as he waved it at her, nearly smacking her in the face with it. "This woman? Your precious 'Mommy', with those eyes and those hips and those *lips*? She lied to you, kitten—hideous lies! She made you think I was the bad one, but that was *her*. She betrayed me. She kept you from me, my own flesh and blood. You were *mine!* I would rather you are dead... I would rather end your life than ever let that *suka* have you for herself. She gets nothing!"

The little girl took another step back, away from him, her bottom lip trembling. "Stop saying that stuff! It's not right, so stop it!"

"You do not tell me what to do. I tell you! What *I* say goes!"

"I hate you!" she yelled. "You have no heart in you!"

She ran out, heading upstairs, moving as fast as her legs would carry her, tears streaming down her cheeks. She *hated* him. She hated him *so much*. She went to her room and slammed the door, jumping into the bed.

"He's lying," she whispered, hugging Buster, squeezing her eyes shut. "Mommy loves us. Mommy doesn't lie. He's just mean, and big, and ugly!"

Footsteps echoed down the hallway, coming near, stomping against the wood, determined. *Angry*. Her bedroom door flung open, slamming into the wall, and the little girl curled tighter into a ball. The moment she felt the mattress dip, she saw his face, bitter and bloodshot and *right there*.

"You want to hate me?" he asked. "I will give you reason to."

She held her breath, terrified, waiting for the hurt she thought he'd make her feel, like the way he hurt mother, but it didn't happen.

No, this hurt was *different*.

He grabbed her arm, yanking Buster from her grasp.

She gasped, trying to snatch him back, but the Tin Man was too strong. He clutched Buster, hand wrapped around the bear's neck, and stormed away without another word.

"No!" The little girl jumped out of bed, chasing him. "Please, Daddy! No! Please! I'm sorry!"

She tried to shove around him, to get Buster back, grabbing ahold of his shirt, clutching it tightly as she tried to stop him, but he just dragged her along.

The little girl begged the whole way down the stairs. He headed for the den, still utterly silent, on a mission, she realized, as he neared the fireplace with Buster.

"No!" she screamed, collapsing to the floor. "Please, Daddy! I don't hate you! Please, can I keep him? I'm sorry!"

He walked straight to the fireplace, ignoring her words, acting as if she were invisible. He held Buster out, over the fire, the flames lapping at the bear, a spark setting his foot on fire.

She screeched. "I don't hate you! No! Please! I love you, Daddy!"

He pulled Buster back when she said those words, beating the bear against the wall, extinguishing the small flame on his singed paw. He turned to her as she hyperventilated, her vision blurry but she could see Buster was okay.

He wasn't in the fire.

The Tin Man approached, crouching down, holding the bear up in her face, but the second she reached for it, he pulled it away. "You love me, kitten?"

She nodded frantically.

"Use your words."

"I love you, Daddy."

His eyes scanned her face before he leaned over, pressing a kiss to her forehead, whispering, "You *lie* just like her."

Standing up, still carrying Buster, he walked back over to the fireplace, but instead of tossing him into the flames, he set him on the mantle.

"You touch him, I burn him, and I will burn *you*, too, kitten. You will get him back when I say you get him back. Until then, he will sit right here as a reminder."

The Tin Man walked out, and the little girl just sat there, staring at the mantle, rocking, sobbing, as she whispered, "I'm so sorry, Buster."

26
Lorenzo

"Boss?"

"Yes, Seven?"

"Are you sure about this?"

Whoever said there were no such things as stupid questions was wrong. I've heard some stupid questions in my life. Usually they come in clusters: *Why do you have that gun? What are you doing? Are you going to kill me?* Uh, *duh*. I'm sure as hell not going to shoot *myself*. The fear of death, you know, it tends to override common sense, which makes the end, for some, pretty damn pathetic. *Oh God, why are you doing this? How could you?* BANG.

Certainly not the kind of 'last words' I want to have.

And Seven, well, I have respect for the guy, but he's notorious for asking stupid questions.

"Do I *look* sure about this?"

"Yes," he says right away.

"Well, there you go, then."

Truthfully, I'm not sure at all, but I'd never let anyone know that, not even Seven.

And before you say shit, I'm well aware that I just told *you*, but you don't count so stop trying to inject yourself into the damn story. This is an important moment.

The house before me is pretty damn big. Three stories tall, wide and square in shape, isolated from the other houses in the neighborhood, off toward the waterfront just along the outskirts of Brighton Beach. It's dark out, a pitch-black night where the clouds overshadow everything, but the front of the house is illuminated.

DARHOWER

The top two floors are completely blacked out, but downstairs I see some dim lights on through the blinds in some of the windows. He's home. I know he is. He invited me over. And he's not alone, like I knew he wouldn't be, so that doesn't bother me.

What does bother me, though, is that it all looks so *normal*. Just once I want to show up somewhere and the place be a dungeon, with guillotines and torture chambers. Hell, give me a fucking *dragon*. I'll slay it. But no, it's always this, always a mask of normalcy they wear with ease.

I get it, you know. I'm a hypocrite. Look at where *I* live. But we can't all be soccer moms driving mini-vans, downing prescription pills with entire bottles of Merlot. Some of us are just crack whores swigging fifths of vodka on street corners.

If it walks like a duck, if it quacks like a duck, it's a fucking duck, you know what I'm saying? And just once I want to shoot a goddamn duck.

Figuratively speaking.

Yeah, we've swung back around to the animal metaphors. What can I say? My life is exhausting.

"Come on," I tell Seven. "Can't be late for our date with the Stepford wife."

Seven trails me as I walk the path straight to the front door of the mansion. A doormat lies there, something written in Russian on it. Might say 'fuck off' but it probably says 'welcome', since he's in the business of pretending to be accommodating.

I try the knob out of habit. It's locked up tight. The peephole, I can tell it's a camera, which tells me the whole place is probably wired. A chime echoes through the house when I press the doorbell, loud enough that I can hear it, and it takes damn near a minute for whoever's answering to undo all of the locks on the door and disarm an alarm system.

That's a hell of a lot of security.

The door opens.

Brother Bear is standing there. *Markel.*

He's squinting, his right eyelid swollen, the eye horribly bloodshot. Laughter bursts out of me, making him grow rigid.

"Condolences on the eye," I say, pointing at his face. "You're just a step away from being me, buddy. You ought to be more careful."

"You think this is funny?" he growls, coming at me when a voice shouts out from inside the house.

"Markel! Where are your *manners?*"

"My manners?" Markel asks, stepping back, out of the way, as Aristov approaches the door.

"Yes," Aristov says. "Mister Scar is our guest."

"He laughed at me!"

"I laughed at your eye," I correct him. "I don't really find *you* funny, Baloo."

He looks as if he wants to attack me, but Aristov grabs his shoulder, pulling him away from the door. "Now is not the time, Markel."

Markel grumbles to himself, storming off.

"You will have to excuse my brother," Aristov says. "He is usually our voice of reason, but he is a little upset tonight. A certain little pussycat clawed him when he tried to bring her home."

Seven clears his throat behind me, saying, "Morgan."

"Morgan," Aristov repeats with a dry laugh. "Such a plain name for someone so... *colorful.*"

The way he words that makes my muscles twitch. It was deliberate, without a doubt.

"Anyway, join me," Aristov says, moving aside, motioning into the house.

I step past him, right inside.

I know what you're thinking. *Idiot*, right? Walking into another lion's den, like it's nothing. But something you ought to know is this isn't the first time I've done it. A lion is more comfortable in his home, surrounded by his pride, and when he gets comfortable, his guard goes down. He's confident, which becomes cocky, because he thinks he can't be touched, and cocky turns into careless, which works to my advantage.

Besides, what's the worst that can happen?

He shoots me, BANG, dead?

I'll just come back and haunt the son of a bitch.

Seven follows me inside, and I see him visibly tense when Aristov shuts the door, taking the time to secure all the locks and rearm the alarm system.

"Join me in the den," Aristov says, glancing at me. "We can speak privately there."

I follow him with Seven on my heels the entire way.

As soon as we step inside, Aristov's gaze flickers to Seven. "I will not harm your boss. *Promise.* So you can relax, help yourself to a drink in the kitchen, make yourself at home."

"I'll pass," Seven says, a hard edge to his voice.

Aristov smiles. "Suit yourself, Mister Pratt."

Pratt.

Bruno Pratt is Seven's given name, something they clearly know. Aristov did his homework. He knows more than he *should.*

Reaching to the floor, Aristov grabs a black duffel bag and drops it on top of a square wooden table, surrounded by leather furniture. It lands with a thud. He unzips it, shoving it open, flashing the contents.

Money.

A lot of money.

Stacks and stacks of money.

"A million dollars," he says, matter of fact, answering an unasked question as he takes a seat in one of the chairs. "All hundred dollar bills."

My gaze shifts from the money to Aristov. "You doubled the reward."

He nods. "All you have to do is give me her location so I can bring her home."

"Home, huh? She told me home was a white house with a red door and wood floors. This doesn't really fit the bill, Aristotle."

His expression freezes on his face, his smile like plastic. "That was never her home."

"You sure about that?"

He leans back in the chair, crossing his arms over his chest. "My sweet girl, she does not know what is best for her."

"But you do?"

"Of course. Everything I do is for her own good."

This is for your own good. How many times did I hear those words? Too many, and never once were they genuine. *For your own good* was synonymous with violence in my life for way too many years.

"What do you want her for?" Seven asks, chiming in. "That's a lot of money. She must've done something to deserve it."

Aristov looks at him. "You are married, Mr. Pratt, correct? You have a family, yes?"

Seven doesn't answer, just staring at him, but that's as good as a 'yes' to Aristov.

"I imagine you do everything for them," Aristov continues. "I am the same way. We are not much different. I do what I must for the ones I love."

"You love her?" Seven asks. "That's what you're saying?"

"Oh, absolutely," Aristov says. "I love the *suka* to death."

Suka.

That word sticks to my mind.

"Seven, why don't you go get that drink," I suggest. "Give me a moment alone with him."

Seven hesitates, like he doesn't want to go, but he walks out after a moment, leaving me.

Strolling over, I sit down in an empty chair near Aristov, already tired of this little game he's trying to play. I help myself to a bottle of liquor from the table, examining the label. *Russian.* "Vodka, I'm guessing?"

Aristov regards me curiously. "Of course."

It's half-empty, piss warm, but it doesn't matter. I crack it open, taking a swig straight from the bottle, and hiss at the intense burn that hits my chest when I swallow.

Aristov laughs. "Good?"

"Strong."

He swipes the bottle from me and takes a big drink, guzzling it like he's sucking down water.

"Vodka is like a woman," he says, pulling bottle from his lips.

"The rougher, the better?"

He offers it to me again. "So you understand."

Shrugging, I take it back, taking another sip, letting the burn buzz through my system. My tolerance is pretty damn high, since Cuban rum flows through my blood on the regular, but Russian vodka is a whole different ballgame. It's like gasoline. *Paint thinner.* I can feel it, my body humming. I'm pretty sure that's what he wants. He thinks we're bonding. He thinks if I get drunk, I'll slip up, but he doesn't know me.

I'm not giving him *shit.*

My gaze scans the room as I drink. Aristov is talking, just rambling away about more ways women are like vodka—like how the emptier the bottle gets, the better *he* feels. I pretend to listen until, well, I don't give a shit to pretend anymore. Sooner or later he'll get the message, and I'd prefer it to be sooner rather than later. The only reason I bothered coming is to solve Scarlet's problem.

My gaze drifts toward a fireplace along the wall, feeling the warmth radiating from the flames, smelling a hint of the woodsy smoke. I admire the fire for as he yammers away before my attention again shifts, this time to the mantle above it.

A teddy bear sits there.

I'm not even kidding.

It's obviously old, stuffing springing out of holes, missing a goddamn eye, and filthy from scruffy head to charred foot. It's out of place, surrounded by all of this forced elegance.

Serial killers, you know, they sometimes keep souvenirs. Trophies, they call them, reminders of the shit they've done so they can relive the moments again and again. Jewelry. Panties. Photographs. Body parts. Whatever got them off, whatever got the blood pumping down below.

And this bear, glowing like a beacon on the mantle, is screaming *trophy* at me. My insides coil, my stomach churning more and more the more I look at it. We're talking about a man with a reputation for trafficking women. He's in the business of selling *bodies.* I'm putting nothing past him.

If that bear indicates what my mind is conjuring, I'll burn

this house to the ground with all of us inside of it, just so I die with the pleasure of being able to usher that asshole personally straight to hell in the fire.

"Buster."

The sound of his voice, louder now, draws my attention. I glance back at Aristov, raising an eyebrow in question. *Buster?*

"The bear," he says casually, helping himself to the bottle clutched in my hand, pulling it from my grasp. "It is named Buster."

"You *named* the fucking thing?"

He laughs. "I did not name it. It came with the name. A stupid one, I say, but what do you expect from a little girl with so much *stupid* in her blood?"

He laughs, yet again, the sound running through me, striking something raw and setting me off. I don't think, just react, pulling my gun out and cocking the son of a bitch, aiming it at his forehead.

Seconds. Mere seconds. That was all it took. My finger hovers on the trigger, lightly pressing it. I'll blow his fucking brains out.

What kind of sick fuck messes with a *little girl?*

He stares at me.

He doesn't cower.

Doesn't beg.

Doesn't ask those stupid questions I always get.

No, he takes a swig of vodka, a slight smile on his lips, and just waits, like he doesn't think I'll do it. I'm not a man who hesitates, but I'm also not a man used to dealing with such *fearlessness.*

After a few seconds, while he's still breathing, he pulls the bottle from his lips, pointing it at me as he asks, "Did she tell you about her?"

"Who?"

"My Morgan," he says. "Your *Scarlet.* That is what you call her, no?"

"What about her?"

"Did she tell you about Sasha?"

Sasha.

I don't answer that, having no idea what he's talking about, but that's all the answer he needs.

He laughs yet again.

"Oh, no, of course she has not told you," he says. "Why would she? Silly man, with a gun... go ahead, shoot me. She will be heartbroken when you do. You will be killing her, too. Either way, I win."

Before I can do anything, he shoves up from the chair, his forehead momentarily pressing against the muzzle as he rises to his feet. I keep the gun trained on him as he strolls over to the fireplace. He hesitates, standing there, staring at the mantle, before he grabs the bear. His hand wraps around the thing, clutching it by the neck as he approaches.

He drops it on the table in front of me.

"Take it," he says. "It is only collecting dust here now. I am sure it will make Morgan happy to see it again."

He steps by me to walk away. I keep the gun trained on him, but I still don't pull the trigger.

Color me curious. "Who's *Sasha?*"

Aristov stalls in the doorway, glancing back at me. I don't expect him to answer, figuring he'll give me some line about asking Scarlet, when he lets out a deep sigh and says, "My daughter, of course."

Daughter.

Of course.

Puzzle pieces I never bothered to connect shove themselves together, like I should've already riddled out the bigger picture here. The man has a daughter, and it's not taking a genius to figure out where he might've gotten that daughter.

Or rather, who gave him that daughter.

I saw the scar on her stomach.

I see it every time she takes off her clothes.

It's there, more prominent than the other scars peppering her body, but she's never brought it up, so I always let it go.

Whatever story is behind it must be one she doesn't want to tell. Because I've given her ample opportunity to spill it. *Tell me a story.* But she'd rather spew some bullshit fairy tales.

I know scars, though. I know the kind of scar a bullet leaves behind. I know the kind left from a knife. Gashes, and welts, and burns—the scars are recognizable. I can read a body like a book and tell you everything it has been through. A litany of fucking horror stories written right onto the flesh. I know the story of a metal shovel to the face, blunt force trauma that should've killed a teenage boy but instead turned him into a nightmare.

But the most recognizable scars are deliberate, the ones caused by a carefully controlled cut with a scalpel. I know when you've had your appendix removed, when you've had open-heart surgery, when you've had a tracheotomy...

And I know when you've had C-section.

It's damn near impossible to hide that truth.

Easier to ignore, though.

Believe me, I ignored it.

Can't ignore it anymore.

I'm a fucking fool.

"Where is she?" I ask. "Your daughter?"

He smiles. "Shoot me, Mister Scar, and you will never know."

* * *

I don't take kindly to being threatened.

Blackmail? Coercion? *Not fucking happening.*

I get it, you know... there are consequences to every action. Cause and effect. *If this, then that.* But there are consequences to inaction, too, and that's something people don't often realize.

Scarlet is living the consequences right now because nobody has stopped this from happening.

My stepfather's voice bounces around in my head as I sit in the passenger seat of my car, slouching down in the dark, the obnoxious ding-ding-dinging of the *put on your fucking seatbelt* warning echoing through the small space.

A clear conscience just means you've got a bad memory. He used to say it all the time. And I've gotta tell you, right about now, I wish I could catch a case of amnesia and have my memory wiped, because my conscience is muddled tonight.

"Speak," I say sharply, my voice making Seven jump as he speeds toward Queens. He keeps casting sidelong glances my way, not saying a damn word, subtlety not his strong suit. "Ask your questions or get out of my car."

"What happened?"

"What happened?" I repeat. "You wanna maybe specify a bit? Because a lot has happened in my life, Seven, and I'm not interested in spilling my guts to you like a little bitch."

He hesitates, turning on the blinker to make a left turn. Once he's onto the next road, merging back into traffic, he lets out an exaggerated sigh. "Lets go with why do you have a *teddy bear*?"

"Gift from my favorite philosopher," I say, glaring at the thing as it rests on the dashboard.

Seven doesn't understand, but it's not my place to explain it to him. Hell, I'm still trying to wrap *my* head around it all. I get it, it's all there, but how to deal with it is another matter.

The more he stays out of it, the better off he is.

"Look, they've got history," I say. "He wants her back. She doesn't want to go. He's getting desperate. That's all you really need to know. I was going to shoot him, but I decided not to, so here we are. You're all caught up. Now get me to my house, and then go home to your wife, and don't worry about what else might've happened, because it's not your problem. Just worry about yourself."

He nods once and says nothing else, the rest of the drive complete silence.

Well, except for the seatbelt warning.

The house is lit up when I get there. Seven gives me my keys, and I take my phone, before snatching up the old teddy bear, carrying it by its burned foot.

I head inside, saying goodnight to Seven.

Menace

The first thing I hear when I open the front door is another goddamn song being sung.

Someone put Baby in a corner and Patrick Swayze got pissed. *Blah. Blah. Blah.* You know what it is.

Leo and his girlfriend are cuddling on the new couch. I slip right past them, heading for the library, finding it empty and dark. The first thing I notice, though, is my puzzle has been fixed, the broken pieces stuck back together.

No Scarlet, though.

Walking back out, I head for the stairs, hearing my brother shout out as I pass the living room. "Hey, bro!"

I stall in the doorway, nodding in greeting. "You seen Scarlet?"

"No," he says. "Might be upstairs, though."

"I figured."

"I see you got us a new couch." He runs his hand along the leather arm. "Where'd you get it?"

"Stole it from a strip club."

He laughs, like I'm joking, so I just walk off before he comes to the realization that he's cuddling his girlfriend on a couch where dozens of men have probably jacked off.

I trudge upstairs. It's dark. I think maybe she's trying to sleep, but the bed is empty, as is the bathroom. I turn to leave when my gaze catches something in my reflection above the dresser.

Reaching over, I flick on the light, stopping where I am. Lipstick is smeared on the mirror, two words scribbled in red.

I'm sorry.

She's gone.

I know it.

Those words tell me that.

That's as good as a 'goodbye' as I'm probably getting, as far as farewells go with this woman.

I don't like it.

27
Morgan

Sunrise is coming.

There's a hint of light on the horizon, the pitch black sky a deep purple hue in the east, slowly pushing toward blue. Another hour or so and the skyline will be streaked with colors, orange and pink and white as the sun settles in, daylight arriving. It's weird, the twitch of anticipation I feel.

I haven't watched the sun come up in weeks. I'm still awake whenever it happens, my internal clock set to see it, but the clouds or buildings have blocked my view.

I miss it.

I miss *her*.

I try not to think about it so much. Maybe that's hard for you to understand. But dwelling gets me no closer to finding the end to this drawn-out nightmare. So I compartmentalize. I tuck it away, deep inside of me, locking it up somewhere safe where the world can't touch it, where reality can't reach it or try to take it from me. It gets me through every minute of every hour. Without it, I'm not sure I'd survive much longer.

"Shove your apology up your ass, Scarlet. I don't accept it."

The voice calls out behind me, loud and brash, a genuine hint of anger in his words that makes a chill flow through me.

Lorenzo.

I'm standing on the ledge on the roof of this apartment building again, one of the last places I should be, probably, but I knew I'd be able to catch the sunrise from here.

Guess he knew it, too.

Didn't take him long to find me.

I didn't expect him to bother, to be honest, but there's that little part of me that selfishly hoped he cared. He shouldn't, because I bring nothing but trouble, but still... I yearn to mean something.

Do you know what that's like?

To know you're poison but still be desperate for someone to sip from you anyway?

"Did you kill him?" I ask quietly, staring out at the city, over toward Brooklyn, where I know he went last night. Where I know he heard my truth. How much of it, I'm not sure, but knowing Kassian, it would be *just enough*.

"Wanted to," he says. "Thought about it. Almost did it. But no, he's still alive."

The relief I feel sickens me. The world around me spins. I close my eyes, to take a deep breath, trying to calm my achey chest.

I hear Lorenzo approach. He purposely snuck up on me, making no noise on his way to the roof, but he's being deliberate about it now, warning me he's coming closer.

Opening my eyes again, I carefully turn around, words on the tip of my tongue about how I truly am sorry he got mixed up in my mess, when the wind is knocked right out of me. It feels like a fist slams into my gut. I *gasp*. My heart stalls. My vision grows hazy until I see nothing.

I almost collapse.

My knees go weak, legs starting to buckle, foot slipping on the edge of the ledge. I sway, damn near falling, the sight hitting me like tank.

Buster.

Lorenzo holds the teddy bear upside down by its foot. It's in worse shape than I've ever seen it, but I know that bear.

I'd recognize it anywhere.

"Jesus *fuck*." Something flashes in Lorenzo's eyes. It almost looks like fear. He darts forward, snatching ahold of me, yanking me back onto the roof. I slip again, almost falling, this time onto *him*, but he keeps me upright, slamming me back against the ledge, pinning me there with his body. "I swear, if you throw yourself off this roof, I'm jumping after you, and I'm going to catch you."

Whoa. I don't know what to make of those words.

My eyes widen, my heart racing.

"I'll catch you," he says again, his face so close to mine I can feel his breath on my skin, "because in those few seconds before you hit the ground, I'm going to fucking choke the life out of you for doing that shit. You got me?"

"I got you," I whisper, surprised I can even speak.

He keeps me pinned there, pressed flat up against me, staring me dead in the face. I'm frozen, like I'm made from stone, unable to move... *unable to look.* He's holding it in his hand, and I don't know why, and I don't know what it means, but it's the closest I've gotten to her in ten long months. I need it to be real.

"I got you," he says, his voice low, serious, and I think at first he's just echoing what I said, until he raises his eyebrows, emphasizing them. "I *got* you. It's okay."

I blink rapidly, my eyes burning, a lump in my throat that I'm struggling to swallow back.

"I got you," he says for the third time, "but I'm telling you, if you start fucking crying on me right now, if you start boo-hoo'ing, there's a chance I'll just throw you over the side myself, so don't do it."

"I'm trying not to," I whisper, my voice cracking.

"Good," he says. "You think I can let go? You think you can stand up on your own?"

I nod.

He lets go of me, taking a step back.

As soon as he does, my feet come out from under me, and I slide right down to the roof on my ass. My shirt catches on the ledge, the old crumbly bricks scraping my back, as a noise comes out of me. A loud noise. An *inhuman* noise. I quickly cover my mouth to stifle it.

Tears burn my eyes, obscuring my vision.

Buster is *right there*, inches from my face.

I reach for the bear, grasping hold of its arm, and Lorenzo relinquishes it to me, not hesitating at all. As I clutch it to my chest,

I pull my knees up, folding into myself. Tears break free and stream down my cheeks.

I cry.

Fuck it.

I can't hold it back anymore.

My chest aches, my stomach clenches, and I can't catch my breath because I cry so hard. I'm hyperventilating, a mess, falling apart. Lorenzo just stands there, not consoling me, but he doesn't leave, either. He stays right in front of me, staring out into the city, as I sob.

"I asked one thing of you," he says when I calm down. "One thing. That's it. I said *don't cry.*"

I laugh at that, although my tears are still falling, laughing and crying at the same time, like a maniac. It's not funny, no, but it's so fucked up that I can't help myself. "Sorry."

"*Jesus...* don't apologize, either. Stop saying you're sorry all the fucking time."

I want to point out that I've said it only maybe three times to him total, and that I *should* be apologizing, but I keep my mouth shut as I wipe my face on my shirt, trying to dry my eyes. I know it makes him uncomfortable. Emotion. Remorse. Tears. Apologies. The whole nine yards.

I press my face against the teddy bear, inhaling deeply. Dust tickles my nose. It smells musty. It doesn't smell at all like sunshine or innocence. There's no *her* in the bear anymore.

I don't know what happened.

More tears fall, silent ones this time. I wipe them away and just sit there, hugging Buster.

After a moment, Lorenzo lets out a dramatic sigh before sitting down on the roof beside me, maybe a foot of space between us. We're not touching, but he's close enough that I can feel his warmth.

"Are you done crying now?" he asks.

I laugh again. "You're such an asshole."

"I was going to talk to you," he says, "but you might blow snot on me with all that blubbering."

I shake my head, wiping my nose on my sleeve. I'm a mess, but there's nothing else I can do about it. It isn't like he brought along any tissues.

Turning my head, I gaze at him. The sky is steadily lightening. I can make him out better now than when he showed up. Uneasiness wafts from him as he picks at the skin around his fingernails, out of his element. For the first time since I've met this man, he's letting his nerves show, his guard lowering just enough for me to see it. I can tell he doesn't want to be doing this, but he's doing it, and that's not something I ever expected from him.

He doesn't *owe* me anything.

He glances at me, surveying my face. Reaching over, he grabs my right hand, turning it over, palm up, my wrist bending as he pushes the tattoo there toward me. My Scarlet Letter, he calls it.

I glance down at it. "Sasha."

"Pity," he says. "I hoped it would end up standing for '*salad tosser*'. I was looking forward to it."

I roll my eyes, snatching my hand back away.

"It was different at first," I say, running my fingers along the ridges of the tattoo, feeling for the scar beneath it. I can even still *see* it, if I look hard enough. "He carved an 'S' into my wrist. I hated it… hated seeing it. It stood for something else back then."

"*Suka.*"

I cringe, hearing that word in his voice.

"Yes," I say. "So after I escaped him, I covered it with her… the only good thing that ever came from me being his *suka*."

It's quiet after that, the two of us sitting here, as I stare out along the roof.

He knows my truth.

"What's your first memory?" I ask after a while.

He doesn't hesitate, answering, "The night my father was murdered. I remember coming down the steps and seeing the gun in the man's hand. First time I ever saw one."

"Do you remember your father?"

He shakes his head.

"I don't remember my parents," I say. "My first memory is

of a social worker telling me the home I'd been living in didn't want me anymore. I was five. I remember being so upset. I just wanted a family. I wanted a *mom*, but I never got one. So when I had Sasha, I was determined to give her what I never got. I was going to be the best goddamn mom on the planet."

"I'm sure you're a great mother."

"I tried to be," I say quietly. "I was only sixteen when I had her, and I had no idea what I was doing, but I knew we had to get away from Kassian, so I took her and ran. It wasn't perfect, but we were happy... until he caught up to us. He took her, and he left me for dead. I haven't seen her since. I don't know where she is."

Tears break free again.

I'm trying not to cry, because the man is actually listening, but it's hard holding it back now that I've been cracked open.

I went to the police. I went to Child Protective Services. I've talked to lawyers and social workers and private investigators. Nobody wants to get involved. They all refuse to help.

Kassian is powerful. He's wealthy. He's *terrifying*. So they all just called it a 'domestic problem' and sent me packing.

In the beginning, I staked out his house. I kept an eye on the club. I followed his men around. Not once did I see her, or any sign that Kassian even had her, but I knew.

I *know*.

He's got her somewhere.

"Did you...?" I trail off. "I mean, was she...?"

"I didn't see her," Lorenzo says, answering a question I can't bring myself to finish. "The bear was on a fireplace mantle. He said it was just collecting dust, so he figured you'd want it."

I close my eyes as those words sink in. They hurt, like a punch to the chest, strong enough to knock my heart out of rhythm so it might never beat right again. "Buster was her security blanket. She loved this bear. She carried him *everywhere*. She wouldn't... she wouldn't just give him up. Especially *now*. She's gotta be terrified. She just turned five, and she's never been away from me until this happened, and now... now she's really alone, and there's nothing I can do to help her."

"If she's anything like you, Scarlet, she's resilient."

"But she shouldn't have to be," I whisper. "She doesn't deserve this. She's... perfect. She's smart, and beautiful, and so just *good*. There's this kindness inside of her that is so pure, like they took the sunrise and stuck it in this fierce little body. She's walking sunshine. And ten months is a long time for the sun to go without shining. It's a long time for her to go without being shown she's loved. And I don't know how much longer it'll be, and all I can think is... will she even remember me? And I think that's what terrifies me most, that when my story ends, the very last words will be, '*and she never saw her again*'. Because that could happen."

"Fuck that."

I look at Lorenzo as I brush stray tears from my cheeks.

"Seriously, *fuck* that," he says. "That's not happening."

"How can you be so sure?"

"Because I'm not going to *let* it."

I shake my head, letting out an incredulous laugh.

"Look, I get it," he says. "You have no reason to trust me."

"You have no reason to *help* me."

"Oh, bullshit," Lorenzo says, shoving to his feet. "I've got plenty of reasons to help you."

I stare at him. "Name *one*."

"I can name a *dozen*."

I wave at him. "Well, then, go on, I'm listening."

"One," he says, "I'm bored as shit and it's something to do. There's not a lot else to do right now."

"That's a terrible reason."

"But it's a reason, nonetheless," he says. "Two, I don't like the guy. He thinks he's better than me. That, alone, makes me want to go after him."

"That's a slightly better reason."

"Three, I've already knocked out..." He pauses, counting under his breathing, using his fingers. *Unbelievable.* "...five self-proclaimed mob bosses, and six is a nice, well-rounded number, so number six needs to happen."

"That's just a ridiculous reason."

"Four," he continues, "I don't like kids, don't want kids, but one thing I dislike more than kids are people who *hurt* kids, so *fuck* him."

"Okay," I whisper.

"Five, I raised my brother to save him from a father *a lot* like Aristov. So if I can help save your daughter, to spare her the same way, you're goddamn right I'm in."

"I get it. You've made your point."

"I don't think I have," he says. "Six, I like you."

That one catches me off guard. "You like me."

"Yeah, I mean, you're a pain in my ass sometimes, but you're not half-bad."

"I'm not half-bad."

He gazes down at me, a slight smile on his lips. "You're gorgeous, and smart, and funny... you eat the *whole* orange and don't just suck the juice out and throw it away like other people. That makes you a catch in my book."

I'm not sure how to react to that. Tears swim in my eyes, but now he's got me *blushing*. What the hell? "I'm a catch?"

"Don't let that shit get to your head," he says right away. "Never in there did I say I wasn't still throwing your ass back when this is all done."

He says that, but I'm *still* blushing. "Noted."

"Seven, you just cried like a bitch in front of me, and I never want that to happen again. I don't like it."

"Are you done yet?"

"No," he says. "Reasons eight through eleven, that pussy of yours is *beautiful*."

I roll my eyes.

His leg shoots out, kicking my shin hard enough that I wince.

"I'm serious," he says, his voice sounding pretty damn serious as he says that. "Roll your eyes all you want, but I happen to think pussy is a damn good reason to go to battle."

"Fine," I say, "is that it?"

"Just one more," he says, squatting down in front of me.

"Reason number twelve, you've got a *mini-me* out there somewhere, and I kind of want the chance to meet a little Scarlet."

"You don't like kids," I point out.

"True, I don't," he says. "But she's *your* kid, which means there's a decent chance she's not half-bad, either."

I stare at him.

I don't know what to say.

His words sound so genuine. This isn't the reaction I expected. Not to say I didn't think he had it in him. But I'm used to being kicked while I'm down, and I haven't quite figured out what to make of Lorenzo. Sometimes, when I look at him, I see the dangerous, cold-hearted criminal, the one that has killed *at least* two men since we met two months ago, but other times I see a man with a deep soul, generous and warm, the kind of man a woman could fall in love with if she wasn't careful.

But I *have* to be careful.

"Come on," Lorenzo says, standing up again, offering me his hand. "The sun's up now, which means another day of bullshit is upon us, and I really need to acquire some breakfast if I'm going to do something about your little Pearl."

I take his hand, letting him yank me to my feet. I know I must look like hell, having cried my eyes out and forgone sleep, but he doesn't seem bothered by it. "Pearl?"

"Yeah, the kid in *The Scarlet Letter*? Didn't you read the book in school?"

"I dropped out at fourteen," I remind him. "I was pregnant at fifteen. Reading the classics wasn't really on the syllabus at the Aristov residence."

He doesn't say anything for a moment, his face twisting with a grimace. "I just did math in my head."

"And that disturbs you?"

"When the math I'm doing is how old Aristov was when he knocked you up, *yeah*."

I want to point out that he has no idea exactly how disturbing that time of my life was, but I let it drop. I'm tired of thinking about Kassian. I'm tired of the way he still controls my life. So I pull myself together, tuck Buster under my arm, and glance around, my eyes grazing over the colorful horizon.

The sun is up, shining brightly.

I didn't watch it happen, but I still feel like a weight has been lifted. I almost feel *hopeful* again.

I glance back at Lorenzo, noticing he's watching me. "I still think you're a fool for helping me, but thank you. *Really.*"

He stares in silence for a moment, his expression passive, before he says, "Yeah, well, who's more foolish... the fool or the fool who follows him?"

"Good question, Obi-wan."

I start to walk away when Lorenzo grabs my arm, stopping me, pulling me toward him. "You've seen Star Wars?"

"Of course."

"See, I'm sure now more than ever before that I'm going to help you." Lorenzo's expression cracks with a smile. "Reason number thirteen, Scarlet: I may just be your only hope."

28

The little girl didn't like playing games anymore.

She was stuck in a stupid match of tug-of-war, digging her heels into the ground, trying to hold on, but the Tin Man was too strong for her.

Every time she pulled away, he tugged *harder*.

She locked herself in the bedroom, not wanting to ever see him, so he took the door off of the hinges, giving her no space. She refused to eat, not having an appetite, not even when he got her some peanut butter and jelly, so he force-fed her, shoving the food in her mouth.

He said if she starved to death, it would be because *he* decided it.

So she took up Hide & Seek again, but he'd proven to be persistent. The best part about living in a palace, though, was that there were *so* many hiding places. A new one every day. Sometimes he found her. Other times he didn't even look. She preferred him not to bother, because whenever he sought her, he made her heart hurt. His words got all ugly. He always made her cry with his lies. *'Your mother does not love you, kitten. If she did, she would be here with us.'*

It was a cold night, snowing outside, when the little girl lay beneath a bed in a guest room on the second floor, right above the den. Noises filtered up, reaching her ears. The Tin Man hadn't looked for her because he had visitors, his flying monkeys and some women. It was late, pitch black, when the noise below got louder, chanting, counting backward.

New Years.

The little girl had *really* missed Christmas. No Santa Claus had come. She thought maybe something had stopped him, like maybe the Tin Man scared him, too, or maybe she just hadn't been good enough that year, but a mean voice in her head whispered, '*maybe he's just not real.*'

It was a whole different year now. She tried to remember the one before it, but her memory was being fuzzy.

She didn't like it.

She lay there with her eyes closed, trying to remember her mother, how she laughed, and loved, but the little girl could only seem to picture her sleeping on the kitchen floor.

She wanted to remember the happiness. How could she do that? Maybe she'd just have to go out and find her mother. Seek *her* out, instead of the other way around.

Some of the noise from downstairs came closer. Whispering, footsteps along the second floor. The little girl tensed when it moved into the guest room, feet shuffling in the darkness.

Two people.

High heels and a pair of boots.

They moaned, making kissing noises, before falling onto the bed, hitting the mattress so hard the springs almost squished the little girl's head. She gagged as a cloud of dust surrounded her, tickling her nose. *Oh no. Uh-oh.* She had to sneeze.

She tried to stop herself, so they wouldn't hear, but holding it in only made it come out *louder.*

The sneeze echoed through the room.

The kissing abruptly ended.

Feet hit the floor and the blanket flipped up seconds before an upside down face peeked between a set of legs. *The Cowardly Lion.* He scowled before dropping the blanket again and sitting back up with a groan.

"Everything okay?" the woman asked.

"Can you...?" He groaned again. "Go back downstairs. There's something I need to take care of."

Uh-oh, for real.

The woman didn't argue, leaving the room. As soon as she was gone, the blanket flipped up again. "Get out here."

Menace

The little girl crawled out from under the bed and stood up beside it, frowning. She tried to just leave, but he grabbed her arm.

"Whoa, busybody, where do you think you are going?"

"To bed," she said. "I'm tired."

He cocked his head to the side, giving her a glassy stare. "Me, too. I've been tired for a long time."

"I'm sorry," she said, grateful when he let go of her arm. "You should go to sleep."

"Tried," he said. "Found a little monster hiding under my bed."

She scrunched up her face at that, which made him laugh.

"Come on, tell me," he said. "Why are you hiding?"

"Because he's mean."

"And?"

"And that's all," she said. "He's just not nice."

The Cowardly Lion blinked a few times, like there had to be more answer, but she didn't have anything else to say.

Wasn't that enough?

"You're right," he said. "He's not nice."

Her eyes widened. "You think so, too?"

"Of course. He's a *mudak*. A real piece of work, that one. But hiding from him will not make him nicer."

"What *will* make him nicer?"

"You," he said. "Believe it or not, *you* make him nicer. It softens us, love. It makes us all squishy. But sometimes that same love becomes a liability."

"What does a lie-bully mean?"

He smiled. "It means he can't live with you, but he can't live without you. Either way, it is a problem. So you should give him reasons to live *with* you, because your mother gave him too many reasons to live *without* her, and we see where she is now."

"Where?" the little girl asked. "Where *is* she?"

"Not here."

'*Not here*' sounded good to the little girl.

"Come on," he said, standing up, grasping her shoulders. "Let's go say goodnight."

He led her downstairs, keeping his grip on her, taking her straight to the crowded den. People were drinking and sniffing white powder again. The Tin Man's eyes were straight black as they zeroed in on her. She didn't like his black eyes. They scared her.

"Found this one up in a guest room," the Cowardly Lion told him, "hiding under the bed."

"That is not very creative," the Tin Man said. "Of all places to hide, you choose where everyone knows to look. Did you *want* to be found?"

She shrugged.

"She says you are mean," the Cowardly Lion added. "You aren't very nice. She asked how to make you nicer."

The little girl glared back at the Cowardly Lion. "Nobody even *likes* tattletales."

The Tin Man laughed at that, like she amused him, opening his arms and motioning for her to come closer, but she didn't budge.

"You know, obedience makes me nicer, kitten. Maybe if you give a little, I will give a little back."

"Will you give Buster back?"

"No."

Then no, she wasn't moving. She wasn't giving. She didn't care if he got nice. She'd already decided she was leaving. She didn't need *him*. She was going to find her mother and they were going to stop playing all this Hide & Seek. She didn't need a daddy.

Especially one so mean.

The Tin Man dropped his arms, giving up, waving her away. "Go to bed."

"I'll make sure she makes it there," the Cowardly Lion said, pulling the little girl from the room, leading her upstairs.

The little girl ignored him, pretending he wasn't even there, as she settled into the bed, covering herself up with the blanket, pulling it the whole way over her head.

The mattress dipped, the Cowardly Lion's hand ruffling her hair through the blanket as he sat down beside her. "It is New Years, sweet girl. It is the time for new beginnings. *Resolutions.*"

"There's no point," the little girl muttered.

The blanket was ripped from her head, and she made a face, trying to snatch it back to cover up, but the Cowardly Lion refused to let her. "What is wrong?"

"It's all stupid," she said, tears in her eyes. "I don't like holidays no more! Santa didn't come, I got no presents, and I didn't even get my wish to come true!"

"What was your wish?"

"I want Mommy. I wanna go *home*."

The Cowardly Lion blinked at her for a long moment before throwing the blanket back over her head, covering her up as he stood to walk away. The little girl listened to his footsteps crossing the floor before he called back to her quietly, "Goodnight, sweet Sasha. *Happy New Year.*"

Acknowledgments

Truth be told, I never expected to write a book about Lorenzo Gambini, much less give him his own series, so never in my wildest dreams did I expect him to weasel his way right to the top of the list of my favorite characters I've ever written (I know, I know... we're not supposed to play favorites). So first and foremost, I want to acknowledge *you*... to all of the readers who wrote me or tweeted me or visited me at book signings to tell me they needed more of this man. From the bottom of my heart, I thank you, and I truly hope you enjoy his crazy little journey.

To my friends and my family, I love you all. You know who you are. I'd list you, but then I'd forget someone, and that would suck. And to the book bloggers, bookstagramers, booktubers, facebookers, tweeters, and whatever else I'm missing here in the book community... thank you, truly, for loving reading so much that you put your voices out there. I'm so blessed to be able to live my dream of storytelling because of those readers willing to give my words a chance, and I'm forever grateful for the support.

Last but not least, to Sebastian Stan. You didn't do a damn thing to help me write this book, but the fact that you exist? I like that shit. Keep it up ;)

About the Author

J.M. Darhower is the *USA Today Bestselling Author* of paranormal/erotic/romantic suspense novels about the baddest bad boys and the ladies who love them. Fangirl at heart, J.M. is obsessed with books, music, and all things Marvel, especially the glorious Sebastian Stan. She spends her days in a tiny town in North Carolina, churning out words and chasing down Pokemon.

Made in the USA
Lexington, KY
20 January 2017